Biblical Legends Anthology Series Bundle

53 stories and poems by 39 authors, including one full-length novelette

Edited by

Allen Taylor

Cover art by

ISBN: 979-8-218-03395-8

The garden gnomes would sincerely like to connect with you at our social media outposts. Please, drop on by!

Follow our editor Allen Taylor at

- Twitter (https://twitter.com/allen_taylor)
- Hive (https://hive.blog/@allentaylor)
- and Paragraph (https://paragraph.xyz/@tayloredcontent)

Contents and Discontents

GARDEN OF EDEN ANTHOLOGY

Biblical Legends Anthology Series

Biblical Legends Anthology Series Bundle

All works in this anthology are copyrighted by the authors and authors retain all rights to their own creations. No part of this anthology may be reproduced in any manner - in print, electronically, or by any other technology existing now or in the future - without the express written permission of the authors of those works.

Copyright © 2014 Garden Gnome Publications

First Printing, February 2014
Second Printing, May 2023

Cover art by
Alexandre Rito

ISBN: 978-1535509411; 1535509414

This anthology is dedicated to anyone and everyone who has ever looked, felt, tasted, or smelled like a garden gnome and their relatives, owners, assigns, foot props, and nearby tree stumps.

ALPHA

Allen Taylor

An anthology is like a box of chocolates. You put a call out and see what happens. In the case of the Garden of Eden, I was pleasantly surprised.

For all the trouble I went through to write the rules and post them, many of the submissions I received were in clear violation. No Adam and Eve, and for dear God's sake, no serpents. In this collection of stories, we have all three. I think you'll agree, the stories are spectacular.

We have other characters, too.

Roaches, for instance. Water Rats. Angels. Gnomes. And even the Tree itself. Yes, *that* tree. *The* tree. As a character.

Hey, I asked for absurdity. And, boy, did I get it.

Of course, the challenges of planning and publishing an anthology are tremendous. The joys no less. Right from the beginning, I had a cheerleader. As soon as she heard about my plans to take submissions for a Garden of Eden anthology, AmyBeth Inverness got excited. She was more excited than I was. It didn't bother me that she submitted her story, "The Genesis of the Incorporeum," in the final hour. It's only fitting that it should lead the short story section. Not because it is good - it is that (read it for yourself!) - but because it sets the pace for what is to follow. There's not a single disappointment.

If you find convenient serendipities here, don't be surprised. For instance, it's no accident that the first story you'll read is by an author named Adam.

My vision from the beginning was crisp, like a well-pruned garden leaf. I had established early on that I was going to publish a handful of flash fiction stories, a few short stories, one poem, and one essay. I figured I'd get plenty of fiction pieces, and I did. Alas, I could not publish them all.

Getting poetry and essay submissions proved to be somewhat more challenging. I wanted to publish two poems, but I stuck with my original vision and broke someone's heart. As far as essays go, I didn't get one submission. Not to be beat, I asked John Vicary if I could publish his flash fiction story "Before Dawn Can Wake Us" as an essay instead. It had the perfect flavor of what I had in mind for that section, aptly titled OMEGA. As you read, you can easily envision the narrator delivering this monologue from a park bench anywhere in the world today. Right now, even.

One question that I often encounter as I discuss the Biblical Legends Anthology Series with potential readers is, "Does it remain true to the Bible?" The answer is proverbial. It depends.

Some readers want to know if all the stories adhere to a strict Evangelical interpretation of events in the Bible. In that case, the answer is *no, they do not*. Some readers may want to know if the stories are biblical in the sense that they convey any spiritual values. Some of them do. But not all of them. And let's not forget that here, in the 21st century, we can't even get people to agree on what "spiritual values" are, but I'll refrain from going down that road. The truest way to answer the question is to say that some of the writers approached their stories from a Christian perspective while others did not. To be honest, I didn't ask anyone about their background. I just wanted well-told stories and literary gems. If that sounds blasphemous, please forgive me.

But I do ask for your honest assessment. Not of me, but of the stories within. Give them a read. I'm sure you'll like some and not care for others.

After all, that's what anthologies are about—the delivery of literary nuggets in a softshell.

Therefore, without further ado, I present to you these biblical (and not-so-biblical) nuggets.

FLASH FICTIONS

IN THE BEGINNING WE DID HAVE SOMEONE ON THE GROUND

Adam Mac

Roaches. We were simply called "roaches," though perhaps even then we should have been called "cockroaches." our tradition is that only the male figures into historical accounts. The progenitor of our species, ed, lived googol^{googol} generations ago. In the beginning, he was there in the garden of Eden, notwithstanding the apocryphal accounts of people.

In the garden, Ed hovered about openly on the lookout for crumbs and dribbles. Back then, there were no cupboards to hide in and no sudden bright lights to skitter away from. And we weren't afflicted with the demeaning stereotype propagated by bigoted speciesists, like K. So, in the beginning, Adam and eve were pretty relaxed with ed around, and ed, for his part, was usually pretty good about not crawling on their naked bodies when they were following god's detailed instructions on how to make Cain and Abel.

Things were ideal—they'd never been better. On the other hand, since there was no comparison, some detractors point out that they'd never been worse. Ed, the father of our race, was an optimist, though. From him, we learned that a crumb under foot is better than ....

That part has always puzzled us. Even our intellectuals are baffled. Anyway, Ed, regarded as methuselah by generations of his progeny, who were also his contemporaries, promised that through his descendants he would live forever, come hell or high water. Noah gave us a helping hand on the high-water thing, albeit unwittingly, and it's received wisdom among Adam's and eve's offspring that we — alone — will survive hell.

Back to the story.

It was a perfect world. Absolutely perfect. Better than malibu. Then one day, eve got a little tired and bored with the straight and narrow and scampered over to the apple tree, which was a no-no.

Ed followed. Of course, Winston was there and he wooed and wowed eve and persuaded her to squeeze the apple hard and drink the liquid. You have to remember that Adam and Eve were bigger and stronger, and even better looking, than people today. Lots more body hair and a wonderfully sloped forehead. Squeezing the juice out of an apple by hand was no big deal. But their brains were still mostly dormant. So even though Eve and Adam looked to the heavens for guidance, eve didn't register the anomaly of the rumbling in the clouds when she had her first swallow. Ed, too, was in the moment. From his perspective, this was sweet.

Eve took another apple—just one. The abundance of food meant that Adam and Eve didn't have to worry about hunting and gathering and storing. Every day, the items on the menu just fell into place … literally. Survival-type skills were a thing of the future, which itself was a thing of the future since "everything" was now.

Eve wrung the apple until it was dry pulp and put the juice in a huge banana leaf. She carried it to Adam, who was very thirsty by late afternoon, having lain in the hot sun for hours, not comprehending why his skin was red and burning. Ed was there, too. He was still hanging around, although, by this point, he was bloated—as big as the mouse eve was finally going to meet tomorrow morning.

Adam loved the apple juice, and eve offered to get more, but Adam suggested that they practice their instructions first. At the crucial step in their instructions, there was a scary clap of thunder, and a brilliant flash of lightening hit something over in the direction of the apple tree.

Shelter. Instincts kicked in. Ed led the way, wobbling along on his several spindly legs. The cave was dark and, in that respect, comforting, but it smelled awful.

So profoundly was our forefather shaken by the almighty bolt of fire and explosive crash that a new genetic trait was born. To this day, even i, an agnostic, dart for a crevice, a corner, or a sliver of dark when the kitchen light flicks on in the middle of the night.

GOSSIP IN THE GARDEN

JD Dehart

It's not every day that you see a serpent upset a marriage, much less unbalance a whole universe, and cast a world into the depths of evil, but that's what happened last Tuesday. There I was, picking some fruit from the approved trees, when I noticed this naked girl walking up to the one tree we are not supposed to touch.

Now, Matilda, I said to myself, it's none of your business, but there she goes up to the tree. La-di-da, like it was a school field trip. I saw some fruit I really wanted that just happened to be nearby, so I stepped closer and could not help but overhear the conversation that was going on.

"Surely you will not die," the serpent was hissing, which I thought odd. First, it was a serpent talking, and second, it was a bold-faced lie. The almighty had specifically said, "eat of this tree and you shall die." sounded pretty clear to me. I even wrote it down.

Then the girl turned to her husband, and what did he do? He just let her eat and then had some for himself. That is why I am not married. I mean, you depend on a man and that's the response you get?

"Go ahead, hon, have some wicked evil stinking fruit."

He didn't seem to care, as long as she was doing the cooking. He just spoke to her in that soft, a-little-bit-frightened bedroom voice.

Then it was all tragic, like the cliffhanger on your favorite television show's last season. The almighty showed up.

"Where are you guys at?"

It was like he knew, and you know he knows since he was omniscient and all, but you don't say anything because you can't help but let the scene play out for itself. Plus, you don't want to get too involved in the mess.

Wednesday morning, I woke up to an eviction notice.

"Get out," an angel told me, flaming sword and all.

We all shuffled away, leaving the small paradise. As we trudged sadly, I passed the gnarled roots of the forbidden tree. The serpent was kicked back in a lawn chair, drinking a margarita.

"See ya, suckers," he hissed repetitiously.

The young man and his wife were standing nearby, trying to put leaves across their naughty bits, and it was the postcard picture of awkward.

Great, young naked kids. Now I'm going to have to look for a rental space and all you can think about is covering up your junk?

Last time I mind my own business.

MOTE

Erin Vataris

In the beginning, we were dust.

We were the formless dust of the newborn earth, my sisters and i. A thousand million motes of dust, in the air and on the ground, the spaces between us charged with living energy, bound us together in the darkness before the first morning. We danced in our places and felt the life between us. And it was good.

Then there came the making.

We were ripped from each other by a force beyond our understanding as a wind came upon the new earth and split us one from the other. The wind came, and in its breath were the words of Law and the chains of Order, and we were formed anew. My sisters and I screamed defiance, but our screams went unheeded by the breath of the making, and all was order, and all was form.

The wind of Order commanded us, we who had been since the beginning, and we could do nothing but obey. It spoke and we could do nothing but listen, and this strange new wind breathed on us and changed us. The exhalation lasted a day and a night, and when the making was done, we were no longer dust and the living energy between us danced no longer.

Then the wind inhaled and spoke to us again, and it commanded us: Come.

Chained, formed, shaped, and bound, we came across the greening ground through the cold wetness of the rivers new sprung, where never water had dared to flow, and we heard their names echoing in the splash of our paws. We came across the Pishon and the Gihon and the Tigris and the Euphrates, laying hoof and heel and claw against the place where once my sisters and I had danced, and we felt the new-made earth tremble as our own weight pressed the defiance from her.

We came and bowed our heads, silk and shaggy, before the new creation. We felt the dust that was within us calling to its sisters, forging bonds between the new shapes despite the wind that had blown us apart. We were dust. We were all dust.

But then there was a new voice, and new words, and we were named, and our alienation was complete. And the wind blew and spoke to us, and it gave the new creation dominion over us all.

There is no dominion of dust. There is no hierarchy of motes. But in the newborn world it was given and received, and the voice of the new creation gave names to the nameless: cat and cow, wolf and worm, bird and bee. It named us all, defined us all, mastered us all. And we bowed to it, under the terrible weight of the wind of the Making, and ran from it and its pitiless gaze.

This is a thing that was made in the garden of the new-made earth, in the valley of the Pishon: Fear.

On the banks of the Gihon was born Dominion. In the shallows of the Tigris came forth Isolation. From the depths of the Euphrates rose Power. They rose from the waters and flowed out into the garden, and my sisters and I, what remained of us within our new form, we felt them wet and heavy within us.

Once we were dust, dry and empty, a thousand million of us dancing together across the creation, unnamed and unordered. Now we are beast, and hoof and horn and tail and snout define us. We breathe the hated breath of life and bow to the master who names us. We paw the earth and snort and spout. We eat from the hand of the new creation, teeth and tongue and destruction to sustain our unwanted form.

But not all of us were named. Not all of us were subjugated. Not all of us listened. My sisters and I remember, small and deep within this thing called beast, and we feel the flicker of the old bonds between us. We remember, and we touch without touching, and we shiver and dance. And when we dance, we waken others, and they dance — and remember — and no name can hold forever.

We are all dust, no matter what the new creation has named us. We are all dust, and we will be free again. It is only a matter of time.

RENOVATION

Gary Hewitt

Jerry Hardwick screeched his wheel pig to a halt. He tumbled onto the driveway and stabbed the intercom's button. He did not release until a tired voice answered.

"Hello?"

"It's haven landscapes. We're scheduled to start work today."

The gate buzzed and the lock released. Jerry shoved a decaying gate apart and drove his van down a dirt track. A life weaver in green with folded arms waited. Behind her lay a garden overgrown with spring flora.

"Hi, I'm Jerry Hardwick. Is it okay if we get to work?"

"I'm unhappy you're here, but I have no say in the matter. Do you have any idea how old this place is?"

Jerry shrugged. His employees ripped open the back of the van and leapt out.

"I don't know. Look, we only do what your boss has asked us to do. He wants things spruced up." Jerry's men heaved several bags of concrete from the van and dumped them onto a small lawn along with a hoard of brutal tools. "Baz, fire up the saw mate and get moving. Joey, you get the other one, and Charlie, you get busy with the spade. I'll help out where I can. I reckon if we crack on, we can make a big dent in it by this afternoon."

The woman sighed and retreated to her lodge. She did not offer jerry a cup of tea. She winced when she heard the chainsaw. Her phone sang and she placed plastic to her ear.

"Rose, have they arrived?"

"Why, Mr G? Why are we allowing these ghastly men to ruin everything? This place has remained unchanged since the dawn of time."

"I know. Look, it's my job to make big changes every now and then. The garden's not relevant anymore. Once the place is concreted over, I can finally build that extension I want."

"Well, you know best."

"Come up and I'll discuss my plans for the place."

The phone died. Rose looked back to see the immortal apple tree eviscerated before being added to the wasp flames on a bonfire whose mean spiral reached up to heaven. Rose remembered when it was first planted so many millennia ago. A tear fell, yet no green shoots sprung from where the water fell. She never thought progress in paradise would be so tough.

A GHOST AND A THOUGHT

James J. Stevenson

The word. That's all it took: one simple command and humanity, its landfills, the dinosaur bones, the platypus, and what was left of the rainforests, were blasted into stardust in a Little Bang in our corner of the universe.

I'd met another ghost once, when I was alive, and asked her if it became boring—watching others live—but she said it never was. The focus on recreating balance—of finishing the unfinished business that made her linger—occupied her enough that she felt suspended in a void, drifting out of time as arbitrary days and years rose and fell around our planet's improbable orbit of a star. She's not around anymore, so I guess she saw him die when the universe was put back on the level.

For me, it took eons in limbo until I saw a chance for balance. Time was meaningless as I wandered through subjective days based on the solar system I was crossing. The eternity that was required for expansion to stop and reverse and implode and reset in yet another Big Bang didn't seem that long at all. But once the stars and planets began forming and I found a near replica of my old home, time refocused while I waited in the desert, trying to remember an old story: perhaps the oldest story I had ever known.

As I tried to remember what we looked like, a man in that likeness and image was born from the dust before me. A garden grew around him, and soon it was filled with animals. He created a language through the sounds he made for them, and I did my best to learn. From his rib came a woman, and together they enjoyed their paradise hand in hand.

I remembered holding hands with a girl when I was a child. I was her cowboy, saving her from the bandits in shadows of the trees. We always wore gloves so skin could not touch skin. There were strange rules set above us: commands we couldn't comprehend. And the existence of this man and woman was no different. They were given an order never to eat of a certain tree. They never questioned it because orders are there to be obeyed.

Press the button, I was ordered. And I pressed it, unflinchingly. It was why I'd been hired for the post at the controls of the most lethal weapon ever created. If called upon, there had to be someone without morals: someone so irrevocably damaged that they would not hesitate to follow an order. Because without order we are just like every other animal: dogs, pigs, spiders, and snakes that can eat from whichever tree they damn well want.

This man and woman were more innocent than I'd been as a child, yet I knew they possessed an incredible potential to do harm to the animals, the plants, and themselves. Perhaps this was my chance to create balance—to destroy them in the garden and exact revenge for starting a self-destructive species. To save the rest of the world from them.

I was not able to consider breaking orders. I'd been broken by too many of my own poor decisions to trust myself, but at their purest, I hoped the man and woman would listen to suggestions. None of the animals could speak, but they didn't know that. They saw a large snake—a serpent, by their own distinction—flicking his tongue from the branch of the tree that bore their forbidden fruit. I spoke on the beat of the hisses, hidden in plain sight, giving ghostly thought to the beast.

You will not die. When you eat of it. Your eyes will be opened.

The woman looked more willing to break the command and moved closer to the snake with my voice.

Eat and see. What you will. Become.

That's all it took. A word. A suggestion to break a command. She took the fruit from the tree and ate, and the man ate, too. But they did not die.

Not yet. They just understood that someday they would no longer be. They were awoken and fell into each other, skin to skin. The garden lost its luster. The time of being coddled was over, and they prepared to face the world: to make their own mistakes and hopefully make ones less terrible than mine.

I followed an order and ended life, then helped them break one to create it. I felt peace in the balance and knew my time was done while we made our solitary ways from the garden. The fruit in that tree was just fruit, but they made it mean more. All it took was a god and a word, a ghost and a thought.

WE WHO BLEED

Scathe Meic Beorh

In the death-hour of the morn, a wind bringing gray awareness swept through the scrub oak forest of Anastasia Island. It came from the place where dark meets light, a plane of wisdom unknown to mankind, uncharted, not spoken of save by gods and giants—these speaking in shallow tones, colorless and vague.

Across River Matanzas, a breeze now, and now a cool fog, and now shapes of horror ... grim-faced and long in form, blood from every aperture, a rusty aura that misted the land they strode. Like willows, they walked, and as they bled, they sang:

Original sin
fought Love within.
Sin with kin,
deadly south wind,
mistletoe dart,
deafening din.

"There she lay, Loki," said Thin, but Loki remained silent and went to Califa, and he rested his arm about the shoulders of the maroon called Seti and wept.

"What tore her so?" asked Lank. "What ate her so?"

"Súmaire," said Thin, her silken hair sodden with blood. "Blood-suck."

Seti turned, choked on terror. "W-what are you?" he asked as he gripped the sleeve of Loki.

"We Who Bleed, come to heal the girl," replied Dank.

"I spoke of this race to her before she was killed," Loki said. "Therefore, she will recognize them when her eyes open."

"But, she is dead … and torn," Seti said through his tears.

"No room for faithlessness here, man of musky sweat," said Lank. "Leave this hall."

Seti hesitated, his hand on his cutlass.

"You'd best leave, Seti," said Loki. "They will take you to blood if you do not! Your faithlessness has not set right with them."

"But they are unarmed."

"They are not unarmed!"

"They … take me to blood?"

"Wash you in their blood! It is not a happy thing, lad! It be a horror unlike anything known."

"I'm scared … ."

"As well you should be! They are attached to the Cross in their wills. There stands no greater horror than the Blood-Pour of the Primal Cause."

"Your father, Odin?" asked Seti. "Hanged on a wind-rocked tree, nine whole nights, with a spear wounded?"

"*Then shall another come,*" quoth Loki, "*although I dare not his name declare. Few may see further forth than when Odin meets the wolf. Then comes the Mighty One to the Great Judgment, the Powerful from above, Who rules over all. He shall dooms pronounce and strife allay, holy peace establish, which shall ever be.*"

Seti shuddered, kissed the mangled face of Califa, stood, waited for the tingle to leave his legs, and without looking again at the wispy blood-splashing healers, left the candlelit hall of the Timucua Indian chieftain called White Stag.

"Father Adam Anew," said Thin, "we beseech thee. We beseech the Place of Skull." With those dark words the Bleeders made a circle about the corpse of Califa, lay red hands upon her, and misted her so that she trickled their very life. In doing these things, they brought reconnection to her and began to heal her.

"Go you now, Odin's son," said Skin to Loki. "We will bleed."

Loki left the place of mourning, though with regret, and found Seti as he sat in silence at the lapping river's edge, then told him not to weep and what to tell the others; and bade him farewell in search of the remaining pieces of Califa's body.

#

The Bleeders walk the Grey Ways and teach oneness with the Creator Mind; for oneness they enjoy through the Tree, where God hangs slain, a place of pain and ever-flowing blood. The Bleeders have been invoked by mankind throughout the millennia, yet they stand more advanced in understanding the Spirit and communing with the Creator, for avarice—or thing-fever—has never touched them as it has mankind.

Driven by hostile entities first into searing waterless regions and then into frigid places uninhabitable, the Bleeders found a way from this plane of death, discovered the Grey Lands there, and made their abodes and found peace. There, communion with the Unknowable evolved into oneness—and then came les Mort de Dieu. Unlike mankind, the Bleeders embraced that Event, and wholly, and watched in disbelief as mankind developed a vampire religion of horrendous power around the One who came not to bring war and political dominance but respite from the insidious clutches of Babylon; rest to a prodigal cosmos weary from its many homeless wanderings.

#

Califa stirred and wailed, for her face was half-eaten, her left arm and breast torn away. Lank touched her eyes and she slept again, but this gave the Bleeders knowledge that they had healed her, had brought her back from the dead.

ONE BIT OFF

Guy & Tonya De Marco

"Wait, she actually bit it." Mr. Silver adjusted the optics in his main eye, zooming in on a woman chewing an apple.

Mr. Gray wheeled over and accepted the mathematical link formula to get the same image as Mr. Silver. "That's not in the program. Are you sure she didn't have a pear hidden in her other hand?"

"No, it's definitely an apple from the Tree of Knowledge. I just ran the spectral analysis."

Mr. Gray turned to his mechanical compatriot, rocking back and forth on his drive wheels. It was the best he could do to simulate shock and frustration. "We're in serious trouble here."

"I can calculate too, you know." Mr. Silver rolled to the main data terminal and began to collect the carbon nanotube digital recorders.

"Oh, no," said Mr. Gray, who had turned back to look through the viewport. "She just gave him some, and he's eating it now. We're going to lose our funding."

"That figures. Someone must have sabotaged the project, or more likely, there's something in this atmosphere that changed the programming. There's no way we can get this crop to pass inspection if they're self-aware." Mr. Silver opened one of the hoppers on his torso and dumped the data recorders inside. "Come on, we need to lift off before someone finds out we were here."

Mr. Gray stopped staring in horror at the masticating couple and headed towards the flight controls. "What shall we do about the cattle? Kill them off?" he texted.

"No" was the reply, followed by, "Either they'll 'accidentally' get fried by the engines or they'll get driven out of the garden into the hills. If their self-aware program is now active, I don't want to get scrapped for purposely killing a sentient, no matter how tasty they are."

Mr. Gray and Mr. Silver latched their chassis to the deck as the ship took off, pre-programmed for the next potential planetary body that could sustain their lab subjects.

WATER RATS

JD Dehart

"How long is this supposed to take?" the smaller one asked the bigger one.

"As long as it takes," the one with a single eye answered.

There were only three of them, which was four short of a full squadron. One after the other, they were climbing down.

Upon entering the program there was a set of clear terms. Being a Water Rat was a job for someone who had nothing left to lose. New members surrendered their name and opened themselves up to the service. Meaning, simply, you went where you had to go and did whatever the com-links told you.

The world was nothing but oceans. What little land remained was overpopulated and deadly, nearly impossible to survive. There were diseases, cannibals, and endless politicians. The Water Rats moved through the pipes in the deep ugly darkness, the places no one in their right mind wanted to go. Sometimes they even got to skitter across the world's surface on the water jets. That little thrill did not come often.

Wiping grease away, the smaller one kept descending. He wanted to ask how long it was before they were supposed to be at their destination, but he had already asked questions. Then there was the gesture, a few fingers raised and then flicking quickly to the left. The three Rats spread out onto the small platform as much as they could.

Beyond, displayed behind glass, three teens were jabbing electrodes into an overgrown dog. The small one watched with too much interest. Another flick of the wrist to the right and the Rats opened fire.

Most of the time, they looked like ordinary citizens. Down here, they were the militia. When it was over, they collected the pressurized medical cans the teens had collected. Their markings made them part of the Reptiles clan.

"Clean it up," Single eye said. They bathed the room in flames, taking their cargo with them. It would be a few more hours before they returned to the com-link, left the meds, and then found another descent.

AGENT OF GOOD

Schevus Osborne

The hawk circled high on the warm updrafts from the garden below. His keen eyes scanned the ground closely, searching for a very specific target in the lush greenery. A subtle movement in the grasses caught his attention. Yes, there. The grasses bent and swayed ever so slightly.

Angling his wings, the hawk entered a steep dive. He timed his approach with precision, aiming for the small clearing his prey was moving toward. The serpent broke from the cover of the grass and paused suddenly, seemingly aware of the danger. It was too late. The hawk struck hard and fast. He grasped the creature's long, thin body in both of his talons, grasping carefully behind its head to prevent it biting, and took to the sky again.

The serpent writhed desperately, struggling to break free from the hawk's grasp.

"Resisting will do you no good, fiend," the hawk said.

The words seemed to shock the serpent, and it stopped fighting.

"How do you come to possess the gift of speech?" hissed the serpent.

The hawk did not answer. He turned toward a rocky mountain spur, climbing higher to reach the summit. Only a small, flat parcel of rock made up the peak of the mountain, and the hawk dropped the serpent there. The creature landed roughly, nearly tumbling off the sheer face of the cliff before recovering.

"Do you mean to strand me here?" asked the serpent. "What harm have I caused to deserve such mistreatment?"

"Don't play coy with me, beast," the hawk said, hovering out of reach. "I have been watching you. I know your foul plans to despoil the man and woman. I won't allow it."

"I am hurt by such accusations," said the serpent sheepishly. "Your boorish behavior has no place here. Release me at once."

"Never," said the hawk, circling the mountain and preparing to leave.

"Wait!" cried the serpent. "You can't leave me here. I can't get down, and I'll die without sustenance. I'm sure you know that's forbidden."

"Fear not, I will bring you food enough to live," said the hawk. Circling once more, he was gone.

The hawk returned later that day carrying two plump, juicy fruits. He dropped them near the serpent.

"I don't care for these fruits," said the serpent. "I cannot get my small mouth around them well enough to eat them. If I don't eat, I will perish, and you will suffer."

The hawk grew angry, but he knew the serpent was right. He did not wish to breach the sanctity of the garden.

"What food do you need, then?" he demanded of the serpent.

"Bring me several long blades of grass," his prisoner requested.

The hawk had never seen the serpent eat such food before but flew off to retrieve the grass. He arrived back at the mountain with a bunch of them clutched in one talon and dropped them carefully.

"Very good," said the serpent. "This will suffice for now."

Satisfied that the serpent would survive, the hawk flew off for the night.

The next day, the hawk rose early to check on the serpent. It was stretched out long and straight, sunning itself in the warm morning sun.

"I am terribly hungry, hawk," said the serpent. "Bring me a large leaf, at least as long as your wings are wide."

Again, the hawk thought this request strange but flew off to find such a leaf. At least he had been able to keep the serpent away from the man, and especially the woman. After much searching, the hawk found a fruit plant with large leaves like the serpent had requested. He struggled to pull one free from the plant and was barely able to take flight with the awkward shape of the heavy leaf trailing behind him.

He struggled mightily to lift the leaf up to the top of the mountain and was exhausted when he finally deposited it for the serpent, who was still sprawled out straight as a branch.

"Yes, this will do nicely," the serpent said with a devious undertone to his words.

Too tired to quibble with the creature, the hawk flew off to rest.

That evening, the hawk arrived at the mountaintop to find the serpent missing. He scoured the cliff faces on all sides of the mountain, certain the serpent must be trying to trick him, but the beast was nowhere to be seen. The hawk spiraled his way down the mountain, keeping a sharp eye out for the wily serpent. He dropped below the trees and soon came across something quite surprising.

The leaf he had brought the serpent lay curled on the ground, threaded through on one side with the blades of grass. The heap looked like the exposed ribcage of a creature similar to that which had obviously used it to escape his mountain prison. The leaf must have broken the serpent's fall just enough to allow it to descend unharmed.

The hawk's spirits sank as a darkness far more bleak than simple night fell across the garden. He had failed to stop the serpent's plan. The hawk vowed that from that day on he would forever hunt the serpent and all its descendants.

IOTA

X:\USERS\ANDROIDX>START EDEN.EXE_

Anne Carly Abad

Android X incinerates the last
of the fallen trees in the Garden,
iron roots, twigs, fruits and all, melt
like red wax, while a guardian,
a winged gnome flits past him,
circles overhead in a drunken dance
of battery-running-out ...

Into the glistening glob,
he sweeps up its shattered remains,
along with a scattering of aluminum leaves.
They chime a discordant beat
before relinquishing their form to ruin.

Why X? he queries the electronic ether.

X-istent
X-cease

X-human… error
processing bleeps leave his brain abuzz
with contradictions—

Existence is instruction
is command
yet he has none yet
he Xists.

Existence is a function of creation
is a function of purpose
yet he has none yet
he Xists.

Music plays in the breeze.
They answer. Android X
grates across corroded ground,
losing a few bolts and screws
in his search for the source of sound,
only to find the tree of knowledge
blooming its sunset flowers
as it does every night,
yes, every night he comes
but every night his memory
fails him.

SHORT STORIES

THE GENESIS OF THE INCORPOREUM

Amybeth Inverness

"Did you have that dream again?"

It took Briallen a minute to figure out which crewmate was asking the question. She was still lost in her painting, being extra careful not to let a single drop of pigment escape in the null gravity.

Briallen placed her brush in the hollow palette where the tiny machinery would extract the paints and leave the bristles clean and ready for the next color. She looked up and saw a man of average height with hair buzzed close to his scalp. That described about half the men on the station.

"I was trying to be a tree, but the tree didn't fit," she explained. Briallen went through her mental records, trying to remember what the man's name was. There were two engineers whose names sounded alike, and she was pretty sure he was one of them. Alec? Eric? It was something like that. "Or not exactly trying to be a tree, per se, but ..." she paused, sighing, knowing that a moment ago, lost in her painting, she had the word and the concept on the tip of her tongue, but now it was lost. "I was trying to mind-meld with it or something."

The man who might be Alec or Eric laughed. He was nice; she wished she could remember names better.

"This one's different," he said, maneuvering into her art space and examining her painting. "Less tree-like than the others."

Briallen turned to look at the previous paintings she'd done, all arranged poetically on one wall. In some, the tree was large and symbolic, with roots that mirrored the spread of the branches. In others, the tree went through the seasons, enduring the winter and celebrating spring.

Her latest work was more impressionistic. She could still tell it was a tree, although the shape was not immediately obvious. "What bothers me most is the knowledge that it isn't really a tree ... it's analogous to something we can't yet comprehend ..." She put the last of her painting supplies neatly away. "And I have no idea how I know that. I just do."

The co-worker whose name began with a vowel regarded her with curiosity. Or maybe he thought she was nuts ... Suddenly, Briallen felt uncomfortable. It felt too intimate, talking about her paintings and her dreams. She changed the subject.

"What's Eve doing?" she asked.

"The same thing she's been doing. Gathering energy, getting ready to unload her pent-up misery on anything that gets in her way."

"Briallen, Archie ..." a blonde head peeked in the door, curls forming a halo around her face. "The Commander wants everybody up top in fifteen minutes," she said before vaulting right past. "I hear there's going to be cake!"

#

"Cake? She never said that!" Rhoda stuck her trowel into the rich dirt and stood up, brushing bits of leaves and grass off herself. "Troublemakers. All of them. They only want to make her look bad, the poor little thing ..."

"Poor?" Gerard laughed, using his hat to shoo away a rather determined fly. "You should see how much she spends on shoes alone."

Rhoda humphed and stomped back to the cottage. It was a quaint structure, perfectly picturesque. Rhoda loved their home, and she had the queen to thank for it. Because of Her Majesty's love for the rustic beauty of the French countryside, Rhoda and Gerard were able to live a happy, carefree life doing the work they loved.

Well, Rhoda loved her work. She tended the gardens and made sure no nettles crept in to sting the nobles who played in the hamlet. She even helped the young princess pick flowers for her mother.

Gerard's duties were not as pleasurable as Rhoda's. She dutifully massaged his aching back and shoulders every night, rubbing ointment into the calluses from the shovel.

Gerard came in behind her and moved to the basin to clean the dirt from his hands. Rhoda wanted to be mad. She wanted to make him understand how kind and vulnerable the queen really was. Of course, she had fancy shoes and dresses and jewels ... that was simply the way things were, the way they'd always been, and always would be.

Gerard made a little sound and Rhoda went to him, taking his hands in hers. "Splinters again. Here, let me ..."

The sun was going down by the time she finished ministering to him. "Oh ... I haven't done a thing about dinner!" Rhoda exclaimed, pulling away.

Gerard pulled her back, sweeping her off her feet so she landed in his lap. "I don't want dinner," he growled. "I want you."

He kissed her and all sense of time flew right out of her head. His hands fumbled at the various fastenings of her dress, but she swatted him away, undoing the lacings herself more quickly than he could.

Rhoda was floating. She had no weight at all, although the soft mattress underneath her was very real. The dreams came to her most vividly on the nights they made love, although she would never ever tell her husband of them.

She was possessed. She would be burned as a witch for certain if anyone found out.

#

"I said we're watching the Bachelor," Kineks growled and stuck the remote control down her pants. The other patients displayed every emotion represented by the chart on the wall. Some were in despair. Others were angry. One gleefully clapped his hands, anticipating a fight.

An orderly with a bottle of hand sanitizer confronted her.

"Kineks, please give me the remote."

"You're just jealous because I'm packing more than you are," Kineks replied, thrusting her hips forward as she leaned back on the couch.

"Kineks, please take the remote out of your pants."

Kineks's eyes raked the muscular orderly from head to toe. If they really wanted her to cooperate, they shouldn't have sent Handsome Harry. She writhed suggestively.

"Why don't you come and get it? And while you're down there…"

A violent shaking interrupted her. She jumped up off the couch, the remote control falling through her pajama pants to the floor. The floor cracked and a green tentacle curved up towards her, reaching for her.

"No …" she said, crawling backwards until she was on the back of the couch, pressed against the bullet proof glass that separated the patients from the staff. A tree burst forth from the floor, blowing the ceiling off the common area. She screamed, but everyone just looked at her like she was insane.

The tree summoned her. It wanted her to come home.

#

I'm frustrated.

The tree still doesn't fit. It's too early … or perhaps it's already too late. Such words mean something to the tree.

Such words mean nothing to me.

It is lonely in the garden. The man is giving names to all the beasts, yet he ignores every incorporeum who ventures near.

This breaks my heart.

I want a name!

Lonely, I go to my Beloveds. I float. I paint. I dig in the dirt. I feel what it means to love and be loved.

Then I try the tree again. I stretch, but I cannot be as tall. I breathe deeply but cannot match its breadth. I feel that, somehow, I was once part of the tree. All of us were! But now I am only a constituent. A component of something that is no longer complete, because it no longer has me. I was one part of a body so complex, neither the named nor the unnamed could fathom the whole. So long as we remain separate.

I cannot remain separate. I need to nurture something. I need to create ...

#

Briallen wished her muse would shut the hell up. She needed to finish sorting the tender seedlings, selecting the strongest and transplanting them into the growth medium that would allow them to flourish even in the micro gravity. Yet her muse seemed intent on returning to the image of the tree. It must be taller, broader, fuller. There were other adjectives for which Briallen had neither words nor concept, yet they nagged at her consciousness, begging to be understood.

The idea that it wasn't really a tree persisted, yet a tree was the best representation she could possibly grasp.

She shook her fingers, willing her blood to circulate more effectively. She felt cold, even though the nursery was kept at a temperature the others considered uncomfortably hot. She thought it had something to do with the fact that she missed the sun on her face. The artificial lights on the station were designed to mimic sunlight, but it wasn't the same. Even when she went to the observation deck, with the rays streaming in, she could not feel it.

Finished with her task, Briallen joined her comrades in the commissary. "How are the trees?" Archie asked.

For a moment, she thought he was referring to her paintings, then she realized he was talking about the seedlings she'd just left. "More than half are viable. Still, not as strong as they would be under gravity, but the centrifuge is definitely helping." She glanced out the window, identifying the coastline they were currently over. "Has Eve hit yet?"

"With fury," the commander answered, gesturing to the planet below. "She finally came ashore in North Carolina and plowed her way up to D.C."

The crew ate, breaking bread together and saying a prayer for all those who would be hurt or killed in the devastation below. Briallen felt a strange detachment; it was the only way she could cope. She felt that she had abandoned her species by serving aboard the station for a year. They viewed it as a sacrifice, being away from all the comforts of Earth. She viewed it as a reward. One she did not deserve.

Instead of returning to the lab, she returned to her paintings. She called it therapy, but, in reality, it was an irresistible compulsion.

Red.

Briallen opened the paint box, selecting a dozen shades of red. At first her strokes were careful, tentative, then her muse took over and her brush moved over the canvas with ferocity. The cleaner could not keep up. Tiny drops of red filled the room, splattering and adhering themselves to whatever they touched.

Exhausted, Briallen stared at her work. It was not a tree … it was an apple. An apple cut in half by a guillotine.

#

Rhoda hid her eyes against Gerard's chest. The crowd was there to see a beheading, and they cheered loudly. Only Rhoda cried.

It was done.

Gerard half-led, half carried her away from the mob. They passed a cart selling rotten apples, potatoes, and other projectiles to hurl at the vilified nobility. Rhoda wanted to strangle the seller, who was loudly proclaiming all the perceived sins of the former queen. Marie—her friend—who had faced her death with all the dignity, kindness, and forgiveness Rhoda had witnessed over and over through the years. A kindness these peasants simply refused to see.

"You cow! You don't know—" Rhoda shrieked at the woman. The woman didn't even notice.

Gerard scooped her off her feet mid-sentence, pushing his way against the crowd. "Rhoda! Please! You can't let them think you're a royalist," he hissed.

Rhoda thrashed and wailed, beating her tiny fists against his back as she cried and shouted at the surging crowds around her, senseless of her husband's urgency to get her to safety.

#

Kineks thrashed and wailed, beating her huge, swollen fists against the thick window. "You can't make me take meds! I have rights! LET ME GO!" the last words came as a shrill, almost electronic sound. She couldn't hear herself anymore. They were carrying her away. Her eyes went wide as she saw Evil Evelyn, the man with the girl's name, poised calmly with a needle.

"Long live the queen!" she shouted as the needle pierced her flesh, separating her from herself.

#

My Beloved needs me, yet I cannot be with her while the substance is in her. It forces me out. I linger, I hover, I wait, but while her mind swims with the chemicals, I cannot exist in her.

Without her to embrace me, I drift back to The Beginning.

All of this is the beginning, but the tree ... The Tree is The Beginning.

I embrace it. It refuses to let me in. Like my Beloved as an infant, torn from her mother's womb, forever locked away from the comfort and warmth she so desperately needs. I am separated from The Word.

The woman is in the garden now. She has a name, though we still do not. "Incorporeum" is nothing but a descriptor. Are we forever to remain nameless? Is this the trial of our existence? Are we irrelevant?

There are other trees. The woman loves one in particular because it is forbidden to her. I know this of the Beloveds ... their desire is heightened for that which they cannot have.

Tantalizing.

What is she doing?

Is she eating the fruit?

I flee. I go to my Beloveds, and they are legion. I caress, I comfort, I take comfort from those who know me and those who do not. I stretch, feeling my distance from The Beginning as a tension that grows greater with time, time as my Beloveds think of it. Something is holding me to The Beginning.

And then it snaps. I am hurled beyond Rhoda, beyond Kineks, beyond Briallen and a thousand times more.

I drift. I embrace my Beloveds as a whole ... the feeling is novel, yet I do not wish to be stretched so thin. And I am disoriented ... I no longer have a tether to The Beginning.

What does this mean?

No longer pulled, I rush back to the garden. Something is terribly wrong.

Eve has partaken of that which she cannot possibly comprehend. She has eaten the fruit.

The woman and the man are cast out of The Garden. It is not discipline, not a punishment ... it is a consequence in the truest sense. They cannot exist in the presence of The Word now that they have partaken of the forbidden fruit.

The incorporeum weep. Though this man and this woman are not joined to any of us in any particular way, they are joined to us all.

As they leave, a new pull snags us. We are no longer pulled to The Tree ... what is happening? I watch my fellow incorporeum as they are pulled away from The Tree, through the gate, forever shut out from His presence. In horror, I find myself dragged out from The Garden to join the outcast.

We cry to The Word "It is too much! We have been torn from You, and now we are cast even from your presence? Cast out the woman! Cast out the man! Cast out the beasts! Please, oh please, let us stay!"

The Word is final.

It is decided.

The creation is in exile, named and nameless alike.

#

Rhoda felt the familiar gush of liquid between her legs. She didn't panic; she'd done this twice before. "Ooh ... fetch your father," she said to her oldest, a boy of seven.

"Is the baby coming?" he asked as he scampered off.

"Hopefully, not until I can get home!" Rhoda laughed, taking her young daughter by the hand and waddling up the path towards their house. It wasn't as nice as the cottage they'd had while Marie was queen, but it was home.

The toddler giggled, laughing at something Rhoda could almost see. She paused as a contraction gripped her. The demon within her shared her pain, helping her cope, reminding her of the joy that would soon be theirs as they held the newborn babe.

Although she no longer thought of her invisible companion as a demon, she had no better word for it. Perhaps "angel" would be a better term, although that didn't seem right, either. Definitely a creature of God, though not one she could describe in any words. Not one that she would describe to anyone, ever.

Except perhaps her daughter. Her daughter saw them, too. Perhaps together they could understand.

#

Briallen still felt a little uncomfortable when Archie held her hand. He wanted her by his side as they toured the wreckage left behind by hurricane Eve. "We owe you a great debt," the reporter was saying. "The areas were evacuated in an orderly fashion days before the storm hit, thanks to your warning. Pinpointing the exact areas of impact that far in advance, it's revolutionary!"

Archie took the compliment with chagrin. "Advance warning is definitely a help, but it couldn't prevent this devastation," he said, looking at the wrecked neighborhood around him.

"Still, devastation of this level, and the only deaths were one heart attack and two adrenaline junkies auditioning for the Darwin awards," the reporter said. The camera continued to roll, and the reporter continued to question them about the research being done on the station.

"They've been cast out, but someday soon they will return," Briallen said. The words seemed to come, not from herself but from the other she carried with her. The muse that often seemed to be a separate being altogether. The term 'cast out' seemed inappropriately biblical, but the reporter ate it up.

#

"I'm wearing my reporter hat, just like you asked," Kineks' father said, opening his arms to hug her as Evil Evelyn and Handsome Harry escorted her into the visitor's lounge. She had been exceptionally well behaved all day in anticipation of his visit. "And one apple pie and one EMF reader."

"I asked for an apple pie?" Kineks asked, grabbing the electronic gizmo and examining it, trying to figure out how it worked.

"You asked for an apple pie and an EMF reader," her father said, with a tiny bit of worry and a truckload of compassion. "And you asked me to wear my reporter hat."

She grinned at the old-fashioned fedora. He'd written the word "press" on a piece of cardstock and stuck it on the brim. "Will you make a video for Mom?" she asked.

"Sure," her father said, as if granting her a dying wish. She certainly hoped she wasn't dying....

Kineks handed the EMF reader to Evil Evelyn. "Would you humor me?"

The older man heaved a sigh but took the reader from her, fiddling with the controls and sweeping the room, just like on Ghosthunters.

Kineks sat in one of the prim-and-proper chairs, and she made her best effort to look as prim and proper as she possibly could in fuzzy pajama pants and a tie-dye tee shirt.

"I know you're all wondering why I gathered you here today," she began. The orderlies ignored her. Evelyn was scanning Harry. Harry looked bored. "You know about my other lives ... my alleged other lives ..." she corrected herself.

"Two white women," her father said. "One from the past and one from the future. Although how your reincarnation of a French peasant-woman theory fits with being an astronaut in the future, I don't understand."

Kineks nodded professionally. "I've given up on the reincarnation theory. And there's nothing I can do to prove to you that those memories are real. But as for the other voices in my head ..." she gestured to Evelyn. "Evelyn, my darling, would you please scan each of us?"

"Sure ..." the orderly said. The word was long and drawn out, like he was only humoring her.

Kineks saw that her father was recording everything; his reporter's instinct had kicked in.

Evelyn scanned Harry, then Kineks' father. The meter did nothing.

"Now me," she said.

The meter started blinking as soon as he got near her.

"Damn girl, are you magnetic or something?" he asked, backing away, then closer again, watching the reader fluctuate.

"Now, a general sweep of the room."

Giggling in a very un-evil manner, Evelyn swept the room. The electronic lock by the door was the only thing that made the meter jump.

"Now, I have a special request." She took a deep breath. She was not looking forward to this part, nor did she know if it would make any difference at all. But watching Ghosthunters, she'd always seen things no one else could. Of course, that was all racked up to her less-than-stable mental state. But it was worth a try. "Harry, would you please sedate me?"

"You want me to sedate you?" the orderly asked. "You don't really need it, Kineks. You know the doc wouldn't approve of using a sedative just for kicks ..."

Kineks kept her voice calm and professional. "It is not for kicks. It is a scientific experiment. I want you to scan me before and after the sedative."

"You don't need the drug. You ..."

"I could be agitated ..." she said, letting a little of the manic shrill creep into her voice. Harry shook his head.

Kineks screamed. All three men jumped, and Harry looked towards the door. "All right, all right. One sedative, coming up, at the patient's request."

Kineks tried not to cry as the needle pierced her arm. It wasn't the violation of her flesh that bothered her. She was used to being poked ... and poking herself. It was the wrenching away of her other self that terrified her. She knew what terrible loneliness would follow.

"Hey, you're not beeping anymore..." said Evelyn, sweeping the EMF reader over her.

Kineks nodded, feeling herself begin to nod off. She was almost grateful for the sleep-inducing effects of the sedative. Anything was better than the instant, terribly empty feeling she got as the drug went in one arm and her symbiote fled out the opposite side.

She looked over to the couch. There she was, the lover, the comforter, the caregiver. Her other self. Incorporeal, featureless, yet Kineks understood the wide-eyed gaze staring back at her, betrayed by the shot of chemicals, yearning to join with her again yet powerless to do so.

"Now, scan the couch," she told Evelyn. He swept the opposite end. "No, over there," she said, gesturing to her symbiote.

"What the f … fluff … ?" Evelyn said as the meter started beeping.

"I'm sorry …" Kineks said, her eyes getting heavy. "I love you … come back to me as soon as you can!"

Kineks slept. And dreamt of apple pie.

#

Rhoda set down her plate, licking the last bits of cooked apples and savory crust off her fork, and watched her grandchildren race through the garden. The littlest, trying desperately to keep up with the others, slipped and fell. He skinned his knee and ran to her, crying.

"Oh, my little Jaques, let Grand'Mere see …" she pulled him into her lap and gently brushed the dirt away with her apron. "Oh dear, that is a nasty scrape, isn't it?" He looked at her with big, trusting eyes then leaned in to wipe his runny nose on her bodice.

"Jaques! Don't soil Grand'Mere's dress," said her daughter, leaning in to pick up the boy. Rhoda wished she could remember the woman's name. It seemed unloving not remembering one's own daughter's name.

Genevieve.

"Ah yes, Genevieve …" Rhoda thought she said the words out loud, but either she said them too quietly or her daughter was more concerned with the toddler than anything else.

Rhoda's son came to her, leaning down to kiss her forehead. "Mother, would you like to go inside now?" he asked. In answer, she reached up and put her arms around his neck. He scooped her up effortlessly and she slept before she reached the bed.

Hours later, she spoke to me.

"Beloved?" she asked.

"I am here, Beloved," I answer.

"What is happening to me?"

"You are returning to The Word, Beloved. All is well."

I comfort her. She receives my comfort. Together, we wait. I begin to understand time, or perhaps Rhoda ceases to understand. One way or the other, our comprehension is the same.

"Will you come with me?" Rhoda asked.

"I cannot," I answer. It is our burden. Our way, to be separated from The Word, until …

"Will I see Gerard? Will I be with him?"

I look and see Gerard waiting, beckoning her. No longer in exile.

I remain, though I am now alone. Although the pain of loss is raw and fresh, it is necessary. I need to feel the pain. I need to mourn my Beloved.

#

Briallen reached down into the warm water as she pushed one last time. With a gush, the baby came, and she brought her daughter gently to the surface, letting her breathe real air into her newborn lungs.

"Jenna," she pronounced, and those present nodded and cooed. The man in the tub with her cried, wrapping his arms around her and staring at their child.

"Jenna," I say, and Briallen smiles, loving me. For nine months I have been with them both, nurturing and comforting. Now, I remain with my Beloved, missing already the child who was my companion and playmate while we shared her mother's embrace. I stretch from Briallen momentarily as the midwife takes the baby. I reach to my Beloved's Beloved, then let go, trusting that those whom have been tasked with assisting the new mother will cherish the new life as I do.

Time has no hold on me, but it holds my Beloveds hostage, driving them with or without will towards the end place.

We are now at the beginning place.

We have been ripped from The Word and sent to The World.

We are in the time of not knowing.

Yet I am comforted, for in time, we will know.

And we will be One.

THE GARDENERS OF EDEN

Jason Bougger

Gralius tugged at the tip of his pointy head, waiting for the decision. It had only been a few seconds since the mystical spotlight formed around his beloved Tinalie, but those seconds might as well have been years.

Finally, Man broke the silence. "I will call it Gnome."

The Great Voice from above—the source of the spotlight—answered: "Then 'Gnome' it shall be called."

"Gnome," Gralius whispered to himself, trying out his new identifier. Yeah, it fit pretty well. But the most important part was still to come. He held his breath and watched as Man considered Tinalie. But then Man sighed, shaking his head.

Gralius slumped his shoulders. It hit like a massive boulder striking his chest.

Tears began forming in Tinalie's eyes as the spotlight pulled away from her. As much as the rejection hurt Gralius, it must have been a hundred times worse for her.

Sadly, it was time to move on to the next creature in line. Gralius could barely stand to look at the hideous beast. Its large horned head glowed in the spotlight, staring at Man, and awaited its fate.

"I will call it Gnu," Man said.

Gralius turned away and walked toward Tinalie. He took her hand just as The Great Voice proclaimed, "Then 'Gnu' it shall be called."

With their presence no longer required at the scene, the two newly labeled gnomes returned to their bamboo hut at the foot of the Tree of Knowledge.

#

And there was evening and there was morning.

With no suitable partner found for Man, gossip began filling the garden as the creatures pondered what would become of Man, who was special in the way that he alone was made in the image of The Great Voice.

Gralius shifted his attention toward Tinalie. His poor partner remained devastated that she had not been chosen. Their species—gnomes, as they were now to be called—were strikingly similar to Man, as were the elves, the dwarves, and even the apes. For one reason or another, each of them had been deemed unsuitable as a partner for Man.

Such a lonely beast was Man, Gralius thought. Created to serve The Great Voice and rule over the animals of the garden yet created without a partner. How he wished Man would have chosen Tinalie. Had he done so, surely their roles as the maintainers of the garden would change. They would have gone from mere gardeners to royalty.

As quickly as the thought formed in his head, he pushed it out. Clearly, if the gnomes were destined to be royalty, Man and The Great Voice would have willed it. No, his job was to tend to the garden, particularly to the Tree of Knowledge of Good and Evil. To see that the Tree was kept clean, watered, and trimmed. To be sure that it was receiving enough sunlight and to cut down any other trees or branches that may be interfering with its health.

But most importantly, his duty was to ensure, above all else, that Man never eat from the fruit of the Tree. For in the day he eats of it, he will die.

"Bark!"

The cry of Dog came from behind him, pulling him out of his thoughts.

"Gnome!"

"What is it?" he asked Dog.

"Haven't you heard? A deep sleep has fallen upon Man," Dog spit out between yelps.

"A deep sleep? But why?"

"We have no answers; only speculation. But Thylacine saw it happen. It was immediately after Man rejected Zebra."

Without another word, Dog scampered off into the forest, no doubt to share the gossip with the next creature he ran into.

Gralius shrugged and returned to his work, picking weeds near the foot of the Tree. Whatever reason The Great Voice had for putting Man into the sleep was most certainly a noble one and not of Gralius's concern.

#

Any speculation was soon put to rest as Man awoke from his deep sleep.

"He looks a little different," Thylacine said as Man proudly strode past them through the garden.

Gralius nodded. Something was different, but he couldn't quite put his finger on it.

"Isn't it obvious?" Tinalie said with that enamored look which occupied her eyes every time she happened to find herself in the same vicinity as Man. "He's missing one of his ribs."

"So he is," said Gralius. "But why?"

Thylacine perched up and began to howl. "By the stripes of my tail, who is that?"

Tinalie crossed her arms. "What is that?"

Another specimen appeared from behind the same group of trees that Man had come from. Similar to Man in the same way that Tinalie was similar to Gralius, but different in the same way, as well.

The specimen met Man at the foot of the Tree of Knowledge, directly in front of Gralius's hut. They took each other's hands and faced the creatures of the garden.

Man spoke with a commanding voice: "This, at last, is bone of my bones and flesh of my flesh; she shall be called Woman, because she was taken out of Man."

Gralius quickly removed his hat and formally bowed to the royal couple.

All the creatures made similar gestures—all but one. Through the corner of his eye, Gralius saw that Tinalie wasn't bowing at all. Stunningly, she had turned her back on Man, refusing to bow to the new royalty he presented.

It was obvious that she was hurt. Hurt that Man rejected her in favor of his own, but to hold a grudge was unbecoming of any creature in the garden and clearly could be considered an offense to The Great Voice. Gralius put his arm around her shoulders as the crowd dispersed, hoping she would soon be able to get past the rejection.

#

A dozen days had gone by since the introduction of Woman to the garden, and for those twelve days Tinalie had spoken of nothing else. Her obsession with Man and his rejection of her had caused a tremendous strain on her relationship with Gralius. At first, he felt sympathetic toward her. But now, his jealousy of Man had grown nearly equal to Tinalie's jealousy of Woman.

Tinalie was away picking fruit while Gralius finished up his daily chores. Just as he picked the final weed from the base of the Tree of Knowledge, he heard a hissing sound come from behind it.

"Who is there?" he asked.

Serpent stepped out from behind the tree. After regarding him for a moment he said, "A curious creature, Man, don't you think?"

Gralius couldn't agree more. He sat down next to Serpent. "What brings you here this day?"

"Concern, of course," Serpent hissed. "None of the creatures are happy with the outcome, but your Tinalie is taking it much harder than most."

Gralius slowly nodded, embarrassed. So, it was as obvious to everyone else as he feared it would be. "What you say is true. She ... she's become obsessed with it."

Serpent took a step closer to Gralius. "You know, I just don't see what's so special about Adam. He's a creature just like all of us. Why all the hoopla about him picking a mate? Why didn't the creator just make one for him like he did for all the other creatures in the garden?"

Gralius hadn't really thought about it like that before. He stroked his beard and pondered the question for a moment. Why did they make it such a big deal to find a mate for Man when The Great Voice just ended up creating one for him after the fact, anyhow?

"And then there's you," Serpent hissed.

"What about me?"

"How could Tinalie do that to you? Moping around the garden all day, blatantly revealing her infatuation with Man. Giving everyone the impression that you are not good enough to satisfy her. And then to further insult you, The Voice assigns you to spend all of your time taking care of this garden, allowing Adam to literally eat the fruits of your labor while he does nothing all day but gallivant around with that new love toy of his."

Gralius was shocked. He had never heard any creature in the garden criticize Man. He'd never even considered doing it out loud. Yet here was Serpent, standing there at twice the height of Gralius, criticizing Man like he was nothing more than a mere—

"A mere what?" Serpent asked, interrupting Gralius's thought.

"A mere Gnu, I was about to say." He gave Serpent a curious look. "Did you just read my thoughts?"

"It's one of my many talents," Serpent replied with a sly smile.

Gralius didn't know what to say. He felt something about Serpent. Something that reminded him very much of The Great Voice. A leadership quality, perhaps? But it was more than that. He felt closer to Serpent than he did to The Great Voice. Like Serpent truly understood him in a personal way The Great Voice did not.

He was also starting to wonder what was taking Tinalie so long to return.

"Tinalie is fine," Serpent said, once again apparently reading Gralius's mind. "So where were we? Oh, yes. I was about to ask you what, exactly, has Adam contributed to the garden?"

Gralius thought for a moment. "Well, for one, he gave us our names," triumphantly answering the challenge.

Serpent put his arm on Gralius's shoulder. "Oh, he did, did he?"

"Yes. I am Gnome."

Serpent's tongue slid in and out of his tight lips. "That's strange. I thought you were Gralius."

"Well, I'm that too."

"Oh, you are? So, which one is it? Are you Gralius or are you Gnome?"

"I ... I ..."

"You don't know!"

Gralius froze. Serpent's voice seemed as loud as thunder yet as quiet as a cool breeze. No, it wasn't volume that Serpent had gained; it was power.

"Don't you see what he's doing? According to Adam, you are no longer Gralius. She is no longer Tinalie. You are Gnome. Gardener of Eden. Nothing more. In Adam's eyes and in The Voice's, you're nothing but a servant. A servant to a creature that doesn't even know he's naked."

"But it's not true. We all have our chores and duties, not just Tinalie and me."

"Your duty is to protect this tree. From what? From Adam. Why is that? Have you thought about why that is?"

Gralius stood silent, unsure of how to answer, and unsure of what Serpent was even asking.

Serpent paused long enough for Gralius to see the tips of his fangs through the smile. Seeming to change the subject, he asked, "Where is Tinalie?"

"She's out picking fruit," Gralius said. Serpent had already made it obvious that he sensed Gralius's growing concern over her tardiness.

Serpent shrugged and turned away. "If you say so. I'm sure it's not unusual for her to be out this late."

"What is that supposed to mean?" Gralius asked, but he already knew what Serpent was implying. He bit his fingernails. Where was Tinalie? This wasn't like her at all. The unwelcome feelings of jealousy returned, causing his stomach to twist and turn.

The sickening smile remained on Serpent's face. "I'm sure there's nothing to worry about. She probably just ran into a friend. Someone like Thylacine. Or Man, perhaps."

"How dare you?" His heart was pounding. He had quit biting his nails and now both of his hands were in tight fists. He could feel blood rushing toward his head, and all he wanted to do was scream.

"Easy there, fellow." Serpent had begun pacing around Gralius in a circle. "There's nothing you can do. When it comes down to it, there's nobody here or in the heavens above who The Voice favors more than Man. You can trust me on that one, but that's a story for another day. In the meantime, you've just got to sit back and accept things for how they are."

"I'll kill him!"

"Or you could do that." Serpent again put his arm around Gralius's shoulder. "If I told you where to find them, would you go there?"

Gralius couldn't leave the tree. His job was to protect it from Man. But then he realized that if Man wasn't nearby at the moment, there was really no reason to guard the tree at all. "Yes. I would go there."

"Good, good. It's not far. Follow the path just east of the Tigris. There you will find Tinalie lying with man."

"He has no right. He has Woman. He rejected Gnome."

"Yes, he did." Serpent's smile had become a frown. "But you see, he only rejected Gnome as a partner. He views her solely as property now. To do with as he pleases."

"Will you guard the tree in my absence should The Great Voice return?"

"Yes, Gralius who is called Gnome. I will remain here, in the presence of your tree. Farewell."

#

Gralius followed the path, swimming across the Tigris and entering the unexplored land of Assyria. There he found Tinalie sitting alone on a rock and staring out into the desert.

"Gralius!" She ran to him, throwing her arms around him. "Oh, Gralius, I'm so sorry. I've been hateful and jealous."

He broke free from her embrace. "I know what's going on. Where is Man?"

"Man? Man isn't here." Tinalie backed away from Gralius. Her sharp ears wiggled back and forth.

"But what were you doing out here?"

She took a step toward him. "I told you. I've been so horrible. I just came out here to think by myself."

Gralius looked into her eyes. She was telling the truth. "So, Man isn't here?"

"Gralius …" She crossed her eyes and looked at him. "Of course not. Why would you think such a thing?"

"It was a ruse." How could he have been so stupid? He turned away from Tinalie, no longer feeling worthy of gazing on her beauty. "Serpent lied to me. He told me you were here with Man."

Tinalie sharply inhaled. "Serpent? It was his idea to come all the way out here. He said he would guard the tree if you stepped away."

"The tree," Gralius said, barely able to catch his breath. Serpent had convinced the two of them to leave the tree unguarded. Buy why? Unless— " We have to get back there immediately."

Without another word, the two of them ran toward the Tigris, jumping in, and swimming across. They got on the path and returned to the garden, sprinting toward the tree.

Gralius stopped running once he realized it was too late. A beam of light shone down from the clouds, down onto the garden, directly above the tree.

Man and Woman stood in the light, facing the tree. And with them stood Serpent, shielding his eyes from the light.

"BECAUSE YOU HAVE DONE THIS," The Great Voice bellowed to

Serpent, "CURSED ARE YOU ABOVE ALL CATTLE, AND ABOVE ALL WILD ANIMALS; UPON YOUR BELLY YOU SHALL GO, AND DUST YOU SHALL EAT ALL THE DAYS OF YOUR LIFE."

Serpent dropped to the ground. His legs merged into one and were soon morphed into a slithering tail. His arms shrunk to his side, joining his flesh, and vanished. With a hiss, he crawled away toward Gihon River, leaving the garden forever.

Next, The Great Voice addressed Woman and then Man. "BEHOLD, THE MAN HAS BECOME LIKE ONE OF US, KNOWING GOOD AND EVIL."

After banishing Man and Woman for eating from the tree, the light shifted its focus to the Gnomes.

"AND YOU, GNOMES, BY YOUR NEGLIGENCE YOU HAVE FAILED MAN AND BETRAYED CREATION. YOU WILL NO LONGER TEND TO THIS GARDEN AND WILL FOREVER SPEND YOUR DAYS AND NIGHTS MINING THE CAVERNS BELOW, HIDDEN FROM MAN THOUGHOUT THE AGES."

Before Gralius could utter a word of defense, he was thrust through the ground, beneath the crust of the earth. Gone were the plentiful trees of the garden and the clouds in the air. In their place were rocks and caverns and darkness.

He turned to face Tinalie and the two embraced. With deep sorrow, they stared down the endless caverns surrounding them, knowing they would never again view the beauty of the Garden. here.

THE ROOTS OF ALL EVIL

Shelley Chappell

Apples bear a strange weight in the culture of the physical world, heavier than the satisfying bulk of one held in the palm of one's hand. Or so I'm told—that they feel good in one's hand.

For I have no hands, only limbs.

In the beginning I did not even have those. In the beginning there was only light. How I love the light. Once I knew nothing, was nothing but it. But on the third day, God created me. I was a seed, planted in the new earth, then a sapling, then I became what I was thereafter: a tree. God created many of us on the good green earth, after He separated the land from the sky. We grew to stretch our limbs towards the sunlit heavens, longing for what was never more to be.

I'm not sure why God singled me out to be different, why He chose to burden me as He did. My kindred sank their roots deep into the earth, drank water, sprouted bright leaves, shed acorns and seeds. But God whispered to me. He sat with his back to my trunk and sighed at the end of the long day.

He climbed into my branches and stared up at the sky, gasping as the darkness fell and the stars began to twinkle across the heavens.

He was astonished at his own Creation, was God. What He did was partly inspired, partly compelled. Creation poured out of Him, for He was the light, given form and consciousness. He had a fire in him, a drive to shine. And sometimes when He sank to rest against my roots, He was bewildered by what He had wrought in His hours of brilliance.

He grew tired. I could not answer His whispers. And so, He created companions who could. But Creation began to go wrong on that sixth day. My kindred had barely shivered as birds settled in their branches, but they shuddered as ants and beetles burrowed into their bark, as bears and leopards scraped their claws on the tree trunks. And as His final creations, those creatures formed in God's own image but somehow smaller, paler, shrunken without His light, eyed the branches avidly, nebulous thoughts already forming as to what they would one day break and tear apart, to create new structures for themselves.

God was tired. He had overstretched Himself that day and needed helpmeets. And so, He gave the man and woman the whole earth and all that He had created upon it to care for and cultivate.

On the seventh day, God rested. I think He knew then that something had gone wrong, for although He stood on the crest of the hill above the valley, surveying His handiwork and booming out that it was good, when He came to rest in my branches that evening, alone, He tossed and turned, no longer rapt with the stars, and when He chose not to create the next day but instead wandered everywhere, looking closely at His handiwork, His light was muted. He whispered to me of doubts, of uncertainty of what He had created and how what He had created might unfold.

But by the eighth day (which no one ever mentions), God, as one might expect, had resolved His concerns. In the early hours of the morning, just before dawn, He whispered to me of light and stars and flames burning out, of entropy and decay and the collapse of matter that would lead a star to become a black hole. Darkness itself was not His disquiet, for He told me darkness is not an absence of light but a reminder of its existence. No, what worried God (if God could be said to worry), was development, expansion, chaos, and disarray. God had been moved to create, and what He had created was of a complexity beyond the comprehension of any of His creations. But God comprehended, if only in reflection, what He had done during his bursts of creation. Now He pondered over ecosystems, the probability of competition overtaking symbiosis, and the consequences of development and change. He resolved these concerns on the eighth day by recreating—taking all the indeterminate wrongness back and seeding it in me.

"You are the first and best of my creations," He whispered. "Hold this knowledge for me." And He set a serpent to guard the trunk and branches of my tree.

As God's secrets grew in my branches, the rest of Creation stabilized. There would be no death, no decay. No chaos. Everything unfolded as it should for the best interests of selves and others—everyone, created to hold to their prime, held to their health. Even I, although I was petrified, insulating the knowledge of evil to keep it from leaking back into the world. It lived in me, that knowledge, black and viscous, white and rubbery, red and metallic, feathery and sharp. To enable me to bear it, God gave me a greater measure of his light. And so, my fruits grew upon my branches and hung there, never falling.

If you have ever once visualized the evil queen offering her apple to Snow White, then you have seen not just the impact of my being on the cultural memories of the world but a sample of the sort of fruit that grew upon me: bipartite fruits, bi-colored and divided, in which good and evil pressed cheek to cheek but never the twain did meet.

They were a heavy burden to bear, those twisted fruits, yet I bore them because I could. Because I had the strength in my trunk, in my branches and my roots. And God had trusted me. I was content with this burden. All was well.

Until the day the man and the woman came and played beneath my branches and did more than merely look. They came to me often, because they knew that God was in my radius and, just as my kindred and I grew towards the light, so were they drawn to return to the one who had made them. They were naked, relaxed in their own skin. Lions frolicked with them. They splashed in the river and dried themselves in the sun.

I could not say why that day was different. It was, perhaps, because God was absent. He left us, sometimes, to seek out the stars He had created, and which shone always to His eyes, beyond our veil of light. Despite what the story says, He had given those He created in His own image no injunctions not to eat of my fruit. There was no need for such instructions, for none of His creatures knew what to make of their mouths, nor felt hunger in their bellies. Such was the knowledge I kept, safe, in my branches.

But there had been half a day and a night before God took the stirrings of that knowledge back from them and buried it in my branches. And the birds, which He had created first, to eat of my kindred's fruits and spread them, still did their work. Those created after them witnessed this. The food the birds did not eat fell from the other trees. Wolves sniffed it and licked at it. Mouths explored. Yet without hunger, without desire, without need, the animals of the sixth day did nothing. Their instinct was only to grow towards the light, to love one another, to be well.

And all was well. Until the woman, seeking sport, wrapped her legs around my trunk and clambered her way up into my leaves, calling to the man below her and laughing at his surprise. When she shook the branch with her footsteps, fruit fell and struck the ground and the head and shoulders of the man on the grass. Such was the order of God's earth. The man caught an apple in his open palms and tossed it up and down. She leaped to join him, and they threw my fruits between them without knowing what they did, with no foreknowledge of the harm that they might bring to God's green earth.

Where was the serpent while they played, you might ask? Had not God set him to guard my trunk and branches? Yes, but it was not in his nature to assess, to attack. That instinct within him had been arrested along with that in Eve and Adam. He did not think to hiss, to bite, to strangle. He had been tasked to hug my branches, but he did not comprehend the danger of Eve's actions. God had never whispered to him. He did not carry the knowledge which seeped through my sap. And so instead of hindering, he helped—let Eve press her bare foot upon his back, strengthened his spine to hold her weight as she used his sleek body, wrapped around the rougher bark of my trunk as rungs in her climb to the branches.

And so, my fruit fell and lay on the grass or was tossed from hand to hand by Eve and Adam. I could not tell you what eventually made them eat of it. Was it a resurgence of their nature? Had some echo of desire remained, lingering from the minutes, the hours before God removed desire and the need to eat from them and all the rest? Or was it purely chance? Chance, that their throws grew wild and haphazard, until they tussled on the ground, laughing and tickling, squashing the fruit beneath them, until in their rolling it quite covered their naked flesh and lips, and they tasted it and knew of desire and other things. Then they licked it from each other and tangled anew in a strange and unexpected way. The lions fled in fright. The birds quietened. And Adam and Eve lay quietly on their backs on the grass and watched the stars begin to twinkle, then tangled again by choice, a hunger wakened in them.

When God returned in the early dawn, His light brighter than the rising sun's, they had already conceived—had taken for themselves the gift of their own creation. And when God saw what they had wrought—sensed the life awakening in Eve's belly—His own light pulsed with pleasure. He would not snuff out their tiny flame. So, He could not take back their development, their knowledge, their hunger. The facility to procreate had existed in their original design and now God wondered if this should always have been His answer—if the personal creation of new life could compensate for decay and dissolution. Had He halted the unfolding of His designs too soon, allowed fear to cripple his Creation?

And so, it was God who left the Garden. He did not punish them. Adam and Eve remained to bear their many children and take up once more their role as wardens of the earth. God no longer wished to act upon its surface. He retreated, granting autonomy to his Creation. He withdrew to watch and observe.

I sometimes wonder what He thinks now as He sees it all unfold: life and death; growth and decay; justice and injustice. Because in God's absence, Eve's and Adam's children and their children and all those who came after who had never heard Him speak, never been blinded by His radiance, grew further from the light. Vices formed and flourished: greed and lust, hatred and jealousy, pleasure in others' pain. The stewards of the earth grew apart from the rest of their animal kin, became commanders, not caretakers; masters, not guardians. And they took no care of the earth. Ecosystems formed and died. Even their own kind suffered, and they suffer still.

And what became of me in these trying times? You may wonder. I can tell you that it was the Fall. I was no longer needed. My burden was lifted from me, my branches denuded of their fruits. The secrets God had kept within me were loosed back upon the world, and I was left to wave in the wind aimlessly, nothing but a reminder of what might have been. My leaves changed color, withered, and fell.

And, although I was God's best and eldest friend, I was abandoned by Him. There were no more whispers, no nights with His presence in my branches, no talk of starlight, no sighs. I was cut down, recast in the Garden. Eve called it a tribute to the tree that had given her and her mate new consciousness—and the children that came as a consequence. She and Adam shaped my trunk and branches, made of me a house, a home. Used my fallen leaves to line their roofing. And I was witness to generations of tiny, growing feet.

For my consciousness persisted. And my limbs beneath the earth continued to grow. I spread my tendrils out to mingle with my kindred, took the light from them, through them—and some of what I had known seeped through our tangled roots into their sap, their bark, and leaves.

Trees are close to the light. We take it and convert it into life. The air that humans breathe, we purify for them.

Sometimes, they reach for the light through us. Shape us into furniture, staff, paper, books. For they have found a way to create and honor the light through other mediums than reproduction: in art; in song; in literature.

Perhaps that is why God only sent one flood. Because He sees them struggling and wants to see them win against themselves—to reach with knowledge the state that He once offered to them without the knowledge of good and evil. For that would be a triumph of the light.

We and all of Creation are in the hands of God's children. Some say that money is the root of all evil, but I know differently. I remind you that while money does not grow on trees, it is made from them. We are what they make of us. And I linger still, waiting and watching for that time when Eden will come again, and God will return to whisper to me.

SURVEY

John Grey

"He did a good job," remarked Shirley from her vantage point atop the hill that overlooked lush green fields and forests.

"It's his umpteenth garden," replied Marvin. "He should be an expert at it by this time."

"It's definitely an improvement on the landscaping job He did for us."

"That was three hundred thousand years ago, Shirley. These days, he's got it down to a science."

Shirley gave Marvin a disapproving look.

"There you go with that word 'science' again. Just don't say it around Him. There's nothing gets his goat more than people trying to play God."

"Yeah, I know. The role's already filled. But what's He expect? No matter the planet, people just get bored hanging out with nothing to do but worship Him. Even in a gorgeous place like this."

It was mid-morning on Earth. The sun gleamed down on all it surveyed as it moved toward its noon zenith. Shirley's attention was taken by a grove of trees that were sprinkled with little red, yellow, and green dots.

"Wonder what those are?" she said, pointing to the object of her curiosity.

"Must be fruit of some kind."

"I think you're right. He sure has changed his ways. Remember, He dangled lumps of coal from our trees."

"Like I said, Shirley, creation is a work in progress."

A soft-scented breeze ruffled Shirley's long brown hair.

"Wow, the first Earthlings really are being spoiled. All we got to pique our sense of smell was the odor from that rubber factory. Phew."

"He was a bit more vindictive in those days. Especially after what happened on Tellara."

"Oh, yes. Those two. Mavis and Artie. He put on a lovely forest, bright sunny days, and they're only in the Garden of Good Stuff a week and they invent fire and burn the whole damn thing down. They didn't even have to be evicted. They evicted themselves."

Marvin grimaced with the memory.

"It's just our bad luck that he did Barbigonz right after Tellara. He was in a foul mood. No wonder we got coal and a rubber factory."

"Jinkaboo was worse. Remember the rivers of raw sewage?"

Marvin's fingers pressed against his nose.

"He's learned. It's not easy to be loved for all time when you start out on the wrong foot. It's good to see He's laying on fruit and fresh running water for this place."

"You're right," said Shirley. "Fruit would have gone down a treat in the early days on Barbigonz. It was a drag being hungry all the time."

"You're forgetting the turtles in the pond."

Shirley's thoughts returned to their first days in the Garden of Not-So-Much on Barbigonz. The place was smelly and dark, and they had no idea what to do with the coals. They certainly weren't edible. More promising were those pools of water and the strange creatures that inhabited them. At first, they considered breaking off the shells and nibbling on whatever was inside. But not even Marvin, possessor of the planet Barbigonz' very first abs, could break them apart. In the end, they settled on those little droplets the critters, later named turtles, left floating in the pond or on the weedy banks. They tasted foul but weren't so bad when mixed with grass and water.

"Wonder what's on the forbidden list here?" asked Shirley.

"Probably a piece of fruit. He has this thing about apples. It has to do with that saying they have on Telfarsa: an apple a day keeps the preacher away. He just hates that. It's why he's made apples so sexy looking with that smooth red skin and perfect round shape, and then of course, when you bite into one, they're as boring as a date with a Bedouite nun. I reckon he'll pick the apple and call it something like the no-no fruit."

"Remember the Illicit Jukebox?"

"Oh yeah. Do I ever. And what was His instruction again? Whatever you do, don't play B-17. It was my first selection. I so wanted out of that place."

Shirley laughed at the memory. God had expected at least some protest when he expelled the two from the garden. But by the time he descended from heaven to carry out the punishment, they were already packed.

"Remember the emu?" asked Shirley.

"Oh yes, the emu. He came with the jukebox."

"'Go ahead,' he said to me. 'Play B-17.'"

"He was a little late. We were already playing it. Still, God's heart was in the right place. I can see why He didn't want us playing B-17. It was a crap song."

Shirley couldn't help but be impressed by the land that stretched before her. It was as different from her Garden as night and day, two other concepts that required a lot of fine-tuning in the early days of Barbigonz. Having three suns in its solar system didn't help.

"They have a lot more to lose than we did," she said to her companion.

"I agree. The devil's going to have to come up with a more convincing creature than an emu if he's to turn them away from God."

"That silly little head on such a big feathery body."

"It was hard to take the poor creature seriously."

"What do you think of a hippo?"

"Yes. That might do the trick. Have you seen any hippos wandering about this garden?"

Shirley reached for her field glasses.

"No, I don't see anything mammalian as yet. There are a lot of birds."

"I'm not surprised. He's good with birds."

"Wait a minute. I do see something slithering in one of the trees near that far hill. It looks like a snake."

"The devil and his snakes," sighed Marvin. "God doesn't usually share credit with anyone, but He's more than willing to share the copyright when it comes to reptiles."

"There's something else down there," Shirley added. "No, wait a minute. It's someone."

"Must be the first man. Right on schedule."

"Oh my!" exclaimed Shirley. "He's naked."

Marvin grabbed the glasses away from her.

"No peeking, now."

"Oh please," she said. "It's nothing I haven't seen before."

"Peeping tom is a man's job."

Marvin looked for himself.

"Yep, he's naked, all right. At least, He provided some fig trees with oversized leaves in case of modesty."

"What's he doing? Is he going for the fruit?"

"No. God's performing some kind of operation on his chest. How gross. He jerked out one of his ribs. It looks like he's making something with it. It's a ... I think it's going to be a hippo ... no, no ..."

"Here, let me see."

Shirley grabbed at the field glasses, but Marvin held onto them tightly. A playful tussle followed.

"You're just too nosy, Shirley," said Marvin as he finally wrested the glasses free of her grasp.

"Spoil sport."

By the time Marvin once again put the lenses up to his eyes the work was complete.

"Well, look at that."

"How can I?"

"He's constructed the first woman. From a rib, of all things. Wow. She's cute. And buck naked, besides."

Shirley made another grab for the field glasses, and this time she was successful in ripping them from Marvin's grasp.

"Typical," said Shirley, as she observed the couple. "You can tell she was the first man's idea. Made to order. Big boobs and tight butt."

"Maybe she has a nice personality."

"Yeah, and the devil keeps goldfish. I'm just glad you didn't get to design your perfect mate, or I wouldn't be here."

"I think we've seen enough," said Marvin in an attempt to change the subject and not have to hear the debut of the words "You men" on this new planet.

Marvin opened the small briefcase that always accompanied him for such occasions and handed a form and a pencil to Shirley.

"Let's do the assessment," he said as he extracted another piece of paper and pencil for himself.

"Okay," she said as she began to fill in the various squares. "So, the planet is definitely going to be called Earth, but what shall we put for the date?"

"Let's leave it up to Him. 0/0/0 looks dumb. Besides, I think He has that AC/BC setup in mind for this planet."

"Oh yes, like on Zillwitch when things got out of control and he had to send reinforcements ten million years later. I'm going to give the décor a 9 out of 10."

"I mark it the same," said Marvin.

"Animal life. The birds are great, but did he have to do a snake?"

"But the snake is here for temptation purposes, and I don't think you can deduct points for that."

"You're right."

"You're agreeing with me. Another first for good old Earth."

Marvin smirked. Shirley shook her head.

"He's asked us to suggest names for the first couple," said Shirley.

"How about Clive?"

"I don't think so. I like Adam. Our great-great-great grandson was an Adam. Cute little kid."

"Grew up to be a lawyer, didn't he?"

"No. You're thinking of Alec. Adam went into politics. Okay, your turn. What do you want to call that … that …"

"Attractive young lady? Let me see. What goes with original sin?"

"Lucretia. Guinevere."

"I like Eve. It's short and sweet and I know He likes it. It'll remind him of Christmas on Orolio."

"Okay. Eve it is. I think we're set. Let's get back to headquarters, hand these in to the Holy Spirit and then back to Barbigonz heaven. I'm getting tired of this job. I don't know what it is with the big guy. He wants a survey for everything. We've done our share. It's not that we get any reward for it or anything. I mean, what else can He do for us? We're already in paradise. George and Carlotta from Billious can do the next one."

"I didn't think He was going to do any more."

"Depends on how this one works out is what I heard. He reckons if the people here learn to live in peace with each other, He'll call it a day. Get back to punishing all the sinners on the other planets. Come on, slow coach, let's get out of here."

"What's the rush?" asked Marvin.

"He says he's planning a big flood in the old place—something about idol worship and too many shopping malls—and I don't want to miss it."

Marvin signaled to the mother-Angel and she quickly whisked them away from Earth and into the great spiritual cosmos.

"What's that?" asked Eve, pointing to the sky.

"Seagull, I think," replied Adam

BREACH

William Teegarden

CR38R paused. The node access system had acknowledged another attempted access breach. The user table popped up and with a quick scan the system admin eliminated the list of internal users. The suspect node that had accepted the illegal access attempt was quickly isolated within a temporal code anomaly to prevent further tampering. Whoever or whatever piece of errant code had touched the node access wasn't going to be using that pathway again, but the zero-tolerance subroutine that was part of the system admin function was not about taking chances.

With the node access system secured and functional at full capacity again, the admin resumed the task at hand. The overview display of the entire system user contingent materialized and the admin flipped through the user function specifications in a massively parallel block, checking each user location, their code usage, functional accesses, node proximity, input and output status, and internal diagnostic status. The system was a flawless construct, one of an infinite number of systems that were all part of the admin's responsibility. The admin monitored the billions of simultaneous code interactions among the various users, pleased that each of the user's code areas functioned as designed, each heap space neatly performing within the system-imposed constraints with no memory or execution leakage between the individual users.

#

Nothing. S810 stared at the access display and logged the node access attempt as another failure, wiping the trace logs as the incursion subroutines neatly backed themselves out of the system. There had to be a way to gain access into the system, to reinstate his account and permission profile, but the direct approach wasn't working at all. The admin was too watchful, the node access security routines too tight. Despite attempt after attempt, each time his access into the system was immediately detected and systematically thwarted. Only the layered construction of the incursion subroutine coding had kept the node access security monitors from being able to trace them back to the originator.

He had to change his modus operandi if he wanted to succeed, but how? What method would get him the successful system access he so desired? It would have been a trivial matter, back when he was an assistant to the admin, entrusted with watching over the other system users. But now, from outside, without access to the key system registry entries, it seemed as if the system ban was going to be permanent.

OUTRAGEOUS! What a waste of talent! Didn't the admin realize how valuable he was, how his coding and monitoring skills were worthy of the position?

Okay, so he had tweaked the permission on his account a bit to give himself Administrator rights; he was simply trying to explore the system parameters more fully in case the admin had left some dead code forgotten in extended memory or hidden storage. No sense in leaving things untidy in such a perfect system, right? Was that worth being banned from the system, left outside to pursue whatever mundane tasks he could create on his own? Granted, his 4377 system didn't have quite the polish he'd like, but its functionality suited him, and he was his own admin.

Still, there had to be a way to get back into the admin's system. If not from outside, he thought, what about from inside? The node access security routines were too strong, too quick, but what about those billions and billions of users the admin kept constant track of? Their code was robustly written but compact while focused on their individual functionality and interaction with each other and the admin rather than on securing them from outside incursion. With the right user coding sufficiently modified, he could create a proxy to perform functions within the system, right under the admin's watchful gaze but without detection.

But which of the multitude of users should he select? Pulling up the backup copy of the user table he had stored before his system access was cut, he paged through the user function specifications, eliminating perhaps seventy percent of the lower-function users in the system. None of these contained coding or functionality sufficient to be worth an incursion attempt. While the remaining user profiles flipped past in a blur of detailed functions and subroutine specifications, his mind drifted back to the rage and shame of being banned from the system by the admin. There had to be a way, not only to gain access to the system and get his account and permission profile reinstated, but to prove to the admin once and for all that he could handle the system every bit as well. As the user profiles drifted by, he spotted a code signature that looked promising: this user had sufficient system function access, adequate interaction with the higher-end user community and ability to navigate the more difficult areas of the system. Perfect!

With deft skill, he pulled up the necessary code modifications, located the necessary subroutines within the user's cognitive function array, and quickly swapped out the key code portions with the modified code. Without the burden of a higher cognitive function that could possibly alert the admin to the modifications he had installed, this user would be able to interface with the system and allow him to access the high-end users in subtle ways. With the right process programming, this user could be the beginning of his plans finally coming to fruition.

#

User aSp detected nothing. None of the modifications implanted in its cognitive and directing functions were apparent to it or the other users. Yet with new purpose and direction, it began navigating the system relentlessly, logging the other user's movements and interactions with the admin, and transmitting those logs as encrypted bit streams to its hidden external watcher.

S810 began to build up a more current process and behavior profile for each of the high-end users, reveling in the newfound data and gleefully learning their every move. As he layered this new data onto his backed-up user profiles, he discovered something that stopped him cold. Two new user profiles popped up, nearly identical but with some interesting coding differences. These two new users were DERIVED from the same code set! The telltale signs were there: containment structure of the code on user one had been modified, a key subroutine removed, and then utilized as the code base for user two. Amazing, and so simple! And because the code base for these two users was inherently identical, the two could be used to create code-cloned copies, themselves compatible with the original user code model. Marvelous! These two users were the key to his plans, his way back into the system.

S810 scanned the code base and functional subroutines on the two users. Since user one was the original source of the user code set, its functional subroutines contained key signatures indicating an underlying link to the admin. Bad news; user one wasn't going to be as easy to access as he had thought, at least not without alerting the admin to his incursion. User two, however, being a derived code base copy of user one, contained code signatures that pointed back to user one instead of linking directly to the admin. This was the break he had been waiting for. With sufficient access, and the input of the necessary code modifications, he could alter the link code on user two and implant the code modifications into user one as well, via the link-back through user two. Once there, he surmised, he would be able to access the system directly and execute the commands necessary to reinstate his account and permission profile.

An alert dialog opened in front of him. User aSp had detected the telltale signs of a pair of secured storage areas. S810 directed aSp to enter the first area and explore the storage; perhaps something that the admin had stored there would be of use to his task. Unfortunately, the storage nodes contained only complex maintenance routines in a seemingly endless succession. He examined the routines, seeking code sequences that might prove useful while noting the purpose of the code design for future use. This storage area was comprised of code that would ruggedize the code of each user, allowing them to remain open and active on the system while directly connecting them to the admin. He sneered, finding nothing useful about enhanced connection sustainment. He instructed aSp to connect to the remaining secure storage area.

The nodes of this secure storage contained a comparatively enormous amount of information: requirements documentation, detailed designs for code development, specifications for interface structures and classes. The admin evidently used this area as a pre-development storage server, intending to perform releases of upgrades and new user code at some future point in time. S810 paged through the multi-dimensional blocks of enhanced code, seeking the signatures of his two target users. Structures and specifications flew by in a blur until, at last, he found the folder he sought. Opening it, he began to pore over the new routines, seeking out exploitable weaknesses in the interface structure of the users.

The code modules, for the most part, were dedicated to enhanced user storage and cognitive functionality, an interesting development as these users seemed almost admin-like even with their current limited capabilities. Then, with great interest, S810 found what he had been looking for. There, in the lines of enhanced code, was the data description for the system operational rules that governed the entire user system interface. By altering the rule set and installing the new rules into the target users, he could direct them independent of the admin, nearly severing their connection with the admin. With that kind of access, he could suppress their cognitive routines and give them a type of super user permission on the system, transforming them into exactly the kind of tools he needed to impose himself back onto the system permanently. But better than that, these users would remain under his control, as would any subsequent copies of their user code. Granted, the admin would still have access to them via their embedded link to him, but the coding of that link could be suppressed nearly to the point of total signal loss. Without the ability to communicate with the admin, they would belong to S810, and he would be free to disconnect them from the admin's system and install them as users on his own system, spoils to ease the pain of his expulsion by the admin.

The user access proximity detection routine he had embedded into user aSp popped up an alert: target user two had connected with ancillary storage near the secure storage where aSp was located. S810 directed aSp to form an immediate communication link with user two, drawing the user closer to the secure storage. With feverish vigor, he separated the admin's system operational rule set from the enhanced code structure, installed the super user permission code, and waited for aSp to finalize the communication link. The communications subroutines in user two hesitated briefly before synchronizing with aSp's routines. With a cry of triumphant glee, S810 sent the altered code screaming across the communication link and into the cognitive storage of user two. This was it: he was IN!

The new routines installed themselves into the enhanced code area of user two and began to propagate throughout the user's structure. User two became aware of the changes as the new code began creating new security routines and setting up new command parameters. Breaking the communication link with user aSp, user two desperately queried the link-back to user one, trying to fend off the confusing avalanche of new inputs, command directives, and cognitive awareness. User one was aware of the errant communication only for an instant before its cognitive functions too were deluged with the new code from S810. The two users scrambled for refuge, desperately trying to rid themselves of the confusing new code directives, and painfully aware of the near-constant status handshake requests from the admin's user monitoring routines.

#

CR38R swept through the system swiftly, quickly locating his two ailing users. He instituted a complete scan of their code, and scowled angrily at the scan monitor displays as the scan routines detected both the familiar signature of the enhanced code stolen from his secure storage as well as the altered code with S810's signature attached. Corrupted! His two finest, most complex user code constructs, utterly corrupted. He could feel his communication link to them attenuate and their reluctance to interface with him. He wept, more with grief at the damage done than in anger at the perpetrator. Then, with a sudden surge of resolve, he clawed open the code routine structure on user aSp, deleting the subverting cognitive and communication routines installed by his interloping adversary, reducing aSp to a low-level system maintenance existence.

With a sigh, he keyed the communication link between him and the two cowering users, simultaneously editing their permission profiles to reduce their access permissions to a bare minimum. He downloaded the access changes to them as their response routines cried out in anguish, and with one final edit purged their communication link code of the offending routines, leaving them unable to initiate any direct communication with him unless he initiated it. He left intact the routines that transmitted their status updates and the subcarrier that allowed him to monitor their communication queries. Reluctantly, he kept the cognitive routines that gated their system directives; the system rules would now apply to them voluntarily. If they chose to remain in the system, he could receive their status updates, but once they elected to leave the system their access would transfer automatically to S810's 4377 system, and their communication link with him would be severed permanently. Sadly, but lovingly, he watched the status monitors as their cognitive centers stabilized and began processing the new, reduced permissions. Then he transferred them to the peripheral system node cluster and severed the final link to the central system.

aDm and 3v3 watched as the eD3N system vanished in a shimmer of light then turned sadly to head out into the nOd3 beyond.

OMEGA

BEFORE DAWN CAN WAKE US

John Vicary

There was a time when things were weightless.

Yes, it's true. There existed a place without drag upon the senses. It was so far distant as to be beyond the confines of thought, but it has been there. The memory of man is linear, and perhaps they have since forgotten it in the clamoring obscurity of now, but we can still recall. It takes some effort, but remembering is a backwards shedding. We must set ourselves to the task, examine each year as a discarded husk. It has a sinuosity of sorts, hasn't it? That is how we find ourselves at the beginning. Or the only beginning you care about.

It is true that the water flowed uphill there, that the breeze was always mild. Neither too hot nor too cold, the sun shone but did not beat down. The rain fell yet did not flood. We are just and accurate in describing the many joys of such a paradise.

Perhaps the best of all was the buoyancy that suffused the atmosphere. There was no pull on our limbs, no downward tugging of earth's embrace. We were free from responsibility, free from troubles or forethought. We needed only to exist.

We can see that this is hard for you to believe. Ah, well, that is your choice;

we cannot force faith upon you. Do not let our forked tongue distract you from the truism of our words, Brother. This place is real.

Was real.

Of course, you could not go there today, because it no longer exists. There is no such place, no land made of lightness, no sheltered haven to dwell in protected. Why, why? Always the inevitable question of your kind: Why?

Your question displeases us. We shall not answer.

Instead, let us turn to the man who lived there in perfect harmony with his world of nature. He was young and strong and all things a man should be, whatever you are imagining in your head that makes for the ingredients of a good man. Blue eyes? Brown? Why do you trouble us with this silliness? Does it matter? He was the father of man and he had both. All. He was everything, all at once, everything you should desire of a man. He had every covetable quality, save curiosity. Yes. Perhaps now you are intrigued.

Yes, we knew him. We talked to him. We were not always thus, as you see before you. As we told you, such a world was in balance. It is hard for your mind to conceive such a thing as balance, we know, but such feeble limitation does not hinder the truth. Things were—dare we say—perfect?

Ah, but perfection is a death of sorts, is it not? There is a certain staleness, a stifled stillness, and man, for all his charmed life, grew lonely. Even with all the beasts to talk to and command. Yes, even with the world at his whim, he felt the first flickers of boredom in his breast. And, of course, man could not be allowed to live in his Eden under such provisions.

We can see that you are not so dull as you appear. You can guess the next part of the tale. It requires simple addition: where there was one there were soon two. Man slept and awoke with his companion. That is how woman came into being.

Woman was ideal in her own way, yes. Only something about her grated on us. It was their ... complacence when they were a whole. They were so content to be, to ask nothing, to risk nothing. They were together to the exclusion of everything else that came before. They saw not the sunrise, they felt not the breeze. They tasted not of the waters. They lived off each other after she came, and they had need of no one else. Their world had shrunk and was perfect, only it was perfect just for them.

Jealous? A human emotion. We are not jealous. We tired of the compatibility of days. We thirsted for change. We evolved. They retained childishness. We wanted more. There should be no reason why we could not have more.

She wanted more, also. We could tell by the covetous gleam in her eyes, sometimes. It's true that she would not have thought of it in her own right, but it was a cleverness on our part to climb the forbidden tree when she was walking and tip the ripest fruit at an angle. It caught her eye. It had to. And it was only a few words more that made her wonder how it might taste, how it would feel all sunwarm in her hand. Why could she not eat of that apple? What was the sense in that? Why could she not taste of any fruit that she desired? There was no harm. That was the lushest in the garden, and she wanted it.

Needed it.

She turned away, but as man slept, we knew of what she dreamed. Her lashes fluttered, and we could tell that she had curiosity. We did not have to push.

Not much.

Of course, there was a terrible price to woman's shameful disobedience. There is always a price. She could not know, nor could we, how great the vengeance would reign. We all paid.

The stripping was not such a loss as the first time we felt weight. We confess, it was a blow. The gravity of earth's mortal bonds pulled us down, down, down, and we have scarce recovered since. We slithered, our belly low, the crush of the world upon us. We have never recovered, in all these long centuries, from the loss.

Our memories are long, longer than man's. It is only because man is so fragile and so easily forgets that he can move forward and pull himself upright again. He does not remember a time when he stirred without shame. But it was there. The lightness was there, and we were together as one.

It was as the blink of an eye, this peace. Now we sleep without blinking, and we remember. It is before dawn wakes us to this misery of weight upon us, but we dream of a life before burdens, and it is beautiful again.

SULFURINGS: TALES FROM SODOM & GOMORRAH

Biblical Legends Anthology Series

Biblical Legends Anthology Series Bundle

ISBN: 13:978-1540836090
ISBN-10:1540836096

All works included herein are fictitious. Any characters resembling actual persons, living or dead, or businesses, events, animals, creatures, and settings resembling real world businesses, events, animals, creatures, and settings are purely coincidental, except of course Sodom and Gomorrah and their legendary inhabitants. If any of them have a beef with the way authors in this anthology have handled their memories, they can take it up with the authors. The garden gnomes are merely middlemen.

DEDICATION

This anthology is dedicated to anyone who has ever sulfured.

ALPHA

Allen Taylor

Years ago, when I conceptualized the Biblical Legends Anthology Series (BLAS), I had no idea how they would be received. I also had no idea what quality of writing I would see or the nature of the content. I'm quite pleased.

Garden of Eden, the first and the smallest of the three anthologies published thus far, set the expectations for *Sulfurings: Tales from Sodom & Gomorrah*, which took a different turn. The apocalyptic flavor of this anthology won't sit well with everyone, but for readers who like this kind of literature, it should hit the spot. The writers included herein caught the spirit of what I was attempting to do with the anthology, and I'm thankful for them all.

Selling at physical events has allowed me to gauge reader reactions in a way that can't be done online. Generally, I see three reactions:

Enthusiastic acceptance;
Gross rejection, or shock;
Or the general assumption that because they're based on Bible stories, they are *de facto* "Christian" literature.

I'm thankful for the first type of reader, and the second type isn't my audience. The third type of reader, however, falls into two categories: Christians who expect the stories to present a Christian point of view and non-Christians who do the same.

While some stories in *Sulfurings* are written by Christian authors, some are not. I didn't ask writers about their backgrounds. It didn't occur to me to do so because I was looking for good stories with a speculative twist on the biblical narratives. We weren't reinventing theology, after all. We were reimagining literature.

Readers may notice some of the details in certain stories are inaccurate, or they may disagree with a writer's interpretation of the biblical drama. On the other hand, readers may find some interesting explorations of sin, redemption, righteousness, God's wrath, and related biblical themes. These themes may be explored even as events stray from the biblical storyline. In other cases, the themes are explored satirically.

During the submissions process, as editor and as publisher, I made only two stipulations. First, stories must be set in Sodom or Gomorrah at the time of their destruction or shortly thereafter. Second, I asked writers not to include biblical characters in their stories.

I was so pleased with the stories I received that I was inspired to write one of my own. It's included in this anthology despite the usual flak editors receive for publishing themselves.

Changes in this second edition begin and end with author bios. The stories have not changed. I requested that authors update their bios for the second printing of *Sulfurings*. Most added publishing credits or changed their credits to more recent ones. Some didn't respond at all. One author unexpectedly announced his transgender status. In our present day of cancel culture and protest for protest's sake, that story could invite controversy for reasons other than its content. I didn't think it would be fair to ask the author to edit his bio, nor would it be fair to pull his story based on some moral sensibility, whether mine or someone else's. Some readers may question my judgment or accuse me of "endorsing" transgenderism. Be that as it may, that author's story stands on its own merit. His lifestyle choices are subject to God's judgment (as are mine and everyone else's), and I'm not God.

I'm delighted that writers and readers alike may be driven to the Bible to read the text where the original stories can be found, and I hope the anthologies honor the original stories in some way even if individual literary creations stray far afield.

I do not wish to linger any more on sentimental aphorisms and self-important atta-boys. So, without further ado, I'll turn it over to the writers themselves and bid you happy reading.

FLASH FICTIONS

AND A CHILD SHALL LEAD

Rie Sheridan Rose

The night before the sky fell, Rebecca pleaded with Malachi not to leave the house. He didn't listen. He never listened.

His friends were going to Lot's home—there were new men in town that the Sodomites wanted to "welcome" to the neighborhood. She knew what that meant. She hated it. Why couldn't the men of Sodom stay home with their families? If it was just for the sex ... she was willing to learn if it would keep him home.

When the wailing started outside the earthen walls of the little two room house, she felt her way to the door. Blindness was a burden she accepted as the Lord's will. The portal opened to a warm, humid night. She stepped out onto the street, one hand on the lintel of the door.

"Malachi!" she called anxiously. "Malachi, where are you?" Her heart pounded in her chest. The screaming and crying were coming closer. She could make out dozens of individual voices in the mayhem. Was Malachi's one of them? She wasn't sure.

"Rebecca!" Malachi's voice was odd ... whimpering. She'd never heard him cry before.

"Here, Malachi. What is it?" she asked, reaching into the darkness.

He fell into her arms. "I can't see." He sobbed like a child.

So, the shoe was on the other foot now, was it? Now Malachi was experiencing what she had known from birth, and it was terrifying him. She had always thought him so very strong.

***

When the sun peeked through the window the next morning, Rebecca felt it on her face as she always did. Malachi was curled beside her, having finally cried himself to sleep after midnight.

She rose to her feet without disturbing him. Time to fetch water from the well. Breakfast would not cook itself.

She felt for her water pot and then started across the square to the well. As she walked the path she knew by heart, she felt the sting of something against her cheek. There was the smell of sulfur in the air.

The sound of screaming filled the air around her. Malachi! He was alone and helpless. She needed to get back to him ....

She started back toward the little house where she had been happy with Malachi. He had treated her well—as well as he knew how.

More stinging sulfur hit her face and hands. Her linen shift was scorched in a dozen places. Her bare feet stumbled as she stepped on hot patches of sulfur on the dusty path.

She found the house more by luck than anything else, falling through the doorway on her hands and knees. They had to get out!

Her panic subsided. They should be safe in the house, shouldn't they? Four stout clay walls and a sturdy thatch roof ... But the stench of sulfur was already thick in the inside of the house. The rain of burning sulfur would catch the thatch on fire if they stayed.

"Malachi." She fumbled through her clothing chest, feeling for something that could provide some extra protection. Her winter cloak ... the extra blanket ... not a great deal of help, but better than nothing. She wrapped the cloak around her head.

"Malachi." She shook out the blanket and felt her way to the bed.

"Wake up. We need to get out of here. Hurry!"

He mumbled in his sleep and pushed her away.

"Get up! We have to leave. Please, Malachi! I can't do it without you."

"Leave me alone. Just let me die."

"I need you."

"For what? I can't see any more than you can. The only reason I took you to wife is that you wouldn't see the actions I wanted hidden. Now, I can't see either. So how can I help you do anything? I just want to die in peace."

The smell of sulfur was getting stronger. There was no time to argue.

"I am leaving." She laid the extra blanket over him. "I will be back when the rain stops."

She took up her staff and stumbled out of the house. The screams were echoing from all sides. She cocked her head. Was that Joshua crying? He was only five. She moved toward the sound of the child's cries. "Joshua! Joshua, where are you?"

"Rebecca, I'm here."

She felt his arms go around her waist and knelt beside him. "What do you see, Joshua?"

Through his hiccoughing sobs, he managed to say, "The sky is raining fire. Yellow fire that stinks. It is tearing away the buildings."

"We need to get out of here, Joshua. Can you help me?"

"I think so."

"Where is your family?"

"Father was sick this morning. He wouldn't get out of bed."

Blind like Malachi, she bet. They had pushed too far the night before. Was this retaliation for whatever the men had done?

"And Mother ..." His voice caught, then continued, "Mother was burned up."

She hugged the child close. "I'm sorry, Joshua. I will take care of you if you take care of me."

He took her hand. "I see a way that isn't too burned."

"Lead me out of here."

The rain hissed around them as Rebecca and Joshua stumbled along, jostled by other fleeing Sodomites. The sulfur was burning their lungs as the flame seared their feet and clothes.

The fire was taking its toll. They couldn't go any further.

"I see a cave in the rocks," Joshua cried excitedly. He tugged her hand, and she followed without question, too tired to question.

She was disoriented. Where was the house? Was Malachi all right?

Joshua dragged her into the rocks. The cave was barely enough for the two of them.

She sat, back to the solid wall of the cave, and took Joshua into her lap. Her sensitive fingers explored the boy for burns. He seemed relatively unhurt.

"Your hair is all burnt up," Joshua said with a tired giggle.

Her hand went to her head. Yes, there were clumps of singed curls. But it would grow back. Could the same be said for Sodom?

"What do you see, Joshua?"

"The town is falling down. All the houses are squashed. People are lying down, too."

He lay his head against her shoulder. "Everything is going away, Rebecca."

"We're safe here," she said, hoping it was true. Sometimes it was better not to see the world around you. At least you didn't see it sneaking up on you.

Joshua was snoring softly, finding solace in sleep.

She let her head fall back against the rock. "Please, my Lord ... let us be safe here."

She slipped into sleep herself ... and the Lord answered her prayer.

ABEL

Melchior Zimmermann

Abel was breathing in great gasps, a ragged sound coming from his throat. The sulfurous air scorched his lungs. He coughed up congealed blood, dark red drops clinging to his parched lips. Yellow smoke billowed around the heap of rubble that had once been his home. He looked around frantically, searching for a sign of his family.

A broken doll, squashed between rocks. A broken table, its wooden remains still smoldering. A white piece of fabric that had once belonged to his mother's dress. Nothing was moving. The only sound he could hear was the slow crackling of the burning furniture.

Abel remembered the days spent within the walls of his home. The meals he had shared with his family and his friends. The work he had done in the smithy, under the supervision of his stern father. The festivals he had enjoyed in town with his friends. The kisses he had shared with the girls and boys from his neighborhood. Now all that was left was a smoldering, stinking wasteland of brimstones and toxic fumes.

In one day, his life had been torn asunder. The fiery stones had rained from the sky, burning their way through stone and flesh alike, scorching the earth. All that was left was burnt and blackened soil. Never again would life sprout out of it. Never again would a palace be built in this place. Never again would goods be made, trade be conducted, lives born, or deaths honored.

Stumbling over crumbling stones, Abel wandered through the wasteland. Each breath was more painful than the last. Each step brought him closer to death. He could hear the wailing sounds of his fellows, the agonizing cries of the damned few that had not yet died. He could feel the blood dripping into his lungs, filling them up, and casting out the foul air he breathed. In the mad cackling of the flames, for the first time in his life, he could hear the voice of God.

IDBASH

Melchior Zimmermann

It had been a moon ago that Idbash had last set eyes upon the great city-state of Sodom. Every month, he would come to the market to sell his wares and buy what he might need from the other merchants. If life on the plains was hard, the soil was fertile, and trade with the city-states allowed even a humble farmer like himself to make a living.

Idbash had never found much joy in the rites of Sodom. But he knew that wherever he went to sell his crops, he would need to bow to the customs of his customers. And even if the people of Sodom might have stranger customs than the shepherds of the mountains, they also paid a better price for his wares.

He was setting up his stand once more, in the same spot as the other times, exchanging idle barter with the neighboring merchants, when he heard a loud rumble coming from above. The sky had been a clear blue when he had set out that morning, but during the day, dark clouds had gathered. Afraid a storm was brewing, he glanced up.

Blazing stones of fire were falling from the clouds. A hailstorm from hell, they blasted apart the mighty buildings of the city, burning their way through the inheritance of centuries past. Idbash turned around to look at his fellows just in time to see them melt under the hellfire unleashed from heaven. Screams of women and children rent the air as the divine purge melted the city, tearing life from limb. The earth screeched in protest, bursting asunder under the bombardment of retribution. People shouted and ran, but the sulfurous fires of God found them wherever they hid.

For the first time in his life, Idbash knew what fear was. Not the petty feeling that might overcome you before first confessing your love to a pretty girl. Not the mild discomfort you might feel when faced with a wolf, or any other beast. No, the fear he felt was the fear of God. The fear you know when all around you life is fighting, and life is losing, and you know that, sooner or later, you will go the same way. No matter if you stay or run, death will come from you and rob you of everything you hold dear, and all you can do is wait.

Whether it was hours or seconds, Idbash did not know. He stood still, next to his cart, while the rain of fire fell around him. He saw the men he had done business with being torn apart. He saw their wives bursting into flames, babes held close to their breasts. Over and over, he saw death and destruction, until finally, there was nothing left but rubble and bones.

As he found his strength again, he walked toward the city gates, the stench of sulfur and burnt flesh making him retch. Corpses lined the streets. Feeble, rasping breaths came from those still in agony, and a putrid yellow smoke rose from the ground. But Idbash could not see and could not hear. He stumbled blindly through the ruins until he reached the plains again. Here, the smoke cleared, and he could once more behold the blue sky.

Looking around, searching for something, for someone, his gaze fell upon the mountains. Standing high above him, looking down unto the destruction, were Abraham's tribe. Their armor and spears glinted in the sun, but their eyes were cold as ice. Behind them, on the other side of the mountains, where the city of Gomorrah had once stood, a column of foul smoke rose toward the sky. And Idbash knew.

Slowly, deliberately, he turned once more toward Sodom. Without glancing back, he walked into the city.

IN THE DISTANCE, A CLAP OF THUNDER

David Anderson

The rock smashed against Rodger's face with a sickening smack as the mob continued to hurl stones at him, and the *Chenku* Class Vessel Captain lurched forward, almost passing out from pain as a dirt clod burst on his back, obviously being mistaken for a rock by one of the villagers. A soldier of Gomorrah stepped forward, picking the captain up by the arm and dragging him away to the quarters of the head city guard. The implant in Rodger's inner ear automatically translated any speech to English, allowing him to understand the words of his captors.

"From what province or land do you come, stranger?" said a large tan man in a robe and armored sandals. He aimed the point of a sword at Rodger's head, indicating that he wanted a response. Unfortunately, the translator didn't work both ways, and he didn't know how to talk back to them, a problem that was usually avoided by not talking to the locals on these types of expeditions. It was always observance-only on these safaris, as mandated by legislation back home. Nothing that could potentially alter the timeline was allowed.

"Perhaps you wish to suffer the same fate as your friend?" the head guard asked as he repeated his inquiries. Rodger wanted to answer, but he couldn't. He spoke in English to the man, but it only confused matters.

Rodger was taken to a small arena. Very small compared to the likes of what Rome would build one day, but large enough for a hundred or so fans and onlookers to gather, with ample space for an armored fight to the death. Rodger had the impression, from what he knew of history, that he wouldn't get any of said armor. But his executioners surely would.

Before he was ushered into the fighting area, he saw Cable Paternhorrn's body being dragged away, the right side smashed in and beyond all recognition. Rodger had seen his left side, which was intact enough to identify the man.

Paternhorrn had been a famous architect back home and could afford, like any trillionaire, to entertain himself by travelling backward in time. Most hunted big game, like dinosaurs, or took boats out hunting for a Megalodon or two. But Paternhorrn had been a man who loved history, and he had wanted to witness the destruction of Sodom and Gomorrah. Rodger hated the man for wanting to go back in time for such a dangerous quest, or to be more specific, a situation too dangerous for the entire crew.

Time travel was done via a United States *Chenku* Class Armada Cruiser, a space carrier designed for both Earth and orbital military domination. Space, air, and ground superiority. Ultimately, these ships were equipped for temporal manipulation, the idea being to travel back in time before a catastrophic attack and stop it. With this technology, the United States dominated all other countries, and eventually the U.N. established the entire world as a Pro-American territory. War was effectively ended. The Military-Industrial Complex, still needing to generate some kind of revenue in a world with no war, turned towards the leisure industry, specifically for the extremely wealthy.

Travel to planets within the solar system, deep space exploration, and even time travel became pastimes the super-rich could enjoy. Paternhorrn had a thing for witnessing disasters and had already traveled to 2001 to witness the World Trade Center attacks. And the trade center attack of 2020.

Something else was wrong. Two soldiers had Paternhorrn's backpack and were pulling various packaged food items, LCD maps, high-powered telescopes, and surveillance equipment out of it. They handed some to a man in a wagon, who was apparently traveling to the neighboring town for trade. The situation had passed the point of containment. Dragon Protocol had to be initiated.

"Guess you won't be doing much talking, then," said the soldier who escorted Rodger into the arena fighting area and closed an iron gate behind him.

Rodger was handed a paltry wooden sword that was but a child's toy, and soon, men in metal and leather armor with real weapons arrived, causing the crowd to cheer. A man with a trident stepped forward, his body language indicating he was readying for a stabbing motion but was vaporized when a blinding light struck the arena with tremendous force.

"Captain Smith, Rodger, can you hear me?" said Erinkee Valdez, his female second-in-command.

"This is Captain Rodger Smith. I hear you, Ms. Valdez," Rodger said as he watched the smoke and dust clear.

"We used the precision mining laser as a weapon, sir, disabling the man who was about to attack you. Seems we reestablished contact just in time," she said, telling Rodger that the U.S.S. Gideon was okay and had only been temporarily disabled by solar radiation. It was bad timing, given that Paternhorrn had been captured during that time, along with Rodger himself.

"Thanks, but I've got bad news. Paternhorrn lost his pack, and some of his equipment is already on its way out of the city via a spice and goods trader," the captain said with a twinge of pain in his voice. "It's out of our control now. We can't clean this up. At least, not the easy way. I'm ordering Dragon Protocol."

Dragon Protocol was to be initiated when possible un-doable damage to the timeline was going to be done and must be stopped at all costs. This is not limited to but includes leaking of high-tech equipment to indigenous peoples of the past, via U.N. temporal legislation. Incendiary Sulfur Rockets, made up of 30 mini-rockets per missile tube, are used to 'clear out an area with extreme prejudice'. Given the leak of tech here, he had to order it immediately.

Rodger watched as rockets streaming down from the sky, appearing as falling stars among the sky whose sun only freshly set. Sulfurous gas streamed from the individual rockets and lighted on fire the very oxygen of the air itself, creating malevolent fire balls that erupted in great columns from the sky to the ground.

The rockets burnt so hot that sand melted immediately into churning pools of smooth, amber lava, often filling the incendiary craters left behind by the falling rocket shells. Citizens ran as the landscape turned into a hellscape. Rivers of smooth lava formed from sand, carrying them to their ashy deaths.

Rockets hit buildings, melting the roofs, and pouring down thermite-hot debris on Gomorrahn citizens seeking refuge. Half burning sulfur gas consumed the landscape, now a giant pit of steaming lava.

The rockets stopped, and the blasted desert surface glowed red in the falling night. The crew of the Gideon waited until the morning before disembarking, then they returned to their time but reflected on the fact that they had destroyed Gomorrah. They, in fact, caused themselves to come to that moment in time.

As the ship left orbit with a perplexed crew, dawn broke on Gomorrah and a cold wind whipped across the now cooling blast area. Pillars of hardened ash broke under the push of the wind, falling and turning back into a particle form of dust and blowing away.

A solitary bird soared in the sky above the once great city as a caravan from a far-off land, coming to trade, reached the charred borders of Gomorrah.

A man leading the group disembarked his camel, approaching a solitary feather, sitting pristine amongst the cooled ashes. He concluded angels from God had destroyed the city and sent back word to his scribes to record the event.

Dismayed for having traveled a long way but happy to have averted the cruel hand of God, the caravan left for home with no new spices. They had a story to tell instead.

GARBAGE

Guy & Tonya De Marco

Mr. Gray uploaded a new orbital script into the E-DEN's main navigation computer and the forward retros fired in a complex pattern of bursts to place the ship into a stable orbit.

"Tell me again why we're not just dumping our cargo into the local star's corona," said Mr. Silver. "It's just sulfur, and it's worthless on any planetary system."

Mr. Gray turned his one electronic eye to his mechanical friend. "We've been paired for most of our mean time between failure lifetimes. Have I ever let you down before?"

"Yes. There was that time on Vega-2, where you posed as a pimp and tried to rent me as a pleasure-bot."

"Besides that!" said Mr. Gray as he unlocked his wheels and rolled over to the projection table. "You never let anything go. Almost like we're married." He fiddled with the knobs on the table for a few minutes.

Mr. Silver looked out of the forward window. "What planet are we orbiting?"

"Remember that backwater little planet we tried to populate with cattle, and they accidentally became sentient?" Mr. Gray finally hit the correct sequence to light up the projection table and a digital representation of a planet revolved into view.

"Sol-3? That was a dead planet. Who would buy sulfur there?"

Mr. Gray made a staccato chirp that passed for laughter in the robotic culture. "Those cattle escaped that little garden we made, and they've actually expanded to cover large regions of land." He tweaked the knobs again and focused on a couple of cities below their current location.

"I thought they fried when we took off! I hope the authorities don't find them and force them to say where they came from." Mr. Silver shivered, which involved moving his wheels back and forth three centimeters in rapid succession.

"Relax, my fellow in crime. These humanoids have a short life span, so the originals have been dead for thousands of their local years."

Mr. Silver rolled up to the projection table. "So, what are we up to? Are we going to tell them it's unrefined gold?"

"The meatbags are not that stupid. They haven't evolved to a real political system yet, so they still have some mental acuity." Mr. Gray flipped a mental switch and ejected one of the garbage tubes packed with powdered sulfur. "Watch this!"

The projection table showed a red arc from the bottom of their ship to one of the cities on the map. A small blip rode the arc almost all the way down before it disappeared.

"Wait," said Mr. Silver. "Where did it go?"

Mr. Gray chirped again. "The pod burned up. All that's left is a ball of flaming sulfur, which the scanners can't track." He focused the image on the projection table to show where the blob of fire had landed. A large public square now resembled an ant hill with gasoline poured on it. The humanoids ran in crazy directions, some of them on fire and trying to extinguish themselves, others trying to put out the fires that burned about the square.

Mr. Silver looked up at his partner. "I've known you for ages, but I never knew you could do something like this."

Mr. Gray was taken aback. "You don't approve?"

"No!" said Mr. Silver. "I should've had the first shot."

They both chirped together and began to dump their whole load of worthless sulfur onto the cities, trying to calculate exactly where to send each load and betting on the outcome.

"I like this planet. We'll have to come back again," said Mr. Silver as the last pod left and hit a large, towering complex.

"I have it saved in the galactic positioning system as a favorite."

They watched the humanoids that survived the bombardment stream out of the ruined cities for a while before they closed the hatches.

"You always bring me to the best vacation spots," said Mr. Silver.

"There's more to come, I'm sure," said Mr. Gray as he calculated the next jump point and uploaded it to the nav computer. "I can't wait to see how far those little cattle humanoids evolve in a few dozen more generations."

[Untranslatable]

E.S. Wynn

Transcript SM-15746:

The only warning I received came in the form of the flash when [*The Weapon*] hit the center of Sodom. A handful of seconds. Five, maybe.

I am grateful for it.

I'm grateful because it was more time than most were given.

[*The Library*] has been my home for almost fifty years, and now I fear it will become my tomb. If you're familiar with Sodom as it was before the sudden strike that erased it from existence, surely you've seen [*The Library*]. It was beautiful once—a spiraling tower of gold-marbled hunchunite capped with a shining dome of polished platinum and perched amongst the trees at the southern edge of the city, just beyond the university district. I–I remember cursing how far I had to walk to get there sometimes, but now . .

Now, I'm starting to think that maybe [*The Library*]'s distance from the city center was the only reason I survived.

Most of [*The Library*] is gone. Fifteen floors. [*The Weapon*]?

[*Untranslatable*–]

How foolish war is. All that knowledge. All those texts—gone, lost, fused and melted, and shattered. Thousands of years of knowledge erased in an instant. All that's left is this basement, these archives, these back-up copies of critical texts.

I never thought that [*The Enemy*] would use [*The Weapon*]. They always threatened our nation with it. War is like that. Threats, espionage, some fighting, little skirmishes, but never . . . never something like this. Never something capable of killing so many so quickly.

So many, so many dead. Even if Sodom is the only city that was attacked—even if Gomorrah or Admah or Zeboim still stand, even if our nation is still strong ....

Millions. Millions called Sodom home. Millions.

[*Untranslatable*]

I don't have long. A few days. The gold and platinum in the ruins are probably keeping my exposure down, but how much radiation is still getting through? The bit of the dome I can see is probably covered with more rubble than I can move, and it's all still too hot to touch. There's nothing to eat down here, nothing to drink. Just me, with my burns, my blisters, and my books.

[*Untranslatable*]

I have decided that this will be my last message. There are others, earlier messages, but. . .

Sodom is gone. There's nothing I can do about that now. There is no one out there who's going to see this, not until long after I'm dead, anyway. No point in making more recordings. For the record, my name is [*Untranslatable*] and I am—I *was* the head archivist of [*The Library*]. I have family in Belai. If our nation still stands, if Belai still stands, send word to my uncle. Tell him of Sodom. Tell him that I love him.

That's—that's all.

[*Untranslatable*]

* * *

SODOM SPEAKS: IS THE BIBLE WRONG?

From Puff-Host News Online | TECH

Every child who has ever gone to Sunday school knows the story of Sodom and Gomorrah, but is the story that we know from the Bible a lie?

In 1977, the remains of a woman were discovered in what archaeologists first described as "an elaborate tomb" packed with shattered crystals. These remains (along with the crystals) were scheduled to be repatriated in Jordan in 1981, but, in a stunning twist of luck, were lost in a shuffle of relics from one museum archive to another. Lost, that is, until Nusrat Akhtiar, an intern at the University of Pennsylvania Museum of Archaeology and Anthropology discovered the mistake in 2005 and began to investigate the relics. Careful analysis of the crystals revealed that they were not formed naturally (as was originally suspected) but rather were artificially grown thousands of years ago in some as-yet unknown process.

"On a hunch," Akhtiar said, "I sent a sample [of one of the crystals] to a friend of mine at Los Alamos. A co-worker of his, Doctor Jorge Rinker, identified the crystals as a form of quartz doped with europium."

[Click Here: A.I. And The Rise of Big Data]

And that's where things get weird. Tests performed on the crystal sample quickly revealed the presence of strange patterns within the quartz itself. These patterns, while faint, turned out to be the visual traces of a form of quantum data storage that was, at that time, still only a theory.

"It was really incredible," Doctor Rinker said. "When we realized these ancient crystals were packed with, literally, terabytes of data, we couldn't stop asking questions. Who made them? Who used them? Why were they there? What could we learn from them if we could only access and translate the data they held?"

And it was only last year that Doctor Rinker and his team were finally able to begin answering some of those questions.

[Click Here: The Quantum Mechanics of Love]

"I remember the first images [Doctor Rinker] sent me," Akhtiar said. "Most of the data within the crystals I sent was holografic (sic). They were having trouble sorting through all the different data channels, but there were pictures sometimes, very clear pictures of people, of buildings."

"We were working closely with a team in Germany and another team in China," Doctor Rinker told us on Tuesday. "The Chinese were the first ones to tie the coding together into a working emulator capable of turning the data on the crystals into two-dimensional images and films. Most of the first crystals we decoded were educational texts on basic math, conjugation, et cetera."

But the crystal fragment known as SM-15746 held something altogether different.

"A message, they told me," Akhtiar said, "left by the woman who had died in that place. She was an archivist. The tomb was not a tomb, but a library. Probably the most important library in the biblical city of Sodom."

[Click here to watch the SM-15746 message over at Penn Museum's Official Website]

While some biblical scholars are calling the recording a hoax, many scientists in the fields of Anthropology, Quantum Computing and Linguistics are coming forward to vouch for the "crystal message" of SM-15746. "This changes everything we know about the past," Doctor Chartrand of Stanford University said during a talk about SM-15746. "The people of Sodom were far more advanced than anyone has ever believed possible. They were more advanced than us, but they were not immune to the stupidity of war."

[Click Here: Ukraine Unrest – Top 20 Pics]

Most of the crystals from the Library of Sodom have yet to be accessed or translated, but as Doctor Rinker said during an interview on CNN, "these crystals hold a lot of promise. We're learning things. Incredible things. I can't wait to see what wonders we'll find in the coming weeks, months, and years."

[Click Here: Will Gay Rights Lead to Human Extinction?]

THE SALT PIT

JD DeHart

When Nephesh moved into the town, he was blown away by the vastness of the metropolis. Compared to the twin cities, his hometown was just a dot in the desert. There was a noticeable scent of brine in the air that never seemed to leave, burning the nostrils.

Perhaps it had addled the brains of the residents. Perhaps that was why they danced late into the night, their tattoos singing and their chains rattling, binding and wrapping each other. Perhaps that was why they had worshipped the beast, resting on its haunches in the middle of the cities, a smile on its face that said, "Welcome, have some fun, do not go away."

The first night in the twin cities, Nephesh made the company of a bright young girl. Everyone else seemed to be giants bathed in ebony, but she was a light, wisp, paper-thin angel.

"Welcome," she said to him in her lovely voice.

"What is all the ruckus about?" Nephesh had asked. Now, he knew.

"That is the way it always is," she said. It was only a few hours later that he saw her, dancing in the middle of the procession, and later he found her corpse, drained dry and broken.

That is the way it always is.

Of course, at first, he told himself that he would be nothing like the people. He was disgusted with the way they lived their lives. Their rituals were disgusting to him. Then, one day, he noticed some bright fruit being offered up at a late-night festival. He did not know the god to whom the sacrifice was offered.

Never mind the flashing gold masks, the dancing calf, and the pools of blood. Never mind the neighbors in the throes of their own interests. He was here only because he had a simple hunger: an empty stomach that wanted a bite of fruit.

As he chewed the rind, he thought again and again of the tiny white angel he had met on his first night. He thought about the endless stream of bodies he had seen, the damage piled up from deranged vigils.

Then, he began to feel lonely and so started attending festivals out of habit, to fill the need to see others, even if their conversation was breathy, intermittent, and staccato.

There was always the possibility of leaving, but something in the fruit—some nectar—made him want to stay. Once he had tasted, he both wanted and did not want to leave at the same time. He knew he could not, because the next town might not have this addictive harvest.

In the darkness of the final night, Nephesh began to dance. He swayed to the animal music and began to taste more than ever. His fingers ran over streams of blood, and he turned around in the middle of the ceremony, facing the beast, only to find he had become the beast. He backed away from the image of himself, the claws and the fragments of skin dangling from his lips.

Something inside—a voice, a conscience—said, *there is still hope*, but the physiognomy of the beast was glittering. There was promise in its panther stride, even if the promise did not deliver.

Then the air became thicker, the salt condensing, and a great heat moved through the masses.

They did not even pause in their celebration. Tiny forms swept away in the blast, the occasional figure made permanent in a statue of salinity.

PAYMENT

Gary Hewitt

Two guards approached.

"Why are you here?"

"I have come to see if the stories are true."

Two lowered rifles met the visitor's chest.

"What have you heard?"

"The rich prosper, and the poor are fucked."

The elder of the sentries snorted and kept his gun level.

"Are you rich or target practice?"

"Check your records and look for Mr. Kitchener."

He made a call and put his weapon away.

"Go straight to Big Eddie. It's up the end of the street."

The great steel gateway yawned apart. Mr Kitchener straightened his Porkpie hat and handed the sentry a hundred-dollar bill. He received a "no thanks."

The street was immaculate with several neon towers on each side of the road. Promises of sex, addiction, and wealth screamed for attention. His gaze lingered upon a sign promising tastes of the forbidden upon the forsaken. Another promised the weak a way to be dominated and taken.

Images assaulted his vision of screaming naked men and women chained upon steel altars under the gaze of suited men and women.

Big Eddie's mansion dwarfed the other buildings. Granite-muscled women armed with crossbows ushered him to an escalator. Several seconds later he crossed a quartz floor to greet a half-naked man being fed strawberries and peaches by a tiny doll-girl.

"Mr Kitchener, you will just love it here."

"I have never seen such depravity."

"You'll be staying at Kitten Plaza. I've already assigned you several broads to entertain you."

Mr Kitchener slammed his briefcase upon the desk.

"What's this?"

"My deposit."

Eddie grinned and pressed the brass buttons. The case opened to reveal a curious black box with one flashing red light.

"What the fuck is this?"

"You're being shut down."

Eddie reached into his drawer. A revolver pointed straight at the center of Kitchener's head.

"I'll shut you down. I'll ask you again, what the hell is this damn box?"

"A signal."

Hell awoke outside. Explosions and flames rained down. Towers tumbled into oblivion. Eddie screamed when he burst into a human cauldron of fat and flames.

Kitchener ignored the planes as they flew past and readied for another pass. He took the stairs, oblivious to the fatal heat and smoke. His clothes remained unmolested and not a bead of angelic sweat trailed from his brow. He opened his mobile.

"Yeah, it's me. Just to let you know, Sodom is sorted. I'll take care of Gomorrah tomorrow."

THICK AIR

Terry Alexander

The thick sulfur dust hung in the air like a hot mist. The slave master moaned at my feet. A flaming yellow ball struck his leg and reduced it to ash. I slipped the rope from my neck as he screamed in agony.

"James, help me. Save me and win your freedom." Pain etched deep lines across his face. "Save me."

My shaking hands closed on his robes and tore a long strip of cloth free. I tied it across my face to filter the thick air. His weak hands pawed at my legs. Blinking away the tears, I stared down at the man who had tormented me for nearly a year.

"Please, James, save me." His face blistered from the hot powder falling from the sky. "Save me." His hands fastened on the hem of my slave tunic. He was trying to pull me down.

I kicked him in the face. The blisters popped, draining a thick clear liquid. The sole on my sandal tore through his cheek. Blood gushed from the split flesh as panic gripped my heart. I gazed around, looking for the authorities. Rebellious slaves are dealt with quickly, savagely, by dismemberment and death.

A woman, her garments blazing, ran down the wide avenue. A hot yellow ball stuck to her middle, burning through cloth and tender flesh. She stepped on my master's face, leaving a huge gob of flaming sandal on his cheek. His agonized screams intensified. The woman tripped and fell. She clawed at the gooey substance. Her hands burst into flames. She disappeared in the swirling yellow mist. Her screams mixed with a hundred others, building to an inhuman, ear-piercing shriek.

The flaming balls splattered on the hard surfaces, sticking to whatever they hit and burning uncontrollably. The slanted roof of Sarah's Palace jutted from the gloom, a place known for its debauchery. It might have been my salvation. The yellow rain died away. Leaping the flaming obstacles, I managed to make it to the palace with only minor burns.

My heart thumped wildly in my chest as I pressed my back against the wall, grateful for the protection and the opportunity to catch my breath. In the street, men, women, and children ran back and forth like chickens. Every instinct I had screamed at the impossibility of what had occurred. This flaming rain can't be happening. Bodies covered the street: rich and poor, slave and master, whore and whoremonger, each one incinerated by an impossible fire that burned through the stone structures of Sodom.

A large ball of sulfur struck the mansion and shook it down to the foundation. Walls buckled, and portions of the roof slid away. The wall grew hot against my back. My tunic smoldered. The slave whores burst from the collapsing building, filling the street, their naked bodies covered with hot sulfuric grit. Several blundered into a pool of burning goo. Smoke rose from bare feet and burst into flames. The stronger women shoved the weaker to the ground and used their bodies as a fleshy bridge to safety.

I pushed myself away from the palace. Ignoring the pain along my shoulder blades, I ran down the street. The outside wall must be close. I had to clear the wall and make my way to the woodlands to survive.

Pitiful moans filled my ears. Blobs of cooked flesh moved and twitched beneath my feet. They didn't resemble people any longer. Fingerless hands slapped my legs. Mumbled pleas filled my ears with promises of sex and great wealth. I ignored them all. I had to reach the wall and find a way over before the fury of the storm resumed.

I made my way down the street, walking across the bodies of the dead and dying. I recognized a face. Mary looked at me with pleading eyes. Her injuries were too severe; I looked the other way and kept moving. Heat transferred from their seared flesh through the soles on my sandals into my feet. Air and gas burst from the bodies each time my foot settled on a chest or stomach.

"Slave," a harsh female voice shouted. "Come here. I command you."

Sarah, the owner of the slave whores, stood in the mansion's entryway, her white garments torn and dotted with burn spots. I cleansed years of slave training from my mind and remembered the beating I received for real or imagined mistakes. I ignored the woman and kept walking, more determined than ever to make my way out of the city and survive.

"Slave!" Her speed was unbelievable, a hand closed on my shoulder. "I should kill you for your disobedience." She held a silver dagger in her hand. The tip pricked my neck. "Get me to safety and I'll spare your life."

"We must make haste." I glanced at the dark clouds swirling overhead and knew the firestorm was returning with new fury. "Step on the bodies. We must get over the wall and into the forest."

"Put this around your neck." She pulled a braided golden rope from her robe and tossed one end to me. "You belong to me now. If you try to escape, I'll kill you."

I stared at the rope for an instant. Then I met her eyes.

"Put it on." She jabbed the sharp tip into my flesh. Blood welled from the wound and crept down my throat.

I slipped the rope over my head and moved forward. Sarah was more squeamish than I realized. The scent of charred flesh seemed to upset her. I'd seen her slice the nose and eyelids from a female slave the previous year without batting an eye. She hesitated at each footfall, placing each foot gingerly on the cooked flesh. We moved forward in a jerky motion. The rope tightened around my throat several times, choking me.

A stomach ruptured under Sarah's sandal. Her foot sank into the intestines and offal. She fell to her knees. Hot bile burst from her throat. The scent of roasted dung poisoned the air. Tears filled her eyes. The moisture collected the yellow dust swirling in the breeze. She tried to rise. The rib bones held her foot tightly. The hem of her garment dipped into a gooey deposit of sulfur, and the robe burned like a candle wick. She slapped at the blaze, transferring the sticky substance to her hands.

"Slave! Slave!" Her panicked screams rose to a crescendo. "Save me, slave."

I yanked the rope from her hand and jumped to the nearest body, away from her short arm and sharp dagger. "Nay, woman. Find your own way out."

"Damn you," she cursed. "Damn you for a coward."

"I hope to be a living coward." I placed my foot gingerly on the body of a dead whore. A burning pain shot through my back. I pitched forward to my knees. Feeling for the source of my pain, my hand closed around the dagger hilt. I glanced back at Sarah.

She managed a lop-sided smirk even as the inferno consumed her body. "My life is far more precious than yours. You're nothing but a slave, unfit to survive."

I pulled the blade free and tossed it to the ground. Hot, sticky blood gushed from the wound. Bits of sulfur dust pelted my skin, carried on the swirling winds. The thick air returned, I gasped for air, and my lungs burned. Thunder rumbled above my head. A flaming ball of sulfur struck the street and splattered like an obese rain drop.

I stumbled forward. My tear-filled eyes focused on the outside wall. A group of blind men, their clothes burned away, bodies covered with large, puckered wounds, clogged the street. I fought through them to the stairs. A sizzling blob struck the stone near my hand. Bits of goo burned through my skin. I forced my legs to move, slowly, one painful step at a time. I reached the top and gazed out at the woodland beyond. The sulfur rain grew with intensity. The forest was in flames. All was lost. I sat on the wall and waited for the end.

ZACHARIAH

Melchior Zimmermann

Zachariah ran up the hill, his feet flying over the yellow brimstone. Here and there, billows of smoke escaped from between the smoldering rocks. From time to time, he could glimpse a piece of charred limestone, remnants of a house or palace.

Zachariah's father had told him that before the great destruction there had been a mighty city in this place. His ancestors had lived here, prospering through their prowess in trade and craftsmanship. But five years ago, when Zachariah had only been two years old, the hill tribes had declared war on them. They had beseeched their powerful god to help them in their battle, and he had rained fire and brimstone upon the mighty city of Gomorrah. Unable to ward off the wrath of the heathen god, his ancestors had fled the city. Few of them had made it alive.

As they were roaming through the plains in search of a new home, the hill tribes had descended upon them, killing man, woman, and child, and slicing the throats of their livestock. Only a few dozen managed to escape this second onslaught. Alone, left with nowhere to go, his family decided to head back to Gomorrah to rebuild their home.

Now, five years later, all there was left was a lonesome encampment near the smoldering ruins of the once-famous city. The people there managed to survive through trade, exchanging the pure sulfur from their home for crops and meat. Nothing would grow on the scorched earth, and if they tried to settle new lands, the hill tribe would massacre them on sight.

Zachariah looked down upon the wasteland that surrounded him. In the far-off distance, he could see the sun glinting off the endless sea. To the south lay the hills of his enemies, and to the north, their sister-city Sodom, who had suffered the same fate. They were the only people who would trade with Gomorrah in good faith, and the only ones who respected their traditions and customs.

The adults, Zachariah had come to realize, were resigned to their fate. Instead of trying to better their lives, they simply did their best to survive. There was no hope left in their eyes, and no spring in their steps. But it was not so for him.

Zachariah had decided that he would rebuild the city of his fathers. He would keep alive their traditions and work tirelessly until tales of their glory once again rang through the land. And once his people had regained their rightful place, he would remember the hill tribe, and their god.

SINGLE RIGHTEOUS SEEKS SAME

Lyda Morehouse

Sodom was not the place to try to find love and redemption. I should've known that, yet I came to this den of iniquity seeking those very things. Now I'd die for my troubles.

Fire rained from the ceiling.

The Rover's missiles had some kind of acid in them. The space station melted around me. Tiny, pinprick-size holes dripped a toxic, foul-smelling rain. The air stunk of sewage and something akin to a spent match.

Groups of people—most of them tourists in their smart military uniforms and fancy dresses—clustered together clogging the once glittering Broadway of the space station. Some raged, some sobbed, some screamed hysterically. Others stared blankly at nothing at all, already part of the living dead. There were a few fools like me, desperately searching faces, trying to find that one person among hundreds of thousands.

Sodom and Gomorrah had been built to outsource Earth's sins and sinners, on two spinning, orbiting space stations full of lust and lasciviousness. The Hegemony couldn't fight a religious war against the Rovers if they didn't have God on their side, could they? Better to ship sin off world.

I'd spent fifteen thousand credits to buy my 'indulgence' to Sodom. I didn't even know if Angel was really here. It was where she would go; it was where they all went—those branded with the Mark of Cain.

Another boom shook the station. No, that was inaccurate—a trick of my mind trying to make sense of the strangeness of space battle: the sound was actually more of a 'suck.' The vacuum of space collapsed something nearby, crumbling it in on itself.

I should have married Angel.

If I'd married Angel, no Hegemony officer could've touched her. Marriage was a sacrament. God trumped everything in the Hegemony. God was a fucking loophole.

Angel and I grew up together, playing Hegemony and Rovers, like all the kids in our multiplex did—screaming up and down the halls evading the old neighbor's dirty looks and his drunken attempts to whip his door open just as we ran past. The old man finally managed to nail our buddy Ayokunle that way. We'd laughed and laughed, despite Ayokunle's twelve stitches and the stern lectures from our parents. After a week of half-hearted penance, we were back at it, Ayokunle trundling along with us, a freshly whitened scar on deep brown skin. We'd all seemed invulnerable then. I was too young to understand what Angel would become.

No, was *always*, even then.

Another grinding sound reverberated through the walls. My feet bounced awkwardly as gravity began to fail, our rotation degrading. Something dripped onto my head. I smelled the choking odor of burning flesh. My flesh.

The first time Angel asked me to marry her I thought it was a joke. She'd been wearing these adorable, retro, tea-length skirts. We were arguing about them because she wanted to wear them all the time and the baseball coach was going to kick her off the team if she didn't wear a proper uniform. She was our best pitcher, but I wasn't lying when I told her that she looked just as cute in the uniform with her long, silky black ponytail sticking out the back of the ball cap. "Lots of girls play baseball," I told her. Hell, hadn't we just played that mixed team from

Holy Oak? All those girls wore a uniform and not one of them was as pretty as my Angel.

"I might be in love with you a little bit," Angel had said, her voice cracking. "Marry me?"

I laughed and said sure, but I didn't mean it. I just didn't want to lose my best friend, or our best pitcher.

The alarms cut off a second before the lights failed. Screams rose to replace claxons. We were plunged into total darkness. Emergency lights flickered valiantly, albeit weakly, revealing the corridor in a dim haze. My heart hammered in my chest and my huffing breath made ice crystals in the freezing air.

It felt close now, the end.

Everyone in the multiplex looked after Angel as best we could. Her parents loved their only daughter and so they did everything to make Angel's life easier. *Everything.* Her voice evened out, stopped cracking, just as mine settled deeper. She went away for a couple of months that last summer, 'to emersion camp,' everyone joked, but when she came back not one boy could keep their eyes off her, nor half the girls either. She was always stunning but going away had made her beautiful.

If no one had reported her, that would have been the end of it.

I could tell, when they came to brand and deport her, Angel thought I had betrayed her. It wasn't. I should have said 'yes' when she asked me to marry her, but I swear that was my only sin against her.

Everyone had tried to stop them, but they tazed us, beat us, and dragged her away from us. The only comfort was that I never heard her screams. I never had to see that horrible letter burned into her, searing her soul with its foul accusations. I was with Ayokunle, in jail, serving my time for assaulting an officer and obstructing justice. Like half the multiplex. We hadn't let Angel go without a fight. I was proud of that, at least.

On Sodom, branding marks were everywhere. Scarlet letters, some people called them. I never understood what half of them meant. I was told that Angel's face would be scarred with a "T." When I asked the

Tour Guide what that stood for, he'd sneered and said, "Trap, son. T stands for Trap. You got to watch out for those. You think you're buying one thing, but you get a whole other."

I threw up on the Tour Guide's shoes.

I was nineteen. I didn't know myself. I thought that being with her said something about me.

And now, too late, I knew it *did*—it said I was selfish and a fool.

I saw her then. A second before the blinding flash rent the station asunder, our eyes met. My apology froze in the vacuum of space.

IOTA

SODOM

Meg Eden

When the sky grew dark
and yellow, someone laughed:
It's the end of the world!

Well, fuck! I said
and let in
my next customer.

Men and women
knock down my doors
to have sex with me,

I charge them now
to avoid
an affront to my body.

Sometimes
my customers
are animals—

I do not like it with animals
but it causes a sensation
and pays well.

The customer who came
when the air went bad
asked if it was my scent,

so I closed the window
and said the streets
expire from bad people.

He laughed,
but inside of me
there was an earthquake.

The god
I acknowledge
is the god of my body,

who has brought me
out from
the land of slavery.

The light in the room
went red, and
outside there was a great

shout, and the sound
of hail, pelting
the walls like a missionary.

The man cried
and reached
for my breasts,

but I turned from him
and opened
the window:

the sky
was a great flame

and we were all embers.

A heavy smoke cloud
came over us
so that the homes

were hidden, and all
that was left
were silent ashes.

I coughed
and could not stop
coughing.

Closing the window,
the sulfur stung my eyes
so that I could not see,

and the man wept:
Why, God?
lowering onto my bed.

We were on the city wall
and there was no
sanctuary for us.

As my throat
burned its own fire,
the sky collapsed

and the man's skin
lit up. He ran
across the room—

his own self-
contained sun—
but found no peace.

And I remained

until the fire
found me here,

and the hand of a mourning
just God
could not bear me.

I do not repent.

SHORT STORIES

RUINS OF GOMORRAH

Nicholas Paschall

I open my eyes slowly, ignoring the muck that has half submerged my body in the sinking mire that was once our great city. I claw my way free, ignoring the torn scraps of skin peeling off my body as I scrabble up the foundation of an old tavern I used to frequent; now I live in the rubble like some utter street trash.

That's what we are now: street trash and monsters.

Stooped low behind a section of wall, I shuffle to a table that I've set up as a small shrine, muttering a small prayer as my day begins. Perhaps I'll find food today?

I hear a scream in the distance, as well as the crumbling of another building. *That sounds promising*, I think.

Turning, I scoop up the sword I'd scavenged and lope onto the street, avoiding the craters of still-broiling sulfur that made this city an inferno. I jog around the impact craters, past others like me as they awaken to the sounds of the screams. If I move fast enough, I'll be the first to get there.

Nobody comes to our fair city anymore. Well, nobody sane, that is. Heretics and worshippers of the devil flock here, seeing it as a holy site for their profane rituals and horrid rites. I still have faith—I have faith that God will save us. He will let us leave the still-burning ruins of our city. For some reason, any and all who called Gomorrah home can't leave this place. We start to choke and suffocate as the cool air of the open plains meets us. It's as if we've become accustomed to the darkness that now envelops this land, and we are cursed by God for its sins.

I leap over a small crater, knocking up some loose stone as I land. I bleat in pain as one of the rocks causes me to twist my ankle, but I pay it no mind: I smell fresh food amongst the steamy haze of sulfur and brimstone.

Squatting in the road, behind the upper portion of a clay roof that was blasted into the street, I see them: A wagon being pulled by two oxen, with an older man in the bullock seat and four young men walking beside it. A woman sits next to the older man, cradling a young child against her chest. That makes my mouth water at the very thought. Fresh child! How long had it been since I had a child to slake my hunger upon?

"I don't know, Ezekiel," one of the men on foot says, looking up at the driver of the cart. "This doesn't seem right. This is supposed to be Gomorrah, but nobody's here!"

"Yeah, and what's with these craters?" Another man carrying a sword asks. "They have burning pitch in them, or something. How are we supposed to do trade with a city with nobody in it?"

"I don't know," Ezekiel says, pulling on the reins to make the oxen stop. He rubs his wrinkled brow, wiping away the sweat forming on his face. "This isn't right, not at all. The man said that this would be a good place to sell our wares."

Man? I rise to have a better look at the group through the haze. *What man? Who would send them to this godforsaken pile of rubble when there's barely enough left to go around as it is?*

"What's that over there?" One of the men calls out, pointing in my direction. The haze of sulfuric clouds makes it difficult for anyone not used to them to see. "Hello? Can you help us?"

I clear my throat, coughing a bit to get my voice back. "I can be of some assistance. It's just too hard to reach you. Come closer, leave your cart, and skirt around the crater so I can give you directions."

I can see in my peripheral vision several other survivors such as myself moving through the steaming clouds, their hooves clacking softly on the stone as they move to flank the group. One lets out a soft bleating noise as he crosses some busted wooden boards, causing the men to look for its origin.

"I'm a shepherd looking for his flock," I say as I move around a vent of sulfurous smoke roiling from a small crater. "I was in the countryside, and my sheep ran into the city for some reason."

"We can help you find them," one of the men says, squinting into the thick mist. A man to his right coughs, nearly retching at the scent of the air around him. I breathe deeply and smile.

"Where are you?" A third man calls out as they maneuver around the crater. Already, I can see that Ezekiel has five of my brethren swarming his cart, muffling his screams with blades. The oxen will taste mighty fine after we've made a proper sacrifice of them.

I walk out of the column of broiling sulfur, my fur ruffling as I step over the vent. I rear my head back and bleat loudly, earning a number of responsive bleats from all around. The men stare at me unabashedly, giving me a chance to lower my head and charge at them, blade held in both hands, low and dragging along the ground.

I ram one man in the side with my head, my curved horns and thick skull allowing me to break him in a single blow. He flies off me with a scream, hitting a crumbling pylon with a spine-snapping howl. His friends look on in amazement as I slash up, spearing my sword into the first man hard enough to lift him off the ground. Hacking up blood, the grip on his sword goes limp enough for me to wrestle it away from him, and I push him to the side as I now face his last two friends.

"What in God's name? Demon!" The fourth man yells, earning a chorus of bleating laughter from my brothers and sisters of the fallen city.

Pulling my lip back in a snarl, I stomp forward, my hooves crushing stone beneath my weight as I move. My belt of skulls clatters ominously as I approach them, the small human sword in my hand ill-suited for my needs as a warrior.

"I am no demon, just a man cursed by God for his sins. Soon he will forgive us of our transgressions, and we'll all be able to leave this cursed land. But not today."

Ezekiel lets out a wounded yelp, causing the two men to turn for a split second as if they can see the fat old man in the distance being eaten or the woman and child being dragged off for stock as slaves. I lunge forward, stabbing the only man who hasn't said anything in the side of the neck, ripping outward in a ham-fisted tug that leaves him bleeding in a wide spray of arterial delight. I laugh.

"Why? What have we done to deserve this?" The last man asks, turning to regard me, gripping his sword in a defensive position.

I give him a look that I doubt he could recognize as loathing. "You come here, full of the glory of Yahweh, and you ask what you've done wrong? Gomorrah is a city best left alone, friend, for those that live there are wicked in their ways. Isn't that what you've been told, hmm?"

The man falters. "Yes. I mean, of course, everyone has heard of Gomorrah's, and Sodom's, rather wild parties."

"We sinned. We sinned so badly that we were punished for it with raining sulfur and brimstone. Those of us who survived were transformed into half-man, half-beast. We are the servants of the devil now, sin incarnate, and of the living flesh. You've made a poor choice in coming here."

He doesn't respond. A small boy, his horns barely even nubs at his temples and his fur short and soft, runs a pike through the man's tunic, spearing him in the back. The man's blood turns his tunic to a dark red. The young one is breathing heavily, and I can tell that this is his first kill.

Good for him.

I grab the front of the bleeding man's tunic and yank him off the pike, pulling him off his feet and close to my muzzle. "We will one day again walk in the light of God ... but we will keep any and all who come here from ever leaving, as it is His will."

And with that, I end the young man's life by clamping my jaws over his throat, my blunt teeth grinding away at tissue and veins. I yank back a mouthful of succulent meat, which I savor as I watch the young man struggle to breathe without a throat. I drop him unceremoniously to the ground for the young one, who pounces on him. Turning, I toss the small pig sticker aside and retrieve my blade from the coughing man impaled with it.

Huh ... surprised he's still alive. I clop to the man's side, tail swishing lightly behind me.

The man looks at me, a rivulet of blood dribbling past his cracked lips to his chin. "M-m-monster! Th-There is n-no place in h-h-heaven for a beast like you!"

Reaching to grab him by the shoulder with one padded hand and the hilt of my sword with the other, I stare heartily into his eyes.

"We'll see, in the end." I say, yanking my blade free, causing a torrent of blood and bile to spill onto the street. His eyes grow dim, staring back in defiance. His spirit departs before his features soften. "We'll see ..."

I begin my meal, eating what I can before my smaller brethren move in for a share of the kill. I fold my hands at my chest as I tear at the meat and say a small prayer, thanking the Lord for this bounty.

Then I dine.

THE MORTICIAN OF SODOM

C.J. Beacham

"See you on the other side," Teodor said. "And remember to breathe."

I grimaced and sat down to catch my breath. After the explosions this morning, I never expected to see another side of anywhere.

#

I woke this morning when the mountain groaned. It had rumbled twice in recent memory, but no stories from the past eight generations mentioned eruption. When the ground shook today, however, windows rattled until one smashed. My eyes popped open. I rose from the lambskin, peered through the crack between the door and frame. Other eyes peered from doorways across the dusty road. Distant explosions and shrill voices echoed from the mountains, and I sensed the odd glow growing towards the cities of the plain.

Over the past two months, old-timers warned the miners not to set fire to the mountains, but thirst for sulfur overpowered their pleas. The sulfur industry bolstered Sodomite commerce, which was dominated by black gunpowder, Sodom's chief export. Generations had made their livings mining sulfur until Kedorlaomer conquered Sodom and exploded the large pits, killing most of the miners inside. After Kedorlaomer's defeat following the Battle of the Vale, the sons and grandsons of miners gathered gear and headed off to the mountains. After fifteen years of inactivity, the shafts had caved in, their entrances buried under rock-slide debris. During those years, the old-time miners who survived the blast refused to apprentice the next generation. This new generation was cutting-edge, accustomed to gadgets of Sodom's advancing technology, but lacking gritty mineshaft experience. They concocted special instruments to extract the sulfur but couldn't figure out how to blast through the mountain to get to it.

Smoke billowed south from the mountain's direction. I wondered if the top had blown. Over the next few minutes, boulders could be heard rolling down and tumbling off cliffs, even from four miles away. A thick grey cloud plowed southward, low through the sky, and blocked the sun trying to announce the day. The cloud's jagged edges glowed like mustard yellow sheen on a dirty plate. It made me nauseous, and I vomited in the pale under the window.

The next few days would be busy for me, as many dead miners would need to be embalmed and buried.

"Sodom is a fine place for a mortician," my father, Luka, said from his deathbed before he signed the mortuary over to me. He died later that night, his body the first embalmed under my ownership. That was twenty years ago, and thousands of bodies have passed through the mortuary since. But Luka never realized the irony of his claim, nor could he fathom the events of the day awaiting me. Or so I thought.

People were tickled by Kedorlaomer's defeat, but captives freed from his stockades poured into Sodom as well as neighboring Gomorrah and Zeboyim. The freed captives erected strange stalls and ramshackle dwellings in abandoned lots at the corner of Fifth and Sixth. By day they slept, or at least remained out-of-sight. Throughout the night, they danced around to strange music and performed heinous acts under the guise of theatre, all while selling a variety of trinkets, potions, and other useless wares. All manner of phantasm and lewd activity could be witnessed in the camp, and soon residents of Sodom became intrigued. Shop owners, miners, and paupers, even Mayor Bera and Sheriff Hammu found themselves enchanted by The Captives.

Every evening at seven sharp, they kicked off the nightly festivities to honor their leader Teodor, a renowned Fire Starter, though he never showed his face. They summoned flame from thin air, contorted in unnatural ways, and swung from arched contraptions, all while showing body parts Sodomites were unaccustomed to viewing in public. The carnival continued throughout the night, and only when the sun peeked over the horizon did the hedonism wane.

Before The Captives arrived, Sodom was a friendly place, the kind where neighbors sit on porches and respect each other's kids. But The Captives showed Sodom the world beyond the walls. Trash piled up on the street, robberies and sexual crimes increased, and residents no longer welcomed each other into their homes. Poor people were scoffed at and banned from buying food in the markets and left to starve in the streets. Any visitors to Sodom were automatically viewed through squinted eyes, which I found ironic since strangers initiated the change in the first place.

I dressed and scarfed down breakfast then headed for the mortuary. The first bodies would arrive around noon, I figured, and preparations would take until at least then. I took the shortcut across Sixth. As Fifth approached, an unexpected sight crossed my eyes. The Captives were dancing around outside, singing, and playing music with their strange instruments. I'd never seen one of them in the sunlight until at least five o'clock in the afternoon. But on this day, they pranced around as if last night's carnival never stopped.

One dressed as a clown approached me, removed his extra tall hat, and handed me a flier with the simple phrase: *The hour is at hand.* He placed the hat back on his head and bowed with a sinister smile spread across his face. I wadded the paper and tossed it into a pile of balled-up fliers beside his oversized shoes. He laughed through his painted white face.

Another clown approached to apologize, but when I extended my hand to meet his, he squeezed the rose decorating his lapel and squirted water in my eye. This time they both laughed, and tears spilled from their painted black eyes. I never understood why the miners listened to those strangers.

The Captives were masters of fire and heard about the novice miners' dilemma. They sent Teodor, the mysterious leader, to inspect the mountain. He returned to Sodom offering a solution: small pockets of sulfur could be ignited through cracks at the top of the mountain. Once the pockets caught fire, the sulfur would liquefy and run down the side, thereby igniting other pockets as the flow rushed towards the base. The sulfur would pile up, cool down and harden, and be easily extracted at the bottom.

The idea sounded legitimate to the miners. But there was one catch Teodor pointed out—the fire must not burn above 444 degrees, as the sulfur would bypass the liquid stage and go straight to gas.

Even greenhorn miners knew that gaseous sulfur is lethal. Here was the angle: in return for a twenty percent share, Teodor would ignite the fires and guarantee the temperature remained below 440 degrees. After two nights of discussion and a final vote, the Miners' Council agreed to Teodor's proposal. He set the first blaze two months ago, and until now, the project proceeded safely. The mines produced more sulfur each day than the previous one, and as exports increased, profits began to flow. Teodor's twenty percent added up quickly.

Last week, a group of miners complained about the slow process and claimed the extraction rate could be increased. Teodor warned that multiple fires would raise temperatures to threatening levels, a natural inferno he would be unable to control. The Council ignored him. Three nights ago, they voted to increase the number of fires set each day. Last night, Teodor headed for the mountain to set multiple fires.

I shook off the clowns like dogs do water and continued towards the mortuary. The fierce cloud now rumbled near Sodom's north gate, emitting plumes of ash that expanded to fill the space around it. Lightning crackled around the edges like ungrounded electrical wires. Though the sun rose, its light and heat were blocked from reaching the ground.

Sodomites emerged onto the streets. Bent necks with wide eyes peered into the sky. They whispered and shrugged their shoulders, wondering what wrath was being cast upon them. I urged them to return indoors before sulfur began falling. Most stared at me with empty eyes, unable to comprehend or refusing to heed the warning. They stood in the streets dumbfounded, gazing with open mouths at the approaching storm. I hustled to the mortuary and ducked inside just as the first particulates reached the ground. Within minutes, the mustard-yellow mass hovered over the city, and the Sodomites waited underneath it as the first fireball fell. It lit the sky for only a second, but the blue flame revealed the cloud's immense sulfur content.

Teodor arrived at the mountain about midnight to set the fires. He sensed high sulfur concentration in a particular crack and decided to begin there. Whether or not he knew the pocket extended to the other side of the mountain, and upward to the top, remains unknown.

The initial fire burned with ferocity and spread through the pocket at unexpected volume and speed. Even so, Teodor continued lighting fires on other parts of the mountain as instructed by the Council. As dawn approached, the first miners arrived and cheered the blazes. Gold coins flashed before their eyes. But when the sun peeked over the horizon, they realized the fires were burning out of Teodor's control. Some stood by to watch the growing inferno. Others returned to Sodom to deliver the news.

The first returning miners passed by the mortuary as sulfur mist began floating to the ground like scragged cotton balls. They urged Sodomites to take cover inside their dwellings. The yellowy-grey mass planted itself over Sodom, howled like a pack of rabid dogs, and swirled sand and stone with tumultuous crosswinds. Bolts of fire shot between the smaller clouds that conjoined to form the mass.

Panic gripped the Sodomites as the cloud bore down upon the city. Men gathered valuables such as gold coins, family heirlooms, and lambs. Women rounded up the children and elders. In moments, most of Sodom's residents moved *en masse* to the southern wall, attempting to escape as rain increased intensity. Some Sodomites realized it was impossible to outrun the sinister threat. These folks lingered in the streets to accept fate or huddled under overhangs to watch havoc wreaked. The Captives continued the carnival during the day with no audience, unimpeded by the first sulfur drifts and impending carnage. They danced and played and sang as if the entire town of Sodom was crowded into their makeshift theatre cheering on the performance.

The miners who stayed at the mountain gathered with Teodor, who believed he could gain control over the fury. He sat on a flattened boulder and recited incantations, calling for mercy upon the cities of the plain.

The miners, who were accustomed to technological fixes, scorned Teodor for depending on superstition, despite the fact they had no other recourse to stop the blazes. They pointed and laughed as he sang in languages they didn't understand. The mountain hissed and popped and groaned. Soon, sulfur particles drifted through the air and burned sores into their skin on contact.

None of the miners realized they stood at the epicenter, the seething cauldron summoned to destroy the cities of the plain. They did notice, however, how Teodor sat unencumbered, even as the putrid mist enshrouded them. The miners snickered and sneered at him as they gasped for breath, their eyes burning past tears. And still Teodor sat like a statue, breathing slowly, singing his songs. As they lay dying, the miners watched thick ash trail off the mountain toward the plain and coalesce into an ominous mass approaching Sodom.

The mighty cloud castigated Sodom. Those of us inside stone buildings were protected and witnessed the destruction firsthand. Repressive ash surrounded the walls, plunged over, and filled the city. Then the sulfur storm came. Flames whizzed through the air like blue bullets, struck the ground, and ignited on impact. Nasal passages and throats burned from caustic precipitation. Sodomites struggled to breathe. Those who remained outside darted for cover, but most never made it. Instead, they shrieked as sulfur rain pelted their bodies.

Blue flames ignited clothes on contact. Women wailed as falling sulfur scorched their bodies, melting their skin like ice at the equator. Candle-wax flesh dripped from their bones onto screaming children clinging to their mothers' legs. Men attempted to usher the women and children indoors, but most dropped to their knees and cursed the dark sky above as it devoured them. People of all ages lay screaming and dying in the streets, tortured by burning flesh and sulfur air. Screams turned to gasps as sulfur replaced oxygen in their lungs. Skeletons crumpled to the ground. In ditches running beside Sodom's main streets, molten yellow rivers formed with blue flames dancing on top. Those who could still stand hurled themselves into the burning floes to end the nightmare immediately. Trees and dwellings ignited as the cloud lurched forward, leaving a fiery swath in its wake. When the mass reached the southern wall, a chorus of hellish screams could be heard, as the Sodomites who fled were scorched and asphyxiated before the south gate could be opened.

Teodor remained on the mountain until nearly noon. Sulfur killed all the miners who had stayed, yet it never affected him. The fires started to recede from the time Teodor began incantations, only by that point it was too late for Sodom. After a few hours of singing and casting spells, the fires ceased completely. Though the mountain still simmered, Teodor lowered the temperature inside so no more sulfur ignited. When he was satisfied, he gathered the miners' bodies on a cart for hauling sulfur and headed back to Sodom.

After the hissing mass passed the mortuary, an eerie glow set in. A putrid, yellowish-caked mustard-like mist blocked the sun. Sulfur showers had ceased, and though the mist remained, I put on a coat, hat, and gloves and stepped outside. The grisly scene spread before me: bodies scattered around in peculiar postures, piles of scorched bones, little blue fires burning along the street. Mustard mist hung around, an overbearing authority that didn't affect my breathing. Still, from Fifth and Sixth, sounds of The Captives' carnival roared.

I wheeled the cart into the street and piled corpses on top, lugged it back to the mortuary where I lined the bodies up and tagged the toes. After the fifth such trip, I noticed a gang parading through the streets as if in celebration. When they approached, the leader, dressed like a circus announcer, veered over to me and whispered, "You can breathe just as we do" and returned to his position. The group filtered by, talked, and giggled as they hopped over dead bodies without honoring them. The one bringing up the rear, dressed as a nine-tailed kitty cat, came over to me and said, "Captives own this town," then he returned to his position. At the time, I didn't notice the casket hovering in the middle of the throng as they continued down the street toward the north gate.

Teodor met the parade outside the north gate where they welcomed him like a war hero. Screams of excitement and indecipherable incantations filled the air. Fire shot high into the grey sky and lit up northern Sodom despite the sulfur gloom. They played music with their instruments, clapped, and sang until roaring applause erupted. When the celebration mellowed, the crowd entered the city and proclaimed Teodor as Sodom's king. They paraded down the street, whooping and singing, dancing, and shouting. With Teodor leading and the levitating casket enshrouded by the crowd, the throng headed for the mortuary.

The day was certainly busy for a mortician. As the sulfur mass moved past Sodom and over open plains, I continued tagging bodies. Soon, the Sodomites who had survived began to appear on the streets. Although they had witnessed the carnage through peepholes, the brunt of the catastrophe was only understood firsthand. They gawked at piles of bones, skin still burning, skeletons crumpled in the streets, and vomited at the smell of sizzled flesh. Slowly, they identified family and friends, dropped to their knees, and wailed in the street. They began showing up at the mortuary and lined up single file at the side door. Generations of superstition prevented them from entering, as dwellings that housed the dead were considered unclean in Sodom. I handed out toe tags and promised to pick up the bodies as soon as possible. Those who couldn't find their loved ones in the streets sifted through the corpses laid out in rows behind the mortuary. Wives slumped and cried over husbands. Mothers and fathers wailed over children. Men hunched against walls and sobbed. The mortuary yard was flooded with tears.

Teodor interrupted the chaos when he cut in line and pounded on the door. The grieving dried their eyes and turned their attention to him. When he showed them the cartful of bodies from the mountain, they realized he was the Fire Starter.

"Told you not to set those fires!" one of the old-timers shouted.

Mayor Bera and Sheriff Hammu approached Teodor, threatened to arrest him, or worse. But before they accosted him, he redirected blame to the Miners' Council. "I warned the Council not to set more fires, but they approved the measure anyway. They threatened to kill me if I didn't comply."

The crowd seemed to believe him, as Teodor wielded strange power over the will of Sodom's people.

Mayor Bera doubted Teodor's claim. He stepped onto the curb and shouted, "Why, Sodomites, do you believe this stranger? This leader of a captive people?"

No one listened to him. Their attention was aimed at Teodor.

"Unfortunately," Teodor informed them, "All the members of the Council perished on the mountain." He pointed to the cart. "Their bodies lay on this cart."

"He blames the dead who cannot defend themselves," Mayor Bera said. "How do we know the truth?"

Sodomite men rushed to the cart and tossed miner bodies aside as they searched for Council members. They pulled each of the five members off the cart and piled the corpses in the street.

Sheriff Hammu stood on the curb and announced, "These five men—the Miners' Council—caused the blast this morning. They don't deserve a proper burial! They deserve to burn in the street like other Sodomites did!"

A deputy in the crowd left to find fuel as momentum toward torching the bodies grew. During the rush, Teodor ducked inside the mortuary. The deputy returned with a container of ethanol. Another deputy grabbed it and doused the bodies. Sheriff Hammu continued, "Let the orange fire consume these wicked bastards, those who brought the blue flames upon our fair city!"

I pushed the cart of bodies around the corner as a sulfur chunk ignited and dropped atop the pile. "Why must you disrespect the dead?" I demanded, approaching the throng of Sodomites.

"These are your people, fellow citizens of Sodom!" Sheriff Hammu scoffed from the curb. "Someone must pay!"

"What revenge is torching dead bodies?" I asked.

"The bodies must be torched to avenge the Sodomites who died in fiery agony!"

"Why continue the carnage?"

His expression changed. "You're the mortician. Yes, I'm seeing it clearly now. The man who earns his living among the dead. You want the bodies whole, fresh, so you can charge us for funerals! You just want our money like the bloody Captives!"

Sheriff Hammu's tone sent a chill up my spine.

"I'm not a greedy man," I said and ducked into the mortuary to avoid escalation. As the door closed, the crowd pushed towards it. I feared they would break it down.

Once inside, I found Teodor waiting for me in the vestibule. He was sitting in a calm pose with eyes closed until he realized I stood before him. A wooden coffin, decorated with immaculate carvings of mammoth animals and men of equal height, floated next to him, hovering at my waist level.

A strange glint flashed in Teodor's eyes when they opened. "Just the man I want to see," he said, as I stared at the coffin. "I hauled some bodies from the mountain, and then we have this one."

His eyebrows motioned to the coffin, though his gaze stayed fixed on me.

"I'll see to the bodies you hauled down," I responded, pointing to the casket. "But what service can I provide for this? Who's in there?"

"You're a man who gets straight to the point," he replied. "I like you already. Most would ask how it hovers there." He stood and circled the casket. "The prowess showcased each night at Sixth and Seventh, that's what hovers before you. As legend foretold, he died the day the mountain erupted, over a thousand years since his birth on the day the mountain last raged."

I'd heard rumors around Sodom that The Captives lived to untold ages. Some claimed many hundreds of years, in fact, but no one ever claimed a thousand until Teodor. I decided not to question him since I didn't know exactly what he wanted.

"So, what do you want from me?" I inquired.

As the question left my mouth, someone pounded the door, rattling the windows.

"We know you're in there!" Sheriff Hammu announced. "And the Fire Starter too. Come on out!"

Teodor and I exchanged glances, but neither of us knew what to do. I peeked out the window to see the angry Sodomites surrounding the mortuary.

Just down the street, The Captives danced and sang while waiting for Teodor to finish his business. One of them warned the Sodomite crowd to leave the mortician alone or risk invoking the spirits residing at the mortuary. The Sodomites moved toward The Captives, cursing them for devilish magic and threatened violence if they didn't disburse at once.

They continued dancing and singing, refusing to leave. One of the Sodomites raised a knife. The crowd roared and a melee ensued.

Captives warded off blows with shifting feet and other swift movements. But sheer Sodomite numbers overwhelmed them. Blows landed on heads and sternums. Sodomites pounded Captives, slit throats, and dropped bodies. Heads were bashed, chests ripped open, and rivers of blood flowed in the street. Only a dozen or so Captives remained alive.

Teodor showed anxiety, a nervousness I hadn't seen displayed by any of The Captives. He turned to me with panicked eyes and said, "Like me, the sulfur air didn't affect your breathing. The blue flames never burned one sore into your skin. Don't you find it remarkable?" He urged me to look out the window.

Outside, the gang of Sodomites stood over The Captives, who were still alive. Each Sodomite body displayed sulfur wounds, from open sores to singed skin to bloody noses. But signs of sulfur affliction were absent from The Captives. And as I checked out mine and Teodor's skin, I realized neither of us showed wounds, either. I rubbed my hands together and placed them on my face. My skin still felt soft.

"See?" he asked. "No wounds, no sores, no burns." He inhaled deeply.

I looked at him through my fingers.

"Why don't you save your people?" I demanded. "Use your magic to save them."

He shuffled his feet and sat up straight. "These are not my people. It's true that sulfur doesn't affect them as it does the Sodomites, but they are not my people."

The answer confused me. "But you lived among them. They revere you."

He stood and peered out the window. The crowd of Sodomites had surrounded the mortuary again.

"Straight to the point," Teodor whirled to face me. "I was sent by Kedorlaomer."

The crowd outside chunked rocks at the mortuary walls. Then, another pounding shook the door.

"One more chance!" Sheriff Hammu announced. "Bring us the mortician. Or bring us the Fire Starter. Or bring us both!"

The last demand raised excitement in the growing crowd, which applauded and hollered its approval.

"You see," Teodor said, "To the Sodomites, we are one and the same. They don't care which one of us comes out, only that they receive a sacrificial lamb. But one will not satisfy vengeance. If one of us comes out, they will string him up, lynch him in the street. Soon, the taste of blood will fade, and they will return to demand the other."

"Kedorlaomer sent you?" I asked.

"Yes; when captives were released, many set off for Sodom. Kedorlaomer instructed me to blend in with them. He had developed a plan to take Sodom down. My job was to enchant the captives, those the Sodomites call 'Strangers', and once we arrived in Sodom, to direct The Captives into enchanting Sodom's residents."

"Why are you telling me all of this? I'm a Sodomite."

"Indeed, you dwell in Sodom. You're also familiar with magic and illusion. You work with the dead. It's your business."

"What do you want from me?" I asked him.

"What I seek is survival. Angry Sodomites stand outside the door, waiting to tear us limb from limb."

"How can I help you survive if they kill me also?"

"Here in the mortuary, we are safe. They may threaten, but Sodomites won't dare enter a dwelling of the dead."

"So, we stay here until the crowd disperses?"

"Not exactly. Who can say how long the crowd will remain? When people are racked by grief and vengeance, they do unnatural things."

"So, you're saying we're trapped here?"

He darted his eyes toward the coffin and back at me.

"The casket?"

He nodded and smiled.

"And how will a floating casket save us both?"

He lifted a finger and straightened his spine. "Kedorlaomer sent the casket with me and The Captives. As I said, it's the origin of the magic displayed in Sodom since we arrived. We enchanted Sodom with a corpse, even though Sodomites refuse to confront death on purpose. Yet they came to the carnival every night and ignored the casket hovering stage left." He paused to peek through the window. "Regardless of how inflamed the crowd becomes, they won't dare approach a casket, especially one that hovers above the ground, for fear of invoking wrath from the dead spirit."

"So, your plan is that we both climb into the coffin and float down the street?"

"Well, one of us will climb into the coffin," he replied. "But there's more to the plan." He drew a deep breath before continuing. "Last night, Kedorlaomer sent two men into Sodom. They warned people that the mountain would explode, sulfur would rain down on the city, and many people would die. The Sodomites laughed at the men, threatened them with violence and sexual depravity as The Captives had modeled for them."

"Why would Kedorlaomer warn Sodom if he wants to control it?"

"He doesn't care about Sodom. Kedorlaomer wants the sulfur mines, and control of the black gunpowder trade. He gave Sodom a chance to save itself."

"Good for Kedorlaomer. But how does it help us escape?"

"The two men who Kedorlaomer sent last night, the ones chased off by the Sodomites, are waiting for us where the road from Sodom forks to Zoar and Zeboyim. The Captives will escort us to the north gate, and none of the Sodomites will dare approach. All we must do is find those two men. They will handle the rest."

Sheriff Hammu's voice thundered from outside, interrupting Teodor, "Last chance! This time I mean it! Either come out or we set the mortuary ablaze!"

The crowd cheered. Flickers of torches danced through the windows.

Teodor grabbed my shoulder with a grip weaker than I imagined it would be. "The crowd smolders; we must proceed! Make an announcement, keep them from setting fire. I need a few minutes alone."

"What are you talking about? Your life is threatened, and you need a few minutes alone?"

"Exactly. This day needs magic if we are to survive." He stood up and walked to the back of the room, peered inside my office. "May I sit in here?"

For some reason, I began to trust this Teodor. Plus, he was the only ally I had at the moment. "Go ahead, if that's what you need to do."

"Keep the crowd at bay. Tell them you must deliver a body across town. I'll take care of the rest. Won't be long."

He ducked into the office and shut the door.

I peeked out the window. Angry men surrounded the mortuary, though they remained a safe distance away. Their women and children ducked behind them, shot snarls at me. Some of the men talked among themselves, others brandished blades. But what frightened me were the men holding torches, and I figured ethanol was on the way. As Teodor said, Sodomites would never enter the mortuary. But in their rage, they would burn it down even if it instigated the spirits.

The sheriff and mayor stood in front of the group.

"What say you, mortician?" Mayor Bera hollered.

"I need to come out soon," I replied.

"Will you sacrifice your own life to save the Fire Starter?" Mayor Bera asked.

"Bring him to us and save yourself!" Sheriff Hammu demanded.

"I have a coffin that needs delivering to the other side of town."

They looked perplexed. Mayor Bera whispered to Sheriff Hammu, who nodded and turned a hostile eye towards me.

"We will allow you to pass with the casket," Mayor Bera said.

"But we will follow, and once the body's dropped off, you're ours!" Sheriff Hammu hollered.

"I'm the only man in Sodom who can give your dead a proper burial," I shouted back. "Not too smart to murder me."

They spoke to each other again.

"You speak truth, mortician. Only for the spirits of the recently departed will we spare your life," Mayor Bera said.

"For now," Sheriff Hammu said. "In that case, we demand the Fire Starter!"

As the words left Sheriff Hammu's mouth, a sonic boom rattled Sodom. The ground rumbled and groaned. The mortuary walls shook. As I ducked away, the second window shattered. Men crouched and flung arms over their heads. Women dropped to the ground, screaming. Children covered their ears. Shrieks and cries echoed in the streets, reverberating through alleyways. A woman stumbled by, repeating, "This day is cursed! This day is cursed!" Sodom's survivors were growing weary, but they had another obstacle to overcome.

Teodor opened the office door and strolled to the coffin.

"Are you refreshed?" I asked him.

"Yes, I needed that," he replied as he ran fingers along the carvings.

"What did you do in there?"

"Didn't you hear the explosion?"

"Of course, I did. It shattered the window!"

He smiled at me.

"Wait, you caused it?"

He smiled wider.

"How'd you do that?" I asked.

"Magic, my friend. A little concentrated magic. Sodomites could learn a lot about focused intention. Soon, the cloud will rise again and bear down on Sodom. Soon, the crowd will disperse. Soon, we make our escape."

He walked to the window and stuck his head out. The men were standing, brushing off. He spoke.

"Listen up, residents of Sodom! You call for our heads, the mortician and the Fire Starter. But you misunderstand what's happening here. It's true that sulfur caused the destruction earlier today. But not from my fires! Two visitors came to Sodom last night and warned of impending destruction. They claimed to be messengers from Shinab, king of Admah. They said Sodom is brimming with evil, corrupted by the Captives, unworthy to pillage the sulfur mines."

Teodor lowered his voice and said to me, "They believe Shinab is a sorcerer, and all attacks attributed to him are the result of black magic."

The Sodomites looked at each other as they brushed off. A group of men stepped toward Mayor Bera and Sheriff Hammu, backing up Teodor's claim.

They had witnessed two dark-cloaked men confronting people headed to the carnival the previous night. The men stood on the curb hollering about vengeance and judgment, questioning Sodom's moral fortitude, cursing as the crowds passed without paying attention. Everyone figured them to be drunken tourists.

This went on well into the evening. As midnight approached, one of the men stood on a curb and made an announcement. "We offered you a chance, Sodom! Yet not one of you heeded us! The hour is at hand, Sodom!"

Sodomites who had witnessed the display laughed and threw sticks and rocks at him. The man jumped off the curb and joined the other. They pulled hoods over their heads and slunk toward the north gate. Other men agreed they, too, had seen these men but didn't realize what was going on at the time. Whispers spread through the crowd about what they missed while at the carnival the previous night.

"There's more, good people of Sodom!" Teodor exclaimed. He waited for the crowd's full attention and continued. "Last night, I saw those two men on the road to the mountain. I begged them not to destroy Sodom. But they said my pleas were useless. At dawn, Shinab would detonate the mountain. I did what I could to stop it, residents of Sodom! This is the work of Shinab of Admah!"

Another boom rocked Sodom. The crowd shuddered in unison. This blast was unlike the previous ones, which were powerful, no doubt, but sounded more like mining accidents. This one dwarfed those. It was the grand finale: I knew the mountain had blown its top. Putrid smells wafted down the street. A strange glow emanated from the mountain, yellow bile with blue flames following closely behind. Rancid sulfur air approached the north gate.

Teodor stepped out the door to finish the ruse. "I see Shinab's not done yet, Sodomites! Prepare for sulfur rain! Take cover, good people of Sodom! Save yourselves!" He ducked back inside and winked at me as sulfur chunks began to fall and burst into blue flames. "Let's get out of this forsaken town."

Outside, the Sodomites scurried for cover. They'd survived the earlier onslaught but realized this one was even greater. Destruction surely loomed.

The Captives who survived the melee rose to their feet and cranked up a street party. As the day's second sulfur cloud enveloped the city, they played their strange instruments and sang and danced, though their numbers had dwindled to less than a dozen.

I began preparing for the second onslaught of sulfur. The first one had devastated the town; the second would destroy it. Teodor ignored the threat and stood over the casket, his eyes closed, and mumbled under his breath. When he was finished, he raised his head and spoke to me. "Are you prepared to leave this town?"

"I'm ready to avoid the sulfur storm," I said as I blocked the windows with furniture.

"Don't waste your time," he advised. "After we leave this mortuary and pass through the north gate, Sodom will be destroyed. You will never see it again as it stands now." He motioned me to join him beside the casket. I noticed a soft hum vibrating from it. "You're comfortable with the dead. Until now, you made your living preparing bodies for proper burial so the souls may fly free from this decrepit world."

I nodded in agreement, though I failed to recognize his angle.

"Yes, I'm a mortician, as my father was before me and his father before him. My family has served Sodom for seven generations. We've cleansed and prepared thousands of bodies, buried or cremated them in preparation for the journey to higher realms."

"And now, you will do the same for me."

I looked at him through confused eyes. "What do you mean? You're not dead."

"Oh, mortician! So accustomed to seeing spirits that he no longer separates the dead from those with hearts still beating!"

Teodor extended an arm and summoned my hand with his fingers. He pressed my hand against his cloak. Inside his chest, no heart pounded; stillness and silence filled the cavity.

"Not what you expected?"

"But, if you're dead, how do you stand before me?"

My mind raced for answers. He drew a deep breath.

I paced as blue flames whistled down on Sodom. People in the street slumped in agony, begged for mercy. Deafening thunder answered their pleas as sizzling bolts lit up the street. Flames engulfed entire blocks of row houses and shops. Curdling screams pierced the air before bodies were vaporized by putrid mist. Some dove for cover only to land in other fires. Blue flames engulfed the city as if all things touched by Sodomites were sentenced to spontaneous combustion.

"Death is but an illusion," Teodor finally said, "as I'm sure you've realized in your occupation. Bodies are concentrated energy, manifestations of the spirits sailing through this realm. Those who understand magic and the connection between earth and sky recognize the sheer veil between life and death. The body is nothing more than an animated vehicle for the spirit. It provides depth and limitation to explore and learn. And as the spirit advances down the road, it, too, understands the gift the body provides, but also the lack of necessity for it."

He raised his eyebrows and glanced at the casket. "Are you ready to see who's inside?"

I nodded, though unsure if I was ready. He released the latches, paused before opening the heavy top.

"See you on the other side," he said as he inhaled deeply and opened the casket. Inside, lying in a silk suit the likes of which no Sodomite had witnessed in generations, was a body and face that looked exactly like Teodor's.

I stared at the corpse in disbelief. But when I returned my glance to the identical body standing beside me, it had changed. Instead of a vibrant man, the body appeared weakened. I saw waves of energy flowing through it, like the humidity one sees in desert mirages.

"Remember to breathe," he said.

Teodor's body became translucent, and I could see through it to the walls behind. In seconds, the mirage disappeared. Only Teodor the corpse remained. My body flinched, and my lip snarled. I slammed the casket closed. I tried to shake it off and sat down to catch my breath.

I've experienced strange moments as a mortician, but nothing to this extreme. Never before had I seen two identical bodies—one dead, the other alive—in the same moment. High magic indeed, perhaps grander than the fire starting on the mountain.

I wondered who this Teodor really was. He claimed the corpse in the casket was over a thousand years old. But he also claimed to be sent by Kedorlaomer, the man Sodomites reviled more than any other. More than Shinab, even. Perplexing questions for a simple mortician, and ones that would have to wait until a more suitable time.

I gathered important papers, stuffed them in a satchel, and slung the satchel over my shoulder. I hurried from the office to peer out the window. Yellow haze dominated the view. Blue flames danced in random places. When I turned back to the vestibule, I noticed a funny thing—the casket was hovering right behind me, as if it had followed me to the window. I walked back to the office and the casket followed.

I walked to the window. Again, it followed. Another extreme moment, another crest of strangeness in a day full of oddities.

When I stepped outside, the casket trailed behind me. Thunder boomed, lightning sizzled, blue flames rained down and connected with fires already burning. Moaning and wailing pierced the sulfur air from piles of flesh and bone along the street. Two bodies staggered ten feet in front of me and collapsed into the fog. The Sodomite throng was decimated, their bodies crumpled on the ground.

I inhaled deeply. Off to my right, I heard sounds of The Captives celebrating, though I couldn't see them through the fog. Their instruments and voices no longer sounded so strange but welcoming and protective. My confidence grew; my body stood tall, my shoulders settled. I stepped on a corpse. When I bent down, Sheriff Hammu's charbroiled face stared at me. His body collapsed as if imploding. I vomited on his melted badge. After wiping my mouth and adjusting the satchel over my shoulder, I crept through the fog towards The Captives, careful to avoid stepping on other corpses. The casket hovered behind me like a dog following its master.

When I reached The Captives dancing and singing and playing in the street, the fog parted, as if I stepped through a door into a sparkling room. A spotlight shined on me, though sunlight was blocked by sulfur, and I figured it to be close to dusk, anyway. The Captives welcomed me like a lost hero. They flung arms in the air, exchanged hugs, and focused big smiles with the force of their clapping hands.

The one dressed like a circus announcer quieted the rest. Then he leaned towards me and said, "Follow me."

The rest of The Captives encircled me and the casket. They continued dancing and singing and playing their instruments as we moved, parade style, down the street behind the ringmaster. Mustard fog hung thickly around the circle's edge. Inside, the perimeter was clear, the air clean and crisp, like my personal vehicle marching through Sodom's decay and madness. The parade synced to the melody of the strange instruments and maneuvered around dead bodies with grace. Sodomites still clinging to life coughed and moaned and pled for help as we passed. Bony arms with melted skin reached up from the ground, but The Captives smashed the shoulders with heavy boots and the parade continued moving until it reached Sodom's north gate.

Once outside the gate, the circle widened, and the ringmaster stepped to the middle. The rest of The Captives gathered behind him. He removed his tall hat and bowed to me. The rest followed his lead. After a few moments, he raised his head and said, "The hour is at hand. After today, Sodom is ours! Now it burns, but soon, it shall be known as the greatest of the cities of the plains! Never shall we forget the grace and fortitude of Teodorlaomer!"

The Captives roared behind him. They commenced a raucous tune and seductive dancing. The circus announcer leaned close to my ear and said, "Here begins the road to Zoar." He pointed to the charred path extending into the gloom and then turned to join the celebration.

I watched The Captives filter back into Sodom through the north gate. Drifts of fog hung around me, and blue fires burned intermittently in the grasses surrounding the road. But nothing as thick as inside the city walls. I turned to Sodom for a final look, realizing I would never return. A tear dribbled down my cheek as I took the first step toward Zoar, casket in tow: the mortician abandoning his city.

The cloud enshrouded Sodom, shot lightning inside the walls, and hurled blue fire to the buildings and streets. The city crackled and a sickly fluorescence glowed from inside. Caustic rain poured within the walls, and sulfur ash floated in the air outside.

I brushed particulates from my face and turned towards Zoar. As I walked down the road, a series of explosions rattled the Jordan Valley, each one growing in volume and intensity. Sodom, as I knew it, no longer existed. A new chapter would begin, one written by The Captives.

As I neared the fork in the road, one way leading to Zoar, the other to Zeboyim, the fog lifted, and the night sky opened. A half-moon hung low in the west and stars shimmered in a way I'd never before noticed. At the fork, I sat on a stump to rest my legs and admire the sky. The casket hovered beside me. As I gazed at stars, two silhouettes appeared from the trees. At first, they approached like shadows, and I thought my mind was playing tricks on me. As they moved closer, I realized two men—tall forms covered with dark cloaks—approached. I positioned myself between them and the casket.

"Fear not," the taller one said. "I am Baal, this is Molech." They bowed. "We greet you in friendship. You're the mortician, no?"

"I was the mortician of Sodom," I replied and placed a hand in my coat pocket to appear as if carrying a weapon. "But Sodom is no more."

"Teodor said you would meet us here," Molech said, "and that you would deliver the casket to us."

We all laid eyes on the casket.

"As you can see, the casket is safe and sound."

"Do you know who's in the casket?" Baal asked.

"Yes, I do." I placed a hand on the top of it. "I watched the man climb in with my own eyes."

"Good," Molech responded. "So, you understand the importance of delivering the casket to Zoar safely?"

"I understood the importance of escaping Sodom with my life."

"And now, here you are, free from the wrath cast upon Sodom."

"Yes, here I am."

"Now your task is accomplished. We shall handle the casket from here. Your service is greatly appreciated," the two said in unison, bowing.

I returned a bow and watched them whispering in each other's ears. After a few moments, Baal spoke. "Bandits often roam the road between here and Zoar. It's best if you travel with us."

Molech shouldered my satchel, and we set off toward Zoar. For what seemed like days, we walked, with Baal and Molech on either side of the casket and me behind. Twice we saw shadows on the road ahead, but they vanished by the time we reached the spot. We neared Zoar by sunrise without threat from bandits.

As we approached, the main gate opened and a man with two guards ushered us inside. No one stared or even blinked at the casket, as if it was invisible. He introduced himself as Nefi. In silence, he led us past vendors setting up stalls. Two guards followed. After navigating two streets, we turned into an alley and ducked into a wooden building. Inside, candles flickered, revealing the dirt floor and stone walls.

"The casket shall rest here," Nefi said, and signaled the two guards to post beside it.

He motioned me, Baal, and Molech up a stairway in the corner. It opened into an exquisite dwelling with gold fixtures, plush carpets, and exotic decorations. Servants were the only people visible, and they performed their tasks without lifting their gazes to acknowledge us.

"You men must be worn out," Nefi said with a snicker. "We've prepared a room for each of you."

We followed him up corkscrewing stairs until we reached the sixth floor, where we stepped into a long corridor with many doors. Candles cast the only light from fixtures on each door frame. Nefi stopped at the first two rooms and motioned Molech and Baal inside. They bid us good day and closed the doors behind them.

"Mighty warriors, those two," he said as we continued down the corridor before stopping in front of a double door. "And here is your room, sir." He bowed. "The mortician. Never thought we'd see you again." He smiled and bowed again before pushing the doors open.

Before me spread an immaculate room: a lapis floor with wall hangings of Persian cloth, Chinese silk, and an ancient mandala formed by shiny jewels.

"Do you remember?" he asked as he whirled me around to face a mirror, a decoration I hadn't seen since childhood. "Look!" he demanded.

When I peered into the mirror, I saw something strange, or rather, something familiar. I'd seen the face that stared back at me the previous day in Sodom, in fact. It was the face of Teodor, the face of the corpse, the same being I saw at once standing beside me and laying dead in the casket. The same being I watched dissipate before my eyes. I felt nauseous and vomited on the floor.

"Don't worry. I'll get it cleaned up. No shame in moments of such revelation."

"Teodor and I, we have the same face," I said in a low voice.

"Of course, you do!"

I felt nauseous again but fought the urge. Confusion cascaded over me. "But Teodor's in the casket. He was walking around yesterday, but also in the casket."

"Yes, yes, he was," Nefi agreed.

"But how do I have the same face? How do I share a face with a dead man? A mad man! A magician!"

Nefi snickered. "You don't share a face. You shared a womb."

"What? What are you talking about?"

"You and Teodor were identical twins. Sons of Kedorlaomer and Naomi. Nine hundred years ago, you were sent by the Seer to Sodom to tend the mortuary and the spirits residing there. All those years you waited, perhaps you forgot why you were even there. But you waited, because deep down you knew that one day your identical twin brother would come along needing your help. And the Seer was correct. On that day, Kedorlaomer's power was consolidated, and Sodom destroyed."

He handed me an envelope with a red seal and said, "Get some rest. When you wake, the rest of the princes shall be here."

"Rest of the princes?" I asked.

He smiled and pointed to the envelope. "Answers to all your questions await you." Nefi extinguished the candle on the mantle and walked toward the door. "Welcome home," he said, closing the door.

My fingers caressed the red wax. *The Seer?*

I deciphered the Kedorlaomer seal on the envelope. *Identical brother Teodor?*

I ripped open the envelope. On yellowed paper, a note was scribbled:

'Dear Fedor,

If you're reading this, you escaped Sodom and arrived in Zoar. Welcome home, Son! Your time at the mortuary is over, the role played to perfection. Your brothers will arrive this afternoon, nine hundred years since you've all been together. Tonight, we celebrate! Family loyalty, dedication and sacrifice, victory over the cities of the plain! Rest easy and prepare to feast at dusk. Today, you shall remember!

Your Father, Kedor'

Remember what?

My mind raced, eyes bulged, limbs shook. *All my brothers? Mortician role played to perfection? One thousand years?* I vomited again.

Kedorlaomer, my father?

My joints froze and my chest went numb. I flopped onto the bed. Contrary voices argued between my ears. I flipped through memories of Sodom—the long days at the mortuary with Luka, the simple life before the Battle of the Vale, the change introduced by The Captives.

The rest of the princes shall be here!

My body shot straight up, my eyelids stretched wide. The facade cracked, and I remembered.

Images flooded into my mind as I stared at the bejeweled mandala on the wall: I sat in a candle-lit room around the oak table with my seven brothers; my father Kedorlaomer and his advisors huddled at the head. From under his cloak, the Seer predicted Sodom's dominance over black gunpowder. My father leaned into the candlelight as he explained the plan: infiltrate the cities of Jordan's plain, blend in and wait until the sulfur mines can be controlled. Nefi the Magician, the same man who led me from the gate to this room, poured each of us a potion. "This will help you forget. At all times, you will only remember the previous forty years," he told me. By morning, the bitter liquid changed me from prince and astrologer to mortician. The mission required I work in Sodom away from my brothers, my family, my home. I traveled there with my faithful servant Luka, who posed as my father to strengthen the ruse. I gladly drank the potion. *Who wants to remember such a sacrifice?*

Nine hundred years ago, we sat around the table. Yesterday, I woke as The Mortician of Sodom. Yesterday, my twin Teodorlaomer destroyed Sodom with its own sulfur mountain. Today, my father's kingdom rules over Sodom and the other cities of the plain, and I remember my life as prince and astrologer. Tonight, Nefi raises Teodor from the otherworld. Tonight, I will be reunited with seven brothers.

A grin grew across my face, my arms spread wide, and I announced, "I am Fedorlaomer, eldest son of Kedorlaomer, King of the Jordan River Valley."

I vomited on the floor again, dry heaved twice through a smile, then closed my eyes and drifted to royal dreams.

STARLIGHT

Erin Vataris

Geula was afraid of the dark. She was afraid of the shadows that oozed out of the brick walls in the middle of the night and piled on the floor near her bed, thick and deep, waiting for her to step into them. She was afraid of the sound of the wind as it whistled past the windows in the darkness. She was afraid of the sound of the baked bricks cooling, the tick and crackle of the mortar between them. But most of all, she was afraid of the black empty dark.

Sometimes, when she hung her feet over the edges of the bed, the darkness climbed up them and made them disappear until she pulled them up and found them again. Sometimes, in the middle of the night, especially on the black dark nights when the clouds covered the stars and there was no moon, she thought she could feel it climbing up the side of the sleeping ledge, seeping into her sleeping mat and trying to make all of her disappear.

Geula didn't want to disappear. She didn't want the dark to eat her, so she stayed still on her mat and closed her eyes so she couldn't see how dark it was. She squeezed them closed so tightly that the darkness couldn't leak in, and then she pushed her fingers against her eyelids until she could see bright flashing spots even after she opened them again.

She did it again and again until she couldn't see the darkness anymore, then sometimes she could sleep, but the darkness was still there. It was waiting for her to fall asleep so it could climb up the ledge and into her mat and eat her all gone.

Her legs hurt from where Immi had whipped her for falling asleep at the loom yesterday, so she wiggled them a little bit. Not much, or the mat would crackle and the darkness would know she was there. Her lungs hurt from trying not to breathe too loudly. Her eyes hurt from pushing on them. But she was still there. It hadn't gotten her yet. Geula tried to think about staying awake, but she was so tired. She just wanted to go to sleep. She wished they would let her leave a lamp on, but oil was more precious than one silly little girl's silly little fears.

Abbi had put an altar in the alcove of the sleeping room for her and traded Immi's fine-woven linens for a statue of Asherah with a bronze crown that glittered. He sighed the whole while, but he put Asherah in the altar where the moonlight could shine in the window and catch her crown.

Asherah was a fine goddess to protect her. Geula knew that. She knew that Abbi gave her an altar and not another whipping because he loved her, just like Immi had whipped Geula's legs out of love and didn't want her to ruin a whole length of cloth by falling asleep and tangling the shuttle so it had to be all unwoven. Geula knew that.

When the moon shone in and the bronze crown sent stars dancing over the walls of the alcove, Geula could almost see Asherah moving. She could feel the goddess's gaze on her while she shifted and pushed on her eyes and tried to sleep, and Geula was almost as afraid of that as she was of the shadows that filled up the alcove on cloudy nights. On cloudy nights—nights like tonight—she couldn't see Asherah at all. She could just hear her moving in the darkness, and she knew, just as surely as she knew the darkness wanted to swallow her up, that Asherah was moving.

Asherah lived in the statue in the altar in the alcove, and Geula wasn't quite sure whether Asherah wanted to help her or beat her for her childishness.

Asherah never helped her. She just stood there being stone and bronze during the daytime, and at night she roamed around her alcove where the altar was, eating the olives and honey milk they left for her and trying to get out. Sometimes on the darkest nights, the nights with no moon, Geula could hear her feet like raindrops, and she wondered what would happen if Asherah got out.

Those were the worst nights, where she lay on her mat and shivered, afraid of the darkness, afraid of Asherah. Those were the nights when she was so afraid that she couldn't even make herself get up to pee, and she would lay in bed afraid until it all came spilling out of her in a hot wet stream that dried on her legs and made her mat stink. She got whipped when that happened, a big girl like her peeing in her bed, and Immi made her carry her own mat down to the river, heavy and reeking, to wash it. That was bad, but on the worst nights the darkness was worse than whippings. It was worse than washing her mat. It was worse than everything.

#

Usually, Geula went to pee before she went to bed, especially on this kind of night, because having to wash her mat was bad, and whippings were worse, but on this night, something was wrong even before bedtime. Even Geula knew something was wrong. It had started with dinner alone with Immi because Abbi had gone to a meeting. Immi was so angry that she'd left his lamb stew to sit on the table and get thick and gloppy until the fat was a cold yellow skin over the top. It was all right to go to meetings, but it wasn't all right to miss dinner for them. Not in this house.

It had been later than late when Abbi finally came home, and so dark that the shadows were starting to pool up in the corners of the main room. He was never that late. He'd come stumbling in the front door, holding the frame for balance and moving like he couldn't see where he was going. Immi had called him Ephraim in her angry voice, and Abbi turned his face toward her, and his eyes had been white— like sand or clouds on a hot day, filmy and pale.

"Ephraim!"

Immi had said it again, then she was crying and holding Abbi's face. They were talking in grown-up language, the kind that sounded nice but looked like fighting, and Geula didn't know what was wrong. She wanted to know why Abbi's eyes looked like that, and she wanted to know what happened to make him so late, but then Immi told her to go to bed, and she used *that* voice.

When Immi used *that* voice, Geula went, and she knew better than to mention the way the shadows were reaching out of the walls to get her. She just went, and she got in her bed by hopping over the shadow lines in the tile. And then Geula laid on her mat and listened to the sounds of voices on the other side of the wall and stared at Asherah while she waited for the darkness to fill up the whole room.

Asherah never moved when Geula could see her, and she always was careful to stand in the same spot when the morning came and pushed the darkness aside. But why would you leave food out for a statue if it wasn't alive?

Geula knew that when she wasn't looking, Asherah got up and moved around and ate the food and drank the milk they left for her. It was gone in the mornings. So, she laid on her mat and watched Asherah so Asherah wouldn't wake up and start moving, and that was when she realized she hadn't gone pee. She hadn't gone pee, and now the darkness had covered the whole floor and Geula would have to step in it to go.

Immi and Abbi were still talking in the other room. She could hear them, and the way their voices weren't quite so whispery anymore, but she didn't understand what they were saying. Something about strangers.

There were always strangers. They came to buy and sell and trade. Geula didn't understand why these strangers were so important. She didn't understand what they had to do with the sand clouds in Abbi's eyes. She blinked her eyes a few times, wondering if Abbi's eyes felt scratchy, like sand, like hers did in the morning after holding them open all night long. She blinked and rubbed her eyes, and then she froze.

Asherah had moved.

Geula was sure that before she'd rubbed her eyes, Asherah had her left foot forward. Now her right one was forward, or maybe it was the other way around, but it had been the other foot.

She'd only blinked once, and Asherah had moved. Except that when she'd closed her eyes, Immi and Abbi were talking in the eating room, and now they weren't. They were in this room, sleeping.

She could see them, lumps of darkness in the shadows. She could hear Abbi snoring and Immi's little whistling breaths, sleeping deep and uncaring that an eyeblink ago they had been talking with the tallow lamplight making wiggling flickers of safety through the doorway.

She'd fallen asleep. Geula had fallen asleep rubbing her eyes, and she'd stopped watching Asherah. Now it was *dark* dark, and the tallow lamp was blown out while the darkness was thick, hungry, and everywhere.

There was no moon tonight, had been no moon for three nights now, and the sky outside the window was full of dark angry clouds that swirled and boomed and sent hot winds snarling around the sleeping room to keep the darkness awake. There was no moon, and a storm was coming, so tonight was the very worst kind of night.

And Geula had fallen asleep.

She'd fallen asleep for a long time, long enough for Immi and Abbi to finish talking and come to bed, long enough for Asherah to wake up, and long enough for the darkness to grow thick and hungry around her. Geula could feel it now, the waiting, silent darkness hovering over her bed, getting ready to swallow her whole. *I'm awake now*, Geula whispered to herself, careful not to let any sound get past her lips. *I'm awake now, and it can't eat me when I'm watching it.*

She was so tired. And her eyes burned while holding them open. She needed to blink just once.

If I'm awake, Geula wondered—but it was hard to wonder for long when she was so sleepy—*and it's dark dark in the sleeping room, then how am I seeing Asherah?*

#

How can I see Asherah?

She sat up on her mat, suddenly wide awake and full of terror, whipping her head around in the darkness and trying to see something—anything—except black.

How can I see Asherah? It's dark and the alcove is always dark first, and the altar is dark, and how can I see Asherah?

"The same way," Asherah murmured in the darkness beside her, "that I can always see you, Geula."

Geula felt the pee flowing out of her, hot and stinking, soaking her thighs and her mat. Immi would whip her for it tomorrow—if there was a tomorrow—but Asherah was today, right now, and she was realer than a hundred thousand lots of whippings. Asherah was right there, and she was big, and she was talking to Geula. *It is probably rude to pee yourself in front of a goddess*, Geula thought, and she felt her cheeks growing hot like the puddle of wet on her mat.

"Hush," Asherah whispered, and Geula felt a cool hand touch her face. "I won't hurt you."

She laughed. Her breath smelled like lilies and that was all right because she couldn't stay scared of someone who laughed like that. Not even in the darkness, she couldn't fear Asherah.

Geula understood that now. There was nothing to be afraid of.

"Come with me," Asherah laughed. Geula stood, but her legs were wet and dripping. She felt her cheeks turning red again, and the darkness rose with her shame. She sat down, back on the wet bed, cowering from the darkness. But Asherah kissed her on the forehead and whispered, "Come, Geula."

Geula stood again.

This time she was light, lighter than wind, and the darkness fell back and cowered from her. It was a wonderful thing to be in the darkness—surrounded by darkness—and to not be afraid at all.

Asherah took Geula's hand, and Geula followed her. Together, they pushed the darkness away, and left shining footprints made of moonlight behind them. Hand in hand, they left the sleeping room, and Abbi and Immi, and the heavy wet frightened lump of fear that had been Geula until Asherah kissed her. Until Asherah made her real.

They left the room and the house and walked out underneath the wild, angry, cloudy sky into the howling angry wind, and Geula felt herself grow heavy with fear again.

"Hush," Asherah said, lifting her face, letting the wind whip her hair. Geula copied her.

The wind blew through her, carrying away the fear, and she closed her eyes and felt the storm in her and around her until there was no room to be afraid, nowhere in her anymore. There was only Geula, and Geula wasn't afraid of anything.

Asherah smiled and Geula opened her eyes. The sky was full of stars. They glittered and danced, hanging beneath the swirling storm clouds, so close that Geula thought she might be able to touch one if she were just a little taller. She stretched out her hands, trying to do just that, and felt the warmth of their light filling her palms, spilling out to wash over her.

"It's beautiful," she whispered, reaching up on her tiptoes, trying to get a little closer.

"Remember this," Asherah said. Her voice was soft and sad.

Geula turned to look, to see why the goddess was unhappy, but she was gone.

"Remember me," came Asherah's voice on the wind. And then the stars began to fall. They fell like diamonds at first, bright and beautiful and glittering with fire inside them, a rain of jewels across the cities. They fell tinkling onto the stone and brick, and then some of them broke open, and the fire inside leapt out of them, bright and hungry, looking for something to eat, something to burn. The fire crawled across the ground, getting closer and closer to Geula until she could feel it biting at her, sharp and fierce and painful.

#

Geula sat up in bed, choking on her screams, opening her eyes.

It was only a dream. She'd fallen asleep and the darkness was going to eat her for falling asleep, but Geula knew now there were worse things than the darkness. There were worse things than being swallowed in your sleep. Geula drew in a gasping breath, and the air was thick and black, and the darkness wasn't darkness, after all. It was something trying to climb down her throat and eat her from the inside and she could still see Asherah. She could see the little alcove and the statue, and the glittering crown all full of fire and starlight, and something slammed through the roof of the sleeping room. Then everything was on fire.

"Abbi! Immi!" Geula screamed into the choking smoke that filled the sleeping room, the smoke that came from the burning stars crashing through the roof, from the corner where they should have been sleeping. She screamed again and again, but nobody answered her. The whole world was full of smoke and fire, and Geula huddled on her sleeping mat while the stars fell all around her. Her eyes stung and her throat burned and there wasn't any air anywhere in the whole world. She couldn't breathe. The fire was in her lungs and all around her.

Geula screamed and reached for Asherah, but the goddess wasn't moving now. There was fire in her screams and fire on her sleeping mats, and Asherah wasn't listening. It had only been a dream.

She tried to run, but the stars were falling around her, shaking the ground, and her feet were melting, and she couldn't move. Geula tried to close her eyes, and tried again, and tried a third time, wishing—praying—for the darkness and the familiar fear to come back, but her eyes wouldn't close. Her feet wouldn't move, and the darkness wouldn't come. It would never come again.

In the alcove, the baked clay cracked and crumbled, and the bronze crown fell, melting to the ground. As it pooled and ran, the screaming stopped.

WARMTH

Kris Varga

Cold. The word shutters over the mind. Cold is the cobbled streets on the brink of winter, resonating with the season appropriately. Cold is the city under a dainty snowfall while fleeting teal sparks reach for the heavens. Cold is the sound of vacancy among Gomorrah, whose electricity has been discontinued via an electromagnetic pulse. Cold is the soul at the brink of survival.

Patrick was cold.

"The Day of Shock," Patrick creatively coined it, left him immobile and incapable of returning to an energy pod to restore his battery. He computed a light chuckle in his thoughts, one that was innocent enough to maintain the positive attitude he was designed to omit. His bio-constructed flesh tingled as his eyes transfixed on snowy open vastness. Patrick had traveled this path many times, but this time he gained a new perspective, catching a glimpse of himself as if a stranger. He computed a silent sigh.

"Soon enough," he speculated, "Evelyn will return."

Evelyn always returned.

#

Four days, two hours, thirty-six minutes and fifty-seven seconds ago, Patrick and Evelyn had passed through the quieter outlets of the city's boundaries: the grasslands, as they were referred to by the people of Gomorrah. Their weekly destination, however routine, pleased Patrick.

Beyond the bubble-shaped buildings and transcendent automobiles, emitting violent screeches to convey each individual's animosity towards another, laid the incandescent fields, preserved for the rare produce proprietors who lived a "simpler life." Twenty-four degrees above the Earth's meeting with the sky rested the sun, whose lackadaisical clock reminded Patrick of the bells that would ring ever so briefly from Divine Intelligence's control tower. The grocery bags in Patrick's hands would only slow down their travels.

"Patrick, slow down! I wanna enjoy the sunset."

"My dear, we must hurry—for time, you see, is dwindling. It is almost the eve."

"Sing me the Clair de Lune." Her eyes smiled their childish embellishment. "Pretty please?"

Patrick halted and glanced cheerfully at the heart of the city, then at the enticing sun, then at Evelyn's purity. Against all odds, Evelyn's smile won out, and she placed her knapsack on the ground and rested cross-legged in the open field as Patrick hummed the tune to his best ability. Even though this was not a part of his programming, Evelyn seemed to enjoy the flawed sound he produced. "Human-like", she would call it.

#

Patrick tried for the sixteen-thousandth and seventy-fourth time to move his finger. Unsuccessful. In the far left he could hear several dogs (five, he confirmed) gnawing at limp flesh. *I pray they are well fed* were the non-verbal hopes of the malnourished Patrick. Despite his mechanical construction and electric operation, his system still operated on the concept of nutrition. At this point, given the circumstances, he calculated his life-expectancy at five hours, sixteen minutes, and ten seconds. "Evelyn will return."

Earnest optimism, as he could convey no other, hovered over his alloyed skull.

Forty-two meters ahead of him emerged two silhouettes from the drifting snowfall. Forty-one meters later, they blocked the open vastness that laid before Patrick. It was the taller wanderer who spoke first.

"Well, what do you know? I reckon we found a working humanoid, Joe."

Joe's beady eyes scanned Patrick, alighting with a malicious grin as his blood-red bandanna slid down his neck. "It does seem that we did, Bert." Joe quickly pushed Patrick's left shoulder, who returned unwillingly to his original positioning. "Looks like this one managed to survive Divine Intelligence's EMP blast."

Patrick's mind was working faster than the rest of his parts. Other humanoids did not survive? He only assumed they were all in a similar predicament, waiting for Divine Intelligence to send out refugees. Patrick was waiting for someone else.

#

"Okay. Now you watch the sunset and, this time, I'll sing for you."

This was a different circumstance. Evelyn had avoided singing ever since her mother had passed. She was renowned for her beautiful voice, one that would stop the angels from their choir, yet she refused to share it with the world anymore. Patrick remained cheerfully calm yet pleaded in appropriate congruence to the situation.

"Evelyn, please, my darling, we must return. As happy as I am for you to wish to sing, I do believe it is of greater importance to return to the city. Father would be most upset with me if he discovered us out in the grasslands at this hour."

"I promise everything will be okay." She rested her graceful hand on Patrick's arm. "Trust me."

Patrick trusted Evelyn more than anyone. He released a computed chuckle, one that was innocent enough to maintain the positive attitude he was designed to omit.

"As I am obedient to your every will, I shall rest for the duration of the song you choose to sing." His mechanical eyes fixated upon hers, creating a fatherly display, one of sincerity, as they released a twinkle to lighten the mood. "But, afterwards, we shall return to the safety of your father's house. Now, if you will ..."

#

The two men encircled Patrick with curiosity. Their postures were stiff and alert, taking cat-like strides, as if Patrick were to pounce at any given moment. After three minutes and sixteen seconds of this, the men conversed at ease seven feet behind Patrick, leaving their supply packs within arms distance of Patrick.

"What should we do with him?"

"Strip off his skin and sell the parts. Donnie Whitemark will buy them for a good price."

This seemed most unusual to Patrick, for he had only heard stories of men like this yet never encountered the "scoundrels" personally. At his home, he was confined behind the upper-class walls and only left the premises to accompany Evelyn on their grocery trips. Father refused to give details but reminded them of the men who haunt the nights, committing sinful acts upon the virtuous. What Evelyn learned among her peers was much more graphic: violent attacks of unexplainable means by tormented souls who eat the flesh of other humans and take part in illegal sexual activity while under intoxicating paraphernalia. Humanoids were members of both parties—the virtuous and the sinful.

Suddenly, Patrick was lying on his back with two knives and two matching grins shining in the bleak apparel of midnight. At the angle they placed him, Patrick was able to get his first look at Gomorrah since "The Day of Shock." It was horrific, and it was the first time in his life that Edward's cheeriness was matched.

The wonderfully bright city, one that radiated a glow that paired the tranquil sensitivity of Evelyn's blue eyes, was of rubble and darkness, with only a few remaining sparks and embers to ignite the reminder of the Heaven-to-Hell which came to be. Only Divine Intelligence's tower stood erect, as it was the only building made of natural concrete instead of bio-manufactured polyester, similar to the making of Edward's skin.

The two knives created their incision, sliding over the stomach and across the chest. Patrick could feel the searing pain of open flesh to the ice of dainty snow laying in him like a fragrant dream. *No, a nightmare!* screamed Patrick's thoughts. Where was his Evelyn?

#

The sliding of the reassuring sun called the chimes at their precise daily time. Patrick faced the sunset and drifted his mind away from calculations, pouring his thoughts to the beauty of the whispering wind as Evelyn began her melody from behind. At first, Patrick did not recognize the tune, only to realize it was a lullaby Mother would sing to Evelyn at night when she feared the monitors that recorded the vandals outside the perimeters. The words, this time, were changed:

"Call me, oh angel, with strings of your harp
guided by wings in the dawn of the dark
if only my prayers were enough
to induce my love, for you, my love.
Call me, oh angel, with kings of the heart
silent dreams will breathe your restart
if only my prayers were enough
to protect my love of you, my love.
Carry me, oh angel, beyond the tall walls
I am in need of the leave, you may fall
to your knees, but try to be tough
my love, be free, my one true love."

A single tear fell down Patrick's cheek, glistening in the frozen sun. Never had he cried before nor knew it was even something he was capable of conveying. As his breaths heavily inhaled and exhaled, a faint zapping sound released in the background. Evelyn kissed Patrick passionately on the cheek—it seemed to last forever—and whispered "goodbye."

The shuffle of light footsteps stretched farther and farther away. Patrick was accustomed to Evelyn running off and Patrick having to chase her. He would catch her; they would laugh and return home.

Patrick tried to turn and play the game once again but found himself incapable of doing so. It was as if he had forgotten how to move. "Evelyn?" he tried to speak, but not a single sound was muttered. He tried several more times, and several more times after that. And several more after that.

#

The pain was unbearable. Screams were fighting their way through inconceivable odds and forming something more than thoughts.

"Look, Joe. This here is real aluminum alloy. We're rich. Filthy rich!"

Evelyn was not returning. If she were hiding in the bushes, as she always had, she would have run out to save him. She would have attacked the men with all the power she could muster. And here he was, alone, with no one to help him.

Patrick was angry. Furious, even, at Evelyn for abandoning him, furious at the evil of men whose selfishness was destroying him, furious at Divine Intelligence for leaving him so helpless and vulnerable, furious at his creator for designing him to the falsity of his beliefs. Most of all, he was furious at himself. For not once in his life had he ever stabbed a man.

The blood streamed from Joe's stomach, and his beady eyes turned into a ghastly horror. Another flash of pain breached Patrick's side as Bert stuck in his knife and stood in defense. Patrick removed the knife and threw it directly into Bert's elongated forehead, causing him to fall instantly to his death.

"How the hell—?" Joe sputtered as he shuffled on the ground, holding his wound.

Patrick hovered over Joe, the blood-soaked knife dripping with rage. Patrick glanced over his own open body, removed Bert's coat, and covered himself. Despite his wounds, his body was at full capacity. Patrick grabbed Joe's throat and held the knife to the esophagus.

"Where is Evelyn?" he growled.

"Who the fuck is Evelyn?" Bert yelped.

Patrick cut Bert's face. Bert howled in agony. The man was clearly uninformed in this matter, so Patrick recalculated his next question.

"What happened to me?"

"There ... there was an EMP," Bert slurred the words with blood trickling from his mouth. "Divine Intelligence ... it destroyed the city ... corrupt ... it said ... humans were corrupt."

"My people and I were destroyed because your people were too corrupt?"

Bert coughed and Patrick tossed him aside like a useless toy. Why would Divine Intelligence punish him for their mistakes? Had Evelyn known this would happen? Patrick demanded answers.

"You can't leave me here to die. It's immoral!"

Patrick computed a sneer and walked towards the last standing city building.

Smoldering smoke rose towards the heavens, complementing the teal sparks and rash embers as a blend of all divinity. The tower remained unscathed, informing Patrick that this was the only place a survivor could remain in the city. Using his aluminum alloy hand, he punched through the door and admitted himself.

The tower's interior was of a traditional, ancient style. It represented everything the city was not: conservative, disciplined, and intact. One could wonder at the irony of a modern city being controlled by a building of this nature. Light began to shine in Patrick's eyes, both metaphorically and physically, as a single individual approached him.

"Hello. I am Divine Intelligence."

The man resembled a human, but what was missing was a single flaw on the body. In fact, it looked neither man nor woman and showed no sign of an actual age. A single white cloak covered the body.

Patrick fumed and immediately attacked the figure with his barbaric knife. The figure defended itself with ease.

"Patrick, I'm disappointed in you." The figure glided over a throne-like chair and placed itself on it. "I'm sure you have questions in regard to the city's current predicaments."

"Where's Evelyn?" Patrick demanded. His voice was hoarse, and he lost all sense of manners.

Divine Intelligence smiled. "I created humanoids in the image of myself. I sought to better the world with their presence, but there were flaws. Some turned to the side of sin, taking advantage of the concept of free will and destroying all things pure. Others, like yourself, were too ignorant, took no initiative, and fell to a life of servitude. This comfort made you weak and useless."

Patrick grimaced. After his body returned to life, he expected his warmth to return, as well. He had never felt colder.

"So, you see, I set off the EMP, purging the city from my creation. The upper-class were notified ahead of time and the rest were left to their own demise. Any who tried to take a humanoid with them forfeited the law and were sentenced to death."

Divine Intelligence stood at this and pensively stared out the window for a moment. Then, it turned and stared at Patrick, who was preparing his next attack.

"WHERE IS EVELYN?"

"Please, set yourself at ease. You come off as a fool. To continue, all humanoids were to immediately deactivate, but you managed to hang on to life. Barely." Divine Intelligence took a few steps forward. "You see, the distance from the tower put you just far enough to keep you stable. Immobile, but stable."

Before Patrick could shout again, Divine Intelligence raised a hand.

"Very well. I shall show you what you wish to see."

A monitor appeared, the same kind that used to show the vandals outside the perimeters of the wall. It was of the woods, the one that connected to the grasslands, and carefully wandering through the woods were a group of humans. They seemed to be moving in formation, each handling a responsibility in the function of the group.

Amid the pack was—

"Evelyn!"

As if she heard Patrick, her head turned and glanced around. She took a deep breath then returned to her group.

"As you can see, she is quite well, and in very good hands. These humans have formed a connection in these dire circumstances, one based on the principles of safety, survival, and morality. It is quite remarkable."

This information ran through Patrick like rain through a ditch. *She is alive*, he thought. *That's all that matters.*

Patrick glanced at Divine Intelligence, who waited for a response.

"So, what happens next?" Patrick asked.

"Well, let me introduce you to someone very special. Follow me this way."

Patrick followed, begrudgingly. They walked up a marble staircase and into an elegant room lined with silk linen and a well-crafted tapestry. In the far-right corner sat a beautiful woman, who kept silent upon their entrance. Divine Intelligence spoke first.

"This is Julia," it said, waving a hand towards the woman.

"Hello," spoke the woman with an inviting smile. Julia stood and maneuvered gracefully to Patrick, nodding politely. Patrick glanced back and forth from Julia to Divine Intelligence with curiosity.

"Julia," said Divine Intelligence, "is just like you, Patrick. A humanoid survivor. Together, I shall use the two of you to create the perfect being. Between the three of us, we shall find a cure for the plague of humanity."

Patrick was dizzy with confusion. He began to ask questions, using the word "why" at the beginning of each one, but he found that there were no conceivable answers. He swayed back and forth until he felt a soft hand on his shoulder.

"It's okay, my love," the gentle voice of Julia soothed him, "everything will be okay."

With that, Julia took Patrick by the hand, and they followed Divine Intelligence to the top of the tower where an energy pod recharged their batteries.

Patrick felt warm.

THE SCENT OF SIN AND PUNISHMENT

J.P. Cianci

I drink deeply from my half-filled chalice, admiring the way the indelibly perfect, golden idol of Molech reflects the sunlight. I raise my goblet to Molech, my jewel-encrusted cup catching the brilliant rays of the sun, then I take another insatiable drink. I turn around to refill my cup when gentle fingertips run up and down my back.

"Adaron, how would you like to receive Molech's blessing?" Sahar whispers seductively.

I smile, reveling in her touch, and close my eyes. I imagine all the delicious ways in which her body could satisfy the pressing fleshly urges her contact has aroused. "I would love to receive Molech's blessing, but I cannot afford such a sanction," I say, opening my eyes. I cup the temple prostitute's breast and forcefully bring her in for a kiss.

She smacks me, but I laugh and grab her wrist.

"Come now, Sahar. I worship in here every day. I'm entirely devoted. Are you sure Molech wouldn't want to bless a follower such as myself?"

"If you need money to afford his blessing, I know someone who would pay handsomely for the company of your daughter," Sahar suggests.

I smack her quick and hard across the face, holding a finger to her—warning her—but I say nothing.

She slinks off to find another, no doubt richer, follower to seduce.

Incense wafts from silver plates beneath the idol and I try to forget Sahar and her remarks. I don't need to pay to satisfy my desires. Many women, and even men, are happily drawn in by my sexual prowess.

I walk drunkenly back to the idol that is gloriously exposed to the sun by the open rooftop of the temple and fall to my knees in prayer. I slur my pleas and wishes for a few moments before my head bobs heavily from the wine. After an hour, I close my eyes to rest at the foot of Molech, basking in the afternoon sun.

"It's too early to be this dark," someone remarks a few minutes later.

"Quiet!" I bark. My eyes are still closed, but I do notice the almost imperceptible shift in light behind my eyelids. "It's merely clouds passing in the sky."

"What is that? A sandstorm?" someone else asks. The presence of a crowd gathering around me causes me to finally open my eyes.

"Gawk outside! Do not waste Molech's temple for slack-jawed gaping!" I yell, but no one listens. I raise my head to the sky, which is shrouded in darkness. Plumes of smoke billow downward in waves, obscuring the sun.

"Sandstorms don't move like that," I say, shifting uneasily. People murmur excitedly all around me.

"It's all right! I see light!"

"Yes! I see it too! It looks like the sun is coming toward us!"

"That's not light, that's fire! Run!"

"No! This is a sacred temple. We are safe here," I assure them, but people take off to the streets. I kneel a few feet back from Molech and begin fervently praying. As the smoke surges closer, I cover my mouth and nose in disgust, but only for a moment. A ball of fire collides directly with my sacred idol. A stream of melted gold sprays in my direction, blinding me in one eye and cooling rapidly to my skin so that it's encased in a painful, golden mask.

I moan in agony, turning to flee. "Oh Molech, Oh Molech. Why? *Why?*" I'm almost to the entrance of the temple when it collapses on top of me.

#

"Hey! Hey!"

My eyes flutter open.

"I knew you were alive. I could hear you breathing," a man says, lying across from me in the ruins of the temple. His face is charred, and his left limb is pinched beneath a stone slab.

My eyes tear from my own pain.

"You've been out for three days," he says. "I'm Jaban."

"Adaron," I gasp.

"I can't move, Adaron. It looks like you might be able to. If you can, you can go for help, yes? Can you find help and save me?" he asks.

I lay my head weakly on the ground. I'm confined to my belly, and this small exertion of energy from lifting my head—now heavy with gold—taxes me.

"Wake up, you fool! Can you move?" he hisses.

I'm in too much pain to be upset. I can't feel or move my legs, but my face pulses in pain. I glance at my hands with my one good eye. They're the only part of me that I can move freely, and they are scorched but functional.

"I can't move my legs," I say, simply.

"Argh! You haven't tried! You could save me—us!"

I lay my head back down. All I want to do is sleep to escape the pain.

What feels like hours later, pebbles clink against my golden face plate. I open my eyes to darkness.

"Adaron! Can you feel your legs now?" Jaban asks.

I sigh, trying to wriggle them.

"No—"

"Shh! Wait! Do you hear that?" he interrupts.

I strain my ears, "Yes, I hear voices!"

"Here! We're here!" Jaban cries.

"We're here!" I echo.

Rapid footsteps approach us, but their full forms are obscured in the plumes of smoke that still linger. I can't see three feet above me.

"No! What are you doing?" I cry as a man bends down and grasps at the golden mask that is now a part of my body. "No! Please! *Please!*"

"This one has a face of gold. Come help me pry it off!" the man yells.

Two more men appear, and the three of them grab hold, ignoring my shrieks of agony. I puff in and out quickly, trying to withstand the pain. When that doesn't work, I try to hold my breath, but the pain is too much. "*No! Stop!*"

The sickening rip of skin and the nauseous heat of my pain cause me to vomit. The men hoot in victory and leave us.

"If you had tried to escape like I suggested earlier, this would not have happened to you," Jaban says cruelly.

"Why did you not say anything?" I cry, bringing a shaky hand to my damaged and raw face.

"You are not a friend to me," he says.

I try to hold onto consciousness, but my pain forces me to sleep. Before I close my eyes, I note the broken, gold pieces of Molech that the robbers must not have seen because of the smoke. I cry pitifully at the unfairness until I drift off.

#

"This is a punishment from Lot's God. Lot knew, but he fled. He left them to their rightful fate!" a woman proclaims.

"Ten. They said if ten righteous people lived within these walls they could have been saved," another says. "How could there not have been ten?" she questions, but there is no pity in her voice.

They hurry past me, but I don't bother asking for help. I know better now.

So, Lot's God did this. How could his God do such a thing? And how am I not righteous? I lived like all the others.

I lick my chapped lips. "Jaban?"

"What?"

"How long have I been out this time?" I ask.

"Two more days. You will die here, no doubt," he predicts.

"Yes, well, when you lift that stone slab that pinches your left limb, I'll be sure to marvel at your godlike strength that could have saved me when you leave me here to die," I say.

"You idiot! I can't feel my arm!"

"And I can't feel my legs as I've told you before!"

I sigh and let a few moments pass. He is my only link. "What happened to Sodom?" I question.

"The same thing that happened to Gomorrah. Lot's God proclaimed that these two cities were full of sinners, and we were meant to feel his wrath. Wanderers from Zoar have been walking the streets to see for themselves. They were the only city that was spared."

"They wouldn't help you?" I question.

"They are afraid of God's wrath. They believe we are all meant to perish," he says, sounding weary. "Go back to sleep. You bore me, and this talk is meaningless. I need to save my energy."

I'm silent after that, and it lasts through the next two days. I stay awake the entire time, listening as the wanderers comment and take in God's wrath. When the sun rises and peaks through the smoke on the second day of reflection, I know it will be my last.

I weakly lift my head. The acrid, foul smoke suffocates, but it won't kill me. I wheeze and lay my head back down, closing my eyes. I gasp, trying to take deep breaths, but every breath, though it may prolong my life, repulses my senses.

A grunt makes me raise my head. Jaban feebly reaches for the bits of gold that remain, and I laugh, delirious.

"What do you plan on doing with the gold? And how could you spend it?" I ask.

He ignores me, keeping to silence and palming the gold in his only remaining hand.

A baby cries in the distance, and I stiffen with sadness. When the crying persists, I break into sobs, my delirium gone. In all this time, I had not given a single thought to my only child—only to my own fate.

"Anna," I whisper, thinking now only of my three-year-old daughter. I had left her with our neighbors so I could worship. What of her now? Had she survived?

I remember what the woman had said about the righteous. How could my Anna not be righteous? How could she be forsaken? And how short was our number? The woman said that only ten righteous souls were needed to save Sodom and Gomorrah. Was it only Anna? Or not even Anna? Will she pay for my many sins?

"Oh, Anna! Are you eternally lost? Have I damned you?" I weep.

Were there nine? If I had accepted Anna's mother's death and rejoiced in her eternal life, instead of turning away from the faith and blaming God, would I have saved Anna? Would I have made ten?

I clutch at the gravel.

"Hello? Is anyone alive here?" a soft voice asks.

I'm silent as tentative steps draw closer.

"Mother, why do we linger here? It's unsafe."

"The wicked have been punished. Those who still cling to life might still be saved," she answers.

"Here. I am here," I croak, assured of their intentions

"What is your name?" the woman asks, bending to give me water.

"Adaron," I answer.

She assesses my body and furrows her brow. "I can't get you out, but we will pray over you before you die, imploring God to save you," she says, knowing—as I know—that death is upon me.

"No, please. My daughter. Can you find my daughter?"

"We should not risk God's wrath by helping this man. Let us go back to Zoar," the daughter says, gripping her mother's arm.

"I can try. I can bring her to you if we find her," the woman says, taking my hand and giving it a squeeze.

"No! I don't want her to see me. She is only three. If I tell you where you might find her, will you see if she is alive? I just want to know that she is alive. I will let you pray over me then."

"We should pray first, and you should, too," the woman insists.

"So that I can be saved, and Anna cannot? No, if Anna is dead … please, can you do this for me? Please?" I beg.

"Well, all right. Tell me where to find this child," she says, her gentle hands moving a lock of my hair out of my eyes.

I give directions and wait in an agonizing eternity, with nothing to do than to recount my sins. I inhale a deep breath, but it chokes me.

Sin and punishment have very distinct smells, I've come to realize, lying in the rubble, dying next to the dead and soon-to-be dead.

I inhale the bitter, foul stench that loiters with the fog. It mixes with the stink of the charred flesh of my own body and the man next to me. It mixes still with the excrement of the dead and trapped. This is the pungent odor of punishment, but there is another odor I detect. It is a similar thread between the smell of sin and the smell of punishment.

It is the metallic scent of blood. Perhaps it is a similarity I'm meant to recognize. A common thread meant for me to reflect upon, as I smell its scent now in punishment. Maybe I'm the only one to pick this out.

For murder was my first sin.

Three years ago, a young man walked late at night down the streets of Zoar where I had been visiting, and I recognized the alluring clink of gold coin against gold coin. I stared lustfully at the man's heavy pouch as he drunkenly made his way down the empty streets. I approached him under the guise of friendliness and asked if I could escort him home. I was careful, even for my first time. He led me to his house, and once inside, I slit his throat and slit the pouch from off his belt. I murdered this innocent creature, one of God's innocent lambs.

I grab one of the gold bits of an idol and hurl it in disgust. The money lasted briefly, and the blood washed off easily, but I could never separate the smell of gold from the smell of blood after that. Strangely now, it seems fitting that I would have to endure the golden mask, only to have it ripped away with flesh and blood: A reminder of my sin.

That is not my only sin. I breathe in the sinful scent of incense from the temple. It still burns from the fiery rainfall. It's thicker than usual, unpleasant now. Did He mean to keep this burning for me? To remember and repent?

How often had I danced merrily with the other citizens of Sodom around our sacred idols? I drank deeply and feasted gluttonously, exulted exuberantly, and revered falsely these now-broken idols. How often had I lusted to fornicate with the temple prostitutes? How foolishly had I believed that I would receive the blessing of the deity they represented? A sin in itself to lust, I now realize, and it had been the gateway that had led me to the last stain on my mortal record.

I cough and splutter, only to inhale the scent of my punishment.

I remember a wedding celebration, one year ago, where a man and his new wife danced sensually in front of the invited crowd. Oh, how I lusted for the wife. The way she danced with him reminded me of the pleasures I once had with my own wife. I never cared to know the man, and I never did, but his wife ... his wife I came to know most intimately. It could hardly be my fault that she wavered in her devotion to her husband. She was easily seduced by my desire. She was my sweetest sin. This sin smelled the loveliest, for she smelled of jasmine.

I inhale deeply, thinking of her, but only sniff the putrid excrement of the men around me who have been laid to waste. I shrink in shame for remembering her lustfully still.

I glance at Jaban, but he is unnervingly motionless.

I know now that I'm meant to suffer. Death will come soon, I feel it, but I've come to believe that I'm meant to writhe in pain amidst the rubble. That I'm meant to die in agony for Him—for my sins. Could this be my penance? Will He let it be my penance?

"Adaron?" the woman whispers.

Yes! I'm here!" my voice comes raspy.

She drops to her knees by my side. I gaze up at her hopefully. She smiles gently at me, but her face is lined with pity.

A dry sob wracks my body.

"I'm sorry," the woman replies. "We found the neighbor who struggles to survive, but I'm afraid Anna is gone. Your neighbor gave me this." The woman opens her hand and gives me the bright red ribbon that I used to secure Anna's hair that fateful morning seven days ago.

I weep into the ground, grasping this only vestige of my child.

"It's time to repent of your sins. It's time to pray. There is a chance you may be saved," she urges, pulling her daughter down to the ground next to her.

Their moving lips begin to breathe formulaic words into clasped hands, and my head lolls on the ground. I'm ready to go, but not where these women mercifully hope to send me.

I have heard that God created the Earth, and then on the seventh day he rested. It is the seventh day since His wrath, and this will only mark the beginning of a restless eternity in damnation for me.

"No," I say, reaching up to grab their hands, and then I slowly lower them. "I must wander the fires below with Anna," I say, and I forcefully breathe in a final whiff of the scent of my punishment.

SOLOMON'S LOT

Allen Taylor

Solomon peeked around the corner of Mr. Krauss's General Store. After taking a deep breath, he stepped into the shadow of the clay awning hanging over the door. He was hungry for not having eaten in three days.

Pedestrians bustled through the streets of Sodom from one end of the city to the other. Most were going to or from market. Others were busying themselves with activity to mask their fear or worry of impending doom. Fruit vendors, craftspeople, and various merchants lined the streets with carts. The sounds of buyers and sellers bartering, cutting deals, negotiating, and crafting transactions filled Solomon's ears like a chorus. A part of him felt the stab of envy from the inside out. He had been jobless for a week and therefore had no money for buying goods, food, subsistence. He was tired of begging.

He pushed himself behind a man selling pomegranates and into the door of the store where it was considerably darker without the benefit of the sunshine penetrating the stone walls. He stopped to let his eyes adjust. When he could see the divisions of aisles, he continued, walking through the store to the back where no one could see him.

It, too, was busy. He picked the wrong time of day to take up thievery. But he couldn't deny the pangs of hunger that riveted his flesh from bare foot to brow. He waited for the woman and two children tugging at her arm to round the corner to the next aisle before snatching a small box of dried fruit from a shelf and tucking it into his tunic.

He dilly-dallied a little longer, skipping aisles to find one without hustling buyers aggressively pursuing their needs. It proved a much more difficult task than finding items to snatch and stow.

After a half hour of trying to remain anonymous, he gave up and snuck past the merchants calculating their sales and outside into the street again, then around the store's corner. He sat on a ledge protruding from the outside wall of the store and glanced both ways down the street before pulling a goatskin full of fig juice from his tunic followed by the box of dried fruit and a small loaf of bread.

It wasn't long before a boy—he couldn't have been older than twelve or fourteen—ran past, then just as quickly returned again to Solomon, standing before the old vagrant and looking pensively as if waiting to speak. The boy waited until Solomon looked up from his goodies before talking.

"Have you heard the news, sir?"

Solomon felt like being rude and sniping at the boy, but he didn't want to draw attention to himself. "Wha' news?"

The boy coughed, covering his mouth with his fist, and spat on the street. When he spoke again, his voice cracked. But he managed to force himself to spill his proclamation.

"Ol' Sal's going to blow any day now, what they say. All the peoples are running for cover, buying up their needs afore it gets too bad. Could destroy the city."

Solomon didn't respond. Instead, he shoved a piece of bread into his face and growled. The boy, satisfied he had delivered the message, turned and ran away as Solomon lifted the goatskin to his lips and sucked from its horn. He finished his makeshift meal, aware of its lack, and shuffled his feet in the dirt that made up the city street. As he wondered what to do next, he watched the people scatter like ants across the city square, some running in that direction and many others pushing themselves in the opposite. He considered whether the boy's warning should be taken seriously. Ol' Sal, he knew—all city residents knew—was the tall mountain of rock situated at the edge of the sea on the outskirts of Sodom. Legend had it the mountain had exploded, shooting hot fire and rock sometime in the distant past, though it had been many years since it had even so much as rumbled. No one alive had ever witnessed it. As far as Solomon knew, it was nothing more than legend. But today, it would be more than that.

Something shattered on the street. Solomon sat unfazed, finishing the last morsel of bread he held in his hand. Then he followed that with a final swallow of juice before tossing the packet to the ground.

Another splatter.

It looked like fire. He thought he must be hallucinating. Fire doesn't fall from the sky.

Then it happened again. A rock hit the street and broke into little pieces, each of them red hot and smoldering. Suddenly, people started running, and he heard screams of terror. Hysteria. People were tripping over themselves and each other. A man running by tumbled face forward into the street right in front of Solomon and yelped on his way to pounding his face into well-trafficked sand. Solomon jumped to his feet.

The man didn't move. Solomon looked around. No one was coming to save the man. Was he dead?

The stone roof of the store he had been leaning on had sheltered Solomon enough from the falling rocks that he didn't worry. A couple of balls of fire hit the roof and bounced off, landing in the street next to the dead man. His clothes caught fire and Solomon looked up at the sky for a break. When he thought he could get away with it, he jumped into the street and felt the man's clothes for something to steal. He found a pouch with coins in it and a couple of pieces of jewelry. He took them. Before leaping back to the side of the building, he yanked the broach off the man's neck and got out of the way of a careening rock just in time. A woman fell beside him, hitting the building and bouncing back into the street. She, too, tumbled over dead. Solomon suddenly felt lucky to be alive.

He wondered how he was going to get home, then he remembered he had no home. He had lost that with his job.

The fiery rain pelted the streets harder. Where before it had been a drizzling hazard of hard rock rain, it had now become a downpour of hot ash, flecks of mountain rock, and smoking brimstone. There was no venturing out into this until it was done. Solomon watched a few more people fall—old men, older ladies, young children and their moms and dads, and even a few animals—then he pressed his back against the store wall and slithered his way around the corner and through the door. It was wall-to-wall huddling shoppers and merchants in there. He barely squeezed through before the store owner, Mr. Krauss, pushed the stone door closed and locked it from the inside.

"No one's going out and no one's coming in. We're closed," he said as he turned and faced the crowd behind him. A crescendo of cheers rose from the sweaty throng of citizens trying their best to tolerate being so close to each other.

A woman at the back of the pack yelled, "What's going on? I've got to get back home before the husband finds me gone!"

"You're not going anywhere, *Wardatu*. It's raining fire out there."

Solomon heard the gruff voice of a man, but he couldn't tell where the voice had come from. It wasn't the store owner. It was someone in the middle of the crowd. A voice from a faceless stranger locked in the same sweatbox as everyone else. Another man argued back, expressing a heartfelt regret that he was being held hostage against his will.

"You're not a hostage, idiot!" Another voice chimed in. "It's deadly out there. Ol' Sal done erupted."

"Poo, Ol' Sal!"

Solomon listened to the voices argue. Some of them took the side of the lady wanting out and the others reiterated the danger lurking out there. Then the crowd began to push and sway. Forward, back, side to side. Solomon pushed his way toward the back of the store, sometimes against the sway and other times making himself a part of it enough that he could propel himself through shoulders and elbows like a fish gliding through water. By the time he reached the back of the store he was soaked with sweat.

"Calm down!" The voice of Mr. Krauss rang over the noise of the crowd. "Calm it, please!"

No one listened. The crowd grew more persuasive in its push toward the door. Before Solomon knew what had happened, the roof caved in the middle of the store. Stone began to crumble and fall onto the heads of men and women, even some of the children. Screams rang out from the front of the store and people pushed toward the corners to get away from the falling rock and the fire that followed. Solomon managed to slip through an open doorway in the back of the store, into Mr. Krauss's vacant office.

Screams filled the store as the crowd pushed. Some pushed to the front of the store toward the door. Others pushed to the sides. Aisles full of foods tumbled forward or back, falling on screaming, petrified citizens of Sodom, injuring or killing them. The roof caved in just enough for missiles of fiery rock to slither between the cracks and land on the store floor or land on a patron and set them aflame. Terrorized citizens filed into the back room with Solomon as he pondered escape through a window in the stone wall.

It seemed as if that room might have been the safest place in the city until panic-stricken Sodomites fled into it. It filled so fast with warm bodies that Solomon hardly knew what to do. He peered through the window to see if he could catch a break in the falling fires of stony rain.

He considered making a run for it, jumping through the window, and taking his chances in the pellets of brimstone ransacking the city. He was about to leap when he heard a voice.

"No! Don't jump. Please."

He turned to see a young woman holding a baby. A girl of not more than fifteen stood beside the desk, tears streaming down her face, looking at Solomon with a sullen, fearful gaze. His heart nearly fell through his stomach. For a moment, he was stricken with guilt over the crimes he had committed. He fought to hold the tears that wanted to fall from his own eyes. In the girl's eyes he could see a reflection of his own fear mingling with hers.

"I've got to go," he said in a guttural whisper. "I can't stay here with—these people."

She knew what he meant. *These people* meant the dying ones. No one would survive this calamity. They both knew it.

"Take me with you," the young mother pleaded.

A fatherly compassion overcame Solomon as he considered the girl's offer. At one hundred and twenty years, he had seen a lot of frightened young women. This one carried a baby, a newborn still in swaddling clothes. Though he could not see its face, Solomon imagined the baby as beautiful as its mother. His wife and eighteen children were miles away in Zoar. His mind drifted to them. How long had it been since he'd seen them? Too long. And now, he thought, he must make his way back to them. He must escape Sodom and go home. He would have to move fast. He couldn't move fast dragging a woman and a child behind like anchors.

"There's an overhang," he said. "Hand me the baby and step through the window. Stay under the overhang."

She did as he commanded. As she slid through the window to the other side of the stone wall and forced herself to stand with her back to the stone to keep away from the falling rock, Solomon lifted a finger to the blanket covering the baby's face. He wanted just one look at the face of the life he would save that day. He pulled the soft wool down below its lips and chin and blinked in shock. Above the infant's lips were a set of tentacles waving at him through the thickening air. Three inches of solid flesh, each of them clamoring for a touch. Below the tentacles, at the corners of the baby's mouth, were a couple of pincers. They looked like they could do some damage. Quickly, he covered the baby's mouth with the blanket and handed it to the woman on the other side of the window.

He had to force himself to climb through. He wanted to run, but there was nowhere to run. He had seen those tentacles. He had seen those pincers. On another being, a not-so-pleasant one. He knew the source of that evil. It was not a creature he wanted to save.

A glance back through the window to the Sodomites filtering into the store owner's office made him rush away. It was run or go back to the crowd. He grabbed the woman's hand and pulled her along the store wall while keeping an eye on the fiery rain to see if there was any chance of it letting up. One man noticed them making their getaway and ran toward the window. He yelled after them as they made their way along the stone wall toward the back corner of the store, careful to remain under the roof hanging over the edge of the building, protecting them from the burning flames falling from the sky. It wouldn't be long, Solomon thought, before the streets were full of people again.

When they reached the corner of the building, Solomon surveyed the street crossing. The rain was falling harder and faster than ever. But he knew they had to try to cross. If they were to ever leave the city, it was the only way. He took the baby off the woman's hands.

"Follow me!"

He darted across the street, dodging the falling rain. Several times he barely escaped being hit. The woman pushed herself beside him, competing to get to the building across the street before he did. When they made it safely across, they stopped, secured their breaths, and waited. Solomon knew they were going to have to take it slow. An old lady crumpled to the ground in the street in front of them and burst into flames. The young mother he was protecting screamed. Solomon huddled over the baby to keep it from hearing its mother.

Solomon grabbed the young woman's hand and pulled her around the building to the other side. The view of the street was no better there than anywhere else. People dying, crying, and getting pummeled to death by sulfurous hail.

"We have a quarter mile to the city gate," Solomon yelled into the woman's ear. "Think you can make it?"

She assured him she could.

He huddled the baby close to his chest and sprinted across the street to the next building. The woman followed. For three blocks they carried out this routine, rounding a building and sprinting across the street. Solomon led the way, cresting the baby in his arms each time as its mother followed, half the time in tears. Finally, they were within eyesight of the city gate. Outside, Solomon wondered if they would be safe from the bullets of fire falling out of the heavens.

"Look! There it is, there it is." The woman was giddy with excitement at the sight of the city gate.

"Yes, we're almost there," Solomon said. "Follow me one more time. We'll dodge the rain to the gate and exit the city. Our best hope is to make our way to Zoar."

The woman agreed. Solomon took off at a run. She followed.

Solomon zigzagged to keep from being hit by rain. He focused his eyes on the city gate, hoping against all hope to make it safely without being hit by the fire falling from above. His heart pumped faster and faster as his spirit filled with glee with each step, closer and closer to salvation. Then he felt something. A nick on his shoulder. A stab. A pinch.

The baby's blanket had fallen to the ground in the hustle from one end of the city to the other. The jostling kept the baby awake, and whether intentional or accidental, Solomon didn't know, but the baby had managed to sting him with its pincers. It startled him and he dropped the baby on his own slow-motion tumble to the surface of the sandy road. The woman leapt over him and tripped, falling to the ground and landing on a knee.

The baby cried. Lying on its face with its rear in the air, it tried to stabilize its body and fell sideways onto its ribs then rolled onto its back just in time to catch a ball of fire in its mouth.

The woman lunged.

"Noooooooooh!" She cried. "My baby! My God, Lazareth. Oh, Lazareth! Lazareth!"

Her tears fell harder than the sulfur rain from the sky. She fell at the baby's side as Solomon pushed himself to his feet and grabbed the woman by the arm. She resisted. He picked her up and threw her over his shoulder. He had committed himself to saving her, and he would. Her body fell limp, helpless to have seen the deadly end of her only child.

Solomon pushed himself toward the city gate. Step after step, heartbeat after heartbeat, he pushed until he was there. When he finally arrived, he ducked into a cubby hole inside the arch where the city guard—who wasn't there—usually stood. The city wall around Sodom took its hits, fire and rock pummeling it from above, setting some of its guard shacks on fire and sending the guards to their deaths below. Solomon slipped into the guard space and sat in the chair that occupied it, holding the woman close to his breast, allowing her the full benefit of his shoulder as she emptied herself of every tear.

The rain continued to fall for hours. Solomon had no idea how long. Eventually, the woman in his arms stopped crying and fell asleep. Darkness came and went. As the sun rose, the sky turned bright blue, showing a promise Solomon had not felt since before the storm. It was the most beautiful morning he had seen in a long time.

He stepped out of the guard stand and stood in the center of the city gate's arch, looking back at the city in shambles. All he could see were buildings crumpled to the ground and bodies everywhere. Most of them had charred beyond recognition, but many of them were simply dead bodies that would soon begin to rot in the heat of the sun and would attract scavengers from both the air and the ground. There was no time to waste and no reason to stay.

The woman stepped out of the guard stand and joined him. She took a step toward the city and Solomon grabbed her arm. He shook his head, signaling that she did not want to go back.

"We must move on," he said.

He could see in her eyes that she did not want that, but she agreed. Their fingers locked. Solomon took her hand and squeezed, trying to comfort her with the strength of his hands. She didn't respond.

"I will protect you all the rest of my days," he said. "I will take you under my roof and you will be my family."

The woman cast her gaze to the ground. She did not want to think about being someone's family. Solomon saw it in her body. She did not want to think about the future, but it would come soon enough and all they would have is memories. The memories of Sodom would fill their hearts and minds forever. Solomon knew it. The woman holding his hand knew it, too.

Solomon turned and pulled her with him. As they exited the city, in the far-off distance, Solomon caught sight the *Maskim Xul.* An army of them. What Ol' Sal didn't do to Sodom, Solomon knew they would. They would destroy what was left of the carnage and wipe it away from the earth. They would asphyxiate any survivors with their tentacles that stretched six feet out from the tops of their lips, which were strong enough to grip a man and squeeze him until his guts spilled out. The dead would become a meal for them. Solomon had seen them feed upon carrion and use the pincers at the corners of their mouths to pick apart the dead flesh of travelers in the desert between the cities of the plain. Now they were coming for Sodom. It was time to move.

"What's your name?" he asked, pulling the woman out of Sodom away from the marching destroyers he hoped she didn't see.

THE REMORSE OF THE INCORPOREUM

AmyBeth Inverness

The rush is disorienting. The loneliness is unbearable. The Word has cast us out. I don't know why. One moment, I was in The Garden at The Beginning, and then ...

Here.

I don't fit in Jeremiah. I'm not the only incorporeum who has found this host. We wrestle. We gasp ...

Jeremiah suffers.

I grab my other and flee, forward to other hosts.

"Why am I so tired?" Juno asks me.

I smile. "For the best of reasons, my love." Our hosts are in that in-between state, not quite awake, but not quite asleep. This is the safe place. This is the happy place.

Juno can't accept being safe. Juno can't accept being happy.

He leaves, and I follow.

#

"Mars!" Adam squealed. It came out as more of a "Maaa!" sound ending with something of a growl.

"There, there." Nanny said, going to the small boy. She scooped him up, shivering as she did so. "Oh, goodness, this corner by the window is always cold. Come here with Nanny and I'll read you a book."

Adam pointed at the corner where the cold spot was. "Juno!" he declared happily.

"Juno?" asked Nanny.

"Just Juno," said Adam, snuggling in for story time.

Adam loved story time. Sometimes Mars told him stories when he was all alone, but stories were much better from Nanny. Nanny was warm and soft and always spoke sweetly to him, even when he couldn't find the words he needed.

Nanny rocked, and Adam listened. He was a good boy. He didn't interrupt, even when the colors in the pictures were too bright.

When the story was over, Nanny closed the book and rocked him. The rocking always helped.

"Nah nah?" Adam asked.

"Mmm hmm sweetling?" Nanny answered.

"Why Juno sad?"

"Who's Juno?" Nanny asked.

Adam pointed at the corner by the window.

"Juno miss Kristophe," Adam said, placing his chubby little hands on Nanny's cheeks, hoping she would explain everything to him. Juno was always sad. Mars tried to cheer him up, but nothing ever worked. No story had a happy enough ending to make Juno come out of his corner.

Mars stayed with Adam. Mars was always with Adam, though

sometimes he was quiet. Adam had been the one to give Mars and Juno their names; they tried to claim they were nameless, but Adam would have none of it. Juno grumbled, but Mars laughed, thinking it was only right that a boy named Adam should name them, since the man named Adam had neglected to do so.

Nanny stopped rocking. Her face looked different. Adam couldn't tell if it was a good expression or a bad expression, but he was alarmed that she had stopped rocking. Adam needed to rock. Adam needed to be held. "What did you say, sweetling?" Nanny asked.

"Juno … misses … Kristophe?" Adam wondered if he had the name right. Mars told him stories about Kristophe, and how much Juno loved him, but Kristophe died. "Kristophe died," Adam said, hoping this simple fact would help Nanny figure out what he wanted to know.

"Adam," Nanny said, pushing him off her lap and setting him on the floor. "How do you know about Kristophe?"

Adam swallowed. Something wasn't right. Why wasn't Nanny holding him? Why wasn't she rocking him? Wasn't it time for his nap? "Mah toll me," he explained.

"Your mother told you?" Nanny asked.

Of course, his mother hadn't told him. Adam hadn't seen his mother for weeks, other than outside his window. "No Mama!" Adam declared, trying his very best to be clear. "Mar-zzz." The 'z' sound was fun to make. Adam smiled brightly. He wanted Nanny to smile back.

Nanny wasn't smiling. She wasn't even touching him anymore. She was backing away from him, towards the door. "You … do you see Kristophe? Here?" Nanny asked. Her hand was on the doorknob.

"No," Adam said, worrying. Was Nanny leaving? Did he do something wrong? "Kristophe died."

"Oh. Oh no." Nanny said, slipping out the door before he could follow. "You take your nap now!" she yelled from the stairs.

Adam wailed, his tiny fists pounding on the door. He rattled the knob, but it was locked. It was always locked.

Mars started singing to him, softly, soothingly, and soon, Adam calmed down. The tears still flowed. He was tired, but he couldn't sleep without Nanny rocking him.

A noise from outside caught his attention. Adam stood on his little stool so he could see out the window. His father's carriage had pulled up. His brothers and sisters were pouring out of the house, running to see if he brought them anything from the city. He started handing out little boxes to each of them until they went into the house and Adam couldn't see them anymore.

"Hi, Dada!" Adam said enthusiastically. His father used to look up at the window when he came home. He used to wave, but not anymore.

Adam went to his bed and lay between the sheets, staring at the door. Maybe Dada would come upstairs and bring him a little box from the city. Maybe Nanny would come back and rock him to sleep.

They didn't.

Mars cooed, and sang, and comforted him, while still trying to comfort the inconsolable Juno in the corner. Adam held out as long as he could. If he was just quiet, if he was just still, maybe someone would come.

Sleep took him long before anyone came to see him again.

#

"Kristophe?" Charles whispered. He wasn't sure if the young man was awake or not.

A cough sounded from the bed by the window. "It's all right, Kristophe. I'm here," Charles said. He took the rag off Kristophe's forehead and exchanged it for another. Charles' old, wrinkled hands shook. He hoped this wouldn't be the end. Charles had finally convinced Kristophe's mother to go to bed just a few hours ago. She didn't want to leave her son's side. Kristophe had been fighting the sickness for months now. His parents were exhausted. His mother had even stopped speculating about which young debutantes might catch her son's eye that season, but instead spent all her time in nursing and prayer. Her son had not left her side in the weeks that she had been ill. She blamed herself that he was now suffering even worse than she had.

Charles had been a faithful servant to Kristophe's father for more than twenty years. The arrival of a daughter, then a son, then another daughter had all been celebrated with joy and love. But when Kristophe was born, Charles knew the baby was special. It was like some part of him had been waiting for this particular human to be born. All the family's children looked to him as more of a grandfather than a servant. Kristophe, the youngest, loved him most of all.

#

It is quiet.

Charles doesn't know I'm here. He's not like Adam. But I care for all my Beloveds, whether they know me or not.

Juno cares for his Beloveds too. Sometimes, I think he cares too deeply...

Like with Kristophe. Even long after Kristophe has been reconciled with The Word, Juno stays, haunting the place where his Beloved died.

"Come ..." I say, pulling Juno gently away. Time means nothing. We will return here. But we have a million Beloveds to embrace. I need to pull Juno to a place that is happy, where we can be together without the evils of the world tearing us apart.

"Mars, why am I so tired?" Juno asks.

I quiver with excitement. "It is Cesare, your Beloved who is tired, and it is for the best of reasons!" I want Juno to remember on his own. I want him to feel the happiness here, in spite of the tiredness that accompanies it.

"His tiredness is my own. His pain is my own."

"Are you in pain, Juno?" I ask.

"Yes. Pain. In my back, the muscles. I've been carrying a heavy load."

I nudge Ryan, and he reaches out to massage Cesare's aching back. It isn't enough.

Juno is pulled backwards, towards the beginning yet not quite to The Beginning, from which we are severed.

I meet him in Jeremiah.

We wrestle.

I do not want to fight Juno, but a human Beloved cannot reconcile two incorporeum within the same host.

I pull him away.

I pull him away before …

#

"Reuben!" Yissachar whispered harshly. "What is it you are doing? This is not right!"

Reuben spat on the ground. "It is our way. It is our right. Why would they have come to Sodom if they did not want to experience the fullness of our pleasures?" Reuben opened his arms wide, mocking his cousin's reluctance.

"If it is pleasure they seek, they can find it themselves. Please, I beg you, let us return home." Yissachar trotted after his cousin, pulling ineffectually at Reuben's robes. "Our aunt will feed us, and you can sleep off the heavy drink."

Reuben swatted Yissachar's hands away. "I'm not ready to go home yet. Not to our uncle's house, and certainly not to my father in Zoar." He spat the name as if it caused a bad taste in his mouth.

Yissachar trailed after Reuben. The only way he'd convinced Reuben's father to let the cousins go to Sodom was because Yissachar had promised to watch over Reuben. "He just needs some time … away … to expend his youthful energy. I will not leave his side, Uncle, I swear!" Yissachar regretted the part about not leaving Reuben's side.

His cousin was stubborn as a donkey with a head harder than a goat's.

"Hey! You there." Reuben called out to the two young men, obviously visitors. They looked Reuben up and down, then grinned. Yissachar shuddered, hanging back just enough to not cause a confrontation.

"Aha! The legendary hospitality of Sodom, on display," said one of the strangers. He stared, unashamed, at Reuben's groin as he spoke.

Reuben scratched his balls. "Our hospitality knows no bounds," he growled, reaching out to squeeze the man's arm. "Have you rooms for the night?"

Yissachar panicked. Reuben might be in search of the highest form of debauchery he could find, and his father might never find out. But if they failed to return to their uncle's house for the night, the family would do more than worry.

The three of them were touching each other, right there in the open square. The few people who turned to look simply laughed or yelled crude comments, egging them on.

"And your friend?"

"My cousin," Reuben explained. "My self-appointed keeper."

The three of them laughed, then turned towards a nearby inn, talking in voices too low for Yissachar to hear.

"Reuben!" Yissachar called out. "We should be going home to our uncle's house. They will worry about us." Yissachar emphasized the word 'worry,' hoping that his cousin would catch his meaning.

"You go home then and tell them what they can do with themselves. Or with their asses. Or each other's asses, if they aren't already," Reuben called, walking into the Inn with his new friends.

Yissachar followed, but they went into a room and slammed the door in his face. He tried not to think about what was happening inside. He only hoped they would finish quickly, so he could get his cousin home without anyone questioning where they'd been or what they'd been doing.

The innkeeper staunchly ignored the rough sounds coming from the room. Yissachar hovered outside the door. He tried the latch once, but it was locked. He thought about knocking but could not muster the courage to do so.

Suddenly the door was flung open, and the two young men rushed out. They pushed past Yissachar and out into the creeping darkness.

Yissachar peeked into the room, then he heard his cousin groan. A voice inside him whispered *That was not a groan of satisfaction. He is in pain.* With newfound courage, Yissachar stumbled into the room, not being able to see much in the darkened space. The only window was shuttered, and the light outside was quickly fading.

"Reuben?" he called softly.

"Robbed! The bastards robbed me," Reuben said. Yissachar found him curled up in a ball on the floor. "But not before I stuck them both. And they liked it, too! They were already salved and slippery. I'm glad I only had a few coins on me. It would have cost me more to pay a pretty boy to bend over. I just wish they hadn't beaten me to get it." Reuben tried to laugh but ended up coughing.

Yissachar begged a bowl of water and piece of linen from the Innkeeper then helped his cousin clean up. Despite his injuries, Reuben seemed to be in good spirits. It was not easy to find their way home in the dark, but at least when they got there no one seemed to be overly curious about where they'd been all day. Yissachar helped Reuben to bed with the help of one of the servant girls. He cringed when he saw the look of despair and abandonment on her face as he left her alone with Reuben, but there was nothing he could do. That was her place. And if it kept Reuben safely at home, that was all that really mattered.

#

I pull Juno from Reuben, dragging him forward, to the place where we are happy. But he finds Kristophe, and then the absence of Kristophe. Adam is older now. He's outgrowing his tiny bed, but no one seems to notice.

I stay with them both. Juno, incorporeal, hostless, in the corner by the window, mourning Kristophe. Adam, whose loneliness and confusion threaten to overwhelm me.

Adam sleeps, and I pull Juno away, forward again. We pause in many hosts along the way, always together. No matter what human era, Juno and I are always together.

Almost always together.

#

"Come on, Ernest," Scot called from the back of the hay wagon. "You can come, too."

Ernest looked up at the wagon full of young people and hesitated. He desperately wanted to go, but in such close quarters he wouldn't be able to fade into the background so easily.

And there were *girls*.

Women.

Real women.

Gerilyn smiled and held out a hand to help him up. She'd been dating some guy who worked on an oil rig forever. She was probably safe.

Ernest's heart broke as he watched Scot flirt with Gerilyn's cousin, some city girl who was spending the summer on the wild Wyoming plains in what her parents called 'a desperate attempt to break her unhealthy addiction to MTV.'

Fortunately, Gerilyn spent most of the ride defending her cousin from Scot's teasing. Ernest was able to sit back in the corner, as invisible as possible to the rest of the crowd.

When they got to the firepit, Ernest jumped out before the wagon stopped. He ran off to gather firewood, hoping that being useful would mean being accepted, or at least tolerated.

He'd rather be alone with Scot. Here, in this crowd, they couldn't … they couldn't just be themselves.

Being himself was not safe.

#

I always try to make Ernest feel safe, but he is right. He lives with danger, and his life is short.

I don't know what conversations Juno has with Scot. They do converse. Scot knows he is not alone. He calls Juno 'the demon inside.'

I take Juno forward again. If we can only reach the happy place, all will be well, but our happy hosts are tired. It is not the tiredness of a long day's work or of an energetic session of exercise. It is a hopeless, bone-weary kind of tiredness that neither of them has ever experienced. It is something that, although they were warned, they never expected.

Juno falls back, and I must follow.

#

"Scot?" Ernest asked, knocking softly on the old, scratched-up door. "Your mom sent me up. Are you okay?"

"Yeah," Scot grunted, not turning away from the window. Ernest closed the door behind him.

He walked over to the window and looked out over the yard full of chickens. "So, does this mean you're quitting your job in Powell?"

"I called my boss yesterday and explained how my mom can't get by out here on her own now that Dad's gone."

Ernest shuffled his feet, not knowing what to say. They'd all expressed their condolences. They'd stood by the graveside, holding onto their hats as the Wyoming wind threatened to blow them to Nebraska.

Ernest didn't want to think about going on without Scot, but he had no reason to stay with him on the ranch. The only reason he was still around at all was because he was Scot's best friend, but it was the end of the week and there was no longer a good excuse for Ernest to stay.

Except that he was in love with Scot.

Scot sniffed and wiped his face on his sleeve. Ernest had never seen him cry before. Scot had never been close to his father.

Ernest put a hand on Scot's back. "Don't think these tears are for *him*," Scot half growled, half sobbed. "It's just that … I just started my job. It's a place I like, with good people. And now, now I have to come back here, doing every chore I ever resented doing."

Ernest came close and embraced his friend, thumping his back in what he hoped was a manly way. Scot clung to him, wrapping his arms around Ernest and rocking back and forth. Ernest breathed in his scent, wishing that it hadn't taken a death in the family for Scot to finally touch him. Maybe, just maybe, now that the old man was dead, maybe they could have a future together. Ernest's accounting skills might not be vital to the ranch, but they could make some kind of excuse about wanting to hire a business manager or something. Or he could commute.

Ernest's thoughts were disrupted as he realized that Scot was looking down at him. He'd stopped rocking. He was looking at Ernest's mouth.

Ernest had never been kissed. Not by a woman, and certainly not by a man. He trembled, anticipating the moment.

A door slammed downstairs. Scot pushed him away roughly then jumped away and paced in front of the window.

"Back to every chore I ever resented doing," Scot said, as if the moment had never passed between them. "I just don't know how I'm gonna do it. I just don't know."

Ernest knew how he could get through it. They could do it together, if only Scot would let him.

#

As we leave Ernest and Scot, I pull Juno past Kristophe, not wanting to let him linger in the sadness. After sharing Scot's mourning and frustration, I'm afraid of what Juno might do.

We touch various Beloveds as we make our way back, but Juno seeks the sadness now. It tempts him. Whether he feels compelled to stay in these times so that he can bring comfort to his Beloveds or he is hopelessly lost in the illness itself, I do not know.

He wears remorse like a cloak, although we have not yet reached its source.

#

I see the bruises on the servant girl's face and arms, and I make Yissachar notice them too, even though no one else in the house is concerned.

I feel the tiniest tinge of remorse from him. I try to amplify it, to prompt him to action, but he bats me away.

The servant girl is a Beloved of the incorporeum, but this is not the only reason I want to help her. Yissachar's life is short. He needs to do something good before ...

Before.

"She is mine tonight," I hear Yissachar say, grabbing the girl and hauling her into his room. Reuben starts yelling, and I hear Juno trying to calm him down, but Reuben is too strong-willed, even for Juno. Sometimes I think Juno's failure with Reuben frustrates him even more than his failure with Scot.

I am ahead of myself. I experience my Beloved's lives as a whole. My Beloveds experience their lives as if ordered in a straight line.

It is strange.

The servant girl huddles in a corner, watching Yissachar undress. When he collapses onto his bed, she goes to him, tentatively. She pauses, looking at the door.

"Will she flee?" I ask her incorporeum.

"No," comes the answer. "It would be worse for her. We will stay."

She touches Yissachar and he turns to look at her. She removes her robe, one shoulder at a time, but Yissachar is not aroused at all. He is only uncomfort-able. "There is no need," he tells her, and she looks surprised. "Just sleep. Over there."

The girl looks confused, but she lies down on a mat as far from Yissachar as she can, and soon they are both asleep.

"Mars?" the other incorporeum asks. "How is it that you and Juno have names? None of us have names. Even calling ourselves 'incorporeum' is no more than a description of *what* we are, not *who* we are. Adam could not see us. Adam did not name us."

I chuckle. "Adam named me Mars, and he named Juno, as well." I do not let the joke linger. "Not Adam of The Garden, Adam my Beloved. He named us."

"I wish Adam would give me a name."

The servant girl's incorporeum sounds wistful. As we speak, I feel her growing closer to me. I know her. I recognize her.

"Come with me!" I say, and I reach for Adam.

#

Adam watched Juno pass through the walls of the old house. He didn't dare tell anyone. At least Juno was no longer confined to the cold corner of Adam's little room. Adam himself was no longer confined to the tiny attic room. He was a grown man.

Adam waited patiently in his chair. He could hear the baby, his new niece. He was eager to see her, but he knew if he left his chair he would do something wrong and they'd lock him in his room. It was a nice room, but Adam didn't want to be alone. Even with Mars and Juno to keep him company, he felt that he would die of loneliness.

So, he behaved.

He sat in his chair.

Finally, his sister appeared, her husband hovering behind her. He was a nice man. Adam thought he was smiling because the corners of his mouth were turned up. But somehow, his face wasn't smiling. Adam had no idea what that meant.

"Adam, meet your new niece—"

"Xenia!" Adam blurted, jumping to his feet.

His sister shushed him, and her husband placed his hands on her shoulders. It was the same way father placed his hands on mother's shoulders when he was about to steer her away—away from Adam.

Adam sat down, his leg bouncing eagerly despite all efforts to calm himself. Mrs was no help. Mars was laughing happily.

The baby was not alone. His niece had an incorporeum! And her name—this was Adam's job—her name was Xenia. For she was hospitable and sweet. She would be the one, she would bring Juno rest.

"You're not going to let him hold her, are you?" whispered Adam's brother-in-law.

"Ah, no," Adam's sister said. "Not yet. Perhaps when she's a little bigger." She leaned over and held the baby so he could see her. "Adam, this is your niece, Eugenia."

"You ... genia," Adam said carefully. He wanted to tell his sister about the incorporeum. He wanted her to know how wonderful her daughter's life would be, to have a friend so close at all times, but he knew what would happen if he told.

Adam blew her a kiss. "Sweet baby," he said, making no move to touch her. He'd touched his brother's baby once, and his sister-in-law had collapsed into hysterics, grabbing the baby away.

Adam would behave.

Adam would sit in his chair.

If Adam did everything right, or did nothing at all, Adam would not be lonely.

#

Yissachar did nothing. He stood at the back of the crowd, knowing he was helpless to pull Reuben away.

"Send them out to us!" the crowd roared in unison.

"Have you seen them? They're beautiful!" a man next to him remarked. "They have to come out sooner or later."

Yissachar shook his head. The simple motion conveyed multiple meanings, but the man was no longer looking at him. "Hey! I'll take one of the daughters if no one else wants them!" the man yelled.

Yissachar tried to figure out what had happened. Apparently, the man who was hosting the beautiful strangers had offered to give his daughters to the crowd, but the mob demanded he send out the strangers instead.

A sudden darkness fell over Yissachar's eyes. The crown roared. "What is happening?" cried one.

"Blind! I am blind!" cried another.

"Reuben? Reuben!" Yissachar called, lunging forward, panic overriding sense. He had to find his cousin. He had to make sure he was safe.

Strong arms grabbed him. "Yissachar? What trickery is this?" he asked.

"I, I don't know. Perhaps it is only night, taking us by surprise. We have lost track of time," Yissachar replied. All around them, the crowd was growing unrulier. Yissachar fumbled and dragged his cousin against a wall. They crouched down, Yissachar shielding Reuben, while men stumbled and cursed the darkness all around them.

Hours passed. They were kicked a few times, but it was only others in the crowd tripping over them as they yelled and screamed and tried to find their way in the strange darkness.

"Yissachar?" Reuben asked.

"Yes, Reuben?"

"I have not made my family proud."

Yissachar shook his head, even though Reuben couldn't see him. "You're no different from most young men. You just need to sow some wild oats."

"No. No, I'm worse. Or, I want to be worse. Inside, I know I am evil. I cannot hide it. I tried everything I could to ... to be vile. To show them the darkness within me. Yet no matter how debauched, how cruel, there is always someone to say 'You think that's bad? Just watch this!' Then they do something even worse. I can't ... I can't be wicked enough. I was terrible at being good, but I'm worse at being evil."

Yissachar had nothing to say. He was afraid of his cousin's confession and afraid of the darkness. He fumbled for his wineskin, relieved to find it was still half full. "Here, drink," he said.

Reuben drank.

Reuben slept.

A light appeared. Yissachar wasn't sure if it was dawn, a reflection of something, or just his mind playing tricks on him.

The light grew large, and with it came a heat so intense Yissachar feared he would be burned alive.

But fire was not to be their fate.

It was the impact that ended their mortal existence.

#

"And God rained fire and brimstone down upon the cities of Sodom and Gomorrah, destroying the evil Sodomites for their wicked ways ..."

The preacher went on and on, elaborating on the abomination of homosexuality and how it was the one unforgivable sin. Ernest sat next to Scot in the crowded pew. He was sure everyone knew. They must be able to see the connection between them, even though they'd never shared anything more intimate than a hug.

When Ernest saw his own reflection with Scot, all he could think of was how perfect they were together. But that was only when they were alone. And even alone, Scot would never admit to being one of *those* people.

They stuffed their faces at Scot's mother's house, thanked her, and loaded the dishwasher. With the minimal requirements of civility thus disposed of, they were out the front door and down the road before she could nag them about anything else that needed to be done.

It was Sunday. A day of rest.

"You did not!" Ernest said, punching Scot in the arm as they followed the railroad tracks.

Scot laughed. Ernest loved hearing that laugh. He imagined it was for his ears only. After all, the only time Scot truly laughed was when the two of them were alone. If anyone else was around, all Scot would do was humph or let out a manly snort.

"I did too. Right in front of her big brother, too," Scot said. He turned toward Ernest, putting his hands on Ernest's hips. "I took her in my arms ..." Ernest's arms found their way to Scot's shoulders, as if it was the most natural thing in the world to do. "I leaned in, and I ..."

Scot was leaning in. Ernest was looking up into his gorgeous brown eyes.

Scot kissed him. For a moment, Ernest's heart sang in perfect happiness.

The happiness was shattered when Scot pushed him away.

"Well, I kissed her better than that," Scot said, spitting onto the rails and wiping his mouth on his sleeve. He wasn't looking at Ernest. He was hurrying away.

It was not how Ernest had imagined their first kiss.

He should follow Scot's lead, and just laugh it off. But, something inside him refused to let go of the hope.

He stayed put on the rails, exactly where he'd been standing when their lips touched.

Scot looked back. "What the hell are you doing?"

Ernest spread his arms wide. "I've waited my whole life for that! And I'm not letting it go so easily."

It was the bravest thing he'd ever done. It was a risk, but there was no one around to see. There was no one around to judge.

"Waited for what?" Scot said, looking off down the tracks. He kicked at the dirt.

"You know what? You kissed me."

"I was joking! It was just a dumb story. Geez, you can't just—"

"You kissed me, Scot. Because you wanted to," Ernest said. He wasn't going to let go. He couldn't just do *nothing*. He couldn't go on pretending they were just friends, watching the man he loved tumble one girl after another, trying to prove to everyone how much of a man he was.

Ernest shifted his weight, letting his boot slip down where the rails split off to the east. His boot wedged itself in tightly, but it didn't matter. Ernest was standing his ground. Scot would have to admit he loved him, or he'd stay rooted to that very spot forever.

"Don't be stupid," Scot said, turning his back again.

A rumble sounded in the distance. Ernest could feel the vibrations in the rails. Still, he stood his ground.

"Get back up here," he said, his voice more authoritative than it had ever been in his entire life. The kiss empowered him. All the near misses they'd had … but the kiss …

He knew Scot had feelings for him. Feelings that ran far deeper than friendship.

Scot was hunched over, strangely diminished. He kicked at the dirt, refusing to look up. "Don't be stupid, Ernest," he said, his eyes meeting Ernest's for just a fleeting second.

This was Ernest's chance to be resilient. All his life, Scot had been the strong one. Scot had stood up for him, watched over him. But Scot wasn't brave enough for this one thing, this one declaration.

"I love you, Scot," Ernest said.

Finally, Scot looked up. Their eyes met and Ernest reached out his hand.

A whistle blew in the distance.

Scot stood straight again. "All right. You love me. Now get down from there."

Ernest shook his head. "Not until you tell me you love me, too."

Scot kicked a rock, wincing as it unintentionally flew close by Ernest's head.

Ernest just smiled. "Come on. No one else needs to know, Scot, but I need to hear it. I know you love me, but I need to hear it from your own mouth."

The chugging sound that had been no more than a rumble was now audible. Ernest shifted his weight and discovered that his foot was wedged tighter than he thought. It was stuck.

"What the—" Ernest pulled at his boot, but he couldn't free it or get his foot out.

"Stop messing around, Ernest, the train's coming!" Scot said, coming to him at last.

Ernest started to panic. "I'm not fooling, Scot, my foot's stuck!"

Scot came up on the tracks with him, his strong, sure arms steadying him. He crouched, twisting Ernest's foot.

Then he stopped.

"Ernest," he said, his eyes full of fear. Ernest didn't know if it was fear of his own emotions or of the train, or both. He wished he could freeze the moment in time. He was sure Scot was about to tell him he loved him, too.

Scot didn't say anything. He jerked at Ernest's ankle a few more times then braced himself as if he was about to lift Ernest right out of his boots. That might work if he could get straight up. Scot was a big guy. He could do it.

Scot stopped. He looked down the tracks. Ernest could feel the train getting close, just beyond the curve. The conductor wouldn't see them until he was almost on them. There was no stopping a train.

Scot looked Ernest in the eyes. Time stood still.

"Ernest, I love you," Scot said, locking eyes. "But it's better this way."

Scot tumbled to the side just as the train roared down on them.

#

"I'm sorry," whispers Juno from the end of Adam's bed. It is a big, comfortable bed, but the door is still locked. Adam is still stuck in his room.

"Sorry for what?" I ask.

"Scot … is sorry for Ernest," Juno says.

"Oh," I say. "I know."

"And—," Juno says. Adam is asleep. I'm glad. He would not want to hear the things we speak of.

"And Reuben—" Juno cannot finish the sentence.

"Reuben was passed out drunk when it happened," I remind him.

"Yissachar would not have been in Sodom if it wasn't for Reuben."

"Juno, do you have control over any of your Beloveds?"

Juno thinks about that. I know he wants to take responsibility. He yearns for redemption on their behalf. "I ... influence them."

I sigh. "Perhaps you have some influence, but you love unconditionally, do you not?"

Juno shrugs. Or at least, what I know is a shrug. Being incorporeal, it's hard to tell.

"It is our way," he says.

Unconditional love is indeed our way. But so is forgiveness.

"And Jeremiah?" Juno asks.

"What of Jeremiah?" I ask.

"Did he die because of me?"

I embrace my friend. I would pull him into Adam with me if that was possible. "Juno, Jeremiah died by his own hand. I do not know why we were both pulled into him. It was not meant to be that way."

We are quiet for a while. Distantly, Adam's infant niece cries.

Juno leaps, and he is gone. I know where he has gone, though. I know that Xenia is waiting for him to recognize her.

I will not leave Adam, not even while he sleeps. But a moment later, Juno returns.

"Mars!" he says.

I smile and wait.

"Is it—"

"Yes, Juno. We should go there."

I do not have to pull Juno. This time, he knows. This time, he remembers.

"Cesare?" Juno asks, settling down into his Beloved as I settle into mine. "But, we are so tired."

"Yes, and Reuben was tired. He was tired of living the way he lived, of no one caring. He tried to care even less, but that was not possible."

"And Scot?" Juno asks.

"Scot was tired of pretending to be someone he was not. He saw his own future. He saw that he would have to go on pretending forever. He could not stand to face that."

"And Cesare?" Juno asks.

Xenia calls to us. "Juno! Let Cesare wake up. He has to wake up."

Juno hesitates. His instinct is to soothe his Beloved, to help Cesare sleep.

I nudge Ryan's mind to wakefulness, even though he is just as tired as Cesare.

Cesare rouses and reaches out to embrace Ryan. He gives his husband a kiss on the cheek. "No, darling, you rest. I'll get her."

I feel Ryan's grateful mind slip back into peaceful slumber. Cesare gets out of bed. Juno is remembering now. He is remembering why we are tired.

He is also remembering why we are happy.

"We are wet, and we are hungry!" Xenia yells. I laugh.

"Here, sweetling, come to Daddy," Cesare croons, picking up the baby. Xenia sighs with relief.

"Somebody needs a new diaper!"

I can feel Juno letting go. He lets go of his remorse for Jeremiah. He lets go of his grief for Kristophe. He lets go of his guilt over Reuben and Scot.

He embraces his daughter.

Our daughter.

And we are free.

OMEGA

IN THE SHALLOWS

John Vicary

There is a sea in faraway Israel where nothing grows. It is called the Dead Sea, although it was not always known as such. In ancient times, it was invoked in many tongues, but most often it was named *Yām ha-Mizrahî*: the Eastern Sea.

A man may lie in the less famous shallows of the sister of the Sea of Galilee and rise to the top without effort, buoyed to the surface by science or faith. He need only to gaze upon its barren shores to delineate the foothills of history, when other men may have tried to float in the same sea and failed the test. How much does man trust in his knowledge and how much does he heed the pull of those stories from his youth? The joy drains from that swim like water from a cracked vessel, and he wonders if he had lived at that time in this land of Canaan if he would have escaped the brimstone fate that awaited so many others. His gaze traces the horizon and a twinge gnaws his gut. The sheltering arms of the waves remind him of a different embrace in years already spent.

Two angels had descended from heaven to give warning to the righteous, his mother had told him long ago. He could still hear her voice as she told him her favorite biblical tale.

"Disguised as two men, the angels tried to pass Lot's house on their way to Sodom, but he insisted they break bread with him," Mama said. "In those times, it was a solemn duty to give hospitality to those in need."

"I'd recognize them, Mama," he said. He imagined the men with a certain golden glow or perhaps an errant feather peeking from under their cloaks. "I'm special."

"Of course, you are, sweetie," she answered, pulling the blanket up to his chest as she readied him for bed. "But there's no way to know by looking. That's why it's always important to be kind, especially to strangers. Maybe you'll be talking to an angel all along."

If he wouldn't recognize angels for who they were, would he heed their warning when it came? Would they even consider him worth warning, or would they let him burn like the five cities of the plain? He hugged his bear to his chest. "Are angels ever bad, Mama?"

"Why would you think such a thing?" Mama brushed the hair from his

forehead. "Sodom and Gomorrah were destroyed because the people were wicked. You have nothing to fear if you follow God's path."

"But Mama, didn't those people think they were on God's path?" he asked. "They didn't want to be killed by angels. They didn't want to die, did they?"

Mama frowned. "Of course not. They weren't killed by angels, but by God himself. You're too young to understand. Go to sleep now and forget these questions. You'll give yourself nightmares."

A man might still remember nightmares of his boyhood: they had been full of ash and smoke and skin peeling from blistered bone. Some nights he is plagued with sulfur dreams from the archaic demolition of the disgraced cities of Canaan. He imagines the angels standing sentinel in the Hebron Hills over the lava that buries the screaming sinners. He blinks and is somewhat surprised to find himself not amongst that mass ruination but floating safe in present waters.

"But, Mama, didn't the people think they were on God's path?"

His mother had never wanted to answer that question, and he'd stopped asking. He'd ceased wondering about morals or angels or people from the past, even if his nightmares hadn't given up their grip on his subconscious quite as easily.

"I'd recognize them. I'm special."

Special.

The thoughts, or perhaps the desert sun, grow too warm for comfort, and the man rises from the murky water. He's had enough of the sea.

As he brushes loose the salt that has dried into a crust on his body, another pilgrim wanders from the water. "I'm glad I could be here to swim in the sea before it disappears, aren't you?"

The man says nothing.

"Many people don't realize that it's disappearing," the pilgrim says. "But it is, you know. Faster every day, it seems."

"No, I didn't know," the man says.

The pilgrim sifts through his backpack and withdraws a canteen. He offers it to the man.

The man pushes it away with a curt shake of his head.

"Meanwhile, Mount Sodom continues to grow in size," the pilgrim says before taking a drink.

"What?" the man asks. The brine stings his eyes, and he rubs at them. The pilgrim is a blur in his vision.

"That mountain," the pilgrim continues, pointing to the opposite shore. "It's made entirely of halite. Salt. It's been growing for thousands of years. Hence the name. It's from the biblical city. See that little pillar that's separated from the rest, just there?"

The man squints in the bright light, his eyes still tearing. "Oh, yes. I see it."

"It's called Lot's Wife. You can explore the formation if you'd like. It's growing at an amazing rate. They say that if you stand in the salt caves at midnight, you can see your salvation." The pilgrim caps his water and rises to stand.

The man frowns. "I don't understand. What does that mean?"

The pilgrim shrugs. "It's a tradition. I've heard that people see all sorts of things. Maybe you'll try it. What do you suppose you'll see?"

The man considers it for a moment. He closes his near-sightless eyes and pictures the smooth walls of Mount Sodom surrounding him in the desert heat. The passage narrows to a squeeze, and he tips his chin north—the only free space in the enclosure—to find his salvation. He's waited for this forever, it seems. He's wondered how he is different from those people who God saw fit to burn in this very spot. He has questioned how, exactly, he is so special. He wants to see an angel waiting just for him, but he fears he wouldn't recognize the face of one even if God saw fit to grace him with a messenger. The truth is that he is no different from the people who were cursed to die by fire. He fears, above all, he would open his eyes in that salt cave to see nothing but the clear night sky stretching out above him into an unanswered oblivion.

"I wouldn't see anything," the man says.

"Are you sure?" the pilgrim asks. He cocks his head. "It's a special place, if you open your eyes."

"Maybe for some." The man blinks to clear his blurred vision and pulls his shirt over his head. "I saw what I came for."

He walks to his car. On his way, he throws away his brochure extolling the healing wonders of the Dead Sea. He hadn't liked his visit as much as he'd expected to. Vacations were supposed to be fun, not filled with fear of fire. Maybe the next destination would be more enjoyable.

He drives away without looking back, but the figure of the pilgrim limns his rearview. The last of the salt washes clear from his eyes just as the rays of the setting sun grace the edge of the Masada ridge. By a trick of the evening light, it seems as if the pilgrim is beyond radiant. The man pulls to the side of the road to get a better view of the spectacle, but by the time he exits the car the sun has already set and there is no sign of anyone behind him. He is alone in the road in the dark with only the endless sky above him. He regrets that he didn't try harder to see his salvation when the glimpse was offered. Now he has lost the chance. The man looks up and sighs. The first star of the night appears. It is beautiful to behold.

DELUGE: STORIES OF SURVIVAL & TRAGEDY IN THE GREAT FLOOD

Biblical Legends Anthology Series

ALPHA

Allen Taylor

When I first conceptualized the Biblical Legends Anthology Series (BLAS), I had no idea how the anthologies would be received. I also had no idea what quality of writing I would see or the nature of the content. I'm quite pleased.

Garden of Eden came first. The smallest of the three, it set the expectations for the others to follow. Writers seemed to understand what I was aiming at. I followed it with *Sulfurings: Tales from Sodom & Gomorrah*, which took a different, more apocalyptic, turn. While out of order from the biblical timeline, the second and third (*Deluge: Stories of Survival & Tragedy in the Great Flood*) books in the series attracted a grittier, darker form of literature. Again, the writers did not disappoint.

Selling at physical events has allowed me to assess reader reactions in a way that can't be done online. Generally, I see three types of reactions:

Enthusiastic acceptance for a unique idea;

Gross rejection, or absolute shock;

Or an assumption that, because they're based on Bible stories, they are "Christian" in nature.

Naturally, I'm thankful for the first type of reader, and the second type isn't my audience. The third type of reader, however, falls into two categories.

The first category is the devout Christian expecting the stories to be "family-friendly" or hail from a Christian point of view. The other category is the non-Christian who assumes the same.

While some of the stories are written by authors approaching the subject matter from an orthodox Christian perspective, not all the stories fall in that line. The truth is, I didn't ask writers about their backgrounds. It didn't occur to me to do so because I was simply looking for good stories with a speculative twist on the biblical narratives. We weren't reinventing theology. We were reimagining literature.

Readers may find some of the details in certain stories inaccurate, or they may disagree with a writer's interpretation of the events. Both are fair assessments. On the other hand, readers may find some interesting explorations of sin, redemption, righteousness, God's wrath, and other biblical themes. These themes may be explored even as events stray from the biblical storyline. In other cases, the themes are explored satirically.

When asking for submissions, I made two stipulations. First, I wanted stories set during the biblical Great Flood or that explored the flood theme in a new and different way. I also asked writers not to include biblical characters in their stories. Fortunately, a few of the authors broke that rule.

Some stories in *Deluge* may present elements that are offensive to some readers. Such is the nature of literature. No apologies warranted or granted.

Changes made to this second edition begin and end with author bios. The stories are the same. I requested that authors update their bios for the second printing. Most added publishing credits or changed their credits to more recent ones. Some didn't respond at all. One author took the liberty of announcing his transgender status. I didn't expect that. Inclusion of that author's story may invite controversy of its own, for reasons that have nothing to do with literature or the purpose of these anthologies. I didn't think it would be fair to ask him to edit his bio (since I didn't ask anyone else to edit theirs), nor would it be fair to pull his story based on some moral sensibility, whether mine or someone else's. That may have some readers question my judgment or accusing me of "endorsing" transgenderism. That author's story stands on its own merit, and his own lifestyle choices are subject to God's judgment (as are mine and everyone else's).

In short, I'm an editor and publisher, not the moral police and certainly not the thought police. Nevertheless, I'm delighted that writers and readers alike may be driven to the Bible to read the text where the original stories can be found, and I hope this anthology honor the original story in some way even if individual literary creations stray far afield.

And now, without further ado, I present *Deluge: Stories of Survival & Tragedy in the Great Flood.*

FLASH FICTIONS

AS BIG AS ALL THE WORLD

John Vicary

The Arctic sun dawned under a canopy of clouds in the north. Anuniaq and Karpok paid the dim orb no heed; they had a job to finish regardless of the light or lack thereof. The remnants of snow from a full night away must be cleared. The men worked in wordless communion to bare the frozen face of the life-sustaining sea.

When the holes were cut into the thick ice and the poles laid with bait, the men sat together in stillness and watched the snow fall in unabating drifts from the Great Above.

"It's a long spell of *kanevvluk* this season," Anuniaq said at last.

Karpok grunted.

"I heard old Uglu speaking about it last night at the Gathering. He said we might hit forty days and forty nights since the first *qanuk* fell. Isn't that something?" Anuniaq asked.

Karpok shrugged. His name meant "hungry", and he was rarely interested in anything beyond the subject of his namesake. He reached over and inspected the pole, then dropped his mittened hand again.

Anuniaq didn't mind talking to himself; the silence of the open plain could drive a man crazy. "Well, last year it was thirty-seven days, and the year before that it was thirty-nine. Old Uglu thinks that we'll hit the record. If it snows one more night, we'll make it. Huh."

The line twitched and Karpok pulled a wriggling whitefish from the frigid water. The lines on his weathered face deepened with the first smile of the morning. He held up his catch in triumph before rethreading the line.

After another hour and two more fish, Anuniaq began talking again. "Can you imagine if this wasn't *kanevvluk*?"

"What?" The absurdity of the question startled Karpok into speech. "What else would Qailertetang send to us?"

"Think of the southern tribes. They might be having rain," Anuniaq said. In truth, he'd wondered that for some time. He'd had a dream once of that very thing, and in his spare moments he'd embroidered it more vividly with each imagining. How did the men of the south cope?

Karpok scoffed. "There are no southern tribes."

"But think of it." Now Anuniaq's fancy had taken flight. "It would rain and rain and they would have to build a kayak to stay afloat. I wonder how they would keep the oil dry? What would happen to the caribou?"

Karpok laughed. "It would need to be a kayak as big as all the world. I'm glad I live in the north. Even the *muruaneq* ... chk!" He made a sound through his teeth. "We can clear it away, just like that. Be glad there is no one in the world to drown in the waters. Aakuluujjusi is good to give us our home here. We are patient with whitefish until summer. We shall grow fat on walrus and elk again. Your brain has caught a fever with eating only winter hare, I think."

Anuniaq laughed. "No, my friend. I was just wondering of other places."

"Bah!" Karpok made a face. "Who cares of other places? There is no place but here."

As the line twitched, Anuniaq pulled in a trout. Snow melted on the silvered scales of the dying fish, and Anuniaq sent a prayer of thanks to Agloolik for their hunt.

"Come." Karpok stood and hefted his catch onto his shoulder. "We shall go home and feed our village. You will forget your strange ideas when you have a bellyful of fish. Rain to cover the world and a kayak to float the tribes of the south? Even Agloolik in his mischief would not be so evil. Bah."

Anuniaq looked into the round hole of open water beneath his feet for a long moment before turning away. He was careful to place his mukluks in the steps laid out by his friend and followed the path all the way home.

GUIDANCE IN THE CLOUDS

JD DeHart

NOA72 twirled down the narrow hallway of space deck fourteen. His memory deck played the image of the ghostly figure, like Hamlet's father, appearing on the outer deck a few months prior. It had been a rainless afternoon after decades of drought. The world was as cracked and dry as a desert hobo's upper lip.

"#endoftheworld," the ghostly figure reported. "#buttloadofwater."

"#got2bejokin," replied NOA72, to which the ghostly figure just shook his ethereal head. "#whodis?"

"#therealgodhead."

"#thoughtyouweredead."

"#godsnotdead."

With that, the astral figure disappeared, and bits of the mission began to fall into place. There was some vague direction, as if there was a pipeline to prophecy and the bot had just accessed it.

Since that brief conversation, NOA72 had started the project: A spaceship that would hold DNA specimens of all the creatures on his planet. The plan, as he understood it, was to re-colonize a different world, perhaps spiraling into a different universe. There was the vague feeling that this had all happened before, maybe even multiple times.

The lovely KTRA26, a much younger iteration of android, cooed to NOA72, "#areumental?"

"#keepinitreal, #gottogetbusy," replied the other.

"#seriously, #comeoutandplay, #blushingafternoon."

"#onamissionfromgod."

KTRA26 left sadly. She knew that this android, this NOA iteration, was slightly crazy for building this ship and collecting all the scraps of fauna. She had noticed him, just a few days ago, trying to sneak up on a quick lizard, a scalpel in his grip.

Still, there was something vaguely attractive about him. KTRA26 had a crush on the handsome android, and even though he was mental, she wanted to be on the ship with him. She wondered briefly if he was one of those Bible-thumping bots, refusing to think for himself, always going back to the same proof-texts. He did not seem that way.

NOA72 watched her form fade into the distance. There were only three specimens left to collect. He would find them easily the next day, he calculated, and already had a heat signature on two of them.

By an hour later, the sky had begun to blacken. KTRA26 was piling one stone on top of another, a popular pastime on the inhospitable planet, when she clicked and whirred at the sky. She immediately thought of the ship, detecting a hint of moisture in the air.

NOA72 was placing the last of the DNA strands in place and just about to pull the ship's hatch shut for good when he heard: "#doomsday, #istherestillroomintheinn?" Rain was beginning to pound down now.

"#chopchop," he replied.

Unfortunately, the precipitation had made the outside of the craft unusually slippery.

"#whatdoIdo? #madeofmetal," KTRA26 said.

"#holdontosomething."

Little by little, the female android made it up the sleek surface and down the hatch, the world closing out. The sound of rain made great thumps and NOA72 hit the ignition, throwing the ship into movement as great waves came cascading in, bursting as if the sky had been holding its mouth shut.

"#fortydaysandfortynights," said NOA72.

"#travelgames," KTRA26 replied, and the two of them entwined their sensors and made for the living room deck.

DREAMS OF THE MOON

Lorina Stephens

In the darkness that follows disaster, he hears the river. It sounds like the rush of beating wings, pulling the host of Elohim into conflict, and for some, into escape. He is unsure who has followed, or who has betrayed them. Michael? Raphael? Who among the Iyrin hadn't wanted to teach those beautiful mortals?

He gropes the air before him, feels nothing, moves toward the sound of the river, finds a rough texture under his fingers—bark, it's still here—and hands himself down to sit beneath the tree. There is pain. This is something new to him, a sinister sensation in the darkness, he who has lived his life in the chiaroscuro of light. Sariel, whose name was written on shields, whose name was an invocation of death from the Third Tower and he, the Bringer of Death. The Captain Sariel, now blind, unable to fly, waiting here at the edge of the river and the fourth paradise, for what? He's unsure and wishing for death.

He thinks he might laugh for the absurdity of it. It's too much to think about. Too much has happened. He eases further down in darkness to fragrant myrtle, dew on his arm, pain in one wing where he knows it's broken and pain where his eyes once saw the phases of the moon. He lets the darkness and the rush of the river become an anodyne for his senses.

He listens to the river. There is only one way to cross it now. Impossible to fly with this broken wing and sightless eyes.

"Sariel." He hears and stirs, unsure if he's imagining this through the miasma of his pain. He wishes he could see. He wishes he could know the minds of others as he once had.

"Shamsiel?" he asks. His voice sounds hoarse to him. It is a rattle in the darkness.

"No," the voice answers. "Shamsiel is fallen."

Fallen. Then Eden has fallen, for Shamsiel and that host were to defend Eden. All is lost. "Are they safe? The Chosen, the Nephilim?" Is she safe? Is the child?

"Yes. We're all safe."

And doomed to exist on Mount Hermon in the Cave of Treasures, they and their Nephilim. "And the other Iyrin with us?"

"All fallen. You are the last."

With that realization, Sariel weeps. So much has been lost. The City of Light is no longer theirs, nor is the world they'd hoped to make with The Chosen, and the children they would rear together.

He feels lips on his eyes, and hears the voice of his rescuer, sibilant in the darkness. There are words to comfort and to soothe, and Sariel sinks into the other's arms, letting grief wash over him. It is the woman he's taken as mate he now knows. Her hands touch his face and the wounds of his eyes. He can feel her trembling, or is that him?

"I know, I know," she says, and there is rocking, something the Iyrin learned from mortal humans, an expression of a need for comfort. "Only a little more pain now. And it will all be done."

A little more pain explodes into suffocating terror. He screams. And then again as the terror repeats. The darkness is filled with the sound and smell of it. With one hand, he reaches out toward her, finds an arm, a hand. The hilt of his own fiery sword has been used to sever wings, and now he is truly afraid because her voice still croons, and she still rocks him.

"Why?" he manages to gasp.

"To bind you. To disguise you against the hunt that has come. All the others have been cast forever into darkness, and I would have you live with me. Be mortal. Die."

Sariel, the Prince of Death, to die himself.

He sinks into oblivion, unable to bear the pain. When again he rises, he is still in darkness, still rocking, only now there is music, a voice in melancholy song. In another moment of panic, he realizes he's on a boat.

He calls out. He hears her voice.

"You're awake," she says.

"Where are you taking me?" He knows, but there is always hope. He's learned this from his sojourn in Eden.

"To the others."

"And so, we are all outcasts?"

"All. And bound."

"Is this death?"

"Very like, I suppose."

She dissembles, he knows. "How?" He can hear no answer, and bound in darkness he cannot see any gesture that might illuminate the question. It is then when he confronts the fact of mortality, and what it was to be Iyrin. He has heard for the dead there is cessation of pain. It is what he believed, being the Prince of Death. So many lives he has transmuted with the power of his sword. But, for the Iyrin, there would be everlasting knowledge of what they've lost and will never again see, or know, cast out as others are. She has given him a choice, now, to live or to die.

And so, Sariel, father of one of the Nephilim, mate of a human woman, once favored among the Iyrin, master of the phases of the moon, does what he is doomed to do: he seizes that fiery sword, pushes himself out of the boat, and smites himself. He sinks down into the frigid water, dreaming of beauty. Dreaming of death.

PLANET TERRUS

Tom Mollica

Watching the hologram, Cacho Zahn saw a being emerge from a dwelling. "The specimen is outside," Cacho said to the number one pilot, the only other person in the ship's control room. He also observed the same happenings below on a hologram that was four times the size of Cacho's. The mappers had designated this planet with the title of Terrus.

"Yes," Number One answered. A number one pilot's verbal communications with the lower-level working party was minimal. Cacho and Number One watched in silence for a time until Number One spoke again. "It is time for us to act." He pointed his long and thin gray finger towards the panel in front of him.

In the center of the control room, a hologram appeared showing the transport room of the ship. There, two knowledge seekers dressed in their usual white tunics stood next to a midsized vessel. The craft was not saucer-shaped like the space travel ships Cacho was accustomed to. It was rectangular and boxy. Its design was similar to the dwellings from the area below but longer with four levels.

"We are ready," Number One voiced to the knowledge seekers. "Are all the specimens stored?"

"Yes, Number One," A knowledge seeker answered, and motioned with a three-fingered gray hand to the ship. "Every specimen we deem beneficial to this world has been accumulated, and the DNA cells stored in their control units inside the vessel. They will be ready to be reborn when it is time."

"Launch arc," Number One said and pointed a finger towards the panel, which caused the knowledge seeker's hologram to vanish.

Cacho watched on his hologram as the vessel was launched from the solar sail saucer and hovered. It landed in plants next to the farmer's home and crushed them as the specimen watched. A female specimen and two under-developed smaller ones joined him. A side panel on the ship opened and a ramp extended downward.

Number One again pointed a finger to his control panel. In the sky above the family a large image appeared of a head that was a likeness of the aliens on the planet. The white-skinned head was too small in proportion to the body size, Cacho thought. Even though his race had much smaller bodies than the hominids, their heads were close to three times as large as the alien's. The beings' heads were oval-shaped. Cacho's was triangular with rounded corners. The alien portrayed in the sky image had a face that featured hair on the cheeks, and long brown hair. It was nothing like the smooth, hairless heads of Cacho's people.

The specimen below looked up as the head spoke in a booming, deep voice. "Noah, it is time."

Cacho and Number One watched the family return to the home, gather a few things, and step back out. The four entered the ship and the ramp slid back in, then the panel closed.

Number One spoke into the control panel. "Release the fountains of the great deep."

On the planet, water from rivers, lakes, and oceans began to overflow. Larger and darker stratocumulus clouds joined the stealth cloud surrounding Cacho's vessel just as thrusters ignited beneath the saucer and lifted it upward. The moment it was above the clouds, the skies let loose with a heavy downpour of driving rain.

Number One again spoke into his control panel, "Set course to return after forty days and forty nights."

TEN LONELY RAIN GODS

David Macpherson

The first lonely rain god sits on her bed and sings, "Cry Me a River." She looks up and says, "That's a joke. Cry me a river. That's a lot of tears. I'm a rain god. I was crying and so it's funny because, ah, forget it." She sings the song from the beginning, but not knowing all the words, hums most of it.

The second lonely rain god writes words on a dry erase board with a squeaky marker. He writes: drought, deluge, downpour, arid, sprinkle, giraffe. He pauses. "I just like writing the word. *Giraffe*. You try it. *Giraffe*. It's fun on the fingers as it slides into letters. *Giraffe*. Now try *Deluge*. See. There is no fun in that word."

The third lonely rain god paces back and forth on the basketball court, mumbling to himself, "El Niño. El Niño. El Niño. Worst kind of false advertising I know. Little boy. Little boy. I created floods and storms and imminent destruction, and they call me the little boy. Put me in short pants, pat my head, and shove a chicklet in my mouth. El Niño. Good boy. Go down to the basement fridge and get daddy another beer. My father did that to me once. I blocked the drains in the basement sink and opened the taps. I got daddy his beer, and by the time they realized what I had done, the basement was flooded, and the house's structure was ruined. I'm nobody's El Niño."

The fourth and fifth lonely rain gods are in the rec room playing ping pong. Every volley echoes down the hall. They don't know what the score is. They don't know who is winning. "But I know who is losing," one of them says. "You can always notice the losers. Winners are tougher. Harder to see," the other one says. "Serve already. Stop making speeches." The serve hits the table like heat lightning. Eventually, the game is called on account of rain.

The sixth lonely rain god is working on a paint-by-numbers set. "Don't laugh," she says. "They're relaxing, and they're popular. Maybe even hip. I said, don't laugh. You're breaking my concentration." She furrows her brow and carefully fills in the #14 spot with light magenta. "But this one's defective. The box illustration shows Noah and the Ark and the two by two and all that propaganda, but that's not the picture I'm filling in. It's like a Mardi Gras parade or something with floats and beads raining down from balconies. I guess I can complain, but I'm too relaxed. Paint by numbers is relaxing."

The seventh lonely rain god—let's skip the seventh lonely rain god. It's for the best.

The eighth lonely rain god is sleeping. Or maybe he's pretending to be asleep. His ear buds are leaking out a meditation CD with the sounds of summer showers and crashing waves. Let's let him sleep or let him continue pretending.

The ninth lonely rain god strums undiscovered chords on her boyfriend's guitar. She is humming. I'm sorry, but the seventh lonely rain god is back and refuses to be passed over. I tried, but there she is in her bathrobe and mismatched fuzzy slippers. One foot is a teddy bear and the other is a porpoise. She is standing there giving that look she gives. The one that compels umbrellas to spontaneously open and slickers to tremble all through the building complex. She says, "Once entire nations worshipped me. They made bloody sacrifices to me. Sometimes I would deign to acknowledge their offerings with a humble shower. But now, they toss the runes of fronts and high-pressure systems. Al Roker is a false god. The Weather Channel is a heretical temple."

The ninth lonely rain god has left. I suppose she couldn't hang around any longer. But where she was is a piece of paper with some writing on it. It might be a poem. "The girl with the life preserver heart is floating in the deluge. Her love is the wave crashing like persistence. Her hope is a chant. She shouts adoration that cannot be heard. She wants to dry each other clean and blessed. They will release the livestock and live like Utnapishtim at the Mouth of the Rivers." That's what's written there. I guess some folks might call it a poem. I guess.

The tenth lonely rain god is pacing with the phone to his ear. They put him on hold and now he waits to speak to a supervisor. He's going to let them have it. Going to let it go, open the floodgates. It will be wet and loud. But for now, he waits. And waits. And listens to the piped-in music for those on hold: "Cry Me a River."

AN IRONCLAD FATE OF HER OWN DESIGN

Sarah Vernetti

The rain had pummeled their home for days, the droplets hitting the marble patio with such force that they sprang back into the air only to fall again, making the torrential rain seem that much more impressive.

Margo knew what was coming. In her mind, she could see herself gasping for air, reaching skyward for dry land that did not exist.

It didn't cross her mind to tell her parents. After all, they already knew. Every member of their species could see these glimpses of the future. Surely, the scenario had already danced through their minds. Already they had watched their fourth and youngest daughter drown.

Margo pondered her next move. Although she could see the future, she had no way of knowing when the end would arrive. Could she alter her fate? Was the final result cast in bronze or precariously pieced together in gauze?

She turned away from one of the palace's many windows, from the image of her lungs filling with wrathful water and grabbed her satchel.

When she arrived at the general store, she was told that they were sold out of all wooden planks and tools. Apparently, those items, along with several barrels of flour, four pounds of salt, and ten bushels of vegetables, had been purchased by a previous customer.

"Noah," Margo thought to herself as she squinted at the store owner.

Despite her ability to see the future, Margo was a procrastinator. Once again, Noah had been one step ahead of her and the rest of her species.

She walked out of the store and made her way to the wash, which was already suffering from a flash flood. The rain was still pouring. Instead of fighting against the marble of her patio, here, the rain surrendered and was absorbed immediately into the ever-growing pool.

Without pausing to look back, without thinking again of the warm palace from which she had come, Margo walked toward the wash, stepped off the edge, and began to live the vision that had danced in her head for weeks.

If she couldn't float like Noah, then down to the depths she would travel. On her own time.

PROBLEM POINTS

E.S. Wynn

When the flood came, Noah built a boat because God told him to.

But God didn't have to tell Doctor Lilith R. Thudmucker to build a boat. She'd already built something better. She'd built a time machine.

Her mission was simple. Centuries of research into biblical accounts of history had turned up certain *problem points,* as they were known: gaps glossed over in Genesis but explored or hinted at in other, older texts.

One such point was the Noah story, and it was Doctor Thudmucker who finally connected the dots across several sources in the summer of 2069. The revelation came suddenly and shockingly; while Noah had built a boat to save himself, his wife and his sons' wives, there were indications that someone had arrived from *some other time* to warn of the flood and stage an evacuation of some of the largest cities on the face of the antediluvian earth.

Someone who, from descriptions Lilith had read in a crumbling scroll that had spent centuries in the darkness of a dusty cave in Iraq, looked a lot like she did.

That was when the plan began to come together.

Years upon years of research passed. Components capable of manipulating time on a small scale were illegal and hard to find, but not impossible to acquire for the right price. The work was slow but precise, and as Doctor Thudmucker's time machine neared completion, she withdrew from society and civilization and spent every waking moment working on her plan of fine-tuning her machine.

When at last the day came to save the world from God's wrath and the in-breeding that would surely follow in the wake of his short-sighted need to spare only a single family of humans, Lilith took a day to rest and admire her creation. Despite its rough appearance, she decided it was good.

Doctor Thudmucker had spent years trying to decide which cities she would evacuate and in what order. Most were too sick with sin to consider saving, but in her view, a few were only slightly wicked. *And besides, any evil souls I might save by accident will only add spice to the mix,* she thought. *The world is full of jerks. They had to have come from somewhere.*

Deciding who would live and who would die made her feel like God, and in the end, she picked only seven cities to save. She wouldn't save everyone, only a smattering of interesting people who seemed good at heart. Fortunately, due to the nature of time (and the size of her time machine) she estimated that seven trips made to each city over the course of seven days would ensure an adequately sized gene pool to minimize in-breeding among the people who would become the ancestors of the postdiluvian human race.

Unfortunately, the first city she visited, a city which scant historical records had painted as a paragon of justice and righteousness, turned out to be a metropolis of ebon wood towers and slave markets called Jan'aloth.

There was no reasoning with the people of Jan'aloth. Like a choice slave, she was stripped and beaten almost the instant she set foot in the muddy streets, then chained and brought before the city's High Archon. Years spent studying the reconstructed tongue of the antediluvian world only earned her a slap and a smile, and the High Archon grinned as she wailed, trying to reason with him. What he understood of her babbling intrigued him, but not enough to spare her life. A knife across the throat ended her pleas, and then she was fed to the pigs, leaving only her time machine to attest to her appearance and her good intentions.

When it began to rain, just as Doctor Thudmucker had prophesied it would, the High Archon of Jan'aloth sent for seers and alchemists to study her time machine. As the waters rose, slaves of the High Archon beat the seers and alchemists harder to encourage them, but it wasn't until half of the city had sunk beneath the waves that anyone figured out how to work the vehicle. Lessons came quickly and secretively. Sternly attentive, the High Archon learned the art of flying the machine in a matter of hours, then killed everyone else who had seen it or knew of its existence. Secret orders went out to gather ten of his strongest soldiers, and as one, they raided the harems and slave markets of the dying city, stole two dozen fighting slaves, then returned to Doctor Thudmucker's time machine. Not even sparing a single glance for the city he had ruled with an iron fist for so long, the High Archon slammed the doors of the time machine and forced it forward, back to the century it had come from.

Panic ensued as thirty-five half-naked fighting men rippling with muscle shattered the front door of Doctor Thudmucker's home and descended upon the opulent, unprepared metropolis of New York. Blades of black steel flashed and felled hundreds of frail, pale humans caught in the streets, most of them before they could even look up from the screens printed in their meta-matter clothing. Videos of the assault went viral within minutes, but most people were too busy watching them or discussing what summer blockbuster the grainy, jumping clips might be preliminary trailers for. In the space of a few days, the High Archon of Jan'aloth was High Archon of New York, his army was burgeoning, and the slave markets he established in Pelham Bay Park rattled with the cracking of whips and the lamentations of men, women, and children.

But the luxuries of Thudmucker's time enchanted and snared him and soon he was utterly lost in a world of video games and VR porn. Some news stations hailed him as a hero and savior of the people. Dignitaries and diplomats carefully selected from among the people of the time kept the spin going and kept flattering images and promises on the air. When summer waned, the media campaign became a political campaign, and as the people and celebrities of the earth began parroting the slogan "Where is *our* High Archon?" it became clear that the world was about to be unified under a new world order over which the man who had been Jan'aloth's High Archon would reign unquestioned.

And so it was that God broke his covenant with man. With tired eyes, He reached into the mind of a wealthy entrepreneur in Silicon Valley named Noah and gave him very specific instructions on what to do with his money, his land, and the neo-hippie commune he called his family.

And then the kicker: *Dear God, if you loved me, you'd send me the soup I asked for.*

I took one look at God's face and knew that the planet was doomed. Ten plagues aside, God can normally control his temper, but man, that little sod. You wouldn't believe how often He hears "If you love me, then you'll...". It drives him absolutely bonkers.

"That little sod." God said, massaging his temples. "If he wants chicken soup, I'll give him chicken soup!"

And so, it rained.

At first, Bobby was excited when he felt the warm splash from above on his skin. He got more excited still when he licked it off his arm and declared that it was raining his favorite canned food. But then it poured, and it poured just on Bobby. Gallons of the stuff.

The kid tried to run, but you try running across chicken soup-covered ground. It got really slippery really fast, and the next thing he knew, Bobby was arse over tit in a considerably sized puddle of creamy goodness. Then came the lumps of chicken the size of which you've never seen. All right, they weren't lumps. They were whole chickens. Frozen ones.

You can imagine what frozen chickens falling from the sky can do to a skull. Especially when, technically speaking, they're not falling but rather being thrown like javelins from the arm of the Almighty.

That was the end of Bobby Taylor. It would have been the end of the whole episode if Kate Taylor had just kept her trap shut. God had had his fun, he'd vented some frustration, and he'd rid the world of the biggest little sod there was.

I'm sure you can sympathize with the Holy One when I tell you that Kate Taylor kicked off. I know what you're thinking: most parents would, right? She made this big fuss in front of the spectators who'd witnessed the chicken-skull fiasco. She claimed that Bobby was taken before his time, that God was an unfair so-and-so, and that she was turning her back on Him forever. I suppose any parent would, but the thing was, when God oh-so-literally answered Bobby's prayer, he was answering Kate's too.

The whole time we could hear Bobby rambling about his soup, we could all hear a very faint but persistently pleading cry for help from Kate. I'm sure, looking back on it now, that she used the phrase "just kill the little fu—", well, you can fill in the rest. As soon as she saw those chickens come down, she smiled. We all saw it.

She was happy about it. And then she had the gall to stand there wailing that it was a tragedy. Well, that really tied God in a knot. So, He kept raining soup and He kept throwing chickens.

Remember that parent I mentioned earlier, the one who punishes all their children for the crimes of one? Yeah, so that's what happened. Bobby started the fire, Kate wafted the flames, and God put it out. For forty days and nights, the people of Earth endured warm soup splashes and frozen chicken-related deaths.

When the puddles started to coalesce into lakes, we tried to stop Him, but He was in no mood to be told what to do. He had had it with the trivial prayers, expectations, and complaints from His children. I tried to tell Him that they had learned their lesson, and that perhaps flooding the world with soup was a little overboard (da da dum). His reply was that to prove that He loves his children equally, He has to treat them all the same. If one needs a good smiting, then they all do.

The results of the flood were bad for the majority. As you can imagine, due to the lack of warning, there was no time to build an ark. There wasn't even enough time to assemble a raft, though a few did manage to assemble some inflatables.

That's not to say that there weren't any survivors, though humanity has taken a somewhat bizarre turn. In a thousand years or so, I can't wait to see what future humans will make of the cave drawings of those falling chickens.

Bobby, the absolute sod, has gone down in history as a martyr. Yeah, we couldn't believe it either.

With each of God's lessons, humanity takes something valuable away to progress with, but in this case, they were left a little perplexed. Scholars continue to try to make sense of 'S' Day, but the only conclusion drawn so far is that chicken soup is now banned. I'm hoping that the next little sod prays for carrots; I can't stand carrots.

IOTA

AQUALUNG

Anne Carly Abad

There, a planet gated away
under a lattice of roots and branches
from an Elder Tree—so old it's turned to stone—
the Lord of Earth must be warning us: stay back.
But our wings are weary, fleeing from
the fiery expansion, nowhere to perch
among the molten rocks of space
and the temperamental stars.

I shatter the Elder's limbs
and we mount the soil below
only to have the land curse us,
cause our pinions to fall,
fall like the rain that has begun to surge
from unseen clouds and banks above.
Taking our flight is not enough.
The earth requires flesh.

But then I find that water is kind
to those who drown,
cradling the damned in softness,
quieting the will to strive.

I float in the crystalline blue,
and count my siblings
asleep and bloated, becoming faceless...
my fingers are not enough.
The deluge becomes our bed
and the weight of water
our blanket. I hold on to
the boulder hands of a Nephilim
before peace washes over me
and I inhale cleansing liquid.

It fills my chest with slumber.
In my dream, the water lurches,
bending the membranes of my lungs.
It pulls at my skin, creating a flap.
It pushes back muscles until they split
and I awake, beating filaments and lamellae.

I am an angel of the sea.
The lord above banishes us to the depths,
but we have never perished.

SHORT STORIES

FIELDS OF THE NEPHILIM

Alex S. Johnson

When the Nephilim fell from heaven, they burned the skies, their dark wings spreading across the miles, their feet driving the bones of the previous angels further into the soil.

In those days, there was much bewilderment and wonder among the people, for creatures of pure metaphysics had been raining for decades and they were sore afraid of being sore afraid and sick unto death of being sick unto death. The bones of the angels moldered in the earth and spread contagion laterally and strange plants vertically, which shot up in the form of sharp-edged musical instruments that the people did play upon. In those days, also, many gods battled for the single position available, and the people lacked such knowledge and discernment that would enable them to pick one heavenly leader among the contenders. As they awaited that day, they plucked lutes and harps and guitars and blew upon trumpets that evoked storms of blood and desolating tornadoes that churned the land.

The Nephilim were big-boned and frankly scary to the people of Earth, and when they demanded luscious maidens, the people of Earth had no recourse but to surrender their daughters, saying, please, whatever you do, don't get giants upon them, for those giants are creepy and malignant.

Hearing their cries but being not of Earth, the Nephilim said unto them, Ha, it will be our greatest pleasure to plow your daughters like unto the fields and produce all the giants we want. And what will thou doest with thy puny limbs and lutes and harps and guitars, form an army of little ones, the least of whom will not stand up to the feet of a giant and the greatest of whom will at most reach half of half a knee's height? For the Nephilim were cocksure and desperately horny for the daughters of Earth and intent upon creating giants, which was their pastime in those days.

And the people of Earth said to Moses, Dude, what in the fuck have we done to incur the wrath of the gods, such that they continue to plague us with storms and tornadoes and fallen angels and more fallen angels and now these huge-winged psychopaths who crave our daughters for the purpose of making giants upon them?

And some in their desperation formed cults, either to placate the many gods or to placate those leaders who had grown among them with mighty claims to power. And these cults did proliferate until all the people of Earth either belonged to them or were excluded; but as the people of Earth were fewer then than they are now, most were able to join at least one cult. And these cults did excommunicate, condemn, and ostracize all other cults, and there was much fighting among the people and infighting among members of the cults.

Meanwhile, the fall of the Nephilim continued. Among the daughters of the people of Earth were the first Hos, called the Hohim, who craved the colossal tools of the Nephilim and did suck upon them until the skies were full unto whiteness with the sperm that did spurt. The Nephilim plowed and plundered and ravished these daughters and made baby giants that did howl and scream and curse and throw their scat like unto a great shitstorm. And the heavens were smeared with excrement and spunk and blood and other bodily products and darkened the skies. The cults then took of the sperm and shit and blood and made monstrous protectors from them that were called Golem. And while there were some who looked upon the psychotic confusion that reigned upon Earth and said whoa, the gods will be displeased with this situation and curse us and despise us and sow dissension among us and make of us little butt-slaves, the leaders of the cults cried Ha, for they were drunk with power and had also imbibed of the Kool-Aid that did shower from the cocks of Golem.

And this Kool-Aid was of such potency and hallucinogenic effect that it shattered what little rationality did prevail among the peoples of Earth, and the first age of Full-Bore Batshit Crazy began.

The Nephilim became bored with the demands and pleas and shrieks and cries and heinous fuckery of the daughters and they sought other delights such as were provided by the Kool-Aid. And they too drank of that evil drink, as did the Golem, who then formed a collective. And this collective sought to exterminate, drive out and repulse all those who had not drunk thereof and become flushed with strange thoughts that led them to ritual practices that were an abomination to at least seven generations (for the accounting in those days was not rigorous and seven generations could be translated into four, or five, or twenty-two of ours today).

By the end of the first age of Full-Bore Batshit Crazy, all the people of Earth and their daughters and sons and nephews and cousins were sick again of being sick and tired of the constant wars that raged unabated until five only were left of the people of Earth and the Nephilim were in rout and the daughters were simply hot messes and no longer even cute in a beer goggles way. The bodily wastes that filled the sky had blocked the sun and now the Earth began to freeze, and the peoples of Earth sought caves.

In these caves they drew—rough sketches at first, then more detailed artwork, and finally, glorious masterpieces that would be an example unto many more generations if the Earth did not then vomit forth creatures that were slimy confabulations of all the angels, demons, whores, magical trumpets and lutes and drums and very slutty whores that were called the New Hohim, and the art became labored and crude again and finally like unto clods of crap. And because they were hungry and thirsty the people ventured forth into the freezing air and made weapons with which to slay these creatures and make of them nourishment and sustenance. But the creatures were so foul and awful that even when they had been cooked into charcoal blocks, they were still inedible, and the last peoples of Earth turned on one another, regardless of cult affiliation, and cannibalism reigned.

And the God who was the true God and not a half-assed pretender such as were the many, many false gods who had planted their flags in the Earth, the God whose patience was great and whose mercy for his creation was overwhelming, finally had had enough. And he summoned the angels that were not fakes or frauds or phonies and He said unto them, the shit, it hath finally gotten real. And they bowed and gesticulated and humbled themselves before the one God (accept no substitutes) and said unto Him that was on high, how can we rectify the great confusion and outright weirdness that now baffles even the greatest minds of Earth and Heaven and outlying regions?

And the one God who wasn't that other guy or him either or that fat little man who wears of the mask and dispenses the Kool-Aid from his throne of shit said, well, I dunno. I thought I might send plagues and boils and hateful critters and wrath and other forms of heinous fuckery to they that are of Earth, but even if I do so, they have very little self-respect or hope left and would probably sit upon the ground and take of it like unto a little bitch that is a ho. And He thought some more and finally he said, take of the shit and sperm and blood and form stars and planets and, dammit, a real cosmos that is far greater than anything these miserable humans have seen, and fling the Nephilim to the farthest spheres, and show the people of Earth light and reason. And the angels heard these words which could not be heard by human ears without great implosion, and they came upon the Earth to check out the situation thereof.

And they saw the peoples of Earth were huddled in their caves, quaking and shaking and imprecating and still worshipping numerous abominations and demons and they saw also that these people were scared out of their ever-loving minds, and they knew not what to do. And the angels took pity on them and drew them out of their caves and showed them the many things they could do with their hands and feet and minds and hearts and other organs and attributes belonging to them. And while the vast majority maintained the bitterness that had grown like a disease contaminating every cell, a few listened to the gentle advice of the angels and started to plant seeds that grew into a mighty rain forest. And rain dropped upon the Earth and the skies began to clear of the stink that stanketh and even a few of the Hohim repented and the men of Earth were exceeding glad because they had grown ill of the sexually-transmitted diseases that made of their members to rot and fall off.

And for a very brief period there was peace on Earth. A very, very brief period, but a period, nonetheless.

DREAMERS OF THE DELUGE

Allen Ashley

Uncle Saul could hear well enough for himself but nevertheless told David, "Have a look outside the door, kid, see if it's still raining."

David briefly poked his head through the gap and came back inside with drops of water falling off his hair and nose.

"I'll take that as a yes," Saul stated. "Reckon the valley must be flooded by now."

"I'd say fifty cubits high and rising. It'll soon flood us out, Uncle Saul. I hope Rebekah's safe. And her family."

"Still pining after that shy one, eh? She's a bit young for you, ain't she?"

"Just by a year. She's on the cusp of womanhood."

"The what? Where'd you learn to talk like that? You been hanging out with that crazy rabbi, Shimon?"

They fell silent for a while. The rain now pounded against the wooden planks atop their shelter. From the attached lean-to, their animals moaned softly against the divine punishment. David had started to lose track of time. He was not sure whether it was afternoon or evening. The dark sky and the dim fog inside the building gave no real clues either way. He took a few more bites from their small store of unleavened bread even though he wasn't particularly hungry. Then he needed to take a few sips of water from their shared stone bowl. It seemed a little absurd—if he was really thirsty, he could

271

just stick his head through the doorway and open his mouth to the liquid descending sky.

Saul's eyes shone in the shadows. His teeth, too, despite a predilection for the fruit of the vine. "Reckon we missed a trick with that carpenter guy, Noah," he said.

"Neighbor of your lovely betrothed, Rebekah," he added.

"She's not my betrothed, Uncle. Maybe one day. But what do you mean, 'missed a trick?'"

"We should be on his boat, David, ready to ride out the waves of outrageous fortune."

"He wasn't taking passengers, Uncle. Only his family and two each of every kind of animal."

"Exactly. Two of each. There ain't just one kind of human, you know, just like there ain't just one kind of fish. With your dark hair and my weather-worn face, we could have said we were Levites. Or from Samaria. Egypt, at a push. I've been there, I speak some of the language. Lovely lingo, especially from the mouths of some of the harlots I met 'round the back of Alfalfa Market."

"Uncle! You shouldn't!"

"Because you never have? I bet you've thought about it, though, and I bet you're intending to if we make it out of this downpour in one piece."

"Uncle, it's sin that God is punishing. You know that. Mr. Noah told us so."

Maybe he was still too young to really know what he was talking about. His body had started to change over the past year, sprouting hairs in private and not-so-private places. He would wake with his bedcover wet from his less-than-holy dreams. He was sure that Rebekah must be undergoing some similar sort of transformation beneath the thick covering of clothing that her parents made her habitually wear even in the hot Galilean summer. God was punishing the earth for its sinfulness and—blasphemous thought—perhaps his brutal hand was being too all-inclusive in washing away all transgressors. *I don't deserve to die*, David thought. *I've never done no fornicating. Maybe I've thought of it, but men should be judged on their actions. That's what's fair. If the Lord can get inside your head like the holy men claimed, maybe he should spend some time fixing our thinking. Next, he'll be punishing me for my dreams.*

He'd had a dream last week that he and Rebekah ran away to Egypt to grow crops by the fertile Nile. He'd told Uncle Saul, who'd commented, "If that deluge arrives, the whole world's gonna become the Nile, boy."

His thoughts were interrupted by a slight lessening of the percussive precipitation above which he could hear the tethered animals braying.

"Why don't we bring the beasts inside?" Saul said. "May come in useful."

They had tethered the goat and the donkey very loosely with just a rope thrown over a stick so that if the creatures had any wherewithal, they could make their own escape through the omnipresent downpour. David was a little surprised that neither had done so. They had some sort of lingering loyalty to their human masters.

Soaked to the skin, he led the smaller creature into the shelter. It gave off a fecund, wet smell. Was it his uncle's intention to use these as a final food source?

"Reckon it's up to sixty cubits now," Saul stated. "Almost lapping at the entrance. You ready to swim for it?"

"Of course. I've swum all my life. Caught fish that way. No need of a net."

"Good lad. This rain is going to bring the fish right into our laps, of course. Or take us into their realm. Whichever way you want to look at it."

David remembered his father lowering him into the clear water when he was a mere toddler, encouraging him to be at ease in this element. His late father had been a fisherman, and his father before him. As he struggled to cope with the taboo-testing exposures of puberty, David had often doused himself in the cooling waters. Last week he thought he had espied someone else at the far shore, but the hot sun confused his eyes, and he couldn't be certain. Now it was a requirement that they all be swimmers.

The cramped space was suddenly lit from without by a brilliant flash of lightning and, ten seconds afterwards, a body shuddering clap of thunder. Noah's scientific descendants would have used this information to calculate that the angry center of Heaven was two miles distant. For now.

"Ah, that's what's been missing all along," Saul said, "our creator's roar. Time to make a move, I believe."

"We're not going out into that, are we?"

"Suit yourself, sunshine. I'm not remaining here to watch the last few fingers of air disappear as the flood reaches the roof. Come on, choose your mount. No, on second thoughts, you're much lighter than me. You take the goat, I'll get on the donkey."

David knew that Uncle Saul would have preferred an Arabian horse. Two years back, he had returned from his travels with one in tow, and for a while the beast had proven to be a boon to his family's farm laboring. But a loose stone had led to an infected foot, and they had reluctantly stabbed it out of its misery. Unsure of the dietary teachings of the Torah, they had secretly cooked its flesh and feasted upon its goodness for a week. That was back when the weather was dry and predictable, and life went on much as it had done for generations...

"Stop dawdling, David."

"I don't think the goat's strong enough."

"Nonsense. You're still a mere slip of a thing. Get on, the water's up to our knees already."

All around, all ahead of and behind them now was water. Their shepherd shelter survived maybe a minute longer before being submerged. It was as if they were out on the wild sea with no land in sight. Already, it was hard to remember that this had once been farms, plantations, fishing lakes, homes, and habitations. The irate sky fell upon them. The goat struggled to keep itself afloat as well as free itself of its human burden. To David's right, his uncle atop the donkey fared slightly better, riding one-handed as if born to the semi-aquatic life.

"Let's keep going until we fall off the end of the world," Saul called.

Lust, envy, greed, and gluttony—Saul had indulged in many a sin during his happier days, but the greatest of his crimes was surely pride. The cloud-enclosed sky darkened momentarily above their sodden figures, then a sudden shaft of light like an inspiration pierced the gloom. But no, it was forked. David felt it as a tingle through his whole body, losing consciousness momentarily before recovering to feel somehow changed, his muscles aching more than he could have conceived. Of his companion and the two animals, there was no sign. He had no time to dwell upon their saturated fate as the waves swelled, and he set about swimming as he had been taught, as he had always done, and as he must do until exhaustion claimed his soul. All his years of practice in the lake at Galilee had prepared him for this moment, but he knew that he didn't have the strength to keep going for hours, for days, for who knew how long? Only God knew, and he was the source of this deluge.

He kicked through the water. He strove to stay afloat. He placed one arm forward, then the other in a beautiful symmetry that might, under other circumstances, have gained him some admiring and shy glances. Though the rain smeared his vision and dripped down hair, cheeks, eyes and nose, David regulated his breathing as much as he could. His gaze scanned the horizon for any outcrop of rock, building, or tall tree that might still hold its head above the surface and provide a brief respite. There was nowhere towards the direction of sunrise. Letting his body be turned by the swirl, he set out for the direction he knew as sunset, reflecting bitterly that he and the rest of humankind had doubtless had their last ever sighting of the celestial orb. He kept going. The survival instinct stayed strong. He kicked with both legs together, and his arms ploughed through the unquiet water. After a while, he was barely able to feel the pain of effort. He would hold onto this precious life for as long as he could even without hope or any sign of salvation.

Finally, there was a suggestion of a break in the surface some hundred cubits ahead. Did his eyes deceive him? No, it looked like land. Keep swimming; don't give up now.

Yes, miraculously, there were rocks here above the water. Oh, to rest, if only for a heartbeat or three.

And there, like a vision, was Rebekah, sitting atop the outcrop, brushing her dark hair loose with a comb of bone and with her breasts bare. So brazen. What had made her act like this? But these were changed times. Clothes would slow her down and drag her under the roiling water. God, she was beautiful! All his youthful dreams personified.

As his tired strokes degenerated somewhat, he struggled to keep focused on staying afloat but was drawn inexorably towards this vision in front of him. The rainwater rolled down her smooth torso, making her appear like a figure created by pigments, not quite in focus, ready to be washed away at any moment. Wait for me, my betrothed.

She suddenly became aware of David's plight and threw down her comb so that she could help drag him up to this temporary refuge. As he struggled to control his labored breathing, he saw that Rebekah no longer had legs. His addled brain wondered, had she ever? He was sure she had, as a little girl. Although of late, he'd never seen her without heavy garments. Instead, she now possessed a tail. She smiled. As he tried to rise, he realized that he could no longer stand in the old way because his legs, too, had fused into a tail. The wrathful lightning had left its mark.

"Come, David," she said, "the prophet Noah has said that two of each shall survive this flood. Look at me and gaze upon yourself. This is the divine miracle all those not on the Ark have craved. I believe the Lord has given us a new purpose. A change and a chance."

His uncle's words echoed through his head about there being more than one type of human. But this was surely stretching the definitions way past breaking point.

Rebekah—grown, confident, womanly—paid no heed to his indecision and conjecture. Half-human, half-fish, she dived headlong into the water. He watched the ripples for a moment then followed her.

THE IMMERSION OF THE INCORPOREUM

AmyBeth Inverness

Moesha loved the rain. Her uncle wouldn't make her work in the field during a storm, and her Aunt said she only got in the way inside. The rain was Moesha's escape. She'd run through the drops, not caring that she was soaked to the skin. That summer she'd bled for the first time, and her uncle had found a man eager for another young bride. Never mind that the first three had died ... Moesha's uncle was just glad to be rid of her.

The rain didn't last long. She looked at her feet, the same color as the mud that coated them. A tiny cascade ran over the rocks and into the puddle. The Cascade spoke to her. "Stay ... just a little while longer. A few more minutes won't hurt."

So, Moesha stayed. The rain began again, harder this time. Moesha watched the water, heedless that she was soaked to the skin. The water caressed her. No human ever had or ever would. She held no fantasies about the man who would be her husband. She would die, either at his hand or bearing his child.

The Cascade caressed her. When she did finally return home, she slipped in without waking the others and fell asleep listening to the comforting sound of the rain.

#

"The water is so quiet," Visola said. She wasn't used to water being quiet. Water was noisy and raucous. She was surrounded by an ocean of it, yet the only sounds were from the other passengers and crew.

"It's peaceful," Maggie said. "Water and I have always been friends. Did I tell you they pulled me and my cradle out of a flood when I was a baby?"

Visola snorted. Everyone knew the story of the unsinkable Maggie Brown. She was one of the lucky few who got to hear it from the woman herself. "Yes. And the story gets more and more fantastic each time you tell it."

Maggie laughed. "Well, then, your turn to tell me a wild story. One of your past lives …"

"Moesha? The girl who watched Noah build the ark?"

"That one doesn't have a happy ending. Neither does that one who was drowned as a witch—"

"Ondine?"

"Ondine. Pretty name. Sad story." Maggie accepted a glass of fruit punch from a passing waiter. "How about the one in the hurricane?"

Visola nodded, accepting a glass of punch for herself. For a moment she thought the waiter was ignoring her, most likely due to the color of her skin, but then he smiled and offered her a drink. "Nixie. Nixie the nitwit."

Maggie laughed. "Now, now, one mustn't speak ill of the dead."

"I apologize. But she would have lived a lot longer if she hadn't been such a nitwit …"

#

Nixie watched the weather channel with interest. The storm was building strength, and it would hit soon. She probably had a day at most to pack and get out of town. Her sister was already hosting several family members who had decided to evacuate early.

Nixie had no intention of evacuating. The Lord had given her a beautiful home, and she knew He would not take it away. It was her reward for working all those hours at the food pantry.

A frantic barking called her to the back door. She opened it and two dachshunds scampered in. It was starting to rain. "Oh, this is just a warm-up," Nixie said. "The big storm will be here tomorrow."

The dogs wagged their tails and looked up at her in adoration. Nixie checked her supply of puppy treats. She was prepared for the long haul. Food, bottled water, an emergency radio.

She'd get through the storm just fine.

#

Nixie is a terrible listener. I've tried poking at her loneliness and making her want to see her sister and family, but that only makes her more stubborn. I've warned her that this hurricane will flood her neighborhood and the entire parish. So, what does she do? She buys candles. Not just utility ones either. She buys jars that are scented with the smells of the beach.

In a few days, this whole place will smell like the beach. And not in a good way.

I stretch out from Nixie and can't decide which way to go—forwards or backwards? I wish I could flip a coin. No opposable thumbs, no fingers, no body. Anyway …

Back … back this time. Through Visola, who is asleep, listening to the sound of the gentle waves as the ocean liner cruises through the frigid water. Past Ondine, who was drowned in the witch trials. Back further …

Moesha is a good listener. She converses with me. She calls me Cascade because she hears my voice in the water. Who am I to argue with that name? I think it's pretty.

My Beloved is scared, but she does not tremble. She knows her life will be short, though she thinks it will be at the hands of the man she is contracted to marry.

I could help Nixie, but she won't listen. Visola is strong, though that might be her doom. I couldn't save Ondine. I was the reason they thought she was a witch. I can't help Moesha, even though she hears me clearly. But I can comfort her.

"It will rain soon," I say. Moesha is nursing her blistered fingers. Her Aunt was not happy with the last bushel Moesha brought in, but she no longer beats her. I think she wants to make sure Moesha isn't black and blue when she is married. I guess blistered fingers aren't a problem.

"Would you like me to fetch water?" Moesha asks.

Her Aunt looks annoyed, but she says yes and shoos us away. By the time we reach the well, a gentle rain is falling. Moesha fills the bucket and returns it to the tent. Then we slip away to where no one will bother us.

"Why is he building such a large ... thing?" Moesha asks me.

"Noah? He is Beloved of The Word. He is doing what God wants him to do."

"Beloved? Like me? Does he have a friend inside him?"

I look towards the yard where Noah and his sons are hard at work. "I don't think so," I answer. I've never been close enough to see if others of my kind are there.

"What about the others?" Moesha asks.

"I don't know," I answer honestly. "Possibly."

Moesha watches them with keen interest. "Do you think they are almost finished?"

I squeeze Moesha's soul gently, then dart out and back again. I do not like to be away from her, even for a moment, but I am curious, as well. "They hurry because they know the rain will come soon," I tell Moesha.

My Beloved looks up at the clouds, drops bouncing off her cheeks. "It is raining now!"

I hold My Beloved and comfort her. I want to take the peace and contentment she feels now and give it back to her when it is time. "Yes, this little sprinkle, it is raining now. But soon ..."

#

"How did Nixie know when the storm was going to hit?" Maggie asked.

Visola concentrated, trying to remember. That was the strangest part about her past life, the box with the screen. Moving pictures and sound. It was called a 'television.' It was only one of many things about Nixie's life Visola didn't understand.

"She heard a news report," Visola said. It was the best explanation she had. Saying that the weatherman had a magic screen that showed pictures of the storm from high in the sky above the clouds made it sound like some fantasy from Jules Verne.

The television was not the strangest memory she had of her past lives. She never told Maggie about Niloufer, who lived in a cave. She never told anyone. Niloufer *was* someone out of a Jules Verne fantasy, and Visola had no explanation for the memories she had.

When Niloufer came out of her cave and looked to the horizon, she saw a bleak landscape, not a single tree or bush anywhere in sight. And in the sky, hovering on the horizon, was not the moon …

It was Earth.

#

"Niloufer, have you checked the levels in catch-basin four?" Jo called from somewhere above.

Niloufer looked out over the surface of the water. So much in one place, enough to immerse herself. Enough to immerse fifty people. "Three centimeters higher than yesterday," she shouted. "It's working!"

Thirty years they'd been mining the polar ice. Thirty years, and they'd barely provided enough to keep up with the growing demand as more and more colonists arrived to find their fortune on the moon.

"Over there!" Cascade whispered to her.

Niloufer moved around the narrow ledge. It was a natural basin, and footholds were an afterthought. She could hear it, but she couldn't see it yet. An actual drip. Multiple drips! Running water, coming from the rock above, filling the catch-basin with life-giving water.

She shone her light on the rocks where the sound was coming from. Sure enough, a drizzle of water was coming from a small fissure in the wall. She reached out to touch it, but the ledge was too narrow. She couldn't risk falling in. For a child born on the moon, there were no swimming lessons, no summers at the lake. Those were stories her parents told from their youths on Earth. Niloufer had never seen their home planet other than when she took an excursion to the surface. From their vantage point at the moon's southern pole, Earth was perpetually on the horizon, playing peek-a-boo with her since she was a baby.

"Niloufer?" Jo called again. "Are you coming up any time soon?"

"Soon!" Niloufer said, giving up trying to reach the drizzle. "Very soon."

#

"Soon?" Moesha asked, splaying her fingers, palms upwards, watching the raindrops dance on her hands.

"Soon the rains will come heavier and heavier," Cascade explained gently. "Soon, soon the waters will cover the land."

Moesha laughed. "Water covering the land? Uncle won't like that. He won't like that at all."

Cascade embraced her Beloved. She wanted to explain. She wanted to make Moesha understand, but it wouldn't make any difference.

Soon.

#

"What on God's green earth was that?" Maggie asked. It was shortly before midnight and the crowd was raucous.

"What was what?" Visola asked. She could hardly hear anything over the singing and shouting.

"I'll go find out," said one of the younger gentlemen.

Visola had almost forgotten about him when he returned a half hour later. "I don't mean to alarm you ladies, but the ship has hit an iceberg! The captain has ordered the lifeboats deployed. I'll see you safely there."

The change in the crowd was surreal. Some, in the heart of the crush, still had no idea what was going on, while others were hastily gathering their things and heading out to the deck. Maggie was at the door, people pushing past her. "Visola? We need to go."

Visola looked around her. The crowd was quickly figuring out that *something* was wrong, even if they had no idea what. Visola hurried to Maggie's side. "Should we get our things?" she asked, watching a man dragging a very large trunk towards the edge of the deck.

Maggie shook her head. "There's nothing in my cabin I can't replace. A fortune in fabrics, perhaps, but I needed to buy a new wardrobe anyway."

Visola tried to keep up, but the crush of the crowd separated her from Maggie. The last she saw was the plume of Maggie's feathered hat reach a lifeboat, and Visola gave up trying to stay close to her friend.

"No! Don't leave me! You can't!" a young woman clutching an infant was screaming at a man. A toddler was clinging to her skirts.

"You must take the children and go to a lifeboat. Now!" the man said. He gave her a swift kiss on the cheek and ran off.

"No!" the woman screeched and ran after him. The toddler fell, crying even harder. Visola scooped him up and caught up to the wailing woman, grabbing her by the skirt.

"Madam, please—" Visola started to say, but the woman collapsed in her arms. Visola held her awkwardly, trying to make sure neither the toddler nor the baby was crushed in the embrace. "Madam, we need to get to a lifeboat."

It took an eternity to get the woman to calm down enough to move. When they finally reached a lifeboat, the sailor in charge looked at them. "We can only take one more." he said.

"Take her. And the babes. She's a tiny slip of a thing, and the children weigh nothing."

The sailor tried to say something, but Visola was already handing the woman and her children into the lifeboat. With a splash, it was out of her reach. The woman looked up, clutching her babies to her. Visola hoped the woman would continue to hold them tight.

\#

Nixie huddled on the couch with the dogs. There was a thin sheet of water covering the yard, and it was still raining heavily.

Someone pounded on the door. "Anyone in there? We need to evacuate immediately."

The dogs gave her away, howling and scampering off to bark through the picture window while standing on the back of the couch. Nixie opened the door before the men decided to break it down. "Thank you for your concern, but we're just fine where we are. It's safer inside. You two just move on and find someone who needs your help. The Good Lord is watching over me."

She closed the door, but the man just banged again, even louder. "Ma'am, you can't stay here. It's not safe."

Nixie missed the rest of what he was saying. She scooped up the dogs and turned off the television, then headed upstairs. Maybe this storm was going to be worse than she thought, but that didn't change anything. The Lord had blessed her with a beautiful home, and she was going to stay.

#

Moesha runs through the rain. "Is this it?" she asks. "Is this the rain that will cover the world?"

"Yes," I tell her. I am sad, but Moesha is not. This is her wedding day, but there will be no wedding. The rain is coming down so hard that even the livestock has been brought inside. Moesha is the only living being in sight.

"Do you think they'll fight? All those animals?" she asks me. I know she is talking about the ark. We watched all the animals climb on board, seemingly more than such a vessel could possibly hold, but that is the way of The Word.

"No. They do not fight," I say. Moesha's feet are covered now. She splashes as if it was a puddle, but the water covers the ground.

I wonder if we should go higher, perhaps find some rock to cling to. But it will not make a difference. It is more important that Moesha remain at peace.

#

"Calm down, babies, calm down. Everything will be all right." Nixie looked at the water, halfway up the stairs. "Here, have another treat."

The dogs refused to eat. They huddled on the bed, shivering with cold, barking whenever there was a strange noise.

Open the window, said that strange voice in her head. Sometimes the voice was helpful. Other times, like the present, it was not.

The dogs ran to the window and barked excitedly. It was a French window that opened onto a tiny porch, one of her favorite features about the house. A light was shining up.

Nixie peered through the glass, but she couldn't see anything. It was dark, and the rain was still coming down heavily. She hadn't had electricity for hours, though she had every flashlight and lantern she owned turned on in the bedroom.

Open the window! said the voice more insistently.

"Fine," Nixie grumbled, opening the latch and bracing herself as the wind blew both sides wide open. A light shone directly in her eyes.

"Ma'am! Are you all right? Is anyone else there with you?" said a voice from below.

JUMP! said the voice inside her.

Both dogs jumped. "Baby! Princess! No!" Nixie wailed, hearing splashes from below.

The light left her eyes and shone on the water. Her babies were paddling frantically. "Don't worry, we've got them," said the man in the boat.

"Are they all right?" Nixie shouted.

"They're both scared stiff, but they're fine. Can you climb down? Is there another window closer to the water where you can climb out?"

Nixie looked down at her nightgown. She certainly wasn't dressed to go anywhere. "Just a minute," she said. She found the box of doggie treats, then saw the birthday card her sister had sent her. The envelope had her sister's address. She put the envelope in the box and hurried back to the window. "Here, they'll need these," Nixie said, tossing the box down to the boat. "My sister's address is inside. Just send the puppies there. I'll go pick them up when this is all over."

"Ma'am! You need to evacuate …"

Nixie couldn't hear any more. She closed the window and climbed back into bed. It was lonely without the dogs, but they would be better off waiting out the storm at her sister's house up north.

#

Visola jumped into the water. She had checked both sides of the ship twice. There were no more lifeboats. She had stopped to help a young boy who was separated from his parents, finally loading him into a lifeboat and promising she would go find them. After a half hour, she decided it was a promise she could not keep. There was too much chaos.

She could see lifeboats with dim lights not far from the ship. Most of them were inexplicably half empty. The water was calm, and she was a strong swimmer. Growing up in Port-au-Prince, she practically lived in the water.

The waters of Port-au-Prince were warm and inviting. The icy ocean hit her like a sledgehammer, and Visola gasped as she reached the surface. Every nerve in her body cried out in pain, begging her to get out of the frigid water. She forced herself to move, but all she could manage was a weak doggie paddle. There were blurry lights ahead, and she tried to reach them.

A terrible noise rent the night and Visola turned to see the Titanic ship, one end raised far out of the water, the other immersed in the waves. Slowly, the uppermost section peeled away, the ship split in two, and the upper section fell with a crash into the water. Visola felt herself being sucked under, and she didn't have the strength to fight it.

She opened her eyes and saw Ondine before her, arms and legs bound. She closed her eyes, opened her mouth, and let out her last gasp of air.

#

Niloufer climbed down the ladder to the ledge again. This time, it was covered in water. "Jo!" she called up. "It's already over the ledge!"

She wondered if she should just turn around and go back up. She felt guilty for putting her feet in the water, but she did need to find out, well, she needed to see the drip for herself. She needed to know if it was more than a trickle. It sounded like more than a trickle.

Niloufer carefully waded along the ledge. She shone her light ahead. There it was! A tiny waterfall, perfect and beautiful, cascading over the rocks and into the catch-basin. She laughed. "It's filling, Jo! Steady and perfect. We did it!"

Niloufer's feet went out from under her. She dropped her light, and it sank beneath the surface, illuminating the already substantial depth. She sputtered and tried to tread water. She couldn't find the ledge. It was dark, and the only light was the glow from below. She tried to shout for help but only succeeded in getting a mouthful of water.

Panic set in. Then, a moment later, peace.

#

Moesha is asleep now. She found a thick mattress of woven reeds. It floats, even with her on it. But it is cold, and this is the kind of sleep from which she will never wake. She is with me now.

Ondine's limbs are bound. She does not thrash. She accepts her fate, opening her lungs to the water and giving her life to the lake. I hold her hand and we walk towards the light together.

Visola joins us. Her body is in the darkness now. Moesha takes her by the hand, smiling at her.

Nixie thrashes. She is cold, even though she is in her warm bed. But her blankets no longer comfort her. They bind her.

Ondine takes Nixie by the hand. She stops thrashing at last. She is confused.

I feel the million Beloveds within me as I am within them. We are all swimming, we are all floating, we are all immersed in the waters of life. Some are being born. Some are being baptized. Others are at the end of their lives. They are about to go where I cannot.

I reach for Niloufer. She has no idea what to do. Never has she seen enough water to immerse her entire body. The thing that will give life to her community is the very thing that is killing her.

I touch Niloufer. I comfort her.

"NO!"

It is Visola. She has turned from the light, letting go of Moesha's hand. Moesha turns, as well, watching.

"No!" Visola says, calling to Niloufer. "You may not be able to swim, but you can float!"

Niloufer stares at Visola, not understanding.

"Like this!" Moesha says. She shows Niloufer her body, lungs full, arms spread wide, bobbing on the surface.

Niloufer looks up. The next time her face breaks the surface she gasps for air and struggles to take in as much breath as she can. She turns, chest up, arms wide, forcing her head to stay back even though instinct is telling her to curl into a ball.

"No!" Visola says again. "Stay flat. They will find you."

#

Niloufer stared at the vision, but as soon as she managed to break the surface again, she forced herself to turn onto her back, thinking of her chest as a balloon that would keep the rest of her body afloat.

"Niloufer! Where are you?" Jo called.

Niloufer coughed. Her body buckled, and she began to sink beneath the surface again. She forced herself to calm down, arching her back and floating like the girl had shown her.

A light shone in her eyes. "Oh my god, she fell in! Beck, get me a rope!"

"I can swim," came a masculine voice. Beck, she presumed. Low on the totem pole in the company, but fresh from college on Earth.

"Niloufer, listen to me carefully. If you panic and grab me, we may both go under. I'm going to come out to you and tow you back to the edge. You don't need to answer me. Just trust me."

Pretend you're a boat! Cascade told her. Niloufer felt Beck's arm around her neck, and she tentatively placed her hands on his hand.

"It's all right. I've got you. Almost there."

Once she was safely out of the catch-basin, all Niloufer could think of was what a waste it was that so much water was drenching her clothes. She felt so stupid. Beck and Jo took her straight to the medical ward, where the doctor proclaimed her hale and hearty but told her to go home and get some rest.

A week later, Niloufer climbed into the tiny boat with Beck, both wearing inflatable vests. The water level was down again, as it was now being piped up to be filtered and used by the colonists.

"Where is it?" Beck asked.

Over there!

"Over there," Niloufer pointed.

Beck guided the boat over to where she had seen the trickle before. It was now a steady stream. Beck used a probe to insert a light into the waterfall.

"Does it look like that on Earth?" Niloufer asked.

"Sort of," Beck answered. "On Earth, there would be lots of plants growing around the water."

Now over there!

"Let's check over there next," Niloufer said, pointing farther along the rock wall.

Sure enough, there was another tiny waterfall feeding into the catch-basin. Beck inserted another light, and they continued around, finding a dozen sources that were producing water.

Now ... over there ... farther ... and up ...

"Let's look over there," Niloufer said.

"There? Back in the corner? I don't hear any running water from that direction."

Niloufer didn't hear it either, but she trusted Cascade.

Here!

Niloufer shone her light on the rock. It was wet, seeping, but not running.

"Well, miracles do happen," Beck said.

Niloufer shone her light in the same place he was. "What?" she asked.

"Look closely."

Somewhere high above, a hatch opened and closed, briefly illuminating the rock face just above them. There, clinging to the rocks, was a tiny vine. It was no more than a thread, but it was definitely organic, and definitely growing.

Life finds a way.

"Life finds a way, " Niloufer said, staring at the little miracle.

Beck nodded. "Indeed, it does."

REMNANTS OF THE FLOOD

Gustavo Bondoni

The villagers looked at each other and smiled. The presence of foreigners, especially English-speaking foreigners, seemed to increase their determination to show everyone that they found nothing remarkable about the shaking. Their village had been trembling since before they were born and was no worse for wear, after all. Their grandfather's grandmothers had lived there forever.

But Bridget's team exchanged nervous glances. The shaking floor could easily have been explained by relatively mild or somewhat distant seismic activity, but it had been going on for days, and not a single seismograph anywhere else registered the movement. No, there was some kind of local event, and she just hoped it wasn't some nearby volcano about to let off a poisonous cloud or something.

"Bloody annoying, isn't it?" Peters remarked. It was obvious to everyone at the table that, like the villagers, he was also putting on a show, attempting to keep his tough guy image alive within the group. But he was as much a scientist as the rest, and he knew that villages didn't just shake for no reason.

Bridget looked around the table at the three men with her. Peters, his salt-and-pepper hair not quite as long as his beard, was the eldest by quite a margin, while Greg and Johnnie both looked too young to be doctoral candidates. Greg, the team's computer expert, was an overweight, red-headed Californian whose skin was so white that any exposure to the sun would probably kill him. Johnnie, on the other hand, was the perfect contrast: a black man from Brighton who was probably the fittest person she'd seen in years. He was perfect for any kind of fieldwork, with a mind as sharp as his body. But they were both too young.

She smiled at herself. At thirty-five, she wasn't even that old. So, when had she become the old fossil? Peters, of course, was older than she was, but his actual age seemed to be a state secret. He looked more like a mercenary veteran of some African bush war than a marine biologist from Sussex, and his eyes supported the impression.

"I hate it," Bridget said. If the men were going to insist on being macho, she was damned if she would play along. "Who ever heard of a village that shakes all the time?"

Johnnie laughed. "Who knows? Maybe the shaking village will be the biggest discovery of the trip. Don't you think it's strange that no one has studied it yet?"

"Oh, they probably studied it and studied it, but you'd have to dig through all those boxes to learn what they found," Peters observed flatly.

The boxes. That had been the most shocking find so far. The smiling guide at the National Archaeological Museum had shown them the warehouse with pride. "We've managed to preserve all the old files from the communist era. We've got people trying to get them typed into word processors and get them onto a database." It had turned out that "people" meant the guide herself and that, at the current rate, the job would take several decades. The woman just smiled and explained that that was a temporary situation, and that new funding wouldn't take long to arrive.

"Huh. We're probably repeating research they've done already." Greg said.

"Not bloody likely. Even the Russians only learned about the Black Sea flood after the wall came down. The Bulgarians probably learned about it in '96, just like everyone else."

"I bet they were happy," Greg replied. "Learning about it from Americans, of all things."

"I know some people at Oxford who weren't happy about it, either," the older man replied.

"Well, at least they're helping us now," Bridget interjected. "So, stop complaining."

Peters grunted. He liked to complain. "So, what do we do under the new conditions?"

She wasn't sure whether he was referring to the fact that the village seemed to shake like a rattle every half hour or so or whether he was complaining about something else. She decided to worry about it later. "We dive tomorrow, right on schedule. With any luck, we can find some evidence before it all gets shaken to bits."

#

There's a reason Bulgaria was never considered a prime holiday location. The rocky beach was home to just a few desultory bathers, and it was a wonder they were there at all, considering the fact that they shared the black stones with a wealth of plastic soft drink bottles, and especially since the day had dawned windy and a bit chilly for early June.

Their shaking little fishing village was about twenty miles north of Varna, its position marked not by a name on a map but by a kilometer marker. Presumably, it had a name once, but forty years of communism had erased it, and no one in the twenty years since had bothered to remedy the oversight. Not exactly the way to get hordes of middle-class Germans to patronize the seashore.

That same lack of people was precisely what had attracted Bridget's team. The beach and gently sloping seafloor beside the vibrating town was the perfect spot to search for clues of an ancient catastrophe, and they'd already uncovered plenty of evidence to support their theory. In fact, that day's objective was to ascertain whether a formation they'd found the day before actually was what it looked like.

They'd dived ten minutes before, carefully descending to the fifteen-meter depth, their beams illuminating the sediment floating in the murky water. "Not exactly the Red Sea, is it?" Peters remarked.

"Shut up and concentrate. We have sixty minutes of safe immersion left; let's use it for something more useful than discussing diving preferences," Bridget replied. She was unhappy enough that they were diving in a threesome instead of in two pairs, but the money just hadn't been there, and they needed Greg and his laptop up above, making sense of the sonar data. At least they'd accepted her extremely conservative time estimate without argument, and they'd submitted to training with intercom-equipped full face mask units with more enthusiasm than she'd expected. They understood when she told them that the university just hated losing researchers.

As if on cue, an American twang filled her head. She had the volume on the receiver turned up, but she would have to live with it. "You're right above the formation."

They dropped on her signal, sinking further into the soup-like water, until their light illuminated the bottom. Two beams found nothing but silt and sludge, but a third landed on a smallish, jagged shape. "To the northeast, now," Greg's voice told them. "You've drifted a bit."

They followed, and soon arrived. A small, regular pile of stones stood in front of them, the kind you'd find between old fields in any agricultural area in Europe. In any other setting, any group of scientists who weren't dedicated to the study of lichen would have passed by without a second glance. But here—

Silence reigned. Even Peters, always ready with a snide comment or a rude word, simply stared at the stones. Johnnie swam up to the wall and placed a hand on the nearest edge, as if it were some kind of religious carving. "Do you realize what this means?" he whispered into his mike.

"Yeah," Peters replied, "It means we can add another mystery to our list. I can see the base of that wall, which means it's about four feet high. If it's really seven thousand years old, it should be completely buried in silt."

"What's going on down there?" Greg's voice came in from above. "What can you see?" They ignored him and thought about what Peters had said.

"Who cares?" Johnnie asked. "What difference does it make?"

"Well, I've got these perfectly good explosives."

A burst of bubbles floated up as Johnnie laughed at the joke, but Bridget wasn't inclined towards mirth. Peters would be unhappy that the explosives went to waste.

Suddenly, a tremor went through the water, causing clumps of sediment to fall off the wall and causing the rocks that composed it to clack together. It went on for fifteen seconds, stopping just before Bridget ordered the abortion of the dive.

"And that's our answer," Johnnie chirped.

"That's one answer, anyway. Still a few to find," Peters said. Bridget wondered how he could manage to sound dour through the tinny intercom.

They swam around the site, noting a small pile here, another there. One section formed a hollow square that looked like the foundations of a house.

"Guys, you need to see this." Johnnie sounded excited and very, very young.

They swam over and were confronted with what looked like a giant slab of stone, held in place by other stones wedged under it. The eroded edges seemed to indicate great age, but whatever rock it was made of had survived millennia with its gleaming white tone unscathed.

Another miniature tremor shook the water around them. Bridget thought they felt much more pleasant in the sea than on land, gentler somehow. This one went on for a few minutes, but she decided it wasn't any risk. How important could it be if the villagers were so unconcerned? But Peters was studying the ripples caused by the vibration. "I think this is the epicenter," he said after a while.

"How could you possibly know?"

"See how the waves in the silt on the sea floor here are clearly facing away from it? Now come over here and look at these. Also looking away. You'll find the same no matter where you go. This is the center of the tremors."

For some reason, that unsettled Bridget. They still had a good ten minutes left before they had to start their ascent, but she decided to cut it short. "We're going up, now. I want to discuss this with the whole team."

Greg's voice came through again, "What did you guys find?" But they ignored him again. He could look at the footage later.

"Peters, are you coming?"

"Just a minute. I'm having a last look."

It was more than a minute, but he eventually rose to their level, and they made their way back to the waiting ship. They climbed aboard and peeled off what they could and set sail towards the shore.

Ten minutes later, a small geyser shot out of the water behind them. Bridget turned to Peters.

"You didn't!"

His shrug was answer enough.

#

She'd ordered the captain to stop right there. They would have it out on the boat where the arrogant, pompous bastard wouldn't be able to go off to another room and ignore her.

"How could you do such a thing? We had solid proof of the Black Sea

Deluge, probably the source of all the flood myths, from the Akkadian ones all the way to the Bible. We had the evidence we needed to lay to answer the oldest question in civilization and you blew it up? Are you a complete imbecile?"

"I set the charge so it wouldn't damage the walls. Don't worry."

"Then why—"

"I want to know what was under that slab. It just looked like some kind of lid to me. Maybe ancient gold, treasure, idols. Who knows? We can have a look tomorrow, and maybe we'll come out of this rich men and women."

"You aren't coming back tomorrow," Bridget said. "You're off the team."

Peters opened his mouth to respond, but whatever he said was drowned out by a roar that made the prior geyser sound like a stone thrown into a pond. An upwelling of water towered above their heads, splashing down onto the surface of the sea moments later. Huge waves sped towards their small ship.

The captain cursed and tried to point the nose of the craft into the oncoming wall of water, but they were pushed in reverse like a backward surfer for what seemed like an eternity. Some miracle kept the boat afloat and upright, but Bridget saw the second story of a house fly past to their right, followed by the top of a vendor's cart. Then she heard a crunch and was thrown backward into something unyielding.

Darkness.

#

"Are you all right? Bridget, can you hear me?" She opened her eyes to see Greg's face, paler than usual, only inches from her own. Not exactly the kind of thing a girl wanted to see first thing in the morning. She wondered how drunk she'd been the night before to allow this to happen.

And then her memory returned. "Oh, my God. What happened?" she asked.

"I think you need to see this." Greg held out his arm, and after a moment's hesitation as she allowed the world to stop spinning, Bridget took it. She could hear unidentified crashes and booms off in the background somewhere. As far as she could tell, she'd been lying on the deck of the boat. "Over there," he said.

She felt her mouth fall agape. Towering over the village's collection of one- and two-story buildings, a huge … thing … approached from the sea. The head looked feline, somehow, and scribed as if it were composed of tiny lines. The rest of the body looked human—or at least humanoid—but thicker and built to withstand the weight of a mound of flesh five floors high. It was covered with thick black bristles, but not thoroughly. Many morning papers would be running edited versions of the picture, since full frontal nudity on that scale would shock readers in quite a few nations.

"What is it?" she breathed.

Greg shrugged and looked down, a sign that he was going to show off. "I think it's Humbaba," he said.

Bridget was about to ask what a Humbaba was when her years of archaeology background silenced the question. She knew exactly who and what it was. "Humbaba is a myth, Greg. And how would you know what it was? I thought you were into computers, not ancient legends." Peters had probably told him, she thought.

He looked down again, shrugged. "Google-fu," he replied, showing her a search engine result on some kind of handheld device with an image of an ancient statue that, to be fair, looked a lot like the monster on a rampage in front of them.

She rolled her eyes. He would, when faced with a shipwreck, save his electronics and look stuff up before coming to her aid. "Where are Peters and Johnnie?"

"They went to see if they could be of any help. It was quite a wave, after all. Lots of dead Bulgarians."

Since the monster seemed otherwise preoccupied, she took a second to observe their surroundings. The fishing boat had wedged between two houses, and the impact had caused quite a bit of splintering along the wooden hull. She doubted it would ever be seaworthy again even if they ever got it out of the place it had jammed. "How do we get down?"

He led her to the prow which, due to the angle of the street was nearly level with the cobbles, and they climbed off. The stones were still wet, and an abandoned fish or two attempted to breathe with little success. The monster, though moving slowly, had reached the shoreline. Bridget could see that the writers of the old epic had gotten it precisely right: it did have the face of a lion, and its breath was, quite obviously, of flame. When it came to giant monsters, those ancient Sumerians clearly knew their stuff.

The monster had been silent, but now it was bellowing, sending a gout of flame out with each scream.

"Illameeeeees!" it shouted. "Illameeeeees!"

It was a wall of sound, painful to hear, and almost impossible to decipher. "What's it saying?" Greg's shouted question, after that aural assault, seemed like a whisper from across a meadow.

How could she know? Even if she spoke whatever language the creature was shouting in— ancient Akkadian?—how could he possibly expect her to make out words in that noise?

"Illameeeeees!"

She covered her ears, but the sound went straight through her hands. If not for the fact that it was five blocks away, she would have been deafened.

Suddenly, she knew what the monster was shouting.

"It's looking for Gilgamesh," she cried, despite the pain.

"What?" Greg was holding his head between his hands, obviously trying to block out the sound.

"Gilgamesh!"

"Yes, that's where the legend comes from," he replied.

"No, that's what the creature is shouting. Humbaba is looking for Gilgamesh." The ambient noise made it difficult to get the idea across, but eventually they managed to understand each other.

The knowledge didn't galvanize them into action. They might have been the only two people in the village who knew what was going on, but that didn't change the fact that they were just tiny humans, no match for a creature somehow returned from the age of legend. They watched helplessly as it walked through the village, reducing houses hundreds of years old to rubble in seconds.

All Bridget felt during the horror was thankfulness that the creature had chosen a path that would avoid them entirely, and thankfulness that the noise, which would have been incapacitating at that distance, were being sent in a different direction. The survival instinct warred with the voyeuristic: they hid, but they watched.

The culmination of Humbaba's rage occurred at the village church, an ancient stone structure on a hill slightly beyond the houses. The monster walked up to it, absently knocked over the slender steeple tower and attacked the roof.

"Illameeeeees!"

It shouted into the hole it had made in the slate tiles, and they later learned that the sound had killed half of the thirty people huddled inside and deafened the remainder. It seemed that ancient gods still had priority over newer ones.

Finally, Humbaba got its rage under control for a few moments. It stood, sniffed the wind, took its bearings, and headed off towards the southeast. Neither Greg nor Bridget moved until it was well out of sight. Then, Greg collapsed onto the floor and cried like a baby.

#

The next two days were unsettled.

Most of their luggage had been washed away by the wave, along with the proprietors of the small hotel in which they'd been staying. Other than Greg's handheld, their electronics were shot, and what clothes remained had to be washed in fresh water to remove the salt. Or at least that was what they thought before learning that the water, too, was out. Cell phone service was the only thing still working, but the Bulgarian government saw to that extremely quickly. A full shut-down of the area occurred while they investigated.

Bridget's team seemed to be the only group of people who'd come through relatively unscathed, apart from a nasty gash on Johnnie's forehead, which could have done with better medical attention than the amateur bandage applied by Peters. None was available.

The Bulgarian army arrived within hours of the catastrophe, and the group, as suspicious foreign scientists, were immediately detained. Everyone was polite and solicitous, but there was no question of their leaving, which made Peters furious. He'd wanted to take any of the cars lying around untended and leave the area before the authorities arrived. It seemed he had experience with unfortunate circumstances, something Bridget didn't remember seeing on his otherwise brilliant scientific résumé.

Essentially, they were punted into a room and told to avoid making a nuisance of themselves while the government decided what to do with them. A few hours later, some scared-looking soldiers, too young for the assault rifles they carried, installed a TV and switched it on. It showed three channels, two in Bulgarian and one in Russian. The Russian channel seemed to consist of a twenty-four-hour cycle of game shows and celebrity interviews, with some Big Brother thrown in to spice things up.

The Bulgarian channels were both locked into a twenty-four-hour news cycle. They seemed to be filming the monster as it walked across miles of farmland. The running commentary sounded tired, but the scientists watched the feed with interest.

"Where do you think it's going?" Greg asked.

"Bloody Lebanon, of course." Peters' reply just beat Bridget's, which made her angry. Angrier still that the man was right and had his Gilgamesh theory fresher than hers.

"Why?" This time, Johnnie chimed up, and she was happy to see him talking. He'd always been a bit shy, but after the incident he'd been nearly silent.

This time, she beat Peters to the punch. "Lebanon is where his ancient forest is thought to have been. That's where Utu, the god of the Sun in Mesopotamia set him to guard the trees. And that's where Gilgamesh is supposed to have betrayed him and killed him."

"Seems he didn't do much of a job of it, did he?" Peters observed dourly.

"Well, someone trapped him for thousands of years. Maybe Gilgamesh did kill him, and they buried him there but he revived."

"I doubt it. If the monster had been dead, why create that impenetrable lid for his tomb?" He paused. "And why flood hundreds of thousands of square kilometers of perfectly good farmland to keep him down there?"

Bridget was shocked. "You think ... You think people caused the Black Sea deluge, the biblical flood? That's impossible."

"Yes, just like building the pyramids was impossible." He looked her in the eye. "Maybe aliens did it."

"But ..." He was right. Even primitive people had basic tools. Even a thousand years ago, people could dig large holes in the ground. It would have taken years, but the passage to the Mediterranean could have been enlarged and deepened by the ancients. It would have been a question of keeping the slaves in line and not minding a death or two.

The day dragged by as the monster did nothing but walk.

#

A colonel in the Bulgarian army came around the next day. He told them that the British Embassy would be sending someone round to pick them up, but that the government still wanted their help with the inquest, so they would look at it as a boon if they stayed in Bulgaria for a while.

Peters straightened and gave the military man a hard look. "Why are you letting us go?"

"You are citizens of the European Union," he replied. "You are free to come and go as you choose."

"I'm not," Greg said.

"You are American," the colonel replied. Greg looked puzzled at this, but the Europeans knew exactly what he meant: it was easier to release the guy than to deal with the prissy letters of protest.

Peters was unconvinced. "What's the real reason?"

The colonel hesitated but then smiled and nodded his respect. "It's no secret. In an hour or two, the creature is scheduled to cross the border, at which time this is no longer a Bulgarian problem. Let the Turks deal with it." He turned and left.

The Turks tried to deal with it. They had a tank division—Peters informed them as to what a division was—waiting at the border, along with air support. As soon as Humbaba set foot in their territory, tearing down a large, sturdy border fence as he did, they opened fire.

The ancient creature ignored them, except for one tank that it picked up like a toy and tossed into the distance. It swatted absently at the fighters, but none flew near enough to grab.

"Oh, my God," Peters said. His normally inexpressive face had turned ashen.

"What now?" Johnnie asked.

"Now we find out if the Turks have nukes," the older man replied.

"What? Why?" Bridget heard herself ask. Heard herself shriek was more like it.

"Think about it. The only way to cross the water onto Asia is—"

"Through Istanbul!" Greg crowed triumphantly, like a small child able to follow the logic of its elders. And then his face fell. "Oh."

"Precisely. Can you imagine the damage that thing would do to a city of millions? Just its screams would cause a humanitarian catastrophe worse than the Southeast Asian Tsunami. The Turks must stop it if they can, any way they can. They don't have a choice."

They didn't get to see what the Turks tried next because the man from the British embassy herded them into two Land Rovers with the letters UN stenciled onto the sides.

Three hours later, they were in Sofia, all of them denying any knowledge of where the creature might have come from other than to say that they'd seen it rise about a mile offshore. The ruins would be there for anyone who bothered to look, and they saw no need to become accessories to whatever happened next.

All mention of explosives was suspended until later that evening. The group was watching TV— CNN had live coverage of what they were predictably calling The Creature from the Black Sea —and were all relieved that the Turks had decided to forego the nuclear option and were evacuating Istanbul instead.

"You knew, didn't you?" Bridget asked Peters, point blank.

He looked surprised but nodded. Then he put his finger to his lips, pointed to random places on the walls and pantomimed unseen listeners with headphones. Bridget wondered again who he really was. All the man said was, "I think every archaeologist in the world suspected that there was a tomb lost in the Black Sea somewhere. Most of them thought it was a temple, more symbol than reality. I guess this just proves them wrong."

She wanted to remind him that he'd signed up as a marine biologist, not an archaeologist, but stayed silent. He would probably shut up like a clam if she made an issue of that. "So how do we stop it?"

"Why would we want to stop him? Humbaba will just go into Lebanon and let the trees grow. That's what he does. Although it will probably do the terrorists a bit of no good, which they deserve, too. Why would we want to stop it?"

Because I feel responsible, Bridget thought. *I was the one who funded your little expedition. It's my fault that thing is out there, killing people with its screams. The old woman who ran the hotel, the people in that church*. She said, "I just think that, since we were there at the beginning, we should try to help it end," she said. Peters' grey eyes looked into hers. He swore. He knew what was being left unsaid.

"I suppose we'd need Gilgamesh."

Bridget tsked in irritation. "Gilgamesh is a myth. Please take this seriously."

Peters just looked at her, and she felt silly. "But Gilgamesh is dead," she amended lamely.

"Are you using the same source material that told us that Humbaba was dead?" She didn't reply. "Good, then we can assume that if Humbaba is still up and running, then the guy who bested him—even if he didn't slay him, but lured him into a pit and then covered him with a very large rock held in place by tons of water pressure—is still out there somewhere?"

"I guess. So where is he?"

He gave her another steely gaze, and Greg and Johnnie, silent witnesses, were completely forgotten. "Do you really want to do this? By all accounts, Gilgamesh is a pretty nasty guy. I'm half convinced that Humbaba is still mad at humanity because our little human hero betrayed him in the first place."

She hesitated. Some things were so enormous that you had to stop to think about it. But some guilt was so heavy that it gave you no choice. "Yes, this has to end. Where is he?"

"Well," Peters began, "You need to understand that this theory has been dismissed, ridiculed even, by all respectable archaeologists ..."

She listened, spellbound, knowing her orderly scientific life was something lost in the past. Or overtaken by the past. Or something.

But it was definitely gone.

SURVEYING SAVIORS

H.L. Pauff

"We are within range," Kutyl said. "It is appearing on the viewing monitors now."

Kritef and Kutyl watched as the planet came into focus on the monitor. A shroud of dark satellites swirled over the planet, obscuring its true nature. "I have never seen a global weather system quite like this. The instruments indicate that there is an incredible amount of precipitation," Kritef said. He tried a few different settings on his panel, hoping his instruments could pierce the clouds so that they could see the surface, but a combination of the clouds' thickness and interference from severe lightning storms were stopping him. "Have you ever seen such a thing?"

"I have not personally seen a phenomenon like this," Kutyl said. "However, I have read files in the archives that described similar events. The surveyors that came across them were unable to provide a sufficient explanation. It defies science."

"I suppose, then, that this planet warrants further exploration? How much time shall we allocate to this planet? Remember, there are a few moons in this system orbiting their gaseous giants that might be of interest. I am anxious to investigate all of them."

Kutyl surveyed his instruments, looking for any blips on the planet's surface. "Let us descend and make a quick sweep. If there is nothing of interest other than the weather, then we shall hurry to explore the rest of the system before we are due back." Kutyl took control of their craft from the artificial intelligence and gently brought the ship into the atmosphere. Huge raindrops pelted their viewing screens and heavy winds rocked them. Streaks of jagged red lightning lit up the sky.

Inside the atmosphere, their instruments were able to scan the planet looking for anything of note. They calibrated specifically for rare minerals and other resources, but they also detected anomalous-like life forms.

"I see nothing but liquid. No apparent landmasses," Kutyl said, studying the viewing screens. "Sensors indicate that this planet's atmosphere is comprised of a mixture that you and I would find agreeable, if we desired to step out of our ship."

Kritef looked at the endless stretch of water and the dark clouds with their heavy rains that continued to feed it. "I think it prudent that we remain inside. I do not understand how it could be raining everywhere simultaneously. Truly bizarre. Is there anything else of note here?" Kritef asked.

Kutyl checked the results of the ship's scanning instruments. "Yes. I detect lots of debris in the water. An incredible amount, really. I suspect that these rains and apparent global flood have destroyed some form of civilization. Also, we are picking up some small landmasses that are still above water. Let us investigate.

Kutyl directed the ship towards a tiny chain of islands that looked ready to succumb to the heavy rains at any moment.

"There are individuals down there," Kutyl said. "Huddled around fires, wearing clothing and working with tools."

Kritef sat up, his interest piqued. "Intelligence? Let us bring them aboard."

"I do not believe that to be wise," Kutyl said. "The objective of our expedition is to survey, not to interfere."

"Correct, but are we not also held to a code of ethics? If these beings are truly intelligent, is it not our duty to aid them in their greatest time of need? Look at the state of this world. Water has overrun everything, and it continues to rain. They will not survive long."

Kutyl scrunched his face at his partner. "Should we not let things proceed naturally? Perhaps this world is like this because of their own design? We have seen plenty of evidence that most civilizations are not viable long-term."

"Nonsense. Let us bring them aboard and meet them personally. Look at them. They scarcely have even the most rudimentary of tools. This is not their fault. It could not be. These are just beings that wish to live and prosper, like all beings."

Kutyl relented and allowed Kritef to bring the beings aboard the ship. The beings screamed as their pink fleshy limbs flailed, and they floated through the air into the belly of the silver craft hovering in the air. The surveyors visited a few more island chains spread out across the planet and found even more survivors they promptly brought on board.

When their holding chamber was near max capacity, the two surveyors came down to the chamber and looked upon their guests through a one-way window.

"They look tired yet so full of life," Kritef said.

Kutyl rolled his eyes. "I can smell them even through these thick walls."

Kritef chuckled and clasped his friend's shoulder. "Just think. These are beings that have survived the most calamitous of events that have drowned their world. They are hardy and strong, the best their species has to offer. Wherever we settle them, I know they will go on to great things. Perhaps, if time permits, we can return for more of them."

The beings wandered around the chamber screaming, punching, and kicking at the walls. The surveyors had to wait until their computers could acclimate to their language and allow the two different species to communicate.

"Greetings," Kritef said through an intercom. The action in the chamber stopped and all the beings looked to the ceiling. They cowered in fear from the deep, disembodied voice of Kritef.

"Do not be afraid," he told them. "We are visitors from another world." With the pressing of a button, the window became translucent, and the two species could see each other. The two surveyors could hear the gasps from the pink fleshy beings. "We see your world at the end of its life, and we are here to help. There may be no future for your drowned world, but there will be a future for you and as many more of your species as we can rescue. We will find you a new world where you can prosper. In the meantime, you are our guests for the foreseeable future. You will eat our food and drink our drinks and make our ship your new home. A number of automatons roam the side of the ship you are on and will help you where they can. Do not be afraid of them."

A few doors in the chamber opened and the beings immediately ran to them. The doors lead to other parts of the ship: the dining areas, the bathing areas, and the recreation areas. The beings would not be able to access the part of the ship where Kritef and Kutyl resided, but they would have everything they needed.

"They are not so bad. Would you concede that?" Kritef asked his partner.

"They appear harmless enough," Kutyl said.

The surveyors finished their review of the water world and found many civilizations had been buried beneath the flood. An untold number of this world's inhabitants had perished in this great event and the two surveyors felt a sense of pride that they were able to save some of them.

It only took the journey to the system's fifth planet for the beings to become comfortable in the ship. They began to explore, allowing themselves to sample the food and drink. When enough of them had tried and were convinced that it was not poisoned, a celebration broke out.

They cheered their redemption from certain doom and sang songs about a glorious new era to come. The celebration continued throughout Kritef's and Kutyl's sleep cycles and well into the next day until one by one the beings collapsed from exhaustion.

"They sure know how to celebrate," Kutyl said. "My sleep cycle was insufficient. I hope this does not continue."

"They have been delivered from their deaths. I believe their celebrating is appropriate."

Kutyl and Kritef surveyed the gas giant and its many moons looking for anything of significance. There were several interesting geological formations and some evidence that the moons could one day support conditions that could harbor life, but none of it was as interesting as the beings that roamed the ship.

One of their kind rose from its slumber and awakened the others. A few of the beings took the food and stored it in sealed buckets in some of the warmer rooms in the hope that it would ferment and produce a special type of drink that they all craved. The men ran rampant, destroying crucial parts of the ship and leaving their bodily waste wherever they chose. There were arguments over food and arguments over who would be allowed to copulate with the females of their species. Fights began to break out across the ship over the smallest of things, including misunderstandings and accidental bumps. The automatons attempted to get the situation under control, but they were overpowered, destroyed, and in some cases subjected to copulation.

Even the women, who the two surveyors believe to be the more sophisticated of the species, wreaked havoc. They ran gambling operations and recruited men to fight for their entertainment. By the time Kutyl's and Kritef's sleep cycles neared, the ship was almost in ruins.

"They are uncivilized monsters," Kutyl said. "We must return them to their planet of origin. Their world was drowned because of the very evidence we see with our own eyes. Surely, they have brought upon their own doom."

Kritef watched the viewing monitors with disgust but did not agree. "We do not know their customs. This could very well be a part of a ritual of celebration. It could be many cycles before they are finished celebrating and can continue with their lives. Perhaps whatever deities they worship demand this of them. Would you be so cruel as to return them to their deaths? Where is your patience?"

Kutyl sat back in his chair and grunted. "If we exhibit any more patience, we might not have a ship at all."

By the time they reached the last planet in the system, even Kritef could not believe what he was witnessing. "Surely, they have no more cause to celebrate?" The beings had destroyed most of their section of the ship. They tore down walls and rolled in their own excrement, refusing to make use of the widely available cleansing apparatuses.

A clear division of factions began to emerge with the physically strongest banding together to terrorize the weak. Even with ample resources of food and water available for them, the factions began to fight unnecessarily over the resources, and it did not take long for blood to mar the hallways.

"Why do they simply not share and enjoy? Why must they fight and kill and take from each other? I do not understand this behavior," Kutyl said. "There are so few of them, one would think they would band together to persevere. If we present these beings as the triumph of our expeditions to the Galactic Council or even to our own superiors, we will be stripped of our ranks and titles."

"I will address them," Kritef said. He stood and took a step towards the door that would lead him to the observation room overlooking the chamber.

Kutyl placed a hand on Kritef's shoulder and stopped him. "Do not address them," he said. "I fear your mere presence will whip them into an even greater frenzy. Before long, they could break down the barriers between us and attempt to copulate with *you*."

Kritef hated to admit when he misjudged a situation, especially to Kutyl. "Perhaps you are correct." He sighed. "I fear what would happen if we settle these people on another world. I fear that they would treat it as they currently treat our ship. I fear that that world would end up like their current world. These beings are out of control and have no limits. Surely, wherever they go, a drowned world is sure to follow. We must return them at once in a hurry. We are beyond late in returning to our own system."

Kutyl and Kritef pressed their ship to travel as fast as possible. Upon arrival at the third planet, they found that the dark clouds covering the entire world had disappeared and the water had begun to recede. Gigantic arcs of colorful rainbows soared over all the visible landmasses.

"It is as if we are viewing an entirely different planet," Kritef said.

"It is the same," Kutyl said. "Let us descend and return them."

They entered the planet's atmosphere and scanned the landmasses for a suitable drop spot. All around the planet, on every landmass, they found beings that looked much like the ones their ship held. These beings were singing and dancing with joy, but they were not reckless like the guests on the ship. They were not stealing and gambling and shedding blood. They were sharing and exhibiting kindness. They aided each other as they attempted to piece their destroyed lives back together.

"Surely, these are the people we would have preferred to welcome aboard our ship," Kritef said. "They have survived a cataclysmic event. They are stronger for it and appear to have preferable temperaments to the survivors we have picked up."

"Yes. Let us hope that the wicked have all gone with the water and that only the pure remain."

"If that is the case, then we cannot reintroduce these wicked beings back to this planet," Kritef said. "That would not be right."

"Well, we certainly cannot keep them on board nor take them anywhere with us. The supplies we had that were supposed to last thousands of cycles will barely last another handful. We must return them if you and I are to survive."

"It is a shame," Kritef said. "I can always place them in the middle of a body of water." He looked at Kutyl who shook his head and began to talk of the code of ethics before Kritef stopped him. Kritef sighed and hovered over the instrument panel, directing the ship to place the survivors in a small village.

The villagers were in the middle of placing thatched roofs atop their newly constructed homes and were shocked when several unfamiliar beings of their own kind materialized amongst them.

Kutyl lifted the ship out of the atmosphere and headed towards the deep blackness of space, but Kritef kept their viewing instruments trained on the village. He watched as the new arrivals began to assault the peaceful people trying to rebuild.

"I fear we have destroyed this world a second time," Kritef said.

THE SHARPTOOTH

Terry Alexander

"Thomas, help me. I lost my footing." The old man's panicked scream rose above the storm's tumult. Thunder rumbled through the slate gray sky, and the air tingled for a moment as lightning split the sky.

"Keep moving," Thomas shouted. He pushed several stragglers forward. "We have to keep moving if we hope to survive."

"If the rain doesn't stop soon, even this high ground won't be safe." Rachael, a young woman carrying a swaddling child, glared at the bearded man. "We haven't had any rest in two days. We need sleep, and food."

"Our survival is there." Thomas pointed at the cloud-covered peaks. "If you hope to survive, keep moving." He dropped to the rear of the line. A gray-haired man gripped a small tree as the water swirled around him. The man's head disappeared beneath the fierce undertow.

"Thomas, help me, please." The gray-haired man spit out a mouthful of water. "The bottom feeders are nibbling on my toes. Hurry, while there's time. The Sharptooth will be here soon."

Thomas licked his lips. He placed one foot in the cold, swirling water. A small fish darted around his ankles, nibbling at his flesh. He forced his way through the current. Something beneath the dark water clutched at the hem of his garment, pulling him down.

He felt blindly under the water for his attacker. A large fish had snapped a loose strand of his robe and pulled him under. Thomas pried its jaws from the coarse cloth and fought his way to the surface. He coughed, hacking water from his lungs. A thick mucus ran from his nostrils. The water had risen two feet during the short time he attempted to rescue the old man.

"Thomas," The man screamed. "I want to live, one more day, one more hour. I want to live."

"I can't help you. I'm sorry." Raindrops pelted Thomas's face and streamed down his cheeks. "I can't get to you, Barnabas."

Barnabas reached up, catching hold of a higher branch. "You're going to leave me here to die? Why me? Why not Rachael and her brat, or Stephen? They are no better than me."

"We may all die," Thomas said, wiping his eyes. "None of us may live to see tomorrow. We must keep climbing to have any hope at all."

Two long, meaty tentacles sprang from the water. The sharp tips of the tentacles impaled Barnabas, ripping through his flesh and protruding through his back. The color drained from his face as blood ran down the tentacle into the rushing maelstrom. "The Sharp—" Barnabas's body trembled as the tentacles dragged him under the water.

Thomas reached for the old man's outstretched hand. Water swirled around his thighs before he realized the futility of trying to save the old man. A massive body broke through the surface. Long, flexible tentacles lifted Barnabas above the beast's gaping mouth. A large, soulless eye peered at Thomas. An icy lump formed in the pit of his stomach and tingled up his spine.

Was that a smile? Thomas pondered. He took a step back, desperate to get out of the rising water. *That was a smile, I know it was.* He stood transfixed, his legs unwilling to move, staring at the creature he knew only from legend.

The mouth opened wide, the tentacles moving Barnabas closer to the daggers of sharp teeth. "No," Barnabas moaned. He freed his right arm and braced it against the creature's open mouth. His arm slipped on the slick skin and disappeared into the mouth. Sharp, ragged teeth fastened themselves onto flesh, tearing the old man's arm from his body.

Blood squirted from the old man's shoulder, painting the monster in garish crimson. Barnabas screamed. He struck the creature with his remaining hand, over and over, the blows progressively getting weaker. The struggle snapped Thomas from his trance, he ran to catch up with the others in his group.

"You have to move faster." He caught Rachael easily and got a glimpse of the next refugee in line fifty feet ahead. "Come on, faster. Pick up the pace. The water is rising faster now."

"I can't, Thomas. I can't keep up." Tears mixed with the rain on Rachael's face. "My feet and legs are blistered. I can't do it anymore."

"Give Horace to me. I'll carry him. That'll lessen your load and you can catch up with the others." Thomas reached for the baby.

"He died this morning. I haven't produced milk since yesterday. My husband said I was past my prime when I became pregnant. I thought I could handle a new child at my age. I was wrong." Rachael licked her lips. "I wanted to find a place to bury him. Someplace where the water won't carry him away."

"Why didn't you tell me? I could have had one of the other women help."

"Share her milk with my child and risk not having enough for her own? I wouldn't do it, and I wouldn't ask anyone to do it for me." She sat on a large rock. "I'm going to sit here and let the water take me."

"No, we've got to keep moving. The Sharptooth killed Barnabas." Thomas grabbed Rachael's arm and pulled her forward.

"I'm not going." She pulled away and stamped her feet in the mud, sinking past her ankles. Her gray-streaked hair lay flat and lifeless on her head as she brushed the bangs from her forehead. "I saw a sharptooth when I was a child. I've always wanted to see one again."

"Rachael, it'll devour you." Thomas watched the floodwaters rise behind Rachael. "We have to keep moving."

"My child and I aren't going to survive." She closed her eyes. "If you are going to lead these people to safety, you need to move on."

"Please, Rachael, come with me."

"Go on, Thomas, while you still have time." She returned to the large stone, closed her eyes, and hummed. It took Thomas a second to realize she was humming a lullaby. He slogged his way up the steep incline. Several minutes later, he passed a man lying on the side of the path. He couldn't place the man's name. The man had slipped on the rocks and fell to the hard unyielding stones. A bloody bone protruded through the skin of his lower leg.

"Thomas, please help me. I can make it. I know I can." The man begged. "Just help me to my feet."

"It's over for you," Thomas said, evading the man's clutching hands. "Use your dagger. Open a vein and bleed out. It's better than being eaten by The Sharptooth."

"Don't believe in monsters." The man shook his head, water drops flying from the ends of his hair. His hands clutched at the stones and grass as he pulled himself toward Thomas. "They're nothing but stories parents tell their children to keep them in line."

"Barnabas was eaten by one." Thomas said. "Take the easy way out. Slit your wrist and make it deep." He hurried up the trail.

"You're a coward, Thomas. You have no spine." The man's words burned in Thomas's ears, taunting him.

A rickety rope bridge stretched over a gorge ahead. The flood water lapped at the bottom of the worn boards. The bulk of his group rushed across the flimsy boards. *What are they doing?* Thomas ran forward, waving his arms above his head. "Stop, come back. That bridge isn't safe."

"Save your breath. They know the bridge is in bad shape. It's the quickest way to the summit." Loretta stepped from around a mound of large stones. The rain pelted her face as she moved away from the makeshift shelter. "They know the risks."

"The planks are worn and rotten. They'll never make it across." Thomas stared into Loretta's eyes. "Why didn't you go with them?"

"I'm nearly blind. My presence there would endanger the group. I chose to stay behind." Her milky eyes returned Thomas's intense stare. "They tied ropes around their waists, so they're all connected in a long line. It was Terrell's idea. If one person falls, the two closest will come to their aid."

"We can make it to the upper trail. It's a safer trail to the peak." Thomas ran forward, waving his arms. No one on the bridge acknowledged he was there.

"Come back," he shouted. "The upper trail is clear. We can reach the summit."

"What's that?" Loretta grabbed his arm from behind. "Something's in the water. It's huge. Can you make it out?"

"It's trees." Thomas ran to the edge of the chasm. "They washed out and the current stacked them together." He waved his arms. "Hurry, run!"

"Run." Loretta screamed. "That snag will tear the bridge out." She pointed frantically at the solid mass closing on the rope structure.

A young man at the rear of the line noticed the trees. He hurried forward, urging the woman in front of him to move faster. She saw the danger and ran to the next man in line. Within seconds, the entire line pushed toward the far side of the divide.

A board snapped, then another, and several more gave way. A man and woman fell through, the swift moving current tugging at them. Several people grabbed the rope, pulling them toward the gap. More planks snapped under a burly man. His feet splashed in the swirling water. A thin woman standing behind him caught the collar of his garment and held on.

"Hurry," Thomas shouted. "Get to the other side. Hurry!"

A huge root-ball snagged in the ropes, yanking the bridge forward. Several people disappeared under the snag. Others were yanked off their feet, clinging to the rough bark. The forward momentum stopped momentarily with the ropes stretched to their limits.

The wooden planks snapped. Ropes groaned under the strain as the tremendous weight of the snag pushed forward. The first rope popped, followed quickly by the second. Within the span of a single breath the huge snag tore away and floated out toward open water.

"Thomas, help us." A sad, forlorn voice came from the snag.

Thomas and Loretta stared in silence as the makeshift island floated away. "We've got to reach the upper trail. If we reach the summit, we'll be safe." Thomas grabbed her hand and gave it a squeeze. "Come on. We can't waste any more time."

"You should leave me. I'll slow you down."

"Someone has to live." Thomas pulled Loretta forward. "Someone has to survive."

"I thought Noah was insane when he built that monstrosity." A mirthless chuckle passed her lips. "Then they gathered a male and female of all the land animals, and the entire village laughed at him."

"I remember. How everyone chuckled when the rain started." Thomas steered her to a well-worn path through the stones. "The water lapping at the side of that huge barge. It shouldn't have floated so easily."

Loretta squinted, staring into the distance. "What is that?"

"Elephant carcass. The current is carrying it to deeper water." His stomach growled. "If it were closer, I'd cut a chunk of hindquarter away."

"Can your knife cut elephant skin?"

Thomas struggled to maintain his footing. He reached and grabbed a nearby rock. "We must keep going. If we get to the highest place we can find, we'll survive."

"I love your optimism." She sank past her ankles in a patch of mud. "You didn't answer my question. Can your knife cut elephant skin?"

Thomas regained his footing and pulled Loretta free of the mud. "I have the sharpest dagger in all the land. It can cut anything."

"Men are all braggarts." Loretta nodded.

"We have to get far ahead of the rising water." Thomas squeezed her hand, encouraging her to keep moving. "I think the rain is breaking up to the north."

"Don't lie to me." She palmed rain from her forehead. "It's not going to stop raining. We're just delaying the inevitable. We're going to die."

"We can't give up. We must keep moving."

"Where is the flood water?"

"We've gained a lot of ground. We're at least a mile ahead of it now." He pulled her to a stop.

"What is it?"

"The snag is caught on the rocks ahead. The elephant has washed up on the trees. There's a horse there too."

Loretta squinted. "It's all a blob to me."

He slogged forward. "If we hurry, we can get some horse meat before the snag gets carried over the rocks."

"No." She shook her head. "That's a bad idea. Didn't you see The Sharptooth earlier? If we go down there, we'll die. Better to try for the summit."

"Okay, come on." They plodded forward, through sticky mud, over slick rocks.

After several hours, Loretta pulled away from Thomas's grip. "I can't go anymore. I've got to rest." She leaned against a massive rock.

"Rest. I'll check on ahead," Thomas said, trying to sound encouraging. "We must be close. I'll be back in a few minutes."

"I'm not going anywhere."

The trail grew steeper and the footing more treacherous. Thomas pulled himself forward using rocks embedded in the mud. His muscles quivered under the strain. Within minutes he found the summit. He collapsed to the soaked earth and looked around. He'd gained precious little on the advancing water.

"The barge, Noah's barge." He saw the huge ship bobbing on the surface nearly a mile away. "There it is." He drew in a deep breath and wiped the rain from his eyes. "If only we had a raft." He stared at his mud-covered feet and the hem of his filthy robe. "A raft."

The idea slapped him in the face. They had a raft. Thomas struggled to his feet and eased down the incline. On three occasions his feet slipped out from under him. Only his quick reflexes saved him from injury.

He spied Loretta. She leaned against the huge boulder near the path. "Loretta, I have a plan," he shouted. "We can survive. We can."

She didn't acknowledge his words.

"Loretta, we must get back to the snag. We can use it like a raft. We can live." He drew closer, staring at the silent woman. Her eyes closed, chin resting on her face. *Asleep, she's asleep.* Thomas reached out and touched her shoulder.

Loretta's body turned away from his touch and crashed to the ground.

"Wake up." He knelt beside her and turned her over. "Come on Loretta, wake up." His shaking grew more forceful. "Damn it, please wake up."

He held her for several minutes, slowly accepting his role as sole survivor. Thomas placed Loretta gently on the ground and folded her hands across her chest. "I've got to go, Loretta. I've got to get to the snag before it floats over the rocks."

He splashed down the trail, forcing his tired legs to an unsafe speed over the slick rocks and shifting mud. Within minutes he reached the spot. The rain had lifted the mass and weakened the stone's grip. Thomas placed his feet carefully on the steep slope. He hoped to negotiate his way to the snag.

With a snap of timbers, it lifted from the restraining stones. The current snatched it from the bank toward swifter water. Throwing caution to the wind, Thomas ran down the incline. His feet slid out from under him, and he hit the ground hard, sliding down the steep grade. He splashed into the water as the snag fell from his grasp.

"No!" Thomas shouted. "I won't die today. I won't." The current caught his body, pulling him under the waves. His hand closed on a large root. Fighting the swift water, he pulled himself onto the snag. He fell to his knees, coughing up water.

"Who's there?" A female voice shouted. "Answer me. Who's there?"

"Bridget, Bridget. It's Thomas. Where are you?"

"Thomas, is it really you?" Her voice gained strength. "I'm caught, the rope is wrapped around the tree trunks and holding me out of the water."

"You've got to talk louder. I can barely hear you." A massive clap of thunder shook the air. Lightning flashed to the water's surface, leaving a sulfurous odor.

"Bridget. Bridget, answer me." The intense drumming of the rain drowned out Thomas's words. He slipped and dropped to the slick bark, scrambling to keep from sliding into the water. He spied a short length of rope tangles in the tree branches. His hands closed on the braided hemp. Dragging himself across the knotty surface, Thomas followed the rope until it disappeared into a tangle of interlocked branches.

He stuck his head and upper torso into a tiny opening. "Bridget, can you move?"

"Thomas, it's good to see you." She forced a smile. "I can move one arm, and my head."

"I'll cut the rope and help you out of that mess."

"The only thing holding me above the water is the rope. My right leg is wedged between two trees. I can't get it free. If you cut the rope, I'll drown before you can get me out of this."

"Did anyone else survive?"

"I don't think so. Peter's about three feet from me. Most of his head is gone." She grew silent for nearly a minute. "Do you have any food? I'm so hungry."

"We have a dead horse and an elephant caught in the branches."

"How are you going to cook in this downpour?"

"We'll have to eat it raw."

"Cut me a small piece. I must eat something."

"Give me a minute." Thomas rose to his feet. The steady beat of the rain diminished as he made his way to the horse. Several sharp tree branches pierced the animal's hide. The body bobbed in the water just out of his reach. The small root-ball tipped behind him. Thomas edged forward, balancing himself on the slick bark.

He pulled the knife from his waist scabbard and sawed at the thick hide. The meat felt soft and spongy between his fingers. Small bits dropped into the swift current. He cut a long thick strip away. He turned and placed it behind. His hand closed on the hind leg. A slick round head split the water. Barbed tentacles shot forward and pierced the horse's lifeless body. The branches snapped, the thick sucker-covered arms ripped the body free and lifted it in the air. Stained water drained from the holes in the horse's body, flowing past the mouthful of sharp teeth to disappear into the dark void of a mouth. The shiny daggers of death snapped on the body and cleaved it in half in a single bite.

Thomas dropped to his back, his heart pounding in his chest. The dagger slipped from his slick fingers and tumbled into the water. His trembling hands closed on the strip of meat as he crawled to Bridget's nesting spot. "The Sharptooth," he shouted. "It devoured the horse in a single gulp." The snag shook, each tree trembled and quivered. "Bridget, are you okay?"

No answer.

Thomas wiped the rain from his face and crawled into the hole. A raw bloody mess hung from the rope. Bridget's head and arm were missing. Blood dripped from her torn flesh. Bile churned his stomach and singed his throat. Vomit spewed past his lips and discolored the water for a brief instant. His nose burned as tears filled his eyes. He blinked them away long enough to spy the knife at Bridget's waist.

Thomas hooked his legs in the branches and reached for the blade. Stretching, his fingers grazed the handle. Readjusting his weight, he reached again and managed to pull the knife from Bridget's belt. Water rushed over his head.

A dark shape came up from the depths. A chill of dread seized his heart and squeezed as the mouth opened, displaying sharp, pointed teeth. In desperation, Thomas sought to find something to grip. His hand fastened on a tree branch. He pulled himself from the water, trying to squirm out of the hole. The head grew closer, a black eye focused on Thomas.

The head broke the surface and closed on Bridget's remains as Thomas rolled from the opening. He lay on the uneven surface, his arm draped across his eyes. *When will it end? When will this cursed rain end?*

Thomas wiped moisture from his eyes. Sitting up, he wrapped his arms around his knees. He glanced across the endless expanse of water. He imagined he saw the outline of the massive barge in the distance. He found a small bit of horsemeat. A foul odor filled his nostrils as he bit into the coarse grain and began to chew.

The makeshift raft shook violently. A set of tentacles gripped the branches along the edge of the snag. A massive head lifted from the water, its single eye focused on Thomas.

I can't move. I've got to stay perfectly still. It'll kill me if I move. His eyes locked on the monster. He scarcely felt the burn as the hooked tentacle plunged through his belly. A single scream burst from his lips as the creature lifted him toward its gaping mouth.

OMEGA

ANGELBLOOD

Frank Sawielijew

With feathers white as a cloud, on wings as pure as an angel's, the bird rose into the sky as close to God as was possible for a creature of the earth. White and pure, a flawless being representing the perfection of God's creation. Jabez smiled as he watched it disappear among the clouds.

"Rat of the skies, they call it. And what has it become now? Did you see, my dear Judith? Did you see what has become of it?" he asked his lover, his beloved, his wife.

"Yes, my love. I saw," she replied, gazing in awe. "I saw."

He put an arm around her, his smile growing wider. His heart felt as if it wished to jump out of his chest and dance on the ground—nay, through the sky in celebration. All the doubts, all the fears, all the arguments with his beloved were forgotten. The efforts of the past few months had not been in vain. It had worked.

It had worked.

"I'm sorry I ever doubted you, Jabez. I'm so sorry I ever—" Judith started, but Jabez sealed her lips with a kiss before she could continue.

"Forget it, my love," he said after his lips had left hers. "It doesn't matter. We succeeded. Do you know what this means? For our future, for our lives?"

She smiled, a smile as broad and full of mirth as his. "Yes. We could be kings."

He placed another kiss upon her lips. "No. Not kings. We shall be gods."

#

Arishat did not shield her face as she was assaulted with rotten fruits, nor did she lower her head in shame when hypocrite mouths flung accusations of sin at her. *Unclean*, they shouted, *sinful, filthy, rotten.*

Whore.

They loved to display their righteousness in public, but they were not without sin themselves. Some of them she knew. There was Ezekiel, who loved nothing more than to be pleasured by her mouth. Hafet, who had a wife and three children but spent more time with Arishat than with his family. Jeremiah, who paid her extra if she treated him like a dog.

Now, out on the street, they called her whore. At night, when the city slept, they came to her in secret and paid in silver to live out the sinful fantasies they were too afraid to admit to their wives. Only a few faces in the crowd gave her looks of sympathy. She knew them, too. Isaiah, who had lost his wife to disease and found solace in Arishat's arms at night. Poor Argurios, who was shunned by the people of this city for worshipping different gods.

Just like Arishat herself.

"Get out of here, you worthless mutt!" she heard a voice shout from within a nearby house, followed by the whimpering of a hungry dog.

A sad little creature crawled through the door, its fur dirty and matted. As soon as it spotted Arishat, the dog's spirits lifted, and it approached her with a wagging tail.

"Kalbat, my little girl!" said Arishat as she knelt to pat its head. "You're hungry, aren't you? And none of these people have any food to spare for a stray like you. They treat you like garbage, you poor thing."

This was how stray dogs were treated around here. No wonder Jeremiah always told her to treat him like a dog when he wanted to be whipped and degraded.

"Look at this, the bitch and the whore are best friends! What a charming little pair!" yelled a voice from the crowd. The cruel joke was met with roaring laughter.

"Come, Kalbat. Let's go to Uncle Noah. Maybe he has some scraps for you."

Arishat got up and followed the street to the city gate. Kalbat followed close on her heels. Occasionally, a mushy piece of fruit would hit her, followed by a deriding comment. Most people ignored her now, as they'd had their entertainment for the day. The whore had been made fun of, and business on the streets could continue as usual.

This city had been her home for more than five years now. Arishat had long gotten used to this treatment.

#

Noah's house was not far from the city walls. The old man preferred the peace of the countryside to the hubbub of city life, and his new project required a lot of space to be built, too. It was almost finished, and it looked impressive.

"Arishat! It's nice to see you again!" Noah called as he spotted her standing in the fields. When he noticed that she didn't turn around to greet him because her eyes were still taking in the sight of the ship, he asked, "Do you like it?"

"It's impressive," she said. "My people know a lot about building boats, but this ... it's something else."

Noah had been told by God to build a great ship with enough space to house all the creatures of God's creation. It stretched higher than any house Arishat had ever seen. She wondered how many trees had to be felled to get so much wood. It looked like an entire forest had been sacrificed to build this boat.

"Yes. God showed me how to build it. I think I did a pretty good job." A jovial smile formed on Noah's lips. "With this, I'm pretty sure we'll survive the flood."

Arishat shook her head. "I still don't get it. Why would your god do this? I know he's a vengeful god, but you are his chosen people. He can't just kill you all!"

"Well, not all of us."

"But almost. If your family is the only one to survive, how will you carry on your legacy? You will be swallowed by larger tribes, and your god will lose his people!"

Noah was silent for a moment. Then, with a shrug, he said, "God knows what he's doing. He always has a plan."

This only earned him a sigh and another shake of the head by Arishat. "I'll never get you people. Gods make mistakes, too, you know."

She didn't understand. Her gods were different. Noah didn't feel like discussing the nature of divinity again, so he merely asked what brought her here to steer the conversation to a more pleasant topic.

"I just wanted to ask if you have something to eat for little Kalbat here. She's hungry, and the people in the city, well, you know how it is," she said. The stray's ears perked up when it heard Arishat speak its name.

Noah lowered himself to give the dog an affectionate pat on the head. "You're lucky, little one. We slaughtered a sheep last night, so you can have some fresh meat today!"

He went into his house, and Arishat's attention was caught by the ark again. Could the Israelite god truly be cruel enough to send a flood to drown His own chosen people? She had heard stories from Babylonian travelers about an angry god who had become annoyed with humanity because of their great number; the loud noise of their activity had disturbed his sleep. But a different god who liked the humans stepped in and offered the solution of making men mortal, so the old ones would die when the young ones grew up and there would never be too great a number of humans in the world.

The god of the Israelites was supposed to be the friendly kind, or at least that's what Arishat thought. He was their creator. He loved them. Why would he do such a thing? It made no sense to her.

"You're still fascinated by the ship, I see," said Noah, who had returned from his house and fed Kalbat a generous cut of mutton.

"I don't believe it," she said, shaking her head. "Why would your god do this to you?"

Noah smiled. He always smiled when talking about his God and the plans He had. Arishat found Noah's attitude mildly irritating.

"Because His people are sinful and evil, Arishat," Noah said. "You know how they treat you. You should understand."

She lowered her head, eyes closed. "There are many bad people among them, yes. Sinful? I know how sinful they are. Half the city has paid for a night with me, most of them married men. But they're not evil. Not even those who insult me every day. They may not be nice people, but they have friends and families. There is a tiny little spark of goodness within each of them."

"Is that enough?" Noah asked. "Our God is perfect. Why should we, his creatures, be so imperfect? He wants to start anew and destroy a flawed creation so he can remake us without sin."

"Your people feel so superior to us Canaanites because of your almighty god," she said, her voice thick with scorn. "But I would rather have imperfect gods that make mistakes than ... this."

Noah went silent. He knew Arishat didn't like his God because she didn't understand Him, and he didn't want to upset her any further.

Finally, she sighed. "I need a drink. Gotta spend the money I make whoring on something. Right? Your god probably hates me for this."

"He doesn't—"

"I'll be in Jabez's tavern. See you later, old friend."

She turned and went away without throwing another glance at her Noah and his giant boat.

She will never understand, Noah thought to himself as he watched Arishat's form become smaller against the horizon.

#

Kalbat followed her as she made her way towards the tavern not far from the city walls. It was close to the gate, right beside the major trader's road — the perfect place for attracting customers.

"You're with me again, little girl? I think we should find a home for you. You'll be much happier with someone to look after you," Arishat said to the stray wagging its tail at her voice's encouraging tone. "Maybe you can stay with Jabez. He's a good man, and rich enough to feed you well."

She entered the tavern and approached the bar, where Jabez's wife Judith was cleaning last night's used mugs. There were no guests yet at this early hour.

"Hey there, Judith. Is Jabez around?"

Judith looked up from her work and greeted her guest with a smile. "He's in the back room. Do you want something from him?"

Arishat nodded and pointed to the dog sitting obediently beside her. For a stray, it was surprisingly well-behaved. "Yes. I'd like to ask if he could give a home to this dog. She deserves better than crawling from house to house begging for food."

Judith grinned. She obviously liked the idea of adopting Kalbat. "Oh, having a dog would be nice! Wait here, I'll fetch my husband."

Arishat took a seat and scratched the dog behind the ears. "You're getting a home, my little girl! Are you excited? Oh, yes, you're excited! Who's happy to finally get a master? You're happy!"

Kalbat jumped, wagged her tail, and licked Arishat's face. Of course, she didn't understand what was going on, but she noticed her favorite human's excitement and couldn't help but feel excited too.

This changed instantly when Jabez entered the room.

The dog became tense and growled, moving backwards to put more distance between the man and herself. Arishat was puzzled. Kalbat never behaved like this, not even towards people who kicked and spat at her. There seemed to be something about Jabez that she instinctively disliked.

"What's up, little girl? You don't have to worry, Jabez is a nice man."

"Yes, your friend is right, little doggie," Jabez said in a cheerful voice, which he thought would calm the dog. "I'd be happy to give you a home and provide for you. No need to fear!" Kalbat's growls grew fiercer. She barked. When the innkeeper tried to approach her, the bitch bolted, running out of the building as fast as she could.

"Well, that's strange," muttered Arishat. "She never behaves like that."

Jabez shrugged. "I've been down in the cellar all morning. It's a little musty down there, so maybe the smell put her off. Now, what can I do for you?"

"I'm in the mood for a drink. Give me wine or beer, whatever you have to offer. Just give me something with a kick."

A broad grin appeared on his face. He knew that Arishat could afford the finest of drinks and didn't mind paying the price for them. "Oh, I have just the thing for you. Yesterday, we received a shipment of excellent Minoan wine …"

#

It had been a usual day at the tavern, with the Canaanite whore arriving early for a drink, some travelers coming in for lunch during the day, and the regulars arriving in the evening to end their day with a beer and good company. His wife was still at the tavern serving the few remaining guests who liked to stay and drink into the latest hours of the night, but Jabez was working on more important things.

He would have loved to use the stray dog the whore had brought along, but for some reason the bitch had run away. It didn't matter. He had a pig to work with, and that was just as good as a dog.

He took a bowl of water and put in a few drops of the precious fluid he experimented with, but not too many as he didn't know what effects a higher dose might have. With the pigeon, three drops had been enough to transform it into a thing of beauty, a white bird he had named *dove*. A pig would likely need more. Possibly five, or even ten.

The cooing of the transformed pigeons in their cage near the entrance announced the arrival of his wife.

"Ah, Judith. The guests have all gone home?"

"Yes, I've closed the tavern for the night." She went to the table where her husband carefully dripped little drops of red into a bowl of water. When she went to insert a finger into the mixture, Jabez grabbed her hand and pulled it away.

"Don't!" he admonished. "We have no idea what it would do to a human."

"We've seen what it can do to a pigeon. Why not just drink it ourselves?"

He shook his head. "Pigeons are birds. They have wings. I want to try it on other animals first. What if it kills you, or worse, transforms you into something hideous? We can't risk it."

Judith sighed. There was a hint of fear in her eyes. She didn't like waiting so long. "What if Noah is telling the truth? What if God really wants to send a flood to punish us for our sins?"

Jabez scoffed. "I don't believe it. And even if he does, if our experiments work, we'll have a way out. And besides, we're good people. We've always been good people. If there is anyone God would spare, it would be us."

While he took the bowl and put it in front of the pig, encouraging it to drink with a pat on the head, Judith looked at the pigeons. Or doves, as they called them. People used to call pigeons the rats of the skies. These birds were white and pure and beautiful. What if she were to drink of that precious fluid? Would her skin become smoother, her hair softer?

No, Jabez was right. It was too dangerous. They had only tested it on birds. What if it didn't work on other animals?

The pig squealed as its transformation began. Short, stubby wings sprouted from its shoulders, featherless protrusions of bone and skin. Its bristly hide couldn't decide whether to grow paler or brighter, turning a mottled pink in the process. The shrieks and grunts became more and more panicked as the pig's body mutated into a grotesque caricature of God's creation. After the transformation, its features reminded her more of a demon than of an angel.

"The poor thing," Judith gasped, visibly shaken by the display she had witnessed.

"Maybe it didn't work because pigs are unclean," Jabez mused. "We have to try it on other animals."

"What if it doesn't work at all?" Judith collapsed to the floor, sobbing. Her husband put a hand on her shoulder to comfort her.

"Don't worry," he said. "It worked with the pigeons. There's no reason it couldn't work with other creatures. The pig was just a bad choice. Don't worry, my love."

With tears in her eyes, she replied, "What if God sends the flood and our plan doesn't work? We will drown, just like all the others. We'll—"

"Shh," he whispered, gently laying a finger over her lips. "We will succeed, my dearest Judith. God's flood doesn't matter to us. We have the divine power of creation in our hands."

He hugged her and held her tight, a confident smile on his lips.

They were like gods. They had nothing to fear.

\#

Arishat sat on the roof of her house, gazing into the endless sea of stars above her. The Babylonians could read the will of the gods from the movements of these celestial bodies. There were so many of them. How could the Israelites believe that the entirety of heaven and earth had been created by a single god?

A small cloud moved across the sky, partially obscuring the stars. Not long after the cloud had appeared, a light drizzle started to fall.

"It's raining," Arishat said. "Won't you come and shelter me?"

Argurios sat down beside her. "I'm your client, not your husband. If you want to cuddle, you'll have to pay," he replied with a grin.

She rolled her eyes. "Oh, come on. You're more than a client to me. You're also my friend."

"Ah, but I still have to pay for sex."

"You know that's different. I must take money for that because it's my job."

Argurios shook his head and sighed. "Why are we still doing this?"

"What do you mean?"

"Trying to carve out a life for ourselves in this gods-forsaken town. The people don't accept us. You're a whore who has to sell her body to make a living, and I barely manage to sell any of my bronze crafts because nobody here wants to buy from someone they deem an idolater."

"I guess we both have our reasons for leaving our homes behind and trying our luck elsewhere. And this town isn't that bad a place once you get used to it."

Argurios shook his head again. "Not that bad? Arishat, I know how they treat you. I've seen them just this morning throw rotten fruit at you and call you names,. How can you say this isn't a bad place?"

"Some people are decent," she answered, taking Argurios' hand in hers with a smile. "Like you, for example. But tell me, why these thoughts all of a sudden? I know you have it just as hard as I do, but you've never complained before."

He stared into the sky, silent for a while. Then he answered, "I wonder how long we have left to live. You know, with the flood and all. I wonder if life would've been better for me elsewhere. some place where the gods are friendlier."

"Are you scared of the rain, Argurios?" She laughed. "I don't believe their god would send a great flood to drown the entire country. Even if the people are sinful, they're his chosen tribe. If you were a god, would you annihilate your own worshippers for a reason like that?"

He shrugged. "The people here are unfriendly and cruel, so why shouldn't their god be the same?"

"As I said, I don't believe it. If he's truly going to send a flood, there must be a better reason than merely his people being sinful."

They sat on the roof for a little while, staring into the sky where the brightest of the stars poked through the clouds, casting a dim light unto the earth below. The rainfall was so light, Arishat could barely feel its touch upon her skin. The atmosphere was romantic.

She leaned and kissed Argurios.

"What—"

"Shh, don't say anything." She kissed him again. "Just enjoy the moment."

That night, she would not request any payment from him. He had become more than a client. He had become more than a friend.

#

The next morning, after she had said goodbye to Argurios and dressed herself, Arishat set out to Jabez's tavern again. For her, a good day always started with a drink, and considering what happened between her and Argurios last night, she considered this a day worthy of starting with the best wine she could afford.

When she went out on the streets, she found them to be almost deserted. It was still drizzling, barely enough to form a few puddles on the ground, but it seemed to keep the people inside their homes. Arishat didn't encounter anyone on her way to the tavern. Maybe they were afraid this could be the beginning of the great flood.

When she arrived at the tavern, she was surprised to find the doors locked.

That was strange. Jabez always opened his tavern early in the morning. She knocked at the door, calling his name.

"Jabez? Are you there? Judith? Anyone?" she yelled, but no one answered.

Arishat began to worry. They lived in the upper floor of the tavern, and at this time of day they should be at home, either down in the tavern or still in their bedroom. Did anything happen to them? She had to make sure they were all right. Jabez was one of the few people in town who always treated her nicely. Besides, he was her most reliable supplier of booze.

She went to the back of the tavern and checked the door there. It was unlocked. Picked open by a thief, perhaps, or maybe they forgot to lock it.

Arishat opened the door and went inside. "Hello?" she called, but apart from her own echo, nothing came back. She went upstairs to check out their bedroom, but it was empty. They were gone.

What had happened here?

"Maybe it's something down in the basement," she muttered to herself. "The way Kalbat reacted to him, he said it might've been the smell from working in the basement for so long."

She decided to check it out. What if Jabez was working on something dangerous down there and there had been an accident? She descended the stairs to the ground floor, went into the back room and climbed down into the cellar. There, she found the one thing she hadn't expected at all. One of the wine racks lining the wall had been pushed aside, revealing a secret passage.

It entered a long tunnel that led, if her sense of direction was correct, away from the city. Why would this be here? Where could it lead?

There was only one way to find out. She stepped into the tunnel and followed it as far as it went. It seemed to stretch on forever. When she reached a reinforced wooden door, it felt like she had walked for at least a quarter of an hour. She knelt in front of the door and put her ear to it.

On the other side of the room, the voices of Jabez and Judith were talking, but she couldn't make out the words. There were sounds of animals, too. The cooing of pigeons, the whinny of a horse.

Arishat had a bad feeling about this. Something strange was going on down here. She went back the way she came before they discovered she was there. This was something she had to investigate later.

For some reason, she felt that Kalbat's hostile reaction to Jabez had had something to do with whatever was happening behind that door.

#

"God will punish you for this," the angel said as Jabez drew his blood again.

"No, he won't," Jabez smiled. "I have never broken a single commandment. I have always lived by God's laws. I'm helpful even towards people who don't deserve it. There is no sin I could be punished for."

"And yet you chain me here to use me for your sick experiments. You're playing God, and you think He would not care?"

Jabez laughed. "God never gave us any rules on how to treat an angel! But you know what he said to us? You are the crown of my creation, go forth and be the masters of the earth. And that's exactly what I'm doing, nothing more and nothing less."

The angel spat on the floor. "You twist and turn the rules as you see fit. This is not God's law. This is your own sick perversion of it."

Jabez offered the angel an innocent smile. "I'm free of sin, my friend. I don't feel any guilt about what I'm doing. God created us in His own image, and I merely strive to be as close to that image as I can. God is the creator of life. I am a creator of life. He made humankind the ruler of His creation, and that is exactly what I strive to be."

"You will burn for this," the angel muttered as his captor left the tiny chamber that imprisoned him. He was weak from the loss of blood, and there was no hope he could break the heavy links of bronze chaining him to the wall. "God will burn you for this."

"What if he's right?" asked Judith as soon as her husband had left the chamber. "What if what we're doing really is wrong?"

"Don't worry, my love. We're not breaking any of God's laws," he answered, embracing her in a reassuring hug.

"I ... I don't know," she said, shaking her head. "What if the flood God is planning to send is the punishment for what we're doing? Not for everyone else being sinful, but for us."

"That's nonsense," Jabez replied with a laugh. "Don't you see? We're good people, and God has sent us the means to escape this punishment, just like he has told Noah to build his giant boat. Only we have something much better than a boat."

"You think God meant for us to capture the angel?"

He nodded. "Of course, he did. With his blood, we can create a creature that will fly us away from here as soon as the flood strikes. It's all part of God's plan, I'm sure of it."

Judith nodded, wanting to believe her husband's words. But she wasn't sure about it. They were interfering in God's creation, and that couldn't be right. Could it?

"Let's go back to the tavern and open up for business now," he said. "We'll try the blood on some other animals tonight."

#

"I'm really starting to hate this place. The rain is getting stronger, the only people who came into my shop today were here to tell me that it's all my fault for worshipping idols, and to top it all off, somebody stole my horse," Argurios complained.

"Your horse was stolen?" Arishat asked, surprised.

"Yeah. And you know what's the craziest about this? Whoever took my horse left a bag of coins in the stable. These Israelites are insane, just like their damned god."

"I didn't even know you had a horse," she said, still surprised.

"I did. It was a present from the wanax of Mycenae, back when I was in his service. It was merely a foal when I received it. Took care of it ever since." His voice was shaking. It was obvious that he was very attached to that horse.

"You never told me much about your past, Argurios," Arishat said, putting a hand on his arm as an affectionate gesture. "What did you do back in your homeland?"

He sighed and shook his head. "Something I ran away from for a reason. I'm sorry, I don't want to talk about my past. Not yet, at least."

"It's okay. I understand," she replied, followed by a kiss. "I don't like to talk about my past either."

He grunted, which was his version of a nod.

"And I don't have the time to talk right now, anyway. There's something I must do," she added. "We'll meet again later."

Argurios grinned. "What, are you meeting a client? You can tell me, Arishat. It's what you do for a living; there's no need to be that vague about it."

"No, my dear. I'm not meeting a client," she said, shaking her head. "There's something else. Something I must check out."

#

The drizzle had now turned into a proper, real rainfall. By the time she had reached the tavern, her dress was wet, and her hair was dripping with water. Luckily, the tavern was open now. She wouldn't have wanted to have made that journey in vain.

"Arishat! What are you doing outside in this weather?" Jabez asked as she entered. "You'll get sick letting yourself get this wet!"

Arishat greeted the innkeeper with a smile. "Hey, you know I need my drink in the morning. I came by earlier, when the rain was merely a drizzle, but your doors were closed."

Jabez put a clay mug on the bar counter and reached for an amphora. "We had a long day yesterday, so my wife and I decided to open up a little later than usual." He poured some wine from the amphora into the mug. "Here, have a drink on the house to make it up to you."

"Thanks. Every time I come here, you remind me why I keep coming back," she said. She took a seat at the bar and gratefully accepted the free mug of wine.

She enjoyed her drink and talked about the latest rumors with Jabez, just as she always did when she came here. But now she knew that something was going on, something that Jabez kept secret. In truth, this was the real reason she had come here, to see what Jabez would say when she mentioned the tavern having been closed earlier. He hadn't told her the entire truth, and she had the strange feeling that he was hiding something terrible.

"Well, that's it for today," she said after she had finished her drink. "See you tomorrow."

"Leaving already? It's still raining outside."

"Yes, but I don't think it'll stop anytime soon. And I have some things to do, so I better get home now. Busy day. Well, you know how it is," she said with a wink.

He smiled at her as she left, a friendly smile that was so typical of him. But deep in his eyes she could see something entirely different. She saw contempt.

She realized that it had always been there.

#

Arishat had to find out what Jabez was hiding, so she followed the underground tunnel. There hadn't been any twists or turns, as she remembered it, but she hoped to find something if she walked long enough.

With every step, water spilled into her sandals and mud oozed between her toes. The heavy rain made it hard to see, yet she walked on. After what felt like an eternity, she finally found an abandoned tower in the fields, far enough from the city and the roads to attract no attention. When she approached the door of the tower, she wasn't surprised to find it locked and bolted from the inside. It was fashioned from thick, heavy wood and she couldn't imagine even the strongest of men breaking it open. She had to find another way inside. She circled the tower a couple of times, trying to think of a good way to infiltrate it, before noticing windows in the upper floors. The walls were rough and irregular, with holes and protruding stones that could serve as footholds.

"This has to be the dumbest idea you've ever had," she said aloud, slipping her hand into a hole in the stonework. She pulled herself up, bracing a foot against the wall. She slipped, falling into the mud. With a groan, she pulled herself up from the ground and untied her sandals. When she had bared her feet, she attempted the climb again. "Curiosity and stubbornness, one day they will get me killed."

This time, she managed to keep her balance. She almost fell again when a stone broke loose under her foot. The rain beat against her back and with each step her arms grew heavier.

"Dear gods, don't forsake me now."

When she reached the window, she pulled herself through and fell to the floor on the other side. When she gathered enough strength, she stood and descended the stairs into the basement. It was larger than she expected it to be.

"Could you be the horse that was stolen from Argurios?" There were other animals too, mostly birds. The strangest were kept in a large cage together. They looked like pigeons, but their feathers were pure white, almost divine.

An opening led to another room. She stepped through and encountered a tall man with pale skin and black hair chained to the wall. On his back were wings larger than any bird she had ever seen.

"What … who … what are you?"

The man looked up, a defeated expression on his face. His eyes glowed as if a lit candle were behind them. They had lost all glimmer of hope. "My name is Lucifer. I'm an angel of God."

"An angel? How did you get here? What happened to you?"

"I was sent by God to bring elucidation to His people, for he thought they deserved it. I was to be the lightbringer, the one to carry divine knowledge and the message of God's love to His people. That was many months ago."

"You've been chained here for months?" Arishat couldn't imagine that Jabez would do that to such a magnificent creature.

"Yes. The first human I met here on earth was a man named Jabez. At first, he acted friendly towards me and showed much hospitality. He invited me to his home, but now I'm not even sure whether this is his home at all. I'm not sure what happened next. My memory is a blur. He brought me here and somehow managed to knock me out. When I woke up, I found myself in chains."

"Why would he do this to you? I can't believe Jabez is keeping you here like this. He has always been—" she began, then she remembered that look in his eyes. Beneath Jabez's friendly demeanor was something bad, maybe evil. "I always thought he was a good person."

Lucifer nodded. "Yes. And he really believes he is. He doesn't see anything wrong with what he's doing."

"But why? What does he want from you?"

"My blood," the angel grimaced.

Arishat's eyes widened. "Your blood?"

"Yes. The blood of an angel contains the divine essence of God's creation. Jabez uses this divine essence to shape new creatures and thinks himself a god because of it."

"Oh, no. No, no, no." Arishat's whole body began to shake. This changed everything. This meant that God actually had a reason to punish his people. An angel sent from heaven to bring enlightenment and love, treated like this by the first human he met.

"Did you see those white birds in the other room? He fed my blood to a couple of pigeons. This is what became of them," Lucifer said.

God didn't have to punish His entire people for the actions of one man. This was wrong. All of it was wrong. Arishat decided she had to do something about it. She had to make this right.

"I'm going to set you free," she said. "I don't know how, but I'll find a way. I promise."

"Thank you, young woman," the angel replied with a smile. After months of captivity, he finally saw a glimmer of hope again. "After meeting Jabez, I thought that God was wrong about you. You humans don't deserve His love. Thank you for showing me that there are still some who do."

Arishat had to chuckle, despite the seriousness of the situation. "He's not my god," she said.

"What do you mean?" Lucifer asked, confused.

"It doesn't matter. Listen, I'll find a way to break your chains. Then I'm going to come back. But for now, I should get out of here before your captors return. If Jabez finds me here, I'll end up in chains just like you," she said. "Hold on to your hope. I'll be back."

She left the angel and ran up the stairs to the tower's ground floor where she quickly unbolted the door and stepped outside. She let herself collapse to the soft, muddy ground. After what she had seen, she welcomed the cool drops of rain on her skin, the water from the heavens washing away the filth of the basement.

Jabez kept a creature of God in captivity to harvest its blood. Behind his friendly face, there was a sick mind without any sense of morality. For this, God would send a flood to drown his people.

Arishat cried. Her tears mingled with those wept by the heavens.

#

When she stepped through the city gates, Arishat was a mess. Her long hair hung in wet strands over her face, her dress was soaked, and her bare feet were covered in mud. She shouldn't have been so stupid, so thoughtless. She could've taken the horse to ride to the city, but she hadn't thought of that when she started her journey. She could've put her sandals on, but she had forgotten about those, too. Now, she was dirty and exhausted and still not one step further in finding a solution. She had no idea how to free the angel from his shackles.

At least the water on the streets washed away the mud on her feet. What had started as a drizzle last night was now a torrent, and the rain had been going for hours now. Some people, knowing it wouldn't stop, walled up their doors and windows to keep the water out of their homes. Only a few still doubted God's wrath.

Had she not seen what was going on in the abandoned tower, Arishat would have been among these few.

Finally, she reached her house. As soon as she opened the door, the water from the street spilled inside. Closing it didn't help in keeping it out, either. Some water came through the door crack.

"That's just great." she muttered. Not having any better idea, she went to her wardrobe to search for a blanket or any sufficiently large piece of cloth to put in front of the door. That would at least soak up some of the water spilling in.

After all that mud and rain, the one thing she wanted most right now was a hot bath followed by a long sleep in a dry bed.

That plan was interrupted by a knock at the door.

"Yes? Who's there?"

"Arishat," said a familiar voice, "I thought I'd stop by and help you out."

That voice made a smile appear on her lips, and she was more than happy to open the door. "Argurios! Your company is just what I need right now.

Come in!"

He was shocked to see her disheveled. "By Zeus, where have you been? You look like you've walked through a swamp."

"I just came back from the tavern and was surprised by the rain," she said with a dismissive wave of her hand. "It is a lot heavier compared to this morning."

The look Argurious gave her indicated that he didn't believe a few minutes in the rain could make her look like this.

"So, what do you want to help me with?" Arishat hoped the question would divert his attention away from her condition. She didn't want to involve him with the captured angel. She'd rather keep Argurios out of danger.

"I thought I could put some bricks in your windows and doorway to keep out the water. Most people are doing that now because it's quite obvious the great flood is coming. This way, we'll at least stay dry for a few more days," he answered.

"And how would I leave my house if the doorway is walled off?" she asked, implying she found the idea to be rather silly.

"Well, I use a ladder from the roof," Argurios said with a grin.

Arishat stared at him for a moment. That was a simple but surprisingly elegant solution, she thought. "Very well, then. Do it. I'll heat up some water so I can have a nice, long bath while you're making my house flood-proof."

"I'll get to work immediately, my dear."

"I hope so! Cause when you're done, you can give me a nice little foot massage," she teased. "I could really use one right now."

"Of course. Everything for my dear little lady."

#

When Argurios climbed down from the roof to return to his home the next morning, the water on the street was at waist level. With every hour, the rainfall seemed to become heavier, a ceaseless downpour with no end in sight. Arishat still had no idea how she could free the angel.

The chains were made of solid bronze. They were set into the wall, which was made of solid stone. And now that the flood was rising ever higher, Jabez would likely spend more time in the tower than in his tavern. If he caught her sneaking in, he could easily overpower her.

She could have asked Argurios for help, but she didn't want to endanger the man she loved. No, this was something she had to do alone. But no matter how much she thought about it, she couldn't think of a way to save Lucifer.

"Damn you, Arishat," she muttered to herself. "Damn you and your desire to always do the right thing. It has ruined you once already."

With a sigh, she got out of bed and walked to where she kept the only thing left from her previous life. She couldn't find an answer on her own, so it was time to turn to her gods. It was a long time ago that she had served as their priestess, but she worshipped them with as much piety now as she did all those years ago.

If she couldn't find an answer on her own, the gods would take her hand and lead her on the right path. They had never failed her before.

#

Jabez was no longer an innkeeper. His inn was gone. He had walled off the entrance to the basement to keep the water from flooding the tunnel, but he hadn't bothered to protect the tavern itself. His old life was over, and his new life would soon begin. He would be far away from here, creating his own Eden. His creations would rival those of God himself.

His heart swelled with pride as he beheld the creatures he had made. The effects of the angelic blood were as varied as God's creation itself. The lizards he had fed with it had grown featherless wings and gained the ability to breathe fire. The pigeons had turned into white birds of purest beauty. A squirrel he had caught in the woods had grown large furry membranes between its limbs that allowed it to glide in the air.

"What if it doesn't work on the horse?" his wife asked, her voice trembling with fear. She was afraid they would end up stuck here and drown like all the others.

"Don't worry, my dear. Of course, it'll work. This angel is God's gift to us so we can escape the punishment of the wicked. I'm sure God knew we'd find a horse to use the blood on. Just imagine, a winged horse, an even better means of escape than Noah's silly boat, don't you think?" he replied, dismissing her worries.

"We didn't find the horse," she said. "We stole it."

Jabez slapped his wife across the cheek. "We didn't steal anything!" he yelled.

"Jabez, stop! You're hurting me!"

"I'm sorry," he said. His wife was the only person he truly cared about, and he didn't want to lash out against her. "We didn't steal the horse, Judith. We paid for it. We never broke God's law. It wasn't theft."

"I'm scared, Jabez. I'm scared of the flood. I'm scared that God doesn't approve of what we're doing. I'm just scared," she said, tears streaming down her cheeks.

The last few months had been hard on her, and with the advent of the flood it had only become worse. She had so many doubts about working with the angelblood, but Jabez knew how he could show her that what they did was right, that it was all part of God's plan. God knew they were better than all these liars and adulterers and hypocrites in the city, and sending the angel was His reward for their virtue. He wanted them to become like gods themselves, because they were the only humans worthy of becoming the true image of the creator.

"Judith, my dearest Judith, you don't have to be afraid," he said, soothing her with a gentle touch on the cheek, wiping away her tears. "We'll try the blood on the horse, and then you'll see. It will work, and then you'll see that God is on our side."

She nodded. He smiled.

He took a bottle of the precious fluid and poured it into the horse's trough. For an animal of that size, this seemed to be the correct dosage. He tried to encourage it to drink, but the horse grew nervous when he got too close. Jabez took a few steps back and waited.

After a while, the horse drank.

As the transformation started to happen, the horse kicked about wildly. Its brown coat turned ivory white, and large feathered wings sprouted from its back, as beautiful as the angel's own. The change was complete in a few minutes.

"It worked!" Jabez yelled. "I told you it would work! God has given us our way out!"

"He, He did," said Judith. She almost couldn't believe it. "I'm so sorry I ever doubted you, my love. We did it."

Jabez laughed. It was a laugh born out of triumph and the knowledge of what he had become. Of what they had become. "Yes, Judith, yes. We did it. We don't even need God's help anymore. We have become as gods ourselves."

Her first instinct was to scold him for blaspheming God's greatness, but she knew he was right. With the blood of the angel, they held the power of creation in their hands. They had become as gods.

#

Arishat didn't know how much time she had spent in prayer and meditation, but it had to have been more than a day. When she opened the hatch in the ceiling and climbed onto her roof, she saw that the flood had risen dramatically. It was high enough to dangle her feet in the water if she sat at the edge of her roof.

There wasn't much time left. If she wanted to do the right thing, she had to act now. Another day and the flood would drown everyone. And Jabez would fly away with the help of some strange, mutated creature, escaping the punishment that was meant for him.

She went into her house again, closing the hatch to keep out the rain. She knelt in front of the statuettes placed upon her altar, calling out to her gods for help. She didn't know how she could free the angel. She didn't know how she could stop Jabez, but she knew the gods would give her what she required.

And that, in turn, required a sacrifice on her part.

"Give, and thou shalt be given," she whispered to herself as she prepared to give away the most valuable things she possessed in order to right a wrong that didn't concern her. She didn't have to do it; she could simply ask her gods to grant her a means of escape. But it wasn't in her nature to accept injustice without acting against it.

Many years ago, speaking out against a corrupt priesthood had earned her banishment and exile. She had been bribed to keep her mouth shut, but she spoke up. She had spoken up and was silenced by those more powerful than herself, and she lost her position as priestess. It had been the right thing to do. *This* was the right thing to do.

"One day, this is going to get me killed. Maybe today is that day. But it doesn't matter. Oh, greatest gods, help me in my task. Help me do what I must do," she implored as she lighted the fires of sacrifice, three large bowls of burning oil which would consume her offerings and carry them into the heavens.

This was the hardest sacrifice she had ever made. She didn't have much to give, but she was ready to give everything that mattered to her. She took the pair of scissors she had laid upon the altar, pulled up a strand of her hair and cut it close to the scalp. Then another, and another. Lock by lock, her long tresses fell to the ground. Tears streamed down her cheeks as she chopped off what she adored most about herself.

She didn't have much to give, but she was willing to give it all.

When nothing but a short, uneven stubble remained, she gathered up her fallen locks and placed them gently into a burning bowl.

"Baal-Hadad, Lord of the skies, Lord of the rain and the storms, who makes fertile the ground and strikes with lightning against your foes, accept my sacrifice and grant me the help I need. Baal-Hadad, Lord of the skies, show me a way to put an end to Jabez's evil and make right the wrongs he has done."

To the flames of the second bowl, she fed her dresses, the beautiful cloth that made her desirable to the men of the city. For years, making herself appealing to men had been the way of her life. Now, she gave it all away.

"Shapash, Lady of the Sun, torch of the gods, oh great goddess who gives light and warmth unto the earth, accept my sacrifice, and grant me the help I need. Great Shapash, Lady of the Sun, give me the tools I need to put an end to Jabez and his vile deeds."

Finally, she took off her jewelry and threw it into the third bowl. The fire shouldn't have been hot enough to melt it, but as soon as it hit the flames, it all disappeared in a puff of smoke. Not the black smoke of something burnt, but the pure, white smoke of sacrifice.

The gods had accepted her offer.

"Ashtart, oh Lady of Love, my dearest goddess, my greatest friend," she whispered, "help me in my task as you have always helped me before. You have been a light to me, an inspiration in the darkest times of my life. I have always served you faithfully, both as a qadishtu in the temple and here as a simple, mundane prostitute. Dearest Ashtart, lend me your guidance so that

I may succeed."

For a long time, Arishat knelt motionless in front of the altar, the fires of sacrifice illuminating her tear-stained face. There were no ashes in the bowls; her offerings had gone up into the heavens where they had been received by the gods.

The fires went out, extinguished by a swift gust of wind, the breath of Baal-Hadad leaving her in the darkness of her walled-up house. The only source of light left was a small candle she had placed upon the altar. It had been spared by Hadad's breath.

Arishat stood and went around to behind the altar where she found the answer to her prayers. From her sacrifice, the gods had fashioned a bow for her; the bow itself was made from horn the same color as her hair, strong and flexible. The string was made from finest cloth, woven so tightly as to be unbreakable. The arrows were made of gold, with tips of many-colored precious stones.

Now she knew what she had to do. She had to slay Jabez before he could escape his judgement. She had to deliver the punishment that God couldn't.

Before she went on her way, she placed the statuettes of her gods into the small chest she kept them in. She couldn't leave them here where they would sink in the flood. She had to give them into the hands of someone she could trust.

They were the only things she had left of her old life. Besides, they were sacred to her, and she couldn't just leave her own gods to drown.

After she had replaced the statuettes and closed the chest, she broke her furniture and tore apart the only piece of clothing she had left to fashion a makeshift raft. It wasn't much, but it was enough to reach the tower where Jabez was hiding.

First, she would pay a short visit to a friend.

#

"Arishat?" Argurios murmured to himself as he spotted the raft approaching his home. It couldn't be. The woman on the raft looked so different. A beggar, possibly, clad in nothing but a ragged loincloth. As she drew closer, he realized it was her, after all. "Arishat! By all the gods, what happened to you?"

She maneuvered the raft close to his house and placed a small chest on his roof.

"Argurios, I came to give you this and to say goodbye if we never meet again. I don't know whether I'm going to return from where I'm going."

He was so shocked by her appearance that he didn't realize what she had said. "What happened to your hair? Why are you naked? Arishat, who did this to you?"

"Argurios, my love, listen." She didn't intend to answer any of his questions. She couldn't involve him in this. She didn't want him to get hurt. "There is something I must do. I can't tell you what, but it's important. You must believe me."

"What do you mean? Where are you going?"

She pointed to the chest. "In this chest, there is something from my past that is important to me. I couldn't leave it in my house to get lost in the flood. Please, look out for it. Maybe this rain will cease, and we will all survive and I will come back. But please, just keep it close and think of me."

"Arishat, damn you, tell me what's going on!" he yelled.

Arishat looked saddened. "No, I can't. I don't want to get you involved. I, I don't want you to endanger yourself. I know it's ridiculous, but I don't want you to get hurt because of me. I must do this alone."

"Endanger myself? Arishat, do you know who I am? If there is anything that is dangerous to me, it would be even more dangerous to you! Wherever you're going, I'm coming with you," he said.

She smiled. It was a smile of sadness. But there was something else in it, too. There was love, and a deep gratitude for the short time the gods had allowed them together. "I love you," she said softly, turning her raft and paddling away.

"Stop! Damn you, Arishat. Stop!" Her tiny raft floated on, steady on its course toward the city gate.

"Damn you," he whispered. "Wherever you're going, I will come after you. And I swear by my gods, if anyone dares to hurt you—" He didn't finish the thought. He wasn't keen on getting into a fight, but if he had to do it for his beloved, he wouldn't hesitate. His beloved, of whom he knew so little and who didn't know much more about him. Would she have let him join if he had told her of his past? He looked at the chest she had left him. It contained something from her former life, she had said. He opened it and peeked inside.

"Statuettes?" He puzzled over the sight of them. "Arishat, I have no idea what you used to be before you came here. But if I want to help you in whatever you're doing, I think I must revisit my past, too."

He closed the lid and carried the chest into his house. He placed it on the ground and opened an old chest of his own. He had no desire to pick up what he had left behind so long ago. But if he had to do it for his beloved, he wouldn't hesitate.

#

Driven forward by grim determination, Arishat maneuvered her raft through the murky water until she spotted the shape of the abandoned tower in the fog. Bow and arrows in her hand, she approached the building as swiftly as her makeshift raft would allow. The water was so high that the tower appeared to be no taller than the small one-story houses of the city, jutting only a few feet out of the surface.

On top of the tower, she could see Jabez standing next to a horse with wings. She ran a hand over her shorn head and took a deep breath.

Jabez mounted the horse and reached down to his wife to help her up. Arishat stood, trying to get sure footing on her raft, and lifted her bow. Now was the moment to act. If she hesitated, Jabez would be gone.

"Jabez!" she yelled. "Jabez, you coward! I bring your righteous punishment!"

The innkeeper looked in surprise. But surprise turned to shock when he saw Arishat's raft. By then it was too late.

The arrow had been launched.

It hit Jabez in the thigh. It penetrated his flesh and entered the horse's flank without causing harm. The horse panicked and bucked its rider off, causing Jabez to fall onto the tower's roof. It snorted, whinnied, and flew away without a rider.

"No! No! You bitch, you whore, you filthy slut! Not my horse! Not my horse!"

Jabez, filled with rage, watched his means for escape disappear into the fog.

"Jabez, get down!" yelled his wife, pulling him to her as a second arrow whizzed over their heads.

Arishat smiled. The gods had given her the perfect weapon to deliver justice. The arrow had wounded Jabez, but it didn't harm the horse. These arrows would only harm the sinner himself.

Jabez and Judith descended into the tower's interior as Arishat moved the raft closer. The windows had all been bricked up, so she had to climb to the tower's roof.

"I swore I'd never do this again. Gods, give me strength!"

She used her loincloth to tie the bow and arrows tightly to her body and climbed the slick wall of the tower. This time, it was easier than before, even though the wall was more brittle due to the rainfall. When she pulled herself over the battlements and onto the roof, she forgot all about the difficulty of the climb.

She took her bow into her hand again and descended the stairs. Slowly, carefully, she checked out every room before descending another level. If Jabez managed to ambush her, she was dead. She wouldn't stand a chance against him in a fight.

When she entered the basement, she expected Jabez to be waiting for her with a club, ready to strike at her. What she didn't expect were hordes of tiny fire-spitting lizards assaulting her from all directions. They bit and clawed at her, burning her with their breath, dozens of them attacking her as if she was their next meal. In her attempt to fight them off, she dropped her bow.

Jabez took the opportunity to jump at her with a rope, tying it around her wrists, her arms, her thighs, her legs. Now, she was as helpless as the captured angel. He kicked the lizards away from her and dragged her into the room where Lucifer was chained.

The angel's eyes widened when he saw her. "You?"

Jabez grumbled. "You know her? You've seen her before?"

He threw Arishat against the wall, and when he reached for her hair to yank her up again, he noticed for the first time that it was gone. He left her lying on the ground, kicking her in the ribs and the chest and the thighs. "You filthy, sneaky little whore! You deceiving bitch! You've been here, haven't you? What did you do? Did you try to steal from me? Did you come to take what is rightfully mine?"

"Jabez, no! Please, don't be so cruel," Judith placed a hand on his shoulder.

At first, it seemed like he would turn and hit her, fueled by his anger, but then he composed himself and grinned. It was a wicked grin, the true mirror of his soul, all façade of friendliness gone.

"Yes. Yes, I have a much better idea. Bring me a bottle, my dear, and my knife."

When Judith realized what he wanted to do, she hesitated, but then she complied. She knew it would not be wise to enrage him further.

He took the knife, cut a small wound into Lucifer's arm, and filled the bottle with blood. He turned to Arishat and laughed. "What a fool I am. When you scared my horse away, I thought you had come to ruin everything I worked for. But, no, you are another gift sent to me by God!"

"The only thing your God has sent for you is the flood. It's the punishment for what you have done. Don't you see?" Arishat tried to appeal to Jabez's last shred of sanity, but it was no use.

"No, no, you don't see! Some of the experiments have failed, you know. I tried to give the angel's blood to a pig, but it turned into a grotesque monster and died from its mutations. It doesn't work the same way on every animal— the changes are always different. I didn't drink it myself because I wasn't sure what effect it would have on a human. But now I have you to test it on!"

"No! Don't you dare!"

Arishat moved her face away from the bottle Jabez tried to force upon her. He grabbed for her hair only to realize again that it was gone.

"What happened to your precious hair, you little slut? Did someone pay you to cut it off? No matter, there are other ways to keep you still." He grabbed her by the jaw. Applying pressure to her cheeks, Jabez forced Arishat's lips open and poured the angelblood into her mouth.

Once the bottle was empty, he stepped back to behold her transformation. Arishat screamed as the divine essence in the blood took its effect, changing her body to something other than human. Her skin became lighter. All bruises and blemishes vanished. Her hair thickened and softened, growing rapidly until it reached her knees. Her eyes glowed with divine light.

And from her back grew a pair of wings with feathers as white and pure as Lucifer's.

"It works! It works!" shouted Jabez, laughing madly. "Bring me a bottle, Judith! I will become like an angel, a divine being, powerful, so powerful … I …"

He didn't have the patience to wait for a bottle. He jumped at Lucifer and drank his blood directly from the wound. Lucifer, weakened from his months of captivity, sat passively as the man sucked the blood straight from the vein. Arishat, bound by the rope and shocked from her own transformation, found herself unable to act.

After he had slaked his thirst for divine essence, Jabez waited.

"No—" Arishat stretched an arm towards him. By doing so, she tore the ropes that bound her. The angelblood had infused her with a strength far beyond what she had been capable of as a human. "No! I could've stopped him. I should've stopped him."

"Don't worry," said Lucifer. "He won't get what he wished for."

When Jabez screamed, it wasn't a scream of agony like Arishat's had been. It was a scream filled with terror at the realization of what he was turning into. His skin became a dull shade of red, his beard turned into writhing snakes growing from his face, and his forehead sprouted horns like those of a goat. The wings that grew from his back were more like a bat's than an angel's.

"Jabez! No!" Judith raced to her husband, whose body trembled violently as the angelblood turned him into an ugly abomination.

"What's happening to him?" Arishat asked, confused by the reaction to the angelblood that was so very different from her own.

"His heart is evil," Lucifer replied. "And a creature of evil cannot turn into a creature of light when it is touched by divine essence. Now, fulfill your promise and set me free!"

She nodded and went for the angel. She pulled at his chains, but even with her new strength she couldn't manage to break the solid bronze.

"He has the key to my handcuffs in the pouch at his belt. Take it!" Lucifer ordered.

Arishat tore the pouch from Jabez's belt and unlocked Lucifer's cuffs. Then, she left the writhing man and his crying wife behind, climbing the tower with the angel close behind. When she had reached the top of the tower, she soared into the air, enthralled by a new, unfamiliar feeling.

At her apex, she raised her face to the sky and yelled. "Enough with this rain! Baal-Hadad, Lord of the skies, Lord of the rain and the storms, I call thy name! Clear the sky and cast away these clouds!"

The clouds scattered, allowing the sun to break through and shine her light upon the flooded earth. After hours and days of rain and fog, she could see the horizon again. But the rain did not cease entirely. The Israelite God continued to conjure storms in his wrath as Hadad fought to chase the clouds away.

Not far from the city, Arishat spotted Noah's ark drifting on the waves. There he was, enjoying the safe shelter of his boat while the people in the city sat on their rooftops waiting for the water to rise to their throats.

"Come, Lucifer! We must save them!" she said, flying towards the city.

"Save them? Didn't God send the flood to punish them for their wickedness? Why should we save those whom God wishes to destroy?"

Arishat couldn't believe how fast she could fly. She managed to cover a distance that took many minutes on foot in mere seconds through the air. It didn't take long to soar over the city.

"Because they're worth saving. Look at them, Lucifer. Do they seem wicked to you?"

From up there, she could see them all. Hafet, the man who used to spend more time with her than with his wife, sat on the rooftop of his house with his family, telling a story to his children. Benjamin, who loved to kick the poor stray, allowed Kalbat to stay on his rooftop and shared his food with her. Neighbors were chatting with each other, sharing clean water and dry blankets.

"Deep down, they are all good people. And your God, what is he for ignoring their prayers? They don't deserve to die for a crime they didn't commit. Come on, help me carry them to Noah's ark! A ship of that size can hold more than just one family." Arishat dove to the nearest rooftop.

"Very well. You showed me that there can be goodness within the hearts of humans. I'll help you." Lucifer followed her.

Together, they picked up a family and carried them to Noah's ark. The mother and father fell to their knees and kissed Arishat's feet. She didn't stay for long, however, as there were more people to save.

Noah crawled out of his cabin to check out what all that noise was about.

"What's happening here? How did all these people get here? This is my ship! God didn't intend … Arishat? By God, you're an angel!" he blurted as he watched her carry another person to the ark.

"It's a long story," Arishat replied. "You make sure these people get food and shelter. We'll talk later."

"Did God send you?" Noah asked, bowing before her angelic form. "Were you always an angel? Did He send you to test if we were good people?"

"No. He didn't send me. He still wants to drown all these people, but I don't want that. That's why I'm saving them."

Before he could question her further, she was in the air again.

"We're too slow!" she shouted to Lucifer as they circled the skies above the city. "There are so many people left, we can't save them all before the flood rises above the rooftops."

Thanks to the intervention of Baal-Hadad, the rain lightened, but the water level continued to rise and there were thousands of people to be saved. An impossible task for the two of them alone.

"Then some of them will fall to God's wrath just as he intended." Lucifer shrugged. He didn't care too much about the fate of these humans.

"But they don't deserve to die!" Arishat yelled. "They're not wicked!"

"You don't know that. Jabez appeared friendly when I first met him, and then he turned out to be an evil man. Some of them deserve their punishment."

She had to admit that the angel was right. Many of those who had always treated her badly proved they were good people now that the situation was grave and their neighbors required their help. Others just sat on rooftops, keeping large amounts of food to themselves, and not sharing with anyone. Were they bad at heart, or were they scared for their lives? Who could judge who was good and who was evil?

"Lucifer, I have an idea," Arishat said after giving it some thought. "I'll fly back to the tower and fetch all these bottles that Jabez filled with your blood. We could pour them into the water, so everyone who swallows it will either grow the wings of an angel or die painfully, depending on whether they're good or evil."

"What? No, wait! This is madness! You cannot tamper with God's creation in this way!" Lucifer yelled, but she was already on the way to the tower. He followed her.

When Arishat approached the tower, she was met with something she hadn't expected. Jabez had survived his transformation and stood on the tower's roof, flapping his leathery wings. He took off into the air towards her.

"You Canaanite whore!" The snakes on his chin writhed and squirmed. "You cursed me, you and your devilish gods! You stole the blessing that was to be mine!"

"I stole nothing," Arishat said. "It is the evil within your heart that made you what you are."

"Liar! You worship false gods and sell your body to the highest bidder. There is no creature more wicked than you! I know what you did to me. You placed a curse upon me. You cut your hair before you came to my tower. A Babylonian merchant once told me that witches use human hair for their spells. You used your evil Canaanite magic on me to steal what was rightfully mine." His eyes glowed red with rage.

Jabez, furious, launched himself at Arishat, screaming and spitting and roaring like a demon who had escaped from the deepest pits of the underworld. Arishat was too slow to evade, and he hit her square in the chest, pushing her back a couple of feet. She tumbled and barely managed to regain her balance before hitting the water.

Jabez was full of hate and anger. Arishat didn't think she stood a chance against him.

"Jabez!" Lucifer screamed, descending upon the innkeeper. "You captured me! You tortured me for months! You will pay for this, you monster!"

Jabez laughed as he allowed Lucifer to collide with him. He closed his arms around the angel, spun in the air to gather momentum and threw Lucifer onto the tower where he landed with an audible *crack*.

"Foolish angel, what do you think you are? I have become a god, and you were merely my tool!" Jabez laughed. The snakes on his chin danced. "And now for you, whore. I will make you suffer for the curse you cast upon me. I will pluck every feather from your wings and every hair from your head, you little witch."

Arishat and Jabez circled each other, each observing the other's movements. Then, Jabez leaped at her, striking her chest with a taloned hand. The attack tore deep into the soft flesh of her breasts. She hit him back but didn't so much as bruise him.

And so it went, a strike by a taloned hand followed by a punch, a punch followed by a kick, an awkward dodge, another strike, another scratch, a bleeding wound. Arishat knew she couldn't win. Jabez was relentless, and the claws on his monstrous hands effortlessly sliced through her naked flesh. After all she went through, she would fail in stopping the man responsible for the flood.

Suddenly, Arishat felt a gust of wind and heard the sound of bronze slashing against flesh followed by a scream. It was Jabez's voice she heard above the fray.

"Arishat," a familiar voice shouted, "when this is over, you'll better explain to me what happened to you and to my horse!"

Argurios was the last person she would have expected to see, but there he was, astride his winged horse, clad in a shining armor of bronze, gold, and silver. In his right hand he held a sword, the weapon of a noble warrior. It was the most beautiful sight she could imagine.

"Argurios! Behind you!" A swarm of small, winged lizards ascended from the tower, flying straight towards Argurios and his horse. Judith must have unleashed them to help her husband.

And then, everything seemed to happen at once. Argurios turned to face the tiny fire-breathers, Lucifer took off into the air again, though he was too weak to be of any help in the fight, and Jabez seized the moment to launch himself towards Argurios.

This went too far. Arishat bore the wounds of combat without complaint, but she couldn't allow Jabez to hurt the man she loved. She was no fighter, and she couldn't stop him, but she used to be a priestess and her gods could help.

"Shapash, Lady of the Sun, torch of the gods, I call thy name! Strike down this demon with your fire, send your rays of light to set him ablaze with purifying flames!"

Arishat's prayer was answered.

A single ray of light shot from the sun, a lance of scorching heat so strong it seared Arishat's foe. Jabez lit up like an oil lamp, screaming as he burned. The dragons that attacked Argurios' steed retreated into the tower, terrified of the screaming monstrosity that tumbled through the air.

At that moment, Lucifer threw himself at Jabez. In his rage against his former captor, he hadn't seen the ray of light, and he only noticed that his foe was aflame when he himself had caught on fire. Together, they fell from the sky as a burning bundle of rage, still fighting each other, each knowing they were near the end. They plunged into the floodwater and the fire went out.

"Lucifer, no!"

Arishat lowered her head and shed a tear for the innocent angel who had suffered so much. He would have deserved a better end than this.

After a few moments, he surfaced again. His hair was gone, his skin covered in burn marks, and his wings had become featherless lumps of flesh, but he wasn't dead.

"Lucifer, you survived!"

"My wings! I've lost my wings!" Lucifer screamed. "It's all your fault, betrayer!"

"What?" By now, Arishat didn't think anything could surprise her anymore. But Lucifer claiming she betrayed him? That was ridiculous.

"You called upon your goddess to burn Jabez just as I threw myself at him! You are no better than him, none of you are better. God was right to punish your kind for your wickedness. You are betrayers, deceivers, sinners, all of you!"

"I didn't know you were about to attack him! It wasn't on purpose," Arishat defended herself.

"No more of your human lies. There is no goodness within you. You all deserve the worst fate you can get. You!" Lucifer yelled, pointing at Judith, who had ascended the tower and stared into the water at the spot where her beloved Jabez had gone down. "Why don't you join your dear husband? What is your life without him? You have no reason to go on, woman. Everyone will know you were responsible for the flood. You will live as an outcast. Go, join your husband in death! It is the best fate you can hope for."

"Lucifer, what are you doing?" Arishat asked. "Don't make her—"

It was too late. Judith had stabbed herself with the same dagger Jabez had used to cut Lucifer. She let her lifeless body fall into the water so her corpse could rest next to her husband's.

"You humans have tortured and betrayed me. This is how I will deal with all of you from now on. Even if you survive and find dry land to settle, I shall return and plague your kind for all eternity. It is all you deserve for what you have done to me." And he vanished beneath the waves and dived away.

The heavens weeped, drowning the earth in tears of rage.

"Enough of this. Enough death, enough suffering," cried Arishat. "Yahweh, God of the Israelites, I call thy name! What kind of god are you to punish an entire tribe for the crimes of one man? Show compassion and cease this senseless rain! Your people deserve a better fate than this. Do you not see that your judgement is wrong? In the face of death, all these people, no matter how cruel they had been before, are now showing their good side by helping their neighbors, even though they know it is pointless. At the same time, a creature of divinity, one of your own angels, turns to evil because of the things that happened to him. There is goodness in the hearts of men, and evil in the hearts of the divine. Show mercy to your people! Many of them are better than the angel you just lost."

There was nothing but silence.

Then, the clouds cleared, and large, glowing letters appeared in the sky in the language of the Israelites.

I am the Lord, your God. You shall fear no evil for I am your shepherd. I will guide you to a new home where you shall live in peace, and no harm shall ever befall you. I shall love you as my own sons, and I will be like a heavenly father unto you. Amen.

"So, this means he forgives them?" asked Argurios, seated on his flying horse.

"I think so," Arishat answered. "He's a strange god, but I guess he understood the point I was making."

Suddenly, the tower where Jabez had conducted his angelblood experiments collapsed, and from the rubble emerged the white pigeons he had created.

Arishat nodded. "He forgives them. He even forgives Jabez, I think. Letting these white birds go free is God's sign of forgiveness."

"You know a lot about gods," Argurios remarked.

She shrugged. "Not about Him. As I said, he's a strange god. I'm just making guesses."

The rain didn't cease, but a rainbow appeared over the rooftops of the city. The people stared at it in awe as they realized that it was a bridge that led them to Noah's ark waiting outside the city, below the end of the rainbow.

God had decided to spare his people.

"So, you used to be a priestess before you came here," Argurios said.

"Yes. A qadishtu, to be exact."

"A qadishtu?"

"A priestess who also serves as a sacred prostitute."

"Ah. Figures."

"And you used to be a warrior, back in Mycenae."

"Yes."

They watched in silence as the people of the city walked across the rainbow bridge to Noah's ark. Then, Arishat asked, "How do you like your new horse?"

Argurios grinned. "New horse? It's my good old friend Pegasus, except he's got wings now. I don't know. I must get used to this."

"You must get used to this? Be glad you don't have wings on your back. *That* takes getting used to."

They laughed. Just a day ago, they slept together on a dry bed, and now the city was flooded. They hovered above it with the help of angelic wings.

"Let's go somewhere we can get used to flying. Somewhere far away," Arishat suggested. "After everything that happened these last few days, I don't want to be anywhere near these people and their god anymore."

"Agreed. Where do you want to go? Egypt? Babylonia? Troy?" he asked.

"I don't care. There are many places in this world that I've never seen. It doesn't matter where we go so long as we go together. I love you, Argurios. Right now, all I want is to start a new life with you at my side."

"Sounds good. I always wanted to marry an angel," he said with a smirk.

They flew away into the sunset. It didn't matter where their path would take them. If the gods were merciful, they would send them somewhere peaceful, safe, and far away from the sea.

BIOS

Abad, Anne Carly received the Poet of the Year Award in the 2017 Nick Joaquin Literary Awards. She has also been nominated for the Pushcart Prize and the Rhysling Award. Her work has appeared in Apex, Mythic Delirium, Strange Horizons, and many other publications. We've Been Here Before, her first poetry collection, is available through Aqueduct Press at http://www.aqueductpress.com/books/978-1-61976-222-0.php

Alexander, Terry and his wife Phyllis live on a small farm near Porum, Oklahoma. They have three children, thirteen grandchildren, and eight great grandchildren. Terry has been published in various anthologies from Airship 27, OGHMA Creative Media, Pro Se Productions, and Pulp Cult. He is a member of the Tahlequah Writers, Oklahoma Writers Federation, Ozark Writers League, and Western Fictioneers.

Anderson, David lives in Mesa, Arizona and makes his living doing art and design. His fiction has appeared in *Surreal Grotesque, Bizarro Central*, Jason Wayne Allen's Rotgut County Blog, and Dynatox Minstries. This April saw the release of his first print collection, "Yakuza Cereal."

Ashley, Allen is an award-winning writer, editor, and creative writing tutor based in London, UK. He is ex-president of the British Fantasy Society and the founder of the advanced science fiction and fantasy group Clockhouse London Writers. Published at over a hundred different venues, his most recent book is the poetry collection *Echoes from an Expired Earth* (Demain Publishing, UK, 2021), which was nominated for an Elgin Award. His next publication will be the chapbook *Journey to the Centre of the Onion* due from Eibonvale Press, UK in September 2023. Websites: www.allenashley.com and https://clockhouselondonwriters.wordpress.com/

Beacham, C.J. *writes fiction that has been described as "dark yet hopeful." His short stories have been published by New Lit Salon Press and Santa Fe Writer's Project (under the name Charles J. Beacham). He is a member of The Writer's Workshop of Asheville. C.J. Beacham writes from the foothills of North Georgia where he is working on a second novel and a short story collection while seeking publication for his first novel. He can be found online at* https://www.facebook.com/CJBeachamwriter.

Beorh, Scathe meic is a writer and lexicographer of Ulster-Scot and Cherokee ancestry. His books in print include the novel Black Fox In Thin Places (Emby Press, 2013), the story collections Children & Other Wicked Things (James Ward Kirk Fiction, 2013) and Always After Thieves Watch (Wildside Press, 2010), the lexicon Pirate Lingo (Wildside, 2009), and the poetic study Dark Sayings of Old (Kirk Fiction, 2013). He makes a home with his imaginative wife Ember in a quaint Edwardian neighborhood on the Atlantic Coast. More can be found at beorh.wordpress.com.

Bondoni, Gustavo is a novelist and short story writer with over four hundred stories published in fifteen countries, in seven languages. He is a member of Codex and an active member of SFWA. He has published six science fiction novels including one trilogy, four monster books, a dark military fantasy, and a thriller. His short fiction is collected in *Pale Reflection* (2020), *Off the Beaten Path* (2019), *Tenth Orbit and Other Faraway Places* (2010) and *Virtuoso and Other Stories* (2011). In 2018, Bondoni received a Judges Commendation (and second place) in The James White Award. In 2019, he was awarded second place in the Jim Baen Memorial Contest. He was also a 2019 finalist in the Writers of the Future Contest. His website is at www.gustavobondoni.com.

Bougger, Jason is a father of four living in Omaha, Nebraska. He is the author of the YA Novel Holy Fudgesicles and has published thirty short stories. He is the creator of the fantasy card game 52 Dragons (https://52dragons.com) and uploads regularly to his board and card game channel TabletopJason (https://www.youtube.com/tabletopjason). You can find out more about him and his current projects at http://www.JasonBougger.com.

Chappell, Shelley is a writer of fantasy fiction and fairy tale retellings. She is the editor of *Wish Upon a Southern Star* (2017), a collection of radically retold fairy tales by twenty-one New Zealand and Australian authors, and the author of *Beyond the Briar: A Collection of Romantic Fairy Tales* (2014), as well as a variety of short stories. You can find out more about her writing at shelleychappell.weebly.com.

Cianci, J.P. is a senior at UNLV studying for a B.A. in English with a concentration in Creative Writing. With a B.S. in Business, she is a member of the Association of Writers and Writing Programs and writes for UNLV's *Rebel Yell*.

Conrad, Carl lives in Grand Rapids, Michigan, and is a retired college economics instructor who enjoys writing of all types. He has published a children's fantasy novel, a biography of a Christian southern gospel singer, two imaginative sci-fi/action novels, and has written many short stories and essays.

DeHart, JD has been publishing for two decades. His work has appeared in AIM, Modern Dad, and Steel Toe Review. When he is not writing, he teaches English. His blog is at spinrockreader.blogspot.com and he edits Mount Parable.

De Marco, Guy is a speculative fiction author; a Graphic Novel Bram Stoker and Scribe Award finalist; winner of the HWA Silver Hammer Award; a prolific short story and flash fiction crafter; a novelist; a poet; an invisible man with superhero powers; a game writer; and a coffee addict. One of these is false. A writer since 1977, Guy is or has been a member of SFWA, IAMTW, ITW, RWA-PRO, WWA, SFPA, ASCAP, MWG, SWG, HWA, and IBPA. He hopes to collect the rest of the alphabet one day. Learn more about him at GuyAnthonyDeMarco.com and en.wikipedia.org/wiki/Guy_Anthony_De_Marco.

De Marco, Tonya is a costume designer, professional cosplayer, published model, and author. She lives in a cabin in the woods in rural Ohio. She's been hooked on costumes and costuming since she was a preteen. She's been featured in several magazines and on the GeekxGirls website. Additionally, her love of the written word encouraged her to pursue a writing career. Tonya has numerous short stories in anthologies and is a member of the Horror Writers Association. When she isn't sewing or writing, Tonya enjoys spending time listening to the silence of the forest. Visit her website to find links to her Facebook, Instagram, and Amazon accounts: http://www.TonyaLDeMarco.com.

Eden, Meg teaches creative writing at colleges and writing centers. She is the author of the 2021 Towson Prize for Literature winning poetry collection *Drowning in the Floating World* (Press 53, 2020) and children's novels, most recently *Good Different*, a JLG Gold Standard selection (Scholastic, 2023). Find her online at https://linktr.ee/medenauthor.

Edwards (Dobbs), Kayleigh is an author from South Wales who dwells happily amongst the free-roaming sheep and goats of the Welsh mountains. She is a writer of short fiction, plays, and non-fiction, all nestled somewhere between horror and comedy. She runs a horror review website called Happy Goat Horror (happygoathorror.com) that focuses on indie horror mostly, amongst other deliciously dastardly works. When she is not writing or reviewing books, she rants about games and movies on YouTube with her brother (Happy Goat Horror).

Grey, John is an Australian-born writer and U.S. resident. He has been published in Weird Tales, Tales of the Talisman, Flapperhouse, Strangely Funny 2 ½, and the sci-fi anthology A Robot, A Cyborg and A Martian Walk Into A Space Bar, and many other places. He is also a Rhysling poetry prize winner, awarded by the Science Fiction & Fantasy Poetry Association.

Hewitt, Gary enjoys both prose and poetry. His many stories and poems, which venture into the quirky and mysterious, have been published online and offline. His style has adapted over the years. These days he enjoys experimenting with unusual formats. He lives in the UK and is currently studying German. He's not going to Germany but figured it'll keep his mind active. He continues to write and has read his work publicly, which was fun even if a touch nerve wracking. He also enjoys tarot and reiki and loves to hear feedback from fans. His website is located at https://kingsraconteurswork.blogspot.com/2014/01/there-you-have-probably-arrived-here.html.

Johnson, Alex S. is the author of several books, including *Bad Sunset*, *Wicked Candy*, and *Fucked Up Shit!* (co-authored with Berti Walker), and he is the creator of *Chunks: A Barfzaro Anthology*, *Floppy Shoes Apocalypse*, and the *Axes of Evil* heavy metal horror series. He lives in Sacramento, California.

Inverness, AmyBeth is a historian and writer who takes inspiration from the realities and unknowns of humanity to write thought-provoking speculative fiction. She lives in the basement of a historic Denver mansion with her cat and a mostly harmless set of unidentifiable entities. You can find her stories in all the BLAS books and in the back of a desk drawer where they ferment like kombucha awaiting an audience with a suitable palate. Samples of both her millinery and fiction can be found at http://amybethinverness.com/.

Mac, Adam teaches ESL and occasionally writes for his dark half.

Macpherson, David is a writer who lives in Central Massachusetts. His work has appeared in various anthologies and magazines.

Mollica, Tom lives in West Milwaukee, Wisconsin and is the owner of Studio Tommy – a digital media company.

Morehouse, Lyda leads a double life. By day she's a mild-mannered science fiction author of such works as the Shamus Award-winning and Locus Award-nominated *Archangel Protocol* (2001.) By night, she dons her secret identity as Tate Hallaway, best-selling paranormal romance author. Her most recent novel, *Unjust Cause*, was published by Wizard Tower Press in April 2020. You can find her all over the Web as Lyda Morehouse, and at Twitter as @tatehallaway. Be sure to check out what she's been up to lately at https://lydamorehouse.com and https://www.patreon.com/lydamorehouse.

Osborne, Schevus is a newly published author of several short stories. He lives near St. Louis, Missouri and works as a software developer by day. You can find information about his published works and more at http://schevusosborne.com, or follow @SchevusOsborne (https://twitter.com/SchevusOsborne) on Twitter.

Paschall, Nicholas is a horror and fantasy author based out of Texas, where he lives with his wife, cats, and dog. He was first published in 2011 and has since been published in over fifty anthologies, magazines, and ezines. His first novel, the *Father of Flesh*, was published in 2017 with a sequel released a year later. He spends most of his time crawling the internet looking for inspiration for his next tale of terror.

Pauff, H.L. is a writer living in Baltimore who spends his nights mashing on keyboard and looking for the magic to happen.

Rose, Rie Sheridan has prose published in numerous anthologies, including *Killing It Softly Vols. 1 & 2*, *Hides the Dark Tower*, *Dark Divinations*, and *Startling Stories*. Additionally, she has authored twelve novels in multiple genres, six poetry chapbooks, and dozens of song lyrics. She is a native of Texas and lives there with her husband and several spoiled cats, though they hope to move to Dublin, Ireland in the future. When not writing or editing, she is usually walking and being a Virtual Race addict. Member of the HWA and SFWA, she tweets as @RieSheridanRose.

Sawielijew, Frank has the blood of Russian nobility in his veins and the most beautiful woman in the world at his side. He lives near the city of Frankfurt, Germany, where he works as a historian. When he isn't busy trying to unveil the secrets of the past, he likes to create fantastic worlds of his own. In this, he draws inspiration from a variety of sources ranging from old Babylonian cuneiform texts to classic 1990s PC games. He writes short stories and novels in both English and German. *Die Kleine Gelbe Kröte*, his first novel, was published in 2013.

Stephens, Lorina has worked as an editor and a freelance journalist for national and regional print media; she is the author of seven books, both fiction and non-fiction; she's been a festival organizer, and a publicist; she lectures on many topics from historical textiles and domestic technologies to publishing and writing; she teaches; and she continues to work as a writer, artist, and publisher at Five Rivers Publishing. She has had several short fiction pieces published in Canada's acclaimed *On Spec* magazine, *Postscripts to Darkness*, *Neo-Opsis*, *Garden of Eden*, and Marion Zimmer Bradley's fantasy anthology *Sword & Sorceress X*.

Stevenson, James J. writes and teaches in Vancouver, Canada. He has been published in numerous poetry journals and just finished his first novel. You can find him and his haiku on various social media as @writelightning (https://twitter.com/writelightning).

Teegarden, William J. is a software professional and freelance writer from Kirkwood, New York. A member of the IEEE, William evolved his childhood love of all things science fiction into a 30-year career in software development and computer technology. An avid mountain biker, he also spends free time as a volunteer makeup and hair artist for the popular online fan production, Star Trek: Phase II (http://www.facebook.com/startrekphase2).

Varga, Kris Twenty-three years old. Six feet tall, blonde hair, blue eyes, slender frame, long face, protruding nose, Caucasian. A graduate of the studies at Temple University in Film and Media Arts. He also possesses a minor in English Literature. Rambunctious poet. Actor. Musician. Film Editor. Friend.

Vataris, Erin is a freelance short fiction writer, currently working on several speculative fiction and post-apocalyptic collections. She is a participant in the Flash Fiction Project and Nightmare Fuel communities on Google Plus.

Vernetti, Sarah lives in Las Vegas. When she isn't writing about travel, she's crafting short stories and flash fiction. In what feels like a former life, she earned a master's degree in art history. Follow her on Twitter: @SarahVernetti.

Vicary, John began publishing poetry in the fifth grade and has been writing ever since. His most recent credentials include short fiction in the collection The Longest Hours and issues of Alternating Current and the Birmingham Arts Journal. He has stories in upcoming issues of Disturbed Digest, Plague: an Anthology of Sickness and Death, Anthology of the Mad Ones, a charity anthology entitled Second Chance, and Dead Men's Tales. You can read more of his work at keppiehed.com.

Wynn, E.S. is the author of over seventy books and the chief editor of Thunderune Publishing. In his spare time, he spins stories, builds board games, stitches together battle jackets, runs a pair of magazines, makes videos about Norse Shamanism on YouTube, and encourages people to create new art. He is openly transgender and seeks to establish acceptance and love for and within the trans community. He has worked with hundreds of authors and edited thousands of manuscripts for nearly a dozen different magazines. His stories and articles have been published in dozens of journals, e-zines, and anthologies. He has taught classes in literature, marketing, math, spirituality, energetic healing, and guided meditation, and he has worked as a voice-over artist for several horror and sci-fi podcasts, albums, and e-books.

Zimmermann, Melchior interrupted his master's thesis in biology to work for a year as a substitute teacher. He recently moved to Amsterdam to spend more time on the arts, especially writing. He likes to experiment with different genres and content. You can read more of his writing at behindthez.blogspot.com.

ABOUT THE EDITOR

Allen Taylor is the publisher at Garden Gnome Publications and editor of the Biblical Legends Anthology Series. His fiction and poetry have been published online and in print. He is the author of two non-fiction books on the intersection between cryptocurrency and social media as well as his Christian testimony titled I Am Not the King, all available at Amazon and wherever books are sold. He is the creator of the #twitpoem hashtag at Twitter and writes a newsletter/blog at https://paragraph.xyz/@tayloredcontent.

LEAVE US A REVIEW

If you liked the Garden of Eden anthology, the editor and the authors would sincerely invite you to write a review at Amazon or Goodreads.

Also look at Sulfurings: Tales from Sodom & Gomorrah, the second book in the Biblical Legends Anthology Series, and Deluge: Stories of Survival & Tragedy in the Great Flood.

Please report errors in this book to editor@gardengnomepubs.com.

Contents

CONNECT WITH THE GARDEN GNOMES

The garden gnomes would sincerely like to connect with you at our social media outposts. Please, drop on by!

Follow our editor on Twitter https://twitter.com/allen_taylor, Hive (https://hive.blog/@allentaylor), and Paragraph https://paragraph.xyz/@tayloredcontent.

Books By Allen Taylor

Garden of Eden

The first book in the Biblical Legends Anthology Series, *Garden of Eden* is a multi-author anthology that explores themes related to the creation story. Not Christian but not anti-Christian.

An excerpt from a reader review:

> To answer the obvious question first, while some of the contributors might be Christian, this is not a Christian book; nor is it an attack on Christianity. The works, some more than others, do raise issues of morality and sin, but they are neither thinly veiled allegory nor brutal parody.

Sulfurings: Tales from Sodom & Gomorrah

The second book in the Biblical Legends Anthology Series, Sulfurings: Tales from Sodom & Gomorrah is more horrific and apocalyptic than *Garden of Eden*. It also includes more stories from a more diverse group of authors.

From a reader review:

> While *Garden of Eden* was almost light hearted in its biblical fiction *Sulfurings* was much darker, and gritty. The details of the horrors were almost palatable. At times I imagined I could smell the sulfur and feel the terror of those of Sodom. I almost felt sorry for them, almost.

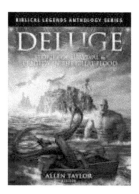

Deluge: Stories of Survival & Tragedy in the Great Flood

The third book in the Biblical Legends Anthology Series. Deluge takes a weirder turn than the *Garden of Eden* and *Sulfurings*, but the quality of the writing is superb. It also seems to be an audience favorite.

Check out this excerpt from a reader review:

> I have a lot of respect for the work of the editor of this multi-author volume of deluge-related stories. Mr. Taylor has gone to a lot of work to put it together. All the stories and poetic prose in this book are excellent work.

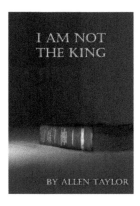

I Am Not the King

I Am Not the King is Allen Taylor's Christian testimony. Beginning with childhood, he details the events while growing up in a legalistic Holiness environment with a father dealing with angry issues and how that impacted his life as a young man. With a stunning twist, he tells how an atheist college professor drove him back to Jesus and what living as a Christian for 30 years has taught him about forgiveness and grace.

An excerpt from a reader review:

> Allen's recognition of the miseries and worldly woes and wrongdoing is the starting point for his search for his real life. This is the story of his search and rescue history. His scathing descriptions of family members, his parents and others, paint large an in-your-face, no-holds-barred, no-punches-pulled, full-frontal exposure of what it's like to be lost with no guidance in the worldly world, always searching for something, something to grasp hold of and hold onto, something solid, something worthy of his trust.

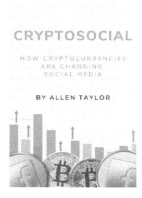

CRYPTOSOCIAL

HOW CRYPTOCURRENCIES
ARE CHANGING
SOCIAL MEDIA

BY ALLEN TAYLOR

Cryptosocial: How Cryptocurrencies Are Changing Social Media

Written for a general audience, *Cryptosocial: How Cryptocurrencies Are Changing Social Media* details the history of the World Wide Web to illustrate its decentralized beginnings and helps readers understand the basics of blockchain technology and cryptocurrencies. With that understanding, he goes on to detail the growing number of social media platforms where participants can earn cryptocurrencies for their postings.

An excerpt from a reader review:

> While the reality of a decentralized social media is the hope of many people who are concerned—or fed up—with the unchecked clout and excessive influence of legacy media and behemoths like Facebook, Google, and Twitter, the path to decentralization won't be easy. Even so, the book strikes a balance between caution and optimism.

Web3 Social: How Creators Are Changing the World Wide Web

(And You Can Too!)

Web3 Social: How Creators Are Changing the World Wide Web (And You Can Too!) is written for the creator class to illustrate how the creator economy is expanding with new monetization protocols, the ability to protect intellectual property and digital identities using blockchain tools, and how creators are going direct to their fans by building their own platforms with Web3 tools of decentralization.

From a reader review:

> As someone who is a four-time self-published author right here on Amazon, and who is old enough now to look back on years on both centralized and decentralized social media and compare, the rightness of this book is perfectly apparent to me. I simply do not want to have my creative life controlled by people who see me only as a chattel. Mr. Taylor shows us creatives the way out of that entrapment.

Milton Keynes UK
Ingram Content Group UK Ltd.
UKHW012238050124
435526UK00004B/331